High Praise for

POPPY Z. BRITE
"A Major New Voice in Horror Fiction!"
—*Booklist*

and her acclaimed novel

Lost Souls

"Poppy Z. Brite combines the sensibilities of a poet with the unflinching eye of a surgeon. . . . Not merely a rising literary star, she is a full-fledged supernova who may well banish paler constellations and make us all far too fond of the night. . . . This young writer takes us to places few will have the courage to visit and none would dare tour alone. Brite's vision is disturbingly dark, deliciously erotic, sweetly savage, and uniquely her own."   —Dan Simmons

"If there is a novelist capturing the dark literary decadence of this waning millennium, that sorcerous poet is Poppy Z. Brite. . . . I can think of few other fantasists who so dangerously evoke the sensual allure of pure evil."
—Edward Bryant, *Locus*

"Poppy Z. Brite strikes out into new uncharted land with a bold original voice; if you don't like her stories, then you haven't read her."   —Kathryn Ptacek, *Women of Darkness*

Lost
Souls

POPPY Z.
BRITE

A DELL BOOK

Published by
Dell Publishing
a division of
Random House, Inc.
1540 Broadway
New York, New York 10036

All characters in this publication are fictitious and any resemblance to real persons, living or dead, is purely coincidental.

ISBN: 0-440-21281-2

Reprinted by arrangement with Delacorte Press

Printed in the United States of America

Published simultaneously in Canada

October 1993

OPM   24   23   22   21   20   19   18   17   16

ACKNOWLEDGMENTS

Very special thanks are due to Monica C. Kendrick. Two of the characters in *Lost Souls*, Arkady and Ashley Raventon, are her brainchildren. She has kindly allowed them to make a guest appearance here.

Other thanks go to the brilliant and ravishing Mr. John Skipp, the urbane and witty Mr. Dan Simmons, and the awesomely generous and talented Mr. Harlan Ellison. These fine writers and even finer people are my trio of patron saints, and I love them very much.

My agent, Richard Curtis, and the good people at Richard Curtis Associates; my editor, Jeanne Cavelos; David B. Silva and *The Horror Show*—I still miss it and always will; to another excellent writer and friend, Brian Hodge, for believing in *Lost Souls* from the beginning; Doug Winter for inducing me to write the damn thing in the first place; Ed Bryant and Tom Monteleone for kind words and deeds; everyone at *Iniquities*.

Craig Spector, Lisa Wimberger, Linda Marotta, Kathryn Ptacek, A. J. Mayhew, J. R. McHone, Jodie and Steve Forrest, Pat Johnson, John Gillespie, John Hughes; Brad and Forrest Cahoon and John Ross for help with temperamental computers; all the fetuses in the Nantahala Street Compound for tearing me away from my work and giving me sustenance to continue it; Paul, the handsomest Ramone-clone in New Orleans, for forcing that first shot of Chartreuse down my throat.

Lastly, ultimate thank-you's to my mother, Connie Burton Brite; Christopher DeBarr, my home sweetie; my father, Bob Brite; and to the Mysterious Multitude for just being their ectoplasmic selves.

The prologue of *Lost Souls* was published in the Summer 1988 issue of *The Horror Show* under the title "A Taste of Blood and Altars."

PROLOGUE

In the spring, families in the suburbs of New Orleans—Metairie, Jefferson, Lafayette—hang wreaths on their front doors. Gay straw wreaths of gold and purple and green, wreaths with bells and froths of ribbons trailing down, blowing, tangling in the warm wind. The children have king cake parties. Each slice of cake is iced with a different sweet, sticky topping—candied cherries and colored sugar are favorites—and the child who finds a pink plastic baby in his slice will enjoy a year of good luck. The baby represents the infant Christ, and children seldom choke on it. Jesus loves little children.

The adults buy spangled cat's-eye masks for masquerades, and other women's husbands pull other men's wives to them under cover of Spanish moss and anonymity, hot silk and desperate searching tongues and the wet ground and the ghostly white scent of magnolias opening in the night, and the colored paper lanterns on the veranda in the distance.

In the French Quarter the liquor flows like milk. Strings of bright cheap beads hang from wrought-iron balconies and adorn sweaty necks. After parades the beads lie scattered in the streets, the royalty of gutter trash, gaudy among the cigarette butts and cans and plastic Hurricane glasses. The sky is purple, the flare of a match behind a cupped hand is gold; the liquor is green, bright green, made from a thousand herbs, made from altars. Those who know enough to drink Chartreuse at Mardi Gras are lucky, because the distilled essence of the town burns in their bellies. Chartreuse glows in the dark, and if you drink enough of it, your eyes will turn bright green.

Christian's bar was way down Rue de Chartres, away from the middle of the Quarter, toward Canal Street. It was only nine-thirty. No one ever came in until ten, not even on Mardi Gras nights. No one except the girl in the black silk dress, the thin little girl with the short, soft dark hair that fell in a curtain across her eyes. Christian always wanted to brush it away from her face, to feel it trickle through his fingers like rain.

Tonight, as usual, she slipped in at nine-thirty and looked around for the friends who were never there. The wind blew the French Quarter in behind her, the night air rippling warm down Chartres Street as it slipped away toward the river, smelling of spice and fried oysters and whiskey and the dust of ancient bones stolen and violated. When the girl saw Christian standing alone behind the bar, narrow, white, and immaculate with his black hair glittering on his shoulders, she came and hopped onto a bar stool—she had to boost herself—and said, as she did most nights, "Can I have a screwdriver?"

"Just how old are you, love?" Christian asked, as he did most nights.

"Twenty." She was lying by at least four years, but her voice was so soft that he had to listen with his whole cupped ear to hear it, and her arms on the bar were thin and downed with fine blond hairs; the big smudges of dark makeup like bruises around her eyes, the ratty bangs, and the little sandaled feet with their toenails painted orange only made her more childlike. He mixed the drink weak and put two cherries in it. She fished the cherries out with her fingers and ate them one by one, sucking them like candy, before she started sipping her drink.

Christian knew the girl came to his bar because the drinks were cheap and he would serve them to her with no annoying questions about ID or why a pretty girl wanted to drink alone. She always turned with a start every time the street door opened, and her hand would fly to her throat. "Who are you waiting for?" Christian asked her the first time she came in.

"The vampires," she told him.

She was always alone, even on the last night of Mardi Gras. The black silk dress left her throat and arms bare. Before, she had smoked Marlboro Lights. Christian told her that only virgins were known to smoke those, and she blushed and came in the next night with a pack of Camels. She said her name was Jessy, and Christian only smiled at her joke about the vampires; he didn't know how much she knew. But she had pretty ways and a sweet shy smile, and she was a tiny brightness in every ashen empty night.

He certainly wasn't going to bite her.

The vampires got into town sometime before midnight. They parked their black van in an illegal space, then got hold of a bottle of Chartreuse and reeled down Bourbon Street swigging it by turns, their arms around one another's shoulders, their hair in one another's faces. All three had outlined their features in dark blots of makeup, and the larger two had teased their hair into great tangled clumps. Their pockets were stuffed with candy they ate noisily, washing it down with sweet green mouthfuls of Chartreuse. Their names were Molochai, Twig, and Zillah, and they wished they had fangs but had to make do with teeth they filed sharp, and they could walk in sunlight as their great-grandfathers could not. But they preferred to do their roaming at night, and as they roamed unsteadily down Bourbon Street, they raised their voices in song. Molochai peeled the wrapper off a HoHo, crammed as much of it into his mouth as he could, and kept singing, spraying Twig with crumbs of chocolate.

"Give me some," Twig demanded. Molochai scooped some of the HoHo out of his mouth and offered it to Twig. Twig laughed helplessly, clamped his lips shut and shook his head, finally relented and licked the creamy brown paste off Molochai's fingers.

"Vile dogs," said Zillah. Zillah was the most beautiful of the three, with a smooth, symmetrical, androgynous face, with brilliant eyes as green as the last drop of Chartreuse in the bottle. Only Zillah's hands gave away his gender; they were large and strong and heavily veined beneath the thin white skin. He wore his nails long and pointed, and he wore his caramel-colored hair tied back with a purple silk scarf. Wisps of the ponytail had escaped, framing the stunning face, the achingly green eyes. Zillah stood a head and a half shorter than Molochai and Twig, but his ice-cold poise and the way his larger companions flanked him told onlookers that Zillah was the absolute leader here.

Molochai and Twig's features were like two sketches of the same face done by different artists, one using sharp straight angles, the other working in curves and circles. Molochai was baby-faced, with large round eyes and a wide wet mouth he liked to smear with orange lipstick. Twig's face was angular and clever; his eyes tracked every movement. But the two were of the same size and shape, and more often than not they walked, or staggered, in step with each other.

They grinned and bared their teeth at a tall boy in full Nazi uniform who had veered directly into their path. From a distance Molochai and Twig's filed teeth were unremarkable except for the film of chocolate that webbed them, but some small bloodlust in their eyes made the boy turn away, looking for trouble somewhere else, somewhere vampires would not trouble themselves to go.

They made their way through the gaudy throngs to the sidewalk, steadying themselves against posters that screamed *MEN WILL TURN INTO WOMEN BEFORE YOUR EYES!!!*, pictures of blondes with tired breasts and five-o'clock shadows. They stumbled past racks of postcards, racks of T-shirts, bars that opened onto the sidewalk and served drinks to passersby. Overhead, fireworks blossomed and turned the sky purple with their smoke, and the air was thick with smoke and liquor-breath and river-mist. Molochai let his head fall back on Twig's shoulder and looked up at the sky, and the fireworks dazzled his eyes.

They left the sleazy lights of Bourbon Street behind, swayed left onto dark Conti and right onto Chartres. Soon enough they found a tiny bar with stained-glass windows and a friendly light inside. The sign above the door said *CHRIS-TIAN'S.* The vampires staggered in.

They were the only customers except for a silent little girl sitting at the bar, so they commandeered a table and slammed down another bottle of Chartreuse, talking loudly to each other, then looking at Christian and laughing, shrugging. His forehead *was* very high and pale, and his nails were as long and pointed as Zillah's. "Maybe—" said Molochai, and Twig said, "Ask him." They both looked at Zillah for approval. Zillah glanced over at Christian and raised a languid eyebrow, then lifted one shoulder in a tiny shrug.

No one paid any attention to the girl at the bar, although she stared at them ceaselessly, her eyes bright, her lips moist and slightly parted.

When Christian brought them their tab, Molochai dug deep in his pocket and produced a coin. He did not put the coin in Christian's hand, but held it up to the light so that Christian might look well at it. It was a silver doubloon, of the same shape and size as those thrown from Mardi Gras parade floats along with the treasure trove of other trinkets— the beads, the bright toys, the sweet sugar candy. But this doubloon was heavier and far, far older than those. Christian could not make out the year; the silver was scarred, tarnished, smudged with Molochai's sticky fingerprints. But the picture was still clear: the head of a beautiful man with enormous sensuous lips. Lips that would be as red as blood were they not carved in cold, heavy silver. Lips pricked by long, sharp fangs. Below the man's face, in ornate letters, the word *BACCHUS* curved.

"How—how do you come?" Christian stammered.

Molochai smiled his chocolatey smile. "In peace," he said. He looked at Zillah, who nodded. Molochai did not take his eyes from Zillah's as he picked up the empty green-and-gold Chartreuse bottle, broke it against the edge of the table, and drew a razor-edge of glass across the soft skin of his right wrist. A shallow crimson gash opened there, nearly obscene in its brightness. Molochai, still smiling, offered his wrist to Christian. Christian pressed his lips to the gash, closed his eyes, and sucked like a baby, tasting the Garden of Eden in the drops of Chartreuse that mingled with Molochai's blood.

Twig watched for a few moments, his eyes dark, his face lost, almost bewildered. Then he picked up Molochai's left arm and bit at the skin of the wrist until the blood flowed there too.

Jessy watched with eyes wide and disbelieving. She saw her dignified friend Christian's mouth smeared with blood, trembling with passion. She saw Twig's teeth at Molochai's wrist, saw the flesh part and the blood flow into Twig's mouth. Most of all she saw the lovely impassive face of Zillah looking on, his brilliant eyes like green jewels set in moonstone. And her stomach clenched, and her mouth watered, and a secret message travelled from the softest fold between her legs to the deepest whorl of her brain—*The vampires! The VAMPIRES!*

Jessy stood up very quietly, and then the bloodlust she had wanted so badly was upon her. She leapt, tore Molochai's arm away from Twig, and tried to fasten her lips on the gash. But Molochai turned furiously on her and batted her away, hard across the face, and she felt the pain in her lip before she tasted the blood there, her own dull blood in her mouth. Molochai and Twig and even kind Christian stood staring at her, bloodied and wild-eyed, like dogs startled at a kill, like interrupted lovers.

But as she backed away from them, a pair of warm arms went around her from behind and a pair of large strong hands caressed her through the silk dress, and a voice whispered, "His blood is sticky-sweet anyway, my dear—I can give you something nicer."

She never knew Zillah's name, or how she ended up with him on a blanket in the back room of Christian's bar. She only knew that her blood was smeared across his face, that his fingers and his tongue explored her body more thoroughly than any had before, that once she thought he was inside her and she was inside him at once, and that his sperm smelled like altars, and that his hair drifted across her eyes as she went to sleep.

It was one of the rare nights that Molochai, Twig, and

Zillah spent apart. Zillah slept on the blanket with Jessy, hidden between cases of whiskey, cupping her breasts in his hands. Molochai slept in Christian's room above the bar with Christian and Twig cuddled close to him, their mouths still working sleepily at his wrists.

Below, far away on Bourbon Street, the mounted police rode their high-stepping steeds through the crowd, chanting, "Leave the street. Mardi Gras is officially over. Leave the street. Mardi Gras is officially over," each one ready with a sap for a drunken skull. And the sun came up on the Wednesday morning trash in the gutters, the butts and the cans and the gaudy, forgotten beads, and the vampires slept with their lovers, for they preferred to do their roaming at night.

Molochai, Twig, and Zillah left town the next evening after the sun went down, so they never knew that Jessy was pregnant. None of them had seen a child of their race being born, but they all knew that their mothers had died in childbirth. They would not have stayed around.

Jessy disappeared for nearly a month. When she came back to Christian's bar, it was to stay for good. Christian gave her the richest food he could afford and let her wash glasses when she insisted on earning her keep. Sometimes, remembering Molochai's blood smeared around Christian's mouth, remembering Zillah's fragrant sperm inside her, Jessy crept into bed with Christian and sat on top of him until he would make love to her. He would not bite her, and for that she beat at his face with her fists until he slapped her and told her to stop. Then she moved quietly over him. He watched her grow gravid through the sweltering oily summer months, lazily shaped her tight distended belly and her swollen breasts with his hands.

When her time came, Christian poured whiskey down her throat like water. It wasn't enough. Jessy screamed until she could scream no more, and her eyes showed only the whites with their silvery rims, and great gouts of blood poured from her. When the baby slipped out of Jessy, its head turned and its eyes met Christian's: confused, intelligent, innocent. A shred of deep pink tissue was caught in the tiny mouth, softening between the working gums.

Christian separated the baby from Jessy, wrapped it in a blanket, and held it up to the window. If its first sight was of the French Quarter, it would know its way around those streets forever—should it ever need such knowledge. Then he knelt between Jessy's limp legs and looked at the poor torn passage that had given him so many nights of idle pleasure. Ruined now, bloody.

So much blood to go to waste.

Christian licked his lips, licked them again.

Christian's bar was closed for ten nights. Christian's car, a silver Bel Air that had served him well for years, headed north. He drove up any road that looked anonymous, along any highway he knew he would not remember.

Little Nothing was a lovely baby, a sugar-candy confection of a baby with enormous dark blue eyes and a mass of golden-brown hair. Someone would love him. Someone human, away from the South, away from the hot night air and the legends. Nothing might escape the hunger for blood, might be happy, might be whole.

Toward dawn, in a Maryland suburb full of fine graceful houses, dark grassy lawns, long sleek cars in sweeping driveways, a tall thin figure draped in heavy black clothes stooped, set a bundle down on a doorstep, and went slowly away without looking back. Christian was remembering the last night of Mardi Gras, and the taste of blood and altars was in his mouth.

The baby Nothing opened his eyes and saw darkness, soft and velvety, pricked with sparkling white light. His mouth drew down; his eyebrows came together in a frown. He was hungry. He could not see the basket that cradled him, could not read the note in spidery handwriting pinned to his blanket: *His name is Nothing. Care for him and he will bring you luck.* He lay in the basket snug as a king cake baby, pink and tiny as the infant Christ in plastic, and he knew only that he wanted light and warmth and food, as a baby will. And he opened his mouth wide and showed his soft pink gums and yelled. He yelled long and loud until the door opened and warm hands took him in.

PART ONE

Fifteen
Years
Later

1

The night wind felt wonderful in Steve's hair. The Thunderbird was *huge*. It always drove like a fucking monster, but tonight Steve felt as if he were piloting some great steamboat down a magic river, a river of shimmering asphalt banked by pine forest and thick, rioting expanses of kudzu. They were somewhere far outside Missing Mile, somewhere on the highway that led up to the Roxboro electric power plant and, beyond that, the North Carolina–Virginia border.

Ghost was asleep beside him, his head hung out the window on the passenger side, his pale hair whipping in the wind, his face washed in moonlight. The bottle of whiskey was propped between Ghost's legs, three-quarters empty, in danger of tipping despite the limp hand that curled around it.

Steve leaned over and grabbed the bottle, took a healthy swig. "The T-bird has been drinking," he sang into the wind, "yes, the T-bird has been drinking . . . not me."

"Um," said Ghost. "What? What?"

"Forget it," Steve told him. "Go back to sleep. Have another drink." He drove faster. He'd wake Ghost on the drive home, to keep him company. Now he wanted Ghost to stay asleep awhile longer; there was bad business ahead. Dangerous business. Or so Steve liked to think of it.

Ghost took the bottle back and stared at the label, trying to focus on it. His pale blue eyes swam, narrowed, sharpened only slightly. "White Horse," he read. "Look, Steve, it's

White Horse whiskey. Did you know Dylan Thomas was drinking at a pub called the White Horse the night he died?"

"You told me. That's why we bought it." Steve crossed his fingers and tried to will Ghost back to sleep.

"He drank eighteen straight whiskeys," Ghost said, awed.

"*You* drank eighteen straight whiskeys."

"No wonder my brain is sailing with the moon. Sing to me, Steve. Sing me back to sleep."

Just at that moment they crossed a bridge that seemed to bow under the weight of the old brown T-bird, and Steve saw moonlight shimmering on black waters, so he raised his voice in the first song that came to mind: "Silver southern moon . . . for ten years I thought I was born of you. . . . Silver moon, I'll be back someday. . . ."

"That's not the way it goes. I should know, I wrote it." Ghost's voice was fading. "Oh, silver southern moon . . . tell me your sweet lies, then let me drown deep in your eyes. . . ."

"Somedaaay," Steve joined in. He and the whiskey sang Ghost to sleep, the whiskey with its somnolent amber song, Steve with a voice that cracked when he tried to hit the high notes. Behind them the river passed in silence; the lowest-hanging branches brushed the water, and the leaves rotted on the bough. The moon spread like butter on the black river, and Ghost's eyes closed; with his head pillowed on the hump between the seats, he began to dream.

They bypassed Roxboro, but Steve saw the power plant on Lake Hyco, lit up all glowing green and white like a weird birthday cake, its million pipes and wires and glass insulators and metal gewgaws reflected in the lake. On the way back, if Ghost was awake, they'd drive up there to a hill Steve knew and look out over the pastures and the lake and all the glittering Milky Way. An hour or so after passing out Ghost was usually raring to go again. His dreams gave him new strength. Or made him laugh or cry, or sometimes scared the shit out of him.

Steve put his hand on Ghost's head, smoothed back wisps of hair from flickering closed eyes. He wondered what was unfolding beneath his hand, beneath the thin bone, inside the orb of ivory that cradled Ghost's weird brain. Who was born and murdered and resurrected inside that skull? What walked behind Ghost's eyelids, what lithe secret phantoms tapped Ghost's shoulder and made him whimper deep in his throat?

Ghost often dreamed of things that were going to happen, or of things that had already happened that he couldn't possibly know about. These premonitions could come when he was awake too, but the ones that came to him in dreams seemed to be the most potent. More often than not they were also the most cryptic. He had known when his grandmother was going to die, but then so had she. Though surely painful, the knowledge had given them the time they needed to say goodbye.

Goodbye for a while, anyway. Ghost had inherited his grandmother's house in Missing Mile, where he and Steve lived now. Steve had spent plenty of time in that house as a kid, watching Miz Deliverance mix herbs or cut out cookies with her heart-shaped cutters, building forts in the backyard, sleeping over in Ghost's room. Even now, five years after her death, Steve sometimes thought he felt the familiar presence of Miz Deliverance in a room, or just around a corner. He imagined this was something Ghost took for granted.

Suddenly unnerved by the prospect of touching Ghost's dreams, Steve put his hand back on the wheel.

They drove past a graveyard full of softly rotting monuments and flowers, an abandoned railyard, a barbecue shack whose sign advertised *GRAND OPENING EVERY FRI AND SAT NITE.* A rabbit darted across the road. Steve braked, and Ghost's head rolled back and forth on his thin neck—so fragile, so fragile. These days Steve was paranoid about something happening to Ghost. Ghost was spacy, sure, but he could take care of himself. Still, Steve couldn't help watching out for him, especially now that Ghost was the only person he felt like spending time with.

They had other friends, sure, but those guys mostly wanted to go out drinking and smoke weed and talk about Wolfpack football at the state university over in Raleigh. All of which was okay, even though the Wolfpack was always pretty shitty, but Ghost was different. Ghost didn't give a flying fuck about football, Ghost could drink everybody else under the table and not get a damn bit weirder, and Ghost understood all the shit that had gone down over the past few months. The shit with Ann. Ghost never asked Steve why he didn't forget about Ann and get himself a new girlfriend; Ghost understood why Steve didn't want to see Ann or any other girl, not for months and months, maybe not ever.

Not until he could trust himself, anyway. Right now he did not deserve the company of women. However lonely or horny he got, he had it coming to him for what he had done to Ann.

He played with strands of Ghost's hair as he drove, winding them around his fingers, marvelling at their fineness, their silvery-gold luster. Just to feel the difference, he ran his hand through his own coarse hair, hair the color of a crow's wing, hair that stood up in wild loops and cowlicks. His hair was dirty, and he noticed that Ghost's was too. Steve hadn't been taking care of himself—he'd gone days without a shower and over a month without washing his clothes; he'd been late for his job at the record store three times last week; he was putting away a twelve-pack of Bud every day or two —but he hoped it wasn't rubbing off on Ghost. There was such a thing as being too damn sympathetic. Steve's hand felt greasy. He wiped it on his T-shirt.

They were here. Steve had no idea where, but he saw what he wanted: the faded light of an ancient Pepsi machine sitting outside a fishin'-and-huntin' store, casting dim red and blue shadows in the dirt of the parking lot. Steve swung the T-bird in and killed the ignition. Ghost's head had slipped onto Steve's knee, and he eased out from under it. There was a little dark spot on the knee of Steve's jeans. Ghost's spit, Ghost's drunken sleeping spit. Steve rubbed it into the cloth, then absently put his finger in his mouth. A faint taste of whiskey and molasses . . . and what was he doing sucking someone else's spit off his finger? Didn't matter. Ghost was lost deep in dreams. Time to go to work.

Steve fished in the backseat. Cassette cases—so *that* was where Ann's damn Cocteau Twins tape had ended up. Steve

had always hated it anyway, the girl's feathery voice that was
supposed to be so angelic and the ethereal-seasick wall of
sound. Empty food bags and a veritable sea of beer cans.
Finally he dug out his special tool, a length of coat hanger
bent into a hook at one end. He wondered if he ought to pull
the T-bird up so it was hiding the front of the Pepsi machine.
No, he decided; anybody out driving this time of night is
probably on business just as shady as mine.

With a last glance at Ghost, Steve knelt, fed the wire into
the coin-return slot of the machine, and wiggled it around
until he felt it catch. He tugged gently and seconds later was
blessed by a shower of silver. Steve scooped the quarters,
dimes, and nickels out of the dirt, shoved them into his pockets, hustled back to the car, and got the hell out of the parking lot.

Twenty fast miles later, Steve had the radio on a rock station and Ghost was trying to decide whether to rejoin the
living. "Are we still in North Carolina?"

"Yeah." Steve turned Led Zeppelin down and waited for
the stories. Ghost always told Steve his dreams, and they
were sometimes coherent, sometimes nonsensical and lovely,
and almost invariably a little frightening. Ghost sat up and
stretched, working out his sleep cramps. Steve saw a flash of
belly where Ghost's sweatshirt parted from his tie-dyed
pants. Pale skin, golden hair sparse and curly. Ghost looked
out the window for several miles, his brow furrowed, his eyes
puzzled. That meant he was remembering. Steve waited, and
Ghost began, haltingly, to speak.

"When they were young . . . they were the world's dar-
lings. The world's opinion meant everything to them, even
though they tried to pretend it meant nothing. Their town
was even grayer and muddier when they pranced along the
streets after midnight, and the rooftops bent to kiss their
dyed hair. They wandered through the shops putting their
delicate fingerprints on the window glass and china, touching
anything colorful or sweet, pinching things between thumb
and forefinger as if to grasp the town in both hands would
dirty them. Sully them." Ghost rolled "sully" over his tongue
as if it were scuppernong wine; in his thick Carolina voice

the word took on a dark, rich flavor. "Sully them. The big
boys at their school shouted things at them, black dirty
things that stank of toilet-wall scrawls and smeared basins.
But those boys never fought them because they knew the
twins were magic. Everyone knew the twins would go away
to the city someday, where they could pick rhinestones out of
the cigarette sludge in the gutter, and the moon would be as
aching and vivid as neon cheese in blue velvet sky. And they
did. They went to New Orleans."

Ghost stopped, looked away down the train track they
were crossing. Tiny colored lights shone far down the line,
fairy lights, Christmas lights, though it was only the middle
of September.

Steve closed his eyes, remembered the road, opened them
again. "Go on," he said. "What happened to them in the
city?"

"Artists put them in films. They were *twins,* and the hip
crowd loved the perversity of that. Their mirror-image por-
nography was art. They were Donatello Davids, skinny and
beautiful, not heavyset like Michelangelo's. Androgynous
striplings who outlined each other's bones in lipstick. And
they were allowed every art and luxury and perversion the
city held because of their overrouged lips and their sluts'
eyes and the poetry of their hands.

"They grew jaded, tired, but still insatiable on their own
mattress. They lived and lived and saw the first lines appear
around their eyes. They saw years of liquor, expensive cigarettes, drugs and passion etch themselves on their movie-
starlet faces. They watched the mirror as they would have
watched a quicksilver film of their death, in a cold heat of
fascination, dread, clutching each other. They bit at each
other's throats in desperation, thinking to regain beauty in
blood, to drink the pulse of life. But their blood was thin,
grainy, mixed with other substances—no longer the rich purple fountain they had once known. They went out less,
spending whole days flat on the mattress like two dry sticks
side by side, forgetting to eat, watching the cobweb cracks in
the ceiling plaster widen, spread like the tracery on their
faces. They—"

The high stupid scream of a siren split the night open. Ghost's voice trailed off. Blue light pulsated in the rearview mirror, turned Ghost's face pallid, made the litter of beer cans seem to whirl and dance.

"Shit," said Steve, trying to decide whether to pull over. His mind spun with the blue light: the store and the Pepsi machine were forty fucking miles behind! No one had seen him jimmy the machine, no one. Would he go to jail? Would Ghost go too, as an accessory to the crime he had slept through? Ghost would lie, say *he'd* planned it, trying to take some of the heat off Steve. Ghost was only twenty-two, Steve a year older. They had their whole lives ahead of them and an open bottle of whiskey in their hands . . . *Fuck! Fuck! Fuck!* Steve's mind raced, and the radio got louder, and the siren ripped the night apart, and he heard Jimmy Page wailing on guitar and then Ghost's voice, not at all panicky, saying, "Pull over, Steve, pull *over*, you dumb fuck!"

Steve wrenched the wheel to the right, braked hard, and they skidded on the surface of the dark road and slowed . . . *slowed* . . . stopped, gravel spraying from the tires, a thin trail of black rubber behind them. But they were whole and safe, and so was the car, and most blessedly of all, the police car was *passing* them, siren still screaming, light still whirling like a cold blue dervish.

"Jesus fuckin' Christ," said Steve, and let his hands drop from the steering wheel, his head fall back against the seat. He was aware of Ghost reaching over to kill the ignition, putting his hand on Steve's shoulder, moving closer across the seat. No questions (why are you so paranoid about the cops tonight, Steve? just carrying a couple of joints? or maybe jimmying Pepsi machines again? or hiding the raped and gutted corpse of your ex-girlfriend in the trunk?), no accusations (we coulda been KILLED!), just the gentle, wordless comfort of Ghost's hand on the back of his neck, Ghost's thoughts inside his head.

For a few moments Steve accepted the comfort gratefully, thirstily. Then he remembered who he was (Steve Finn don't need *nothin'* from *nobody*! No, not much, not much), straightened up, and shook Ghost off. Ghost withdrew, un-

derstanding all too well. Understanding maddeningly. Steve
wanted to hurt Ghost, to stop the waves of complacent sympathy pouring from the passenger seat. But Steve could not
find the words to hurt Ghost, and if he had found them, he
could not have made himself use them. The best he could
come up with was "Don't you call me a dumb fuck."

"Okay," said Ghost, so soft that Steve could barely hear
him.

Up ahead was a riot of lights and movement. Red lights,
blue lights, someone standing in the road flagging the T-bird
down. Steve stopped, and the flagman motioned him forward. *Slow,* he signalled. An ambulance. Two police cars. An
officer talking to a tired country woman in a torn bathrobe
and curlers. The woman held the collar of a Doberman, re-
straining it. The dog snarled at the police, strained toward
the T-bird as it passed at five miles per hour. A brick ranch
house built close to the road, its scrubby yard littered with
broken toys and car parts; on the porch the woman's family, a
man holding four small children back, apparently telling
them not to look. The man was small and red and scrawny as
a chicken neck. The children craned their necks, pointing,
curious.

There was something else in the yard, near the roadside,
something that had excited the dog, something the children
were trying to see. Something naked, dry, withered. A child
—but what could have shrivelled it so, leached its life away?
Steve saw a backpack lying nearby, spilling the kid's life.
Clothes. A couple of toy robots. Transformers, Steve knew
from watching the Saturday-morning commercials. The kid
must be a runaway. Flecks of gravel were embedded in the
soft skin of his face; his head lolled back, half severed, the
dark red cavern of his throat glistening—but there was so
little blood, and the raw tissues within looked wasted,
parched. A gray blanket settled over the planes and angles of
the little body. A small brown hand protruded, thin and
dirty, scraped by roadside grit.

As Steve rolled down his window and handed his driver's
license to one of the cops, Ghost turned his head and stared
back at the blanket, at the body beneath it. His eyes lost their

focus; then, slowly, they closed. Ghost saw through the blanket, through death. He saw how the boy had looked alive, curiosity and intelligence in his young eyes. The name came to him as clearly as a memory: *Robert*. He felt the fury that had made Robert climb out his window, steal away from home and parents who used him as a receptacle for their overprotective love. There was something they had not let him do—go to a ball game or spend the night at a friend's house. Ghost almost had the knowledge; then it slipped away. It didn't matter. The important thing was that the boy need not have died. Ghost felt Robert's fear at being alone under the tall trees and the wide midnight sky, the great glittering impassive sky. He felt the boy almost turn around, almost save his own life, but the wounded pride of adolescence would not allow him.

Ghost felt Robert's terror mount as he caught sounds— insidious whispers, soft laughter—sounds not of the night and its usual spooks but something darker, stranger, more purposeful and far, far deadlier. And then the hands, grabbing him from behind, four strong and sharp-fingered hands, and the hungry mouths all over him, sucking out his strength and his life. At the end there was only pain that spiralled up and up and stretched itself impossibly thin—exquisite pain, pain that precluded all thought, all memory, all identity. To know such pain was to lose one's self, to become the pain, to die borne away on pain, its high soundless song in the ears. That was what had happened to Robert.

Ghost lay quiet, and he knew the insensate loneliness of a corpse on the roadside, growing cold, the taste of blood melting from the tongue, the eyes filming over, the impossibility of human contact ever again, of comfort ever again. Ghost tried to swallow, but his throat would not work, and he made some small gasping sound and felt Steve's big hand covering his own, enfolding his fingers, squeezing life back into him.

"Let it go, Ghost," Steve said. "You can't take on all the pain in the world. Let it *go*, man."

Ghost shuddered, then began to slip back. Warmth. Blood where it ought to be, in his veins, flowing safely and sanely.

The ambulance, the police cars, the lonely dry dead thing under the blanket were far away now, left behind.

"What happened to those twins?" Steve asked as they drove on. "In your dream."

Ghost thought, remembered. Suddenly he didn't want to think about those twins.

But Steve wanted to hear the rest of the story. Ghost hoped it was only a story, only a dream. He never knew, not at first. "They grew weak," he said. "Eventually they had to spend alternate days alive. One would watch over the other, keeping vigil over the still chest, the blotted-out eyes, the drying mouth. At the first tinge of dawn the dead twin would begin to move, and the living twin would lie down and stretch himself taut on the mattress, his skin already crackling on his bones, his hair straggling like grass across his bare hollow shoulders. One day . . . one day . . . One day their eyes were open, but neither of them moved."

Ghost finished in a rush of breath, whiskey and fear breath, upset all over again. Steve kept hold of Ghost's hand. Ghost's fingers twitched.

"Jesus, Ghost," Steve said. "Jeeesus, Ghost."

2

The last dying days of summer, fall coming on fast. A cold night, the first of the season, a change from the usual bland Maryland climate. *Cold,* thought the boy; his mind felt numb. The trees he could see through his bedroom window were tall charcoal sticks, shivering, afraid of the wind or only trying to stand against it. Every tree was alone out there. The animals were alone, each in its hole, in its thin fur, and anything that got hit on the road tonight would die alone. Before morning, he thought, its blood would freeze in the cracks of the asphalt.

On his razor-scarred, wax-scabbed desk before him lay a picture postcard. The design on its front was multicolored and abstract. There were splotches of deep lipstick pink, streaks of sea green and storm gray, flecks of gold embossed in thin bright leaves. He picked up his fountain pen with the graceful heart-shaped nib, dipped its delicate tip into his bottle of ink (pen and ink having been stolen from the art room at school), and wrote a few spidery lines on the message side of the postcard.

Then the boy stretched his legs under the desk and with the bare toes of both feet grasped the bottle he had hidden there. The liquor inside was a darker amber than he was used to, and when he took a swig, there was a sharp taste of smoke behind the familiar musky burn that hurt his throat. He swallowed the whiskey, licked his lips to wet them with liquor-essence and his clear spit. Then he picked up the postcard, brought it to his mouth, gave it a whiskey tongue-kiss, kissed it as hungrily as he had ever dreamed of kissing the sweetest, richest mouth. And he picked up the pen again and signed his name: *Nothing*.

His capital *N* and the loop of his *g* swooped like kites' tails. His *t* was a dagger thrusting down. He took another swig of his parents' Johnnie Walker and realized he could already feel the familiar half-queasy anticipation of drunkenness in his stomach, the floating dizziness in his head. He was getting drunk on two shots of whiskey. Evidently the shit from his parents' liquor cabinet was stronger than the shit his friends poured into empty Pepsi bottles and passed around in cars going too fast on the highway outside town.

He looked at the postcard, frowned at the signature, *Nothing* drying dull and black, wishing he'd signed it in blood. Maybe it wasn't too late. With the pen's tip he jabbed at his wrist until a bead of blood appeared, bright red against his pale thin skin, with a prick of light from the lamp shining in it. He signed his name again, *Nothing* in blood, tracing over the black letters with scarlet. The ink ran into the blood, and the whole thing dried rusty brown-black, the color of an old scab. The results did not altogether disappoint him.

His blood made a trickling path down the inside of his forearm, staining the fine invisible hairs, covering some of his old scars, leaving some of their razor-tracery exposed. He licked the blood away. It smudged his lips sticky, and he smiled at himself in the window's reflection. The night-Nothing in the glass smiled back. The boy in the window had the same long sheaf of dyed black hair, the same pointed chin, the same almond-shaped dark eyes—but his smile was colder, far colder.

Nothing turned off the light and watched the reflection of his bedroom click out of existence, watched the cold night fill the panes. He lay on his bed and watched the stars and planets glowing on his ceiling behind the layers of black fishnet he had hung up. He'd painted them there, the rings of Saturn lopsided, the constellations crazed.

He felt his room gather itself in the dark and stand darkly around him, not frightening but surely full of power. He was never certain what was here. Cigarettes, he thought. Flowers from the graveyard, and that bone, that damned bone, his friend Sioux wouldn't say *where* it came from. Books, most of them stolen from thrift-shop shelves where he left only his finger marks in the dust. Horror stories, thin books of poems. Dylan Thomas, of course, and others. A copy of *Look Homeward, Angel*—on the cover the stone, the leaf, the unfound door, and the angel with its expression of soft stone idiocy. A lily drooped from the angel's hand, dead in stone. Dust. His old stuffed animals. A clay skeleton his friend Laine had brought him from the Day of the Dead festival in Mexico, its eyes red sequins, its ribs dusted with glitter. All the objects here, all the pencil drawings on the walls and pictures cut out of obscure music magazines and secret lists in notebooks, wove a web of power around him.

He pulled his quilt around his legs and touched his ribs and hipbones, liking how thin he was. Then the bedroom door opened, and painfully bright light spilled in from the hallway. He jerked his hand away and pulled up his quilt.

"Jason? Are you asleep? It's only nine. Too much sleep is bad for you."

It might block my channels, he thought.

His parents stepped into the room and he felt the web of power collapse and drift down, broken strands brushing his face. Mother, fresh from her crystal healing class at the Arts Center, looked exalted. Her eyes sparkled; there was too much blush on her cheeks. Father, behind her, only looked glad to be home. "Did you do your homework?" Mother asked. "I don't want you going to sleep this early if you haven't done your homework. You know what your father and I thought of a smart boy like you getting those grades last quarter. A C in algebra!"

Nothing looked at the pile of schoolbooks near his closet. One of the covers was a vomitous shade of turquoise. One was bright orange. The black T-shirt he'd thrown over them blotted them out. He thought that if he stacked them all up, he might be able to build an altar.

"Jason, I want to talk to you." Mother came all the way into the room and squatted next to the mattress. Her sweater was woven of soft iridescent wool, pink and blue. In fascination Nothing watched a smudge of ash from the carpet transfer itself before his eyes onto the knee of her cream-colored cotton pants. He raised his head and checked the quilt; it was covering him decently. He thought he saw the two small ridges of his hipbones poking up under it.

"My support circle meditated with our rose crystals tonight," Mother said. "I thought of you. I don't want to keep you from fulfilling yourself. I certainly don't want to decrease your potential." She paused to glance at Father glowering in the background, then let the great revelation fly. "You can get your ear pierced after all, if you still want to. Your father or I will go with you."

Nothing turned his head to hide the two tiny holes in his left earlobe, made with a thumbtack and several swigs of vodka one day at school. The Jewelry Box at the mall would not pierce the ears of anyone under eighteen without a parent's permission, especially not the ears of a boy in black who looked younger than his fifteen years, who forged signatures on endless homemade permission slips. And no wonder Father was pissed off. This was the final indignity: a son who wanted to wear earrings.

"Wait a minute. Wait one minute. Just what the hell is this?" Father crossed the room in two strides and pulled the bottle of Johnnie Walker from under the desk. The last gossamer strands of the web whispered past Nothing's face and dissolved in the air. He smelled the ghost of incense. "Young man, I think I would like an explan—"

"Just a minute, Rodger." Mother radiated benevolence, spiritual wholeness. "Jason is not a bad child. If he's drinking, we should spend more quality time—"

"Quality time, my ass." Nothing decided he liked Father better than Mother these days, not that he liked either of them much. "Jason is not a child at all. He is fifteen and runs with a gang of punkers who give him a liquor habit and God knows what else. He dyes his hair that phony black that rubs off on the pillowcases and stains my good shirts in the wash. He smokes cigarettes—*Lucky Strikes,*" Father said with distaste. Nothing saw the pack of Vantages poking out of Father's breast pocket. "He throws away the clothing we buy him or rips it to rags before he'll wear it. Now he's stealing from us. Things are going to CHANGE—"

"Rodger. *We'll* talk about it, *among ourselves.* Don't worry, Jason, you're not in trouble." Mother positively floated from the room, pulling Father after her. Father slammed the door. A stack of books fell over, spilling Plath and Bradbury and William Burroughs across the floor in an unlikely orgy of paper and dust.

In the hall Father's voice rose. "What the hell was *that* supposed to mean, he's not in trouble . . . he goddamn well *is* in trouble. . . ."

Nothing closed his eyes for a moment and watched red spangles swirl away behind his lids. Then he got up and stretched his lithe naked body, shaking his hair and his hands to cleanse himself of Mother's touch. Father had taken away the good whiskey, but Nothing had his own bottle of brainrot hidden in the closet. A flask of something called White Horse. He'd gotten his friend Jack to buy it for him because of the name: Dylan Thomas had drunk his last eighteen whiskeys at a pub called the White Horse in New York City.

Nothing lay in the dark and sipped from the neck of the bottle, blinking up at the stars on his ceiling. After a while the constellations began to swim. *I've got to get out of this place,* he thought just before dawn, and the ghosts of all the decades of middle-class American children afraid of complacency and stagnation and comfortable death drifted before his face, whispering their agreement.

In Nothing's English class the next day, Mrs. Margaret Peebles plunged her hypodermic of higher learning into *Lord of the Flies* and sucked out every drop of its primal magic, every trace of its adolescent wonder. Nothing knew half the class hadn't even read the book. If they were judging it by what the teacher said, he could hardly blame them. But he'd read it three years ago, one summer afternoon in bed with a fever, and when he had put the book down, his hands had been shaking. Those wild salty-skinned little boys had tumbled through his head, and he had cried for them, so young, grown old so fast.

He looked at the blank page of notebook paper in front of him. Pink and blue lines, neatly ruled. He began to count them but lost track of the number. The clock said 9:10. Twenty more minutes left of class. His head ached from last night's whiskey, and he wanted to sleep. He began drawing in his notebook. Swirls. The first vestiges of a face. An eye, green because his pen was green. A tooth.

"Jason—"

Outside, far away across the wide green front lawn, past the pink granite sign that looked like a gravestone except for the snarling tiger carved on top (Gift of the Senior Class, 1972), a black van sped by. The road past the school was long and straight, and the van was going too fast for Nothing to catch more than a snatch of the singing that blew back on the wind out the open windows of the van, borne on the wings of the sweet September day. But he was sure it was Bowie. Someone in that van was singing a song by David Bowie. The voices were clear and loud and drunken. Nothing watched the van disappear and wished more than anything else in the world that he were going with it, going with those happy singers, drinking and singing and going away on the open road.

"*Jason.*"

He sighed. Peebles was staring at him. The rest of the class paid no attention; they were elsewhere too, in their own worlds, driving away on their own roads. "What?" he said.

"We were discussing William Golding's *Lord of the Flies.* You have read the book?"

"I have."

"Then perhaps you can tell me about the rivalry between Jack and Ralph. What allows it to grow so bitter?"

"Their attraction for each other," Nothing said. "Their love for each other. They had this fierce love, they wanted to *be* each other. And only when you love someone that much can you hate them too—"

A ripple of laughter went through the class. A couple of boys rolled their eyes at one another—*what a fag!*

Peebles pressed her thin lips together. "If you had been paying attention, instead of doodling and staring out the window—"

Suddenly he was too tired to care what happened to him. This was empty, all empty useless crap. "Oh fuck you," he said, and felt the class suck in its breath and silently cheer him on.

Half an hour later, sitting in the principal's office waiting for the hand of petty academic fate to descend upon him, he thought again of the ghosts that had visited him last night. Visions, or whiskey vapors? It didn't matter. *You've got to get out of here,* they'd told him. *You've got to get out of here.*

After school, a bunch of kids met in the parking lot and went over to Laine Petersen's house to get stoned. Laine's older brother had gone off to college and left behind his water-bong, an elaborate ceramic affair shaped like a skull with worms twining in and out of the empty eye sockets. You put your finger over one of the nostrils to hold the smoke in.

Laine's girlfriend Julie had a bag of pot, real ragweed, the kind of stuff that scoured your throat and made your lungs feel like parchment if you held the smoke in too long. Still, it was all these kids knew, and within fifteen minutes they were stoned out of their minds. Someone put a Bauhaus tape on and turned it all the way up. Laine and Julie rolled around on the bed, pretending to make out.

Nothing had his doubts about how much Laine really liked girls. The walls of his room were plastered with posters of the Cure; he had seen them in concert three times, and once he had sneaked backstage to present Robert Smith, the singer, with a bouquet of bloodred roses into which he had tucked two hits of blotter acid. Julie wore her hair wildly teased in all directions, and she favored lots of black eyeliner and smudged red lipstick. Nothing suspected that Laine liked her mainly because of her superficial resemblance to Robert Smith.

He looked around the room. Several of the kids were groping each other ineptly, kissing each other with sloppy wet mouths. Veronica Aston had pulled Lily Hartung's skirt up and had two fingers inside the elastic of Lily's panties. Nothing stared at this for several minutes, dully interested. Bisexuality was much in vogue among this crowd. It was one of the few ways they could feel daring. Nothing himself had made out with several of these kids, but though he had tasted their mouths and touched their most tender parts, none of them really interested him. The thought made him sad, though he wasn't sure why.

He lay back on the floor and stared up at a poster tacked on the ceiling above Laine's bed: Robert Smith's lips enlarged several thousand times, smeared with hot orange-red lipstick, shiny and sexual. Nothing wished he could fall into them, could slide down Robert Smith's throat and curl up safe in his belly. The marijuana made him feel restless; he wanted to do a hundred things at once, but none of them here. He realized that among these kids he called his friends he felt much more alone than he had felt in his room last night.

The Bauhaus tape ended, and no one put anything else on. The party began to break up. A hippie-looking girl Nothing didn't know flashed a peace sign at Laine as she left. Julie got up to leave too; she was supposed to be grounded, she explained, because her mother had smelled beer on her breath when she came home from a party last weekend. "Bummer," said Laine, not sounding as if he cared very much.

Nothing stared at the floor, feeling depressed. He had seen Julie so strung out on acid that she thought the flesh was melting from her bones, and her parents couldn't even deal with her drinking beer.

As she was about to leave, Julie reached into her purse. "You can have this," she told Nothing. "You said you liked it, and I never listen to it—sounds like shitkicker music to me." She handed him a cheap home-produced cassette tape. The crayon writing on the liner said *LOST SOULS?*

Nothing's heart quickened. When he had heard this tape at Julie's house, something in it had sung out to him. He remembered a snatch of lyrics: "We are not afraid . . . let the night come . . . we are not afraid." The singer's golden voice chanting those words had awakened in him a courage he didn't know he had, a belief that someday his life would be more than this. But to show an excess of feeling in this crowd was considered uncool; as far as Nothing could tell, you were supposed to act bored all the time. He only smiled at Julie, said "Thanks," and stuck the cassette in his back-pack.

As soon as Julie was gone, Laine got up and put on a Cure tape. Then he came and lay beside Nothing on the floor. His bleached white-blond hair fell in long strands over his eyes. His hand found Nothing's and squeezed. Nothing didn't squeeze back, but he didn't pull away.

"Do you want a blowjob?" said Laine. He was one of the youngest of the crowd, only fourteen, but he cultivated ar-cane talents. Nothing had seen the legend *Laine Gives Killer Head* inscribed on more than one bathroom wall at school.

"What about Julie?"

"Julie doesn't turn me on much," said Laine. "I like you, though. I think you're really cool." Lazily he propped himself on his elbow and reached over to touch Nothing's face. Nothing closed his eyes and let himself be touched. The contact felt good. Laine hugged him, buried his face in Noth-ing's shoulder; he smelled of shampoo and clove cigarettes.

"Seriously," he said. "I haven't given you a blowjob since August. I want to."

"Okay," Nothing told him. He pulled Laine's face to his and kissed him, nudging his mouth gently open. Laine's mouth tasted delicately salty, like tears. He suddenly felt terribly sad for Laine, who was too young to know so much. He wanted to show Laine some gesture of tenderness, some-thing that might make them both feel as young as they really were.

But Laine's tongue was already tracing a wet path down Nothing's chest; Laine's hands were already unfastening Nothing's jeans and tugging them open. Nothing stared up at Robert Smith's magnified mouth. The singer's lush clotted voice surrounded him, making him feel again as if he were tumbling between those lips. Laine's hands and tongue worked him with a skill born of practice. Nothing felt some-thing twist inside him. He put his hand down to touch

Laine's brittle hair, and Laine looked up at him with clear, guileless eyes.

As he began to come, Nothing thought again of the black van that had driven past the school today, of the snatch of song he had heard trailing from its windows. He wondered where the van was now.

Wherever it was, he wished he were there too.

3

 The road was long and hilly, the black van was hurtling along like a roller coaster, and the day was fine. Twig drove with an elbow cocked out the window. Molochai hung out the other side, gnawing on his sticky fingers, letting the wind blow in his face. Zillah lolled on a mattress in the back, luxuriating in the clear autumn warmth. The mattress was filthy, parts of its fabric caked with stiff stains that faded from dark maroon to nearly black. They would have to unload it at a dump and find a cleaner one soon.

Molochai swivelled his head as they passed the school. "Hey! Kiddies!"

Twig swatted him. "Small game. How boring."

"There'd be plenty to do at a high school. All those candy boys, all those sugar girls . . ." Molochai pictured himself gliding through shadowy afternoon halls when almost everyone had gone home, his nose and mouth full of the dry smell of paper, the soft scent of years' dust grimed into the corners, the underlying thrill of odor left behind by healthy young flesh shot through with sizzling hormones, greased with quickening blood. Maybe one of them would have stayed behind, kept after school: a bad girl, sulking in an empty classroom, her eyes downcast. She would never see the shape coming down the hallway, pausing at the door. Molochai thought of ripping soft bellyskin, white and firm just above the tangle of pubic hair. That was his favorite spot to bite girls.

"A temple of boredom," Zillah offered from the back. He was braiding his hair. He kept a streak of it dyed purple, gold, and green, and he was weaving the three colored strands together, toying with the braid, then delicately pulling it apart with his fingers. "Boredom is a sin. Boredom is unholy."

Molochai snorted. "What do *you* know about it? When have you ever been bored?"

"I'm a hundred," said Zillah, studying his long fingernails critically. He produced a bottle of black nail polish and began painting his nails, neatly, carefully. "You two are only seventy-five, but I am one hundred years old this very year. I have been bored. I'm bored now."

"*I'm* a hundred." Twig reached under the driver's seat and found a bottle. "And this wine was born last Tuesday! Let's drink to it."

"I'm a hundred," Molochai mumbled around the neck of the bottle. The wine was sticky, sweet as rotten grapes. He licked his lips and took another swig.

They kept driving, kept drinking, never looked at a map. They did not need maps; the possibility of alternate routes, charted yellow and red and green roads, cryptic legends, held no fascination for them. By some warm alcoholic magnetism in their blood they were drawn on to the next city and the next. Twig always knew what roads to take, what highways he could roar along the fastest, what country blacktops were haunted by state troopers and God-fearing folk. They had just come from New York City where they were able to sate their appetites every night on blood rich with strange drugs, where a hophead chick they met had let them sleep the days away in her East Village apartment until they grew careless and left a shredded mess in her bathtub. Kinky stuff was fine, she said, but she wasn't into death. And there were gore stains on her only set of towels. She had still been trying to decide how to get rid of the body when they sneaked out.

Molochai, Twig, and Zillah were good at sneaking out. They had plenty of practice at it: Zillah had taught Molochai and Twig how to act nonchalant, how to wipe the blood off their faces and control their passionate breathing before they left the scene of a kill. Without his guidance, Zillah reflected, they would both have been dead several times over, probably with stakes driven through their punky little hearts. It was true that Zillah was a hundred and the others only seventy-five; even so, they were just teenagers by the standards of their race. Zillah remembered the depthless eyes of Christian, his quiet, almost painful dignity. How old would Christian be now? Three hundred years? Four? But even when Christian had been a mere babe of fifty, Zillah found it hard to imagine him acting as stupid as Molochai and Twig.

Still, they were his charges. They took orders without question, and in return they expected Zillah to take care of them, to do their thinking for them. They had perhaps half a brain between them. They knew Zillah was the smart one. But they were good fun.

Zillah had met them at an elegant garden party in the roaring twenties, a *Great Gatsby*-ish affair with paper lanterns and drunken croquet games on the lawn. Molochai and Twig were huddled in a corner of the garden making fun of the women's fancy dresses. Whenever a waiter came by with a tray of champagne flutes, they would reach out and grab two glasses apiece, one in each hand. When Zillah approached them, they were too drunk to recognize him as one of their own, but they liked his pretty face and his natty suit of white linen. They led him into the big house, thinking they were luring him to his death, and tried to attack him in an upstairs parlor decorated entirely in animal skins and trophy heads. Zillah threw them across the room, hoisted them up, and cracked their heads together beneath the eternally roaring jaws of a stuffed lion. Then he opened a vein in his wrist and tenderly gave them to drink. After that they were his forever. Or nearly so.

Several miles outside the town, they gave up on finding the doughnut shop that Molochai thought he remembered once seeing along this highway. They stopped at a 7-Eleven instead. Molochai filled a big bag with candy and Hostess cakes. Twig chose a package of sliced bologna and stocked up on cheap wine.

The cashier watched them with an absorption that bor-

dered on awe, readjusting her heavy ass on the stool behind
the register, pushing at the colored plastic barrettes that held
her stringy hair in place. When Zillah's eyes met hers, she
felt her insides go runny. The unfamiliar territory between
her legs twitched, suddenly moist.

She had moles on her face, and she was vastly overweight,
and she figured she would reach forty untouched by a man.
But something in his green eyes made her feel the way she
used to when she would look at the *Playboy* and *Penthouse*
magazines that were sold in the store, before she told herself
she wasn't interested and started going to church again.
Something in his eyes made her wonder how it would feel to
let a man lie on top of her, to push his thing inside her. She
felt for her pack of Mores, lit one, and sucked the smoke up
hungrily, watching the black van pull away, wondering if that
green-eyed angel would ever return.

On the road again, Twig peeled off slices of bologna and
stuffed them into his mouth, tossing his head like a feeding
leopard as he swallowed, hardly chewing the soft meat. Molochai gulped sticky mouthfuls of cake and cream. Zillah
licked at a sliver of bologna, nibbled delicately around the
edges of a Twinkie, sipped from the bottle of Thunderbird.
None of them were satisfied.

"Will we be in DC by tonight?" Molochai asked, licking
chocolate off his fingers.

Twig stared at the road. "Shit, we'll be there in an hour.
But you can count on staying hungry till way after dark." No
one bothered asking why. They knew where the best city
pickings were—in the clubs, in the alleys, under the midnight moon.

"Yeah." Molochai managed a sticky smile, thinking of
nights in the city. "So we stay in DC for a couple of nights.
Then what?"

Twig thought. "We could check out California again. You
liked the ice cream shops in Chinatown."

"But that's so far. And the whole desert in between us and
it. Nothing to eat. Nothing to drink. No people. No blood."

Zillah closed his eyes, stroked his eyelashes with the tip of one shiny black nail. "We could drive down to New Orleans," he said. "We could visit Christian."

Twig's eyes lit up. "Christian! Remember Christian?"

"Good old Christian!"

"He doesn't drink—*wine!*"

They all laughed.

"Yeah, but he might still be tending bar. Free drinks!"

"And everyone's blood full of wine and beer and whiskey—"

"And *Chartreuse*," said Zillah.

They paused for a moment, tongues tasting a memory of altars, of the Garden of Eden.

"Let's do it."

"Let's go see good old Christian."

"Good old *Chrissy*," said Molochai.

"*Chrissy!*" Twig collapsed in giggles over the wheel.

Zillah passed the wine up to Molochai. "Let's start saving our empties. We'll need to bottle some up tonight. Things may be quite a bit drier after DC."

Molochai and Twig were quiet, considering the possibility of a long dry spell. Then Twig shrugged and said, "Yeah, but fuck it—we're going to New Orleans!"

Molochai turned the music back on, and they sang along with Bowie, leaning on each other, their voices soft and lilting as they got drunker. Zillah ran his hands through Molochai's hair, pulling out the knots. Twig grinned as the road stretched out ahead, long and smooth and magical, unrolling like a carpet all the way down to Christian's bar in New Orleans.

4

Heading south again, away from the Virginia border toward home, Steve swung the car onto a side road and drove toward the hill. The town of Roxboro usually fascinated Ghost, made him press his face to the window trying to see all its barbecue shacks and barbershops; its Southern Pride car wash whose sign read, mysteriously, *AS WE THINK, SO WE ARE;* its one dilapidated nightclub outside which dark shapes always lurked, regardless of hour or temperature.

But tonight Ghost had been silent all through Roxboro, his eyes open and vacant; he seemed still lost in his story. Steve wanted to take him away from those twins, those dream twins dying or dead. Too often the phantoms of Ghost's dreams possessed him even after he woke, claimed all his attention and a little of his soul.

The visions worried Steve as much as they enchanted him. Ever since they had become friends, Steve had thought of himself as Ghost's protector because he was a year older and because so often Ghost seemed to hover precariously on the edge of reality. Ghost lived with one foot in Steve's world of beer and guitars and friends, the other in the pale never-never land of his visions. Reality was often too much for Ghost; it could puzzle and hurt him.

Sometimes it seemed that Ghost consented to live in the world only because Steve was there, and Ghost would not leave Steve alone. *Please, God or Whoever*—Steve crossed his fingers on the steering wheel—*please don't let him change his mind about* that.

Ghost was so damned important, so valuable. When Ghost was along, ordinary surroundings—a pizza joint, a lonely stretch of highway—became strange, maybe threatening, maybe wild and beautiful. Ghost *tinged* reality. And Steve consented to let it be tinged and saw things he would never have seen otherwise, things he did not always believe or understand. He credited Ghost with saving his imagination from the death-in-life of adolescence.

What about another time you were driving late at night, he thought, *too late at night, driving with Ghost, and he had you convinced you'd driven into the ocean? Saw flying fish, starfish. Saw a swimming pool full of air.* Maybe he'd fallen asleep behind the wheel that time; maybe he and Ghost were lucky the T-bird hadn't wrapped around a tree, creaming both of them. Maybe that was what had happened. But mostly Steve accepted the share of magic the world had given him in Ghost, deluded himself that he, fearless old Steve Finn, was the leader. The protector. Yeah, right.

Because, especially now, what would life be *without* Ghost? He thought he knew the answer to that one. So much shit, that's what life would be. So much lonely, aching, empty shit. Ghost was taking care of *him* nowadays. The thing with Ann had nearly convinced Steve that his life was worthless. More than once he had found himself thinking about death in the middle of the night. *Just drive over to Raleigh and score some barbs, then pick up a quart of whiskey on the way home. Take 'em all at once. There's one cocktail that'll never give you a hangover.* But he could no more swallow that cocktail than he could have shoved it down Ghost's throat. Their friendship was the only thing keeping him sane right now, and he guessed he owed it more of a debt than that.

Somehow the last image of Ghost's dream—the twins lying on their bare mattress, flat, their beauty spent—had gotten all mixed up in his mind with the sight of the dead kid on the roadside thirty miles behind. Both pictures drifted in front of Steve's face, obscuring the road. He shook his head to banish them. When Ghost turned to look at him, Steve saw death in Ghost's eyes, a faint pale shadow.

"Let's drive up to the hill," said Steve. "It'll be nice there. See the stars."

"The stars were waiting for us," Ghost said when the T-bird reached the end of the road and pulled off. They were in a clearing thick with weeds and late-summer wildflowers. In the tall grass, empty cans and bottles shone dully, not marring the weird beauty of the hill but mirroring the huge luminous stars in the sky.

Behind them stretched the road, winding all the way back to Missing Mile; before them, a barbed-wire fence marked the break of the hill, and acres of pastureland fell away, rolling gently down to the shore of Lake Hyco. Miles off—Steve thought it was miles, but he couldn't be sure, the air was so clear—the electric power plant shimmered, all green and white and dimly roaring, reflected in the lake. It was so green here, so lush even after the hot Carolina summer, with the tall grass and the cow pastures and the great oak that spread its branches over the clearing.

Ghost knew all the stories of that oak. He said an Indian had climbed it to escape from a bear once. The marks of the bear's claws were still there, eight feet up the trunk, deep and twisted in the thick bark. The claws had hurt the tree, Ghost said, and it had bled clear sap to fill the wound, to stop the blaze of blind pain. Now the scar was knotted, invulnerable, and the tree sang with the hum of the power plant far away on the lake.

Ghost looked at the tree, silently greeting it most likely. Steve stood watching, one hand on the warm hood of the T-bird. He ran his other hand through his hair, shoving it back behind his ears, trying to tame it. Finally, against his will, he said, "What killed that kid?"

Ghost shrugged, pulled his hair over his face. "Something bad. Something really bad."

Steve started to say *no shit*, then thought better of it. Sometimes you didn't want to say such things to Ghost. They walked to the fence and looked out over the pastures toward the power plant. Steve curled his fingers around the barbed wire. It was cold, colder than the night air, as cold as dead flesh. He shivered. "A psycho," he said. "A dog. Maybe that Doberman the lady had. You suppose there's any wolves left around here?"

Ghost tossed his hair back and slowly shook his head. "It wasn't any wolf or dog. How could they suck him dry like that? And if you think it was a psycho, how come you're not scared to be up here? He would've taken off. He could be anywhere."

"Probably across the Virginia border by now." Steve saw again the cavernous throat, the sad brown hand with road dirt ground into the creases of its palm. He was aware of the cool air against his eyes, drying and chilling them. He squinted at the power plant, making the lights run together fuzzily, dazzlingly . . . and then Ann was in his head again.

He remembered the last time he'd come up here, months ago. With her. They had made love on a blanket in the backseat of the T-bird, hot and sweaty, but the clear cool air of the hill had blown over them, and the lights of the power plant had run together in just the same way.

Steve's shoulders drew up and he clamped his arms across his chest, ready to say *Let's leave, let's get the hell out of here* . . . and then Ghost was offering him a green apple. Distracting him. It worked; Steve had to wonder where in hell the apple had come from. He took a big bite and handed it back, chewing slowly, letting the golden-tasting juice run over his tongue: crunchy, sweet. The taste made him feel better. "You remember the Hook?" he asked after he had swallowed the mouthful. "That old spook story?"

"Uh-uh," said Ghost, eating the core of the apple. Steve watched to see whether Ghost would spit out the seeds. When he didn't, Steve spoke again. "You know, that story about the kids out at Lovers Lane. They're fucking in the backseat, and all of a sudden this bulletin comes on the radio about a crazy man escaped from the asylum outside of town. A psycho killer with a hook instead of a hand."

Steve looked at Ghost. Ghost was leaning against one of the fence posts, head tilted back, staring at the sky. The moon had gone behind a cloud. Ghost's face was shadowed, his eyes dark. He might have been listening; then again, he might have been receiving messages from an agrarian collective civilization somewhere near Alpha Centauri.

"So they hauled ass out of Lovers Lane," Steve went on anyway, "and when they got home, the boy went around the car to open the door for the girl. And what do you think he found? *A bloody hook, hanging from the handle of the door!*" He leaned over and spoke the last words right into Ghost's ear.

Ghost jumped, almost fell over. He stared at Steve for several seconds, then grinned. "Out at Lovers Lane?" he asked. Both of them turned to look at the T-bird parked in the clearing. It sat large and dusty, its engine giving an occasional metallic groan as it cooled.

"How come—" Ghost began, and Steve knew Ghost was about to exhibit the weird, irritating logic that sometimes possessed him. He was going to ask how come the couple had the radio on while they were fucking, or why the psycho killer would have reached to open the car door with his hook when he could have used his hand. But then the moon sailed out from behind its cloud and flooded the hill with cold white light, and Ghost sucked in his breath, sharp and scared.

Steve followed Ghost's gaze to the oak and saw nothing at all. But he knew Ghost saw something there. And somehow that was scarier than seeing it himself.

Ghost felt his feet moving. He hadn't told them to move. He wasn't even sure he *wanted* them to move. He took several steps toward the oak, and when he got close enough, the outline of the twins grew clearer, more solid.

They were balanced on a low branch, their legs swinging, their hands climbing like delicate white insects along the trunk. Closer still, and Ghost could *smell* them: their strange, heady bouquet of strawberry incense, clove cigarettes, wine and blood and rain and the sweat of passion. All the things they had loved when they were alive, the things that dragged them down, drove them to live upon each other's essence until they ran dry. But here on this midnight hill, in the

pallid moonlight, the twins were beautiful still. They wore
colored silks, silks that caught the moon and threw it back in
a thousand shades of iridescence. And Ghost could see no
spiderweb tracery of age on their faces. He saw only their
dark lips, their brittle, false-colored, silken hair of lemon-
yellow and cherry-red, their eyes like silver pearl, filmy and
pupilless.

But they were looking at him, he knew that, and when he
was close enough to touch the trunk of the tree, one of them
spoke to him. It was only his name, whispered through the
branches, "Ghost," but it was like a wind blowing from
across a strange sea, like an unseen rustle in an empty room.
Ghost put his hand on the trunk, near a slender silk-clad leg
so tangible he wanted to stroke it.

Why was he seeing them now, these creatures from his
dream? He had thought they were pitiful, but now they
frightened him. He found himself wondering what they had
become after their death, how death had changed them. If
they were somehow alive even now, what allowed them to
be? And why had he dreamed of them in the first place?

Ghost was used to asking himself such questions. He had
been visited in his dreams by the dead; he had dreamed the
future as clearly as a story in a book; he had been able to pick
up the thoughts and feelings of people he was close to—and
other people if he concentrated—for as long as he could
remember. But he had never been visited while awake by
creatures from one of his dreams.

"What is it?" Steve called from across the clearing.

"Hello, Ghost," said the crimson-haired twin, smiling
down at him with rouged lips. Those lips were too dark in
that pale, peaked face, and there was no warmth in that
smile, only a spasm of muscles long forgotten, a memory of a
smile. But Ghost looked up into those flat silvery eyes, and
he was not afraid for his own safety. Not yet. These twins had
been dead a long time, if indeed they had ever lived outside
his dream.

"Of course we haven't," said the first twin, catching
Ghost's thought. "We're just your dream."

"*We* don't go around killing little niggerboys on lonely roadsides long past midnight just to suck their lives out."

"He didn't taste exquisite, did he, love, at the moment of death? No, we didn't suck out that little boy's life, Ghost."

"Nooo, not us, not so we could stay beautiful. We're just your dream. . . ."

Obviously they did not intend him to believe it. Beneath the twins' exotic scent Ghost caught a whiff of decay, dry and stale, edged with pale brown. Their skin suddenly looked brittle, as if the touch of a breeze would flake it away from fragile ivory bones. Ghost wanted to ask them whether it hurt to rot, whether they grew lonely in the grave. He wanted to know whether they were buried together in a casket big enough for two bodies—big enough for two small dry bodies that knew how to fit together like a puzzle of blood and bone. Or did their graves lie side by side, and did they have to reach through the earth to clasp hands?

He had to find out what they were, whether they were dangerous. Reluctantly he reached out and tried to touch their minds; reluctantly he found them. Their minds were like echoes, like haunted rooms from which all the life had gone. The touch of their thoughts was light, fluttering, as cold and silver as graveyard stone, as voracious as feeding animals. They took Ghost into the grave with them, and he saw the darkest darkness that ever was, darker than a starless night on the mountain where he'd been born, darker than the darkness that swam up behind his closed eyelids when he lay in bed at night, darker than the hour before dawn.

He was lying on rotten satin, and he felt his tissues drying and shrivelling inside him, felt the secret loving movement of the creatures that shared his grave, the pale worms, the shiny beetles with their delicate black legs, the things without shape or name, too tiny to be seen, the hungry things turning his flesh back into new rich earth—

"Ghost! What the fuck are you doing?" Steve's hands were on him, large and strong and undeniably real, Steve's bony fingers digging into Ghost's shoulders.

Ghost leaned back against Steve. "It doesn't hurt," he said —to Steve? to the twins? He knew not, he cared not.

"*What* doesn't hurt? Who are you talking to?"

"Death doesn't hurt," said one of the twins, and a light came into his silver eyes. "Death is dark, death is sweet."

The other twin took up the litany. "Death is all that lasts forever. Death is eternal beauty."

"Death is a lover with a thousand tongues—"

"A thousand insect caresses—"

"Death is easy."

"Death is easy."

"DEATH IS EASY DEATH IS EASY DEATH-ISEASYDEATHIS—"

"*Shut up!*" Ghost screamed. The chant swelled inside his head, became the rhythm of his heartbeat, sucked him in. "*Stop it! Leave me alone!*"

Then Steve's arms were around him, and instead of the twins' rotten-spice odor there was only Steve's smell, beer and dirty hair and fear and love, and Ghost buried his face in the soft black cotton of Steve's T-shirt. When he opened his eyes again, the twins were gone. Ghost heard only the far-away roar of the power plant across the water, saw only the branches of the oak, tangled and twisted, stretching up to the clear, glittering sky.

Ghost didn't talk much on the drive back to Missing Mile. He told Steve only about the lovely feral faces of the twins and their bright silks and their bewitching dead smell. He didn't want to wonder, he said, what kind of an omen those twins might have been . . . or, worse than an omen, if they might have been real. Instead he finished the whiskey and went to sleep with his head hung out the window and his hair streaming in the wind, and Steve looked from the shimmering road to the hill of Ghost's cheek, the dark curve of his eyebrow, the satin scrap of his lashes.

Again Steve wondered what manner of things lived in that pale head, what Ghost was made of, of what substance were his visions. Steve had heard nothing back there on the hill, nothing but the wind and the power plant's faraway hum. He had seen nothing but the old scarred oak tree, wild against the sky. But he believed that Ghost had seen a pair of twins

long dead, the twins that had died in his dream and come
back to life in his waking hours. Steve no longer even considered disbelieving the things Ghost saw and heard, the things
Ghost knew without knowing.

Steve's faith in the high omniscient gods of his childhood
—Santa Claus, the Easter Bunny, and an eccentric creature
apparently designed just for him, the Haircut Fairy—had
been blasted by older, more worldly friends who advised him
to stay awake and see whether it wasn't his dad spiriting
away the carefully wrapped package of dark and unruly hair
clippings, whether it wasn't his mother delivering all those
mystical goodies. The Easter-morning chocolate never tasted
quite so wondrously creamy after he found out that it wasn't
brewed and molded under the roots of a tree deep in some
enchanted forest, in the vast subterranean workshop of a giant rabbit he had pictured as bearing a strong resemblance to
Bugs Bunny, but with bright pink fur.

Years later, when his aunt and cousins took him to church,
he suspected that this was more of the same magical gobble-
dygook updated for grown-ups. With the cynical hope of an
eleven-year-old he prayed for the successful flight of the hyperspace machine he and his friend R.J. were building in the
Finns' garage. But the motors they had salvaged from hair
dryers, refrigerators, and one precious wrecked motorcycle
left them stranded on earth, no matter how many adjust-
ments they made, how many dials they twisted, no matter
how many times R.J. pushed his glasses up on his nose and
checked the spiral notebook from Walgreen's that contained
his calculations, no matter how bitterly Steve cussed and
kicked at the mess of machinery.

Steve thought his belief in magic might well have died
there, at the hands of a God who cared nothing for a hyperspace machine built by the labor and thievery and faith of
two skinny, sweaty boys who had hoped all through a long
summer. Steve's faith might have been shattered beyond salvation, might have died right there on that garage floor, along
with the snips of wire, the scraps of metal, the broken drill
bit that his dad whaled him for.

He might never have believed in magic again. But a few

weeks later—right around this time of year, he realized, twelve years ago to the month—he met Ghost, and everything changed forever.

It was near the end of his eleventh summer, when the season was about to turn, when Steve was poised at the last reach of childhood. The passions and excitements of children no longer seemed so heady to him. He felt faintly silly for having tried to build a hyperspace machine, or indeed for doing anything that was not dictated by the realm of the practical. He cringed now to think how different he might have been. He might never have picked up a guitar, might have graduated from N.C. State with a bachelor's degree in advertising or some such deathsome thing. If he hadn't met Ghost.

The locusts were still singing in the trees and in the long weeds by the side of the road, but their song grew sad, the harbinger of another summer's end. School was in session. The days would be relentlessly hot and sticky for another month at least, but some new coolness in the night air signalled the golden mantle of fall. As at the beginning of every school year, there was a new kid. This year the new kid was a pale, frail-looking boy whose hair was a little too long to meet the current standards, who came to school wearing shirts that were clean but always seemed to hang from him too loosely. Steve sat behind him in class and saw that his shoulder blades were as distinct and articulated as the joints of birds' wings.

By rote the new kid was ignored at first, though there was some discussion of his funny name and his hillbilly origins. Then, by virtue of his appearance, his quietness, and his disinclination to join in the sixth-grade touch-football games at recess, he was judged a fag and thereafter jeered at. Everyone knew he must be smart because he'd come up a grade and was a year younger than the rest of the class. Most of the kids in Missing Mile had something weird about them: their fathers had died in the big fire at the old cotton mill, or their mothers worked as strippers in Raleigh, or they lived out on Violin Road and were so poor, the rumor went, that they had to eat roadkill.

These children were happy to have someone to look down upon. The new kid didn't seem to care, or even really notice; even when the sixth-grade boys zinged him with pinecones and chunks of gravel, he looked around bewilderedly as if he thought they might have fallen out of the sky. He checked out grown-up books about space from the school library and spent his recesses in the fringe of woods at the edge of the yard.

Steve was curious. He'd heard the new kid and his grandmother had moved here from the mountains, and he wanted to hear about the mountains. He and his parents had driven through them once, and to Steve they had seemed a place of dark mystery, of lushness, of a foreboding beauty that verged on the sinister. In the mountains you wouldn't need a hyperspace machine; in the mountains they kept giant possums for yard dogs.

So one day Steve forsook the touch-football game—it was kind of a stupid affair anyway, less concerned with the actual rules of football than with knocking down as many kids as possible and grinding their faces into the dirt—and took his own walk in the woods. He walked with his hands stuffed in his pockets, feeling awkward, half-hoping he wouldn't meet the new kid, who probably only wanted to be left alone, who surely thought he was just a roughneck jerkoff like the others. The woods were sun-dappled and quiet, but Steve kept walking into old strands of spiderweb that stuck to his face and made him think tickly legs were racing down his back. He was about to give it up and go play football after all when he heard a quiet "hey" from above his head.

Steve looked up into the calmest blue eyes he'd ever seen. No wonder this kid didn't mind insults or pinecones. Set in a face that was far too delicate, framed by wisps of rain-pale hair, those eyes were nevertheless at peace. Steve wondered what it felt like to have eyes like that.

The kid was perched comfortably in a tree, his legs stretched out along a low branch, his back snuggled against the trunk. He raised an arm and pointed to a spot along the path just past Steve.

At first Steve didn't see anything. Then all at once it came clear, the way an optical illusion will suddenly resolve itself: an intricate and enormous web that spanned the path, and hanging head-down at the middle of the concentric gossamer circles, a particularly large, juicy-looking brown weaver. Another couple of steps and Steve would have walked right into it. He tried unsuccessfully to suppress a shudder.

"Spiders are spinning all over the woods," said the kid. "That means it'll be cold soon."

This went against the rationality that Steve so loved. It sounded childish. What could spiders have to do with the weather? "How do you know?" he said.

"My grandmother knows all that stuff." The blue eyes did not challenge Steve to believe. The kid had an air of quiet sureness; there was nothing cocky about him, nothing arrogant, but he seemed to know he spoke the truth.

Steve was interested despite himself. Anyway, a kid from the mountains was surely entitled to his share of weird folklore. "Yeah?" he said. "What else does your grandmother know about?"

"Lots of stuff." The kid hesitated. "If you want to meet her, you could come visit us sometime. We live out on Burnt Church Road right by the dead end."

It should have been hard to extend that invitation, being the new kid with no real friends, not knowing whether Steve might just laugh at him and walk away. And it should have been difficult for Steve to accept. But already there was an easiness between them that surpassed any words they had exchanged. Standing on the path in the sun-dappled September woods staring up at the skinny kid in the tree, the kid he had not yet known for ten minutes, Steve felt comfortable, as if he could say anything. It was not quite déjà vu; it was not so unsettling, but it was somehow *familiar*. When he remembered it now, Steve thought that it was not so much like meeting a friend as like recognizing one.

He loosened his grip on the steering wheel and stared ahead into the sparkling night. Christ, but he was tense— first his bad mood and the whiskey, then the spooky shit on

the hill. His nerves were as tight as the thrumming of the
wheels on the road. Ghost mumbled something, but when
Steve glanced over at him, Ghost was still sleeping, his eyes
soundly shut and his hands lying limp in his lap. He was
dreaming again. Ghost always dreamed, but only sometimes
did his dreams come true.

Now they were coming into the outskirts of Missing Mile,
the place called Violin Road, where dark pine branches hung
over the dusty gravel road, where the land was peppered
with heaps of old scrap metal and chicken coops and family
graveyards that sprouted from the tired grass like sad little
crops of stone. Whenever Steve drove out here in the daytime, he saw kids with ragged clothes and faded eyes playing
on rickety jungle gyms, digging holes in the dirt of the
scrubby yards, standing aimlessly, their heads swivelling to
follow the T-bird as it went by. Once he had seen a group of
small kids hunkered down around a dead possum by the side
of the road, poking it and turning it over with sticks, looking
for maggots. That had been a hundred-degree August day,
and Steve had caught a noseful of ripe possum as he'd driven
past.

But now, under the cold September moon, the trailers and
rusty cars and trash heaps seemed to fade, to grow insubstan-
tial. Only the grass and the low-hanging trees appeared to
shimmer and come alive. Steve wondered who lived here,
scratching out a place to exist, holding the kudzu and the
wide empty sky at bay. Were they farmers gone broke trying
to beg crops from this dirt that had gone barren fifty years
ago? Were they field hippies, aging bohemians who thought
living off the land meant a couple of scraggly tomato plants
and Dannon yogurt from the 7-Eleven two miles up the
road?

Steve glanced down at the gas gauge. Nearly empty, but
the change from the Pepsi machine would buy a tankful tomorrow. The T-bird was damn thirsty these days. *Piece of
shit,* he thought with affection.

They were almost home now. Steve would sleep in his
once-cheerful wreck of a room, swathed in filthy sheets, try-

ing to fend off nightmares. In the morning Ghost would make whole-grain banana pancakes and bring him a beer. The presence of Ghost in the next room, drunk and dreaming, would be a comfort. It had been a long night.

5

Fifteen years later, Christian's bar was not so very different than it had been on that last night of Mardi Gras, that night of blood and altars. That delicious night.

One of the stained-glass windows had been broken in a fight, on a rare evening when the bar was crowded and the liquor flowed too freely and tempers reached a sodden white-hot pitch. Christian never found a replacement for the antique glass. The window was covered with black cardboard; it kept the sunlight out during the daytime, kept the shadows in at night.

Upstairs, in Christian's room, the bloodstains Jessy had left on the carpet grew pale brown and edgeless as Christian walked over them in black leather boots, in slippers, with his bare, long-toed, knobby feet. Fifteen years of his footsteps wore Jessy's blood away.

The wood of the bar lost its sheen, grew dull, scarred. Christian forgot to replace the light bulbs in the imitation Tiffany lamps—a curse of excellent night vision. The tawdry, alcoholic, glorious life of the French Quarter went on way up Chartres, far away. No one ever came in before ten.

Later, Christian often thought that the man who called himself Wallace should have appeared at Mardi Gras. There would have been a symmetry to that, a sort of correctness. But of course life was messy, Christian had lived long enough to know that. The man came to the bar one night early in September, during a late heat wave. He had rolled up the sleeves of his white cotton shirt, and the cloth at his armpits was circled with sweat. At first Christian thought he was an old man, by the usual standards at any rate, a very old, sad, tired man. Then he looked again and saw that the man could not be much older than fifty.

But this was a man who carried himself as if expecting blows, a man turned inward, looking out at the world through guarded eyes. His clipped curly hair was only beginning to go from brown to gray. He had a face that might once have been kind—deep careworn lines, brown eyes that had seen too much pain. There was still warmth in those eyes, but it was warmth dampened with weariness and watchfulness. Christian thought that whatever this man chose to drink, he would take it straight, and he would take a lot of it.

"Scotch," said the man. "Chivas Regal." Christian poured it over ice. The man held the glass up to the light, frowned into its amber depths. Then he brought it to his lips and tossed the whiskey down in one practiced motion. Christian heard the ice chitter against the man's teeth. The man spat it back into the glass. Then he looked at Christian and said, "My name is Wallace Creech," and held out his hand.

"Christian," said Christian, taking the hand. He looked straight into Wallace's eyes. Wallace stared back, unflinching. Most people started at the touch of Christian's fingers and withdrew quickly, rubbing their hands against their clothing to rid themselves of Christian's icy touch, glancing away from the cold light of Christian's eyes. But Wallace looked steadily back, grasped Christian's hand harder, and said, "A fine name."

Only then did Christian notice the small silver crucifix that hung on a chain around Wallace's neck, glinting in the dim light of the bar. "I'm afraid I'm not," Christian told him.

"I beg your pardon?"

"I don't belong to a church. I'm not religious." *It is possible to live too long for such comforts,* Christian thought.

"Ah," said Wallace knowingly. Christian expected him to reach into his pocket for a tract. Over the years, Christian had been given hundreds of them and had found hundreds more left on the tables, or under them. Everything from the smudgily printed, misspelled credo of a snake-handling cult from the Louisiana swamps to a lurid pamphlet called *Rock Music Is Worse than LSD!* Christian was curious as to what drew people to these religions; their obsession with their own mortality intrigued him, and he read all the tracts.

But Wallace didn't offer him a tract. Instead, he changed the subject abruptly, asking, "Have you had this place long?"

Christian felt a touch of shame. He had misjudged the old man. From the looks of him, Wallace needed all the faith he could muster. The pain seemed to pour from him. He must be lonely, just trying to make conversation, and talk was part of a bartender's job.

"Twenty years," Christian told him.

"You must have been a very young man when you opened it."

"I am older than I look," said Christian, smiling slightly. His face had not changed, had grown no older, had lost none of its narrow cold beauty since the last night of Mardi Gras fifteen years ago, the night he had slept in the arms of Molochai, his belly heavy and warm with Molochai's blood. Christian had not aged for a very long time.

"So I gather," said Wallace dryly.

Christian paused, looking into Wallace's face. Wallace's expression was no different than before; the eyes were the same, the hurt, frowning eyes, the lines bracketing the mouth as weary and patient as before. Christian dismissed the remark as meaningless—the man only wanted someone to talk to. He was lonely. Religious people always seemed lonely; perhaps that explained their need to be among great crowds of people who believed as they did. Such a great comfort, to be among others of your kind, and such loneliness when there were none. How could humans ever believe themselves truly lonely when there were so *many* of them?

"Another drink?" Christian asked.

Wallace tossed back a second shot of Chivas, then surprised Christian by asking, "Is business always this slow?" Then, realizing what he had said, he tried to apologize. "I didn't mean to be rude—I was only curious. It's a nice place, a good location, the French Quarter—"

The man was babbling, and Christian realized that for
some reason Wallace Creech was terrified. The empty glass
in his hand rattled against the bar; the ice made cold little
chinking sounds. The man seemed on the point of bolting.

Christian dumped the melting ice cubes, scooped in fresh
ones, poured another shot. This one was a double, but he
watched Wallace put it away with the same practiced motion,
not even grimacing. Here was a seasoned drinker.

"Why are you here, Wallace Creech?" Christian asked
softly. "What do you want?"

Wallace's hand went to the cross at his throat. Then, as if
trying to conceal the gesture, he ran a finger around the
inside of his collar, loosening it, though the top button was
already undone. "There was a girl, once," he said. "Jessy.
Small, thin. Short brown hair. Black dress. She used to come
here."

Christian felt a cold fist squeeze shut somewhere deep
inside him. The fist twisted, clenched; it was wrapped
around some vital part of him, tearing him loose inside. He
licked his lips. His mouth tasted of sour blood. He pretended
to think. "Jessy," he said. "Jessy. Such a long time ago . . .
but perhaps I remember. She stopped coming in fifteen
years ago."

"Was that after Mardi Gras . . . fifteen years ago?"

"I think so," said Christian, and tasted the sour blood
again.

"She was my daughter," said Wallace.

Christian swallowed. He was suddenly thirsty. "And she
just disappeared?" he asked. "Didn't you call the police?"

"I didn't, no. Jessy was wild." For a moment Wallace's face
was a Mardi Gras mask of tragedy; then he put his hand over
his eyes, frowned his tears away, and went on. "She was
forever threatening to leave home, saying I didn't give her
enough money, saying I was dull. She liked to go out and
drink. She was angry because I made her continue with
school when she wanted to drop out. She didn't seem to care
about anything . . . certainly not her father."

Wallace covered his eyes again. "A girl needs her mother,
I think, and Lydia—my wife—died when Jessy was only five.

Suicide, a sin. I brought our daughter up myself, and did a poor job, I suppose. When Jessy disappeared, I thought she had run off with a boy. I hoped she would come back when his money was gone. She had such strange notions . . . such very strange notions . . . and sending the police after her would have made her hate me."

"Why are you here now?" Christian couldn't look at Wallace's eyes. He stared at the silver cross, at the soft loose skin of the man's throat behind it.

"Well . . . after Jessy left, I moved all her things to the attic. When I realized she wasn't coming back, I hated to look at them. Recently I happened to think of them, and I wondered whether her old clothes might be good enough to give to my church group. They hold a yearly bazaar for the poor, you know." Christian nodded. "While I was going through the boxes, I found an old diary. The entries mentioned you several times—and your bar. She seemed to have . . . feelings for you. I thought she might have told you where she was going. I'd so love to see her now."

"I don't know," said Christian. "She only drank here. She didn't talk to me. I've no idea where she went." He realized that he was still staring at the crucifix and dropped his gaze to Wallace's empty glass.

Wallace gave a heavy sigh. "I'll have another," he said. He stayed to drink two more whiskeys, getting drunker, wandering around the bar. He examined the stained-glass window and its blind twin, the tables scarred with cryptic patterns of initials and beer-rings, the worn crimson leather of the bar stools. From time to time he glanced back at Christian, who silently avoided his eyes.

When Wallace began staring at the door that led to the staircase and, beyond that, to Christian's room, Christian picked up his rag and started wiping down the bar. "I'm closing up. I'm sorry I couldn't help you with your problem." His voice was sharper than he had meant it to be.

When Wallace was gone—he left with a quiet, swaying dignity—and the door locked after him, Christian turned to his rows of bottles and found a squat embossed bottle nearly full of luminous green liqueur. No one wanted Chartreuse, not anymore, but Christian always kept a few bottles of it in case Molochai, Twig, and Zillah came rolling into town some Mardi Gras night. They would want Chartreuse, Christian knew. Tonight he wanted it too. He wanted the swirling heaviness of alcohol to weigh his mind down, wanted to sleep deep and dreamlessly, with no phantoms to swim out of the recesses of memory, no thin little girls with shadowed eyes and thighs bloody from murderous, innocent birth.

Could he?

Christian uncapped the bottle and started to pour himself a shot. His hand paused over the glass, bony and white, cold on the cold bottle. He smelled the liqueur. A scent as fresh as the new night, as birth. The smell of altars. He wanted so badly to be drunk, to sleep. The others—Molochai, Twig, and Zillah—drank incessantly, even *ate*; they drowned their true natures in gluttony. But they were young. They were of a newer generation. Their chemistry was subtly different; they were hardier, their organs perhaps more thick-walled, less delicate. Christian remembered the time he had drunk wine, the time he had drunk vodka, and the memory of pain shivered up his spine. But perhaps this . . .

Christian clutched the bottle to his chest and carried it up the stairs with him, turning off the bar lights as he went, ascending in the dark. A blessing of excellent night vision.

The Chartreuse burned going down, and Christian sat tensed in the dark, waiting for pain. But when the liqueur hit his belly, a gentle green fire began to spread through him. It was going to work this time. His strange, treacherous body was going to let him get drunk as he had never been before, and he would rest; for a time he would not have to think.

He poured himself another shot and tried to sip it. It stung his eyes and went up his nose, and he threw it back and swallowed hard to keep from coughing. He laughed quietly at himself. He was a good bartender, an excellent bartender, but he certainly did not know how to drink. After the next shot he dispensed with the glass altogether, swigging out of the bottle as he had seen the others do on that Mardi Gras night.

When the first noise floated up from the alley, Christian was drunk enough to ignore it. It was only a bump. But then there was another bump and a scraping clatter that hurt to hear, as if someone were dragging one of the metal garbage cans across the concrete. A stray dog? A bum? Christian crept to his window, which gave him a clear view of the alley and a slice of Royal Street beyond it. He cupped his hands to the glass and looked out.

Apparently Wallace Creech was still drunk too. Nothing else could account for the clumsiness with which he was going through Christian's garbage, mostly empties from the bar. As Christian watched, Wallace let a Taaka vodka bottle slip from his hands. It shattered on the concrete, and Wallace went down on his hands and knees, trying futilely to scoop the glass up, to dump it back into the torn garbage bag.

This was too much. Wallace Creech would have to be dealt with more harshly. The alley was already strewn with broken glass, wrinkled paper bags, and other trash, but what was Wallace looking for? His daughter's bones, picked clean and wrapped in a *Times-Picayune* fifteen years out of date?

Christian straightened and turned away from the window. He would go down and slip into the alley; he would bend that dry old neck back, let flow the old man's tasteless blood—

The first spasm hit him as he was opening the door to the landing. It bent him nearly double. He leaned against the jamb, clutching himself, trying to hold in the blaze of green agony that was burning its way through his belly. This was worse than the other times, so much worse; surely the pain must be ripping him apart inside, webbing his innards with tiny bloody holes. His eyes squeezed shut, and a long shudder ran through him.

Christian moaned and twisted his head, clenching his teeth, trying not to scream. He had to get to the bathroom: it was out on the landing, shared by the other apartments on the top floor of the building. He pushed at the door. It swung fully open, and Christian fell onto the landing, clumsy and agonized, his throat bitter, his eyes hot and streaming.

"Jesus, man, Jesus. Are you all right?" His neighbor,

David, was just going out. Christian rolled onto his back and looked helplessly up at David, the drop-dead suit, the hair kept pathologically short, the sunglasses he always wore, even at night. Another spasm of pain washed over him, incredibly worse than the last, and he curled around himself and whined deep in his throat. Surely the tissues of his body were burning away, dissolving inside.

Then he was aware of David's hands under his arms, David helping him up, half dragging him to the bathroom where he bent Christian over the toilet. Something deep in Christian loosened, and all the Chartreuse came up—green, hot, churned into a foamy mass now. Christian sobbed at the sight of it and turned his head away. Thick strings of saliva webbed his lips.

"Jesus, barkeep, are you going to live? Have to close up early tonight?"

Christian managed to nod. He leaned against David. The warm pressure of David's hand on his shoulder kept him from collapsing. He vomited again, having to force it this time. After that, he felt almost good. "I'm going out," he told David.

"Jesus wept, are you sure? How about I help you to your room? Don't you even want to brush your teeth?"

"No. I need a drink to kill the taste. I must have eaten something bad."

"I'm meeting a girl. Why don't you come and have a drink with us?"

At the mention of alcohol, Christian had to suppress a moan. The idea of having a drink with David and his girl made him feel terribly lonely. He could never do such a thing. And besides, now he was ravenous.

They walked downstairs together, and David headed up Conti toward the lights of Bourbon Street. Christian checked the alley, but of course by now Wallace was gone. All that lingered was a breath of whiskey and fear. He would meet Wallace Creech again, though, with his old tired eyes and his silver cross. Christian knew it, and he smiled, feeling the night gather around him. He slipped away toward the river.

* * *

Nothing sat on his bed, naked and cross-legged, the quilt pooled around his waist and a candle before him. He cupped his hands around the flame and kept them there until his palms began to sweat. Then he raised his hands to his face and rubbed the heat onto his cheeks. He had his music turned up loud—Tom Waits, loud and splendidly drunk tonight, wishing he were in New Orleans. Nothing wished *he* were too.

He looked toward the window. Outside, he could see a few lights: other windows in other houses, more houses beyond; houses with well-kept lawns and shade trees, like the one he lived in; houses with swing sets and poured concrete driveways and half-baths and redwood sundecks; streets travelled by Volvos and Toyotas picking the kids up from day care, going to the supermarket, the health club, the mall, or, if they were bored enough, the liquor store. Suburbs, stretching forever or until the end of Maryland, whichever came first. Nothing shivered, then swigged from the White Horse bottle next to his bed. He had refilled it from the supply in his parents' liquor cabinet, watering down their bottle, but now it was nearly empty again.

He kept looking toward the window. Most of the lights had gone out. He shivered again.

Christian still wore a cloak, long and black and lined with silk, whenever he went out. Old habits died hard, if they ever died at all. The night had cooled. A black iron railing under Christian's hand was warm, still saturated with the heat of the day, but a dark-smelling breeze wound its way up from the river, brushing Christian's face, reviving him. Now he had nearly forgotten the burning in his stomach and the vomiting that had made his throat bloody and raw.

His step quickened. His boot heels clocked along the sidewalk. He fell to wondering how many times he had walked along these ways, how infinitesimally his steps had worn down the sidewalks of these old streets, these exotically named, haunted streets—Ursulines, Bienville, Decatur. He wondered how much of his substance he had left here, how much of his substance was made up of the dust of these streets.

There had always been New Orleans. Christian had lived in other places, far away across sunless seas, places older and darker and just as strange, with ghosts aplenty. But where else did slave spirits still lament in the Royal Street house of sadistic Madame Lalaurie, where else could one still smell the lingering sweat of a slave woman chained to a stove all the years of her life? Where else did crows flap over the crumbling ruins of St. Louis Cemetery and settle, inky and baleful of eye, on a tomb slashed with hundreds of red X's— X's in faded crimson chalk, X's still fresh and glistening, X's for voodoo curses, X's to invoke the wrath of Marie Laveau, the voodoo queen who had stayed young forever?

Christian passed a dark doorway. Inside, pale shapes moved through dull blue light. He remembered when this hole-in-the-wall had been a jazz club, when bright brassy music floated out late at night and spiralled up to the sky, when smoky-skinned women with ripe lips and red dresses stood outside smiling dark smiles at passersby. Once he had seen Louis Armstrong standing there on the sidewalk with his shirtsleeves rolled up, talking to a crowd of friends.

Christian remembered the slow laughter, the white eyes that shone out of faces blue-black with sweat, the flasks of illicit liquor raw enough to burn a hole in the guts of even Molochai, Twig, or Zillah. Now the figures that waited uneasily on the sidewalk were as white as white could be, with eyes smudged black and ripped black clothes, little ghosts, like photonegatives of the dusky dancers who had once swirled all night to bright jazz. Now the music that drifted out of the doorway and up toward the moon was sparse and dark and strange, the anthem of all the lost children who began their lives at night, when the bars opened and the music began to play.

Right now it was sainted Bauhaus, the pale long-boned gods of this crowd, doing "Bela Lugosi's Dead." The eyeliner eyes glazed and the black lipstick lips moved in time with the words, and the children danced slowly, for their blood was

thin, and they were under the spell of the DJ and the music
and the night.

Christian went in. As he passed the bar, he heard a girl
say, "God, how tall *is* that guy?" He turned but could not
search out her eyes. He rose like a narrow, pale beacon
above most of the children in the club, and he could look
down on leather-clad, studded shoulders, on earlobes hung
heavy with chains and crucifixes and tiny silver skulls, on
heads of hair dyed every unnatural color possible—blue-
black, orange, red, white. The club smelled of sweat and
melting hair mousse and hot leather, all underlaid with the
sweet, spicy smell of clove cigarettes. A veil of smoke twisted
gently around Christian's shoulders.

He stood against the back wall, not smoking, not drinking,
just watching the children move, watching their faces lift and
their hands flicker in the blue light. A boy came up to him
and said, "Will you watch my leather?" When Christian nodded, the boy dumped the jacket on a chair near Christian and
danced back into the crowd, lithe and T-shirted, his thin
arms raised above his head. These children trusted one another; the adult world was obtuse and threatening, but in one
another they had absolute faith. Still, a leather jacket was
nothing to be left unattended. Each one was an individual
masterpiece marked by its owner with intricate arrange-
ments of studs and safety pins, arcane band logos, patches
and chains.

Bela Lugosi was still dead. The singer's voice was low and
smooth and insidious as throat cancer. Christian imagined
him gaunt and bone-white, writhing onstage. When the song
was over, the boy danced back and slung his jacket over his
shoulders. He offered Christian a cigarette and lit it for him.
Christian inhaled once: a clove, tasting of the Orient and ash,
its paper sugared. Then he held it between two long fingers
and let it burn, raising it to his lips occasionally, pretending
to smoke. The taste nauseated him; all tastes nauseated him
save one. And now he was so hungry, so thirsty.

When the boy cupped his hand around his mouth and
went on tiptoe to shout something in Christian's ear—his
name, perhaps, though Christian never caught it—Christian

laid his hand flat against the small of the boy's back. Through the T-shirt damp with sweat, the boy's skin was hot, alive. Christian felt the little ridges of the spine through the thin cloth. The boy looked at Christian for a moment, his eyes darker than before. Then he smiled and moved so that his hip was touching Christian's. Their hipbones met and spoke to each other in a secret bone language. The boy's smile was heartbreakingly sweet.

"Mind-eraser," the boy shouted when they were at the bar. Christian paid for the concoction. It was the drink of a child alcoholic, a sweet fizz with a deadly bite. "Share with me," the boy offered, holding up the cup. There were two straws in it.

"No," Christian said, remembering the nausea, imagining how Molochai, Twig, and Zillah would howl. "You have it."

For a moment he thought he heard them laughing raucously behind him, thought he saw them from the corner of his eye: three clumps of hair, three smudged faces. When he turned, there were only three girls in leather dresses giggling and staring at him. Christian turned back to the bar, but the boy was sharing his mind-eraser with the girl on his left. The girl's teased red hair tickled the boy's face, and Christian saw him laugh and brush strands of it away.

But when the drink was gone, the girl went off on the arm of a skinhead, and the boy turned to Christian. "Do you want to go somewhere?"

The air outside was amazingly cool and fresh after the haze of smoke and liquor in the club, and the boy stood still for a few seconds, gazing up at the stars, breathing deeply. He smiled at Christian. "It's nice. Let's go down to the river."

As they wandered down to the river's edge, Christian watched the boy, saw the ripe shine of his eyes and mouth in the dark, the softness of the blond hair that was cut short at the sides and tumbled in a pale cascade down the boy's back, the grace of the boy's drunken hands and the unconcerned, achingly lithe motion of his hips, the soft place under his jaw where his pulse beat. He smelled the leather and the clean sweat and soap and skin of the boy, and he smelled the French Quarter around them, the spice and the garbage, the grainy golden smell of beer, the deep brown fish smell of the river.

The water shone dark and still tonight. Near its edge, the boy spread his jacket and pulled Christian down with him. Their tongues melted together. The boy's spit was as sour and sweet as wine. Christian sucked at the boy's mouth, let the spit flow down his throat, warming him, awakening his hunger even more.

The boy twisted and stretched under him, hugging him close to bony childish chest and soft thin skin, and then the boy sat up and pulled his T-shirt over his head. The moonlight made him a creature of white and silver, striped dark with jutting ribs. He slipped back into his leather. "I like to feel it against my skin," he explained shyly.

Christian held the boy close, cradled him, kissed his throat. The boy moaned very softly when he felt the first touch of the long needle-sharp teeth that curved over Christian's lips now, drawn out by the night and the smell of the river and the delicious beauty of the boy in his arms.

The boy twisted his head to look at Christian. His eyes were big in his thin face, and very dark. "What are you?" he asked.

Christian was silent. But his teeth had pricked the boy's skin, and the first faint scent of blood reached him.

"Are you a vampire?"

Christian stroked the boy's hair back from his forehead, kissed the side of the boy's face tenderly, flicking the tip of his tongue across the smooth skin.

"Make me into one too," said the boy. "Please? I want to be one. I want to walk at night with you and fall in love and drink blood. Kill me. Make me into a vampire too. Bite me. Take me with you."

Christian nipped the boy's throat gently, not breaking the skin this time. He ran his hands along the length of the boy's body under the jacket, caressed his smooth bare chest, slipped one hand beneath the belt of the boy's jeans and found molten trembling heat there. The boy's back arched; he made a low gasping sound. Christian's tongue found the tender spot under the jaw, and he sank his teeth in. The boy whimpered and went rigid in his arms. The raw yolky taste of life spilled into Christian's mouth, bubbling out of the boy fresh and strong.

Christian eased the boy's body to the ground, held him, and sucked. The taste was all he remembered, all he dreamed about, all he would ever need. The boy pressed himself up against Christian. His hands found the long black hair that spilled down over Christian's shoulders and tore at it in a passion born of pain.

Then suddenly Christian's vision blossomed red, black, red again, great gauzy flowers of light and darkness that blotted out the French Quarter, the river, the boy's face. He clasped the boy more tightly, and their bodies locked together in a final wash of ecstasy, Christian's belly warming and filling, the boy beginning to die. The boy's sperm flooded warm over Christian's fingers. Christian brought his hand up to his lips and sucked at that too. The two tastes mingling in his mouth, creamy and delicate and bitter and salty, raw as life, were almost too exquisite to bear.

When the boy's veins ran dry and his hair and hands trailed limply on the wet ground, Christian picked him up and held him like a baby, gazing into the face gone paler than before, the rapturous half-closed eyes. For several minutes he held the boy, and then he turned his cold eyes to the cold moon, and something passed between them, between Christian and the moon, something as ancient and implacable as the tides, as the distances between the stars.

And had the moon been able to look into Christian's eyes, it would have seen that Christian did not love what he had done, but now he was no longer hungry. He was no longer sick and cold. The drinking of a life left him a little less alone than he had been before, and if the boy had died thinking he would rise again as one with Christian, that could not be helped. It was kinder to let the children die believing as they did. He could not turn the boy into one of his kind any more than the boy could have bitten him and turned him human. They were of separate races, races that were close enough to mate but still as far away from each other as dusk and dawn. But the dead slept, and did not know.

Christian kissed the white forehead and eased the empty
little body into the river. The weight of the leather dragged it
down, and for a moment Christian saw it hanging beneath
the surface, limp and cold as a dream. Then it was gone.

6

Nothing cupped his hands around the candle again. He felt the heat biting into his palms, the bright point of the flame embedding itself in his eyes. When he looked away, yellow light burst out of the darkness and melted across his vision. He knuckled his fists against his eyes and rubbed hard.

The candleholder, an ornate thing of black iron as fluted and curlicued as a balcony in some exotic city, tipped and spilled. Only when the hot wax touched his foot did he realize that something was wrong. The flame had begun to lick at the quilt. Small tongues of fire shot up, blackening the bright cloth, dazzling Nothing's eyes. He watched the flames for several seconds, caught in their hot thrall, as still as a boy drugged. Then, slowly, he put out his hand to touch them.

The pain yanked him out of his trance. He grabbed a dirty T-shirt off the floor and threw it over the flames, beat at them, smothered them. Then, cautiously, he lifted the shirt and examined the mess. There was a large black-edged hole in the quilt, and the room was filled with the smell of charred cloth. It smelled almost like burnt marshmallows, but he couldn't say he had been toasting marshmallows in his room; that would be pushing things too far.

"Fuck," he said softly, without conviction. He would catch hell for burning the quilt, but he couldn't make himself care. His father's impotent anger, his mother's puzzled eyes held no dread for him, only a dull guilt. A sadness that he dismissed as stupid.

If his parents watched him with bewilderment and a little fear, if they seemed happier when he asked to be excused from supper and shut himself in his room, that was all right with Nothing. He was strange to his parents, and they were incomprehensible to him. He rejected their world. There was not a thing in it that touched him, not a thing he could claim as his own. Sometimes he wondered whether there was a place for him outside the elaborate juju of his room, whether there was anyone in the world who would belong to him, whether he could ever belong to anyone. Who would want him? Not his parents, for sure. He had never belonged to them. They should never have taken him in from the doorstep that cold dawn fifteen years ago.

Nothing pulled the quilt around him again, picked at the edges of the burn. They didn't know he knew about that. Long ago they had told him he was adopted, making it all sound proper and respectable, watching him for signs of childish trauma. Maybe the knowledge that he was not of their blood assuaged their guilt when they saw their son looking at them and knew that he had caught the distance in their faces. Maybe then they were able to justify their longing for a normal son who would keep his hair brushed out of his eyes, who would be elected student council president instead of sitting in his strange bedroom reading strange books, who would bring home little fresh-faced girlfriends in clean skirts and pink blouses. Maybe they looked at him and thought, *We did not make this creature out of our seed. He is not our mistake.* And they were right.

They would never show him the adoption papers. They said he had been left at the orphanage as a newborn, that his parentage was unknown. But one day in early June, when he was twelve, he brought home an end-of-term progress report from school:

> Jason is a highly intelligent child. His achievements in areas where he chooses to apply himself, such as art and creative writing, are considerable. However, he seems unable to relate well to the other children; his remoteness and his apparent determination to be "different" keep him

from becoming a successful member of the classroom com-
munity. Due to this, though all his marks are above aver-
age, I cannot call his passage through the sixth grade a
fully satisfactory one.

Yours,
Geraldine Clemmons

Two or three years later he could have laughed. But all
through his sixth-grade year he had had no real friends, no
one who would come to his house and play games of pretend
in the woods, no one who offered to trade sandwiches at
lunchtime or asked him to one of the boy-girl parties that
were beginning to be all the rage. Through the girls' thin
T-shirts he saw their sore budding breasts. When he undressed for gym with the other boys, he tried to look at their
bodies without seeming to look. On some of them he noticed
those same fearfully secret hairs he had begun to find upon
himself.

He could not laugh at Mrs. Clemmons's stupid progress
report because he had begun to know how alone he was. All
through his childhood he had amused himself without really
thinking about it—reading, playing alone or with neighbor-
hood children, never noticing that they were uncomfortable
with the stories he liked to make up, that they seldom came
back more than two or three times.

But at twelve he became aware of himself, painfully so. He
became aware that he did not know who he was. He
dreamed often of a strange boisterous family who laughed all
the time and cuddled him and took him along wherever they
went. He discovered how to masturbate, thinking at first that
it was something he had made up. Then he connected it with
things he had read, and he learned how to turn it into a
highly sensual experience, biting himself at first gently and
then harder, thinking of other children in his class, imagining
how it would be to hold them, taste them, feel their flesh
between his teeth. It did not seem strange that he thought
about these things.

But on the day he brought the progress report home, he

knew that he was alone and that he might be alone for a very long time.

His parents were both at work, his mother counselling disturbed children at a day-care center, his father doing something that had vaguely to do with finance. The house was sunny and still, and all that afternoon he searched through their desk drawers, through their files and boxes, looking for his adoption papers. He had to know who his real parents were. He had to know where he had come from and whether someday he might find his way back.

His parents' papers were remarkably dull. There were no old love letters scented and tied with pastel ribbons, no scandals, no bloodstained lace handkerchiefs. There were no adoption papers. The shadows in the house lengthened. He became frantic, knowing with the terrible conviction of a twelve-year-old that these strangers named Rodger and Marilyn would murder him if they caught him going through their things; they would have an excuse at last. But he opened one final dresser drawer in their bedroom, not really expecting to find anything, and under his mother's old granny glasses and McGovern buttons was the note. It was tucked into a corner of the drawer, not hidden very well. By this time he was sweaty and a little breathless. His hand shook as he extracted the note, trying not to disturb the rest of the mess.

The paper was thick and cream-colored, with two small holes at the top as if it had been pinned to something. Slowly he deciphered the spidery handwriting: *His name is Nothing. Care for him and he will bring you luck.*

All at once the story fell into place around him. A baby in a basket, abandoned on two strangers' doorstep some night. That was what he had been. Surely this note had been pinned to his blanket. But the strangers had taken him in, changed his name, tried to make him into one of their kind. If he had brought them any luck at all, that luck had surely been bad. It was all so clear now. It was all so *right.*

He slept with the note under his pillow that night and dreamed of a place where the buildings were gay with scrolled ironwork and the river flowed darkly past and soft laughter went on all night, every night. He roamed the streets and the alleyways and courtyards, a sweet, rotten, coppery taste on his tongue.

The next day he put the note back in the drawer in case Mother ever looked there, but when he was alone in the house he took it out and read it again and again, holding the paper to his face, pressing it against his mouth, trying to catch the scent of the place it had come from. For that was where he had been born. He closed his eyes and tried to imagine the hand that had shaped those spindling black words, for that hand belonged to someone who knew him, who had held him. In the veins of that hand, his blood might flow.

And he ceased to be Jason. He became Nothing, for that was what the note named him. He still answered to Jason, but the name was like an echo of a half-forgotten life. *I am Nothing*, his mind whispered. *I am Nothing*. He liked the name. It did not make him feel worthless; on the contrary, he began to think of himself as a blank slate upon which anything could be written. The words he inscribed on his soul were up to him.

He grew taller, and some of the flesh of childhood melted from his bones. He was truly Nothing now; he knew it. When in junior high school he finally made friends—not friends who could share his soul, but friends who understood a little better than anyone else ever had, other skinny pale kids, hippie and punk kids, kids in black T-shirts and leather jackets and smudgy makeup shoplifted from the drugstore at the mall—he told them to call him by that name.

The house was cold tonight. His room was the coldest of all. He shivered again, then threw off the quilt and pulled on gray sweatpants and an old black sweater with holes at the elbows. The Tom Waits album had finished playing and turned itself off. The hiss of the empty speakers filled the room, too loud here in the dark.

Nothing rummaged through his backpack and found the cassette Julie had given him. It came from far away down south, and only five hundred copies of it had been printed— it was numbered on the liner, *217 of 500*. But somehow one copy had ended up in a record store in Silver Spring, a nearby town, where Julie had picked it up.

He put it on now. The singer's voice wove in and out of the jangly guitar line, now losing itself in the music, now as strong and golden-green as some Appalachian summer mountain stream.

> Does your road go no place?
> Does it go someplace where you can't see?
> If you follow it anyway
> It just might lead you here to me . . .

Nothing sat on the edge of the bed and hummed the words under his breath, his head tilted back, his eyes searching the stars and planets on the ceiling. He thought of Julie taking the tape from her purse and handing it to him; he thought of Laine, sucking him off with innocent abandon.

Somewhere in the music, perhaps outside the window in the cold night, somewhere above the melody and under the moon, those lonely little ghosts started whispering to him again: *You've got to get out of here. You've got to find your place, your family, before you rot and die.*

"All right," he said after listening for a while. "All right." All at once he knew he had to leave. It was inevitable, and he wondered what he had been waiting for. He would go south, looking for what he wanted, hopefully knowing it when he found it. Maybe he would even hook up with the musicians from Lost Souls? The name of their town was fascinating: he pictured it as a mysterious southern crossroads, a hamlet where the ordinary became exotic. He had found it on a map of North Carolina, a tiny dot between the mountains and the sea, a town whose streets Nothing pictured as dusty and strange, whose shops were crammed with dark secondhand treasures, whose graveyards were haunted, whose moon rose full and honeyed behind the lacework of towering pines.

He said the name to himself and shivered: Missing Mile.

Nothing crossed his dark room and let himself into the hall. His parents were out somewhere—a consciousness-raising group, a holistic health class, an expensive dinner with other people like themselves. Their bedroom door was ajar, and the room within smelled of perfumed soap and after-shave. The odors struck him as stinging and chemical. They said *his* room smelled bad.

His fingers searched the bottom of the dresser drawer, familiar by now, and found the note at once. Its presence in his hand was comforting, its ink faded, its edges soft and ragged from all the times he had held it over the past three years. He slipped it into his pocket. He considered the col-lection of crystals on top of the dresser, then picked up the one he liked best, a piece of rose quartz. He curled his hand around it. No, he decided; it was too tainted with Mother's touch, with her antimagic. After a few minutes of hunting he found Mother's cache of emergency money in her jewelry box and took that instead. A hundred dollars. It wouldn't last until he got where he was going, but it would help. After that —*Well, after that I'll find something else,* he told himself.

Next he used the phone. Jack wasn't home, but Nothing called around and found him at Skittle's, the pizza shop downtown where his friends hung out at night. "Can you drive me to Columbia?" he asked.

"Gas isn't free, dude." Jack was eighteen, had a fake ID that got him served at the liquor store, and considered him-self the lord of the local scene.

"I can pay you. I have to catch a bus. I'm getting the hell out of here."

"Folks giving you too much shit, huh?" Jack didn't wait for an answer. "Okay, I can take you tonight. Five bucks for the gas if you got it. Meet me here at midnight."

How far could you ride a Greyhound for ninety-five dol-lars? Far enough to start with. "Thanks, Jack," he said. "See you at midnight."

"Hey, Laine wants to talk to you," Jack said, but Nothing was already hanging up.

Back in his room he huddled under the quilt. It was only nine o'clock; he could sleep for a couple of hours before walking into town to meet Jack and the others. But his mind would not shut down. His eyes would not stay closed. Even

the whiskey didn't help; he realized he was maddeningly
sober.

He rolled over, hugged himself, then felt under his mattress and pulled out a single-edged razor blade. Gently, lovingly, he pulled the edge across his wrist. A thin line of
crimson welled up, beading and running, bright against the
pale tracery of old scars. Nothing lay under his charred quilt
in his own safe room for the last time, and he sucked at his
own blood because that was what comforted him, what he
had always done when he grew too lonely, too hungry for
something he did not know. He lay there with his mouth
tight against his wrist, praying to the juju in his room: *Come
with me. Stay with me on the road until I find what I'm
looking for, because now I'm going to be more alone than
ever.*

At last, when his lips were stained red and a thin pink line
of blood and spit trickled from the corner of his mouth, he
was able to sleep.

7

I'm going to be a vampire, Daddy.

Wallace shut his eyes tight and shook his head. "Begone, Jessy," he muttered. "Torment me no more." His hands came up hard against the side of the brick building that housed Christian's bar, and he pushed himself away from the wall and staggered out of the alley.

The palms of his hands stung dully. He had left some of his skin on the bricks, and he could feel dust and grime embedded in his lifelines, his heartlines. The pain did nothing to soothe his mind, nothing to stop the cursed past from rushing back. The streets and alleys and buildings around him swam and grew dark. Now he could actually *see* Jessy, see her as she had been that day. . . .

"I'm going to be a vampire, Daddy."

It was all she had spoken of for weeks. Finding a vampire to bite her, turning into one, drinking the blood of others (her lovers, Wallace supposed, the lovers he didn't know) and turning them into vampires as well. Her things spoke of this obsession too. Jessy had always been quite a reader, turning the pages of *Charlotte's Web* and the Bobbsey Twins books with scowling concentration, but now the stack of books by her bed was all vampire stories. *Dracula* was there, dog-eared and heavily underlined. Wallace had looked at the book one night while Jessy was out at one of her haunts. Some passages were circled over and over, in pencil and lipstick and what looked like blood.

Wallace began reading, but after a few paragraphs he was too disgusted to continue. He hadn't known the novel was pornographic. He touched the marks on the page. They *were* blood. Jessy's blood. She had been cutting herself to get at it. Wallace found razor blades between the pages of the book. There were other novels that looked just as lurid, and a vial of some sort of red dust that must have come from one of the voodoo shops in the French Quarter, though he'd told her not to go to those places. There were all the posters from the movies she saw, cruel eyes and gaping, razor-toothed mouths all bloody, and the walls and ceiling festooned with black lace . . .

"Daddy."

Wallace forced his eyes open. He was not at home, standing in the hallway outside Jessy's room. He was weaving down Bienville, breathing in the cool night air, heading for the river. But the past sucked him in again, and it was that day. . . .

Jessy was calling him. For ten years they had been alone except for each other, ever since the day Wallace had found Lydia in her cooling red bathwater with her forearms slashed open from wrist to elbow. He was Jessy's father, and he had to go to Jessy when she called. She might need him.

"Daddy," she called softly. *"Daddy . . ."*

Wallace looked at the old sign on Jessy's bedroom door—a cartoon rabbit in rainbow-spattered overalls painting the words *GENIUS AT WORK*—then turned the knob and stepped out of the dark hallway into brightness. Jessy's room always caught the morning sunlight.

She'd just come out of the shower, and her skin was as pink and white and dewy as spring. Her hair fell wet and straight along her cheeks. As he stared at her, she let the green towel fall from her breasts. Wallace had not seen his daughter's body since she was a young child, plump and androgynous, with pink buttons for nipples and a tiny clean fold of a sex. But now her breasts were round and smooth, with a girlish heaviness to them, and Wallace wondered how it would be to cup their weight in his hands, how it would taste if he took one of those creamy strawberry peaks in his mouth and sucked.

"I'm going to be a vampire, Daddy."

He could not find his voice. There was no spit in his mouth. "Put your clothes on, Jessy." It was a dry whisper, weak and useless.

"I'm going to bite people, Daddy. I'm going to *feed* on them. I need blood. Hot . . . rich . . . red blood. I need your blood, Daddy. I'm hungry. Your Jessy's hungry. Come to me."

He did not know how he got to the bed. Surely if she had not cajoled so, if she were not his daughter, his only joy, if he had not always tried to give her everything she asked for . . . surely if he had lain with some other woman in the ten years since Lydia was gone . . . surely then, if the ache in his groin had not come bursting forth, he would not have let her lay him out and undo his trousers and straddle him, slipping around him as smooth and tight as sea anemones. Surely he would not have groaned and squeezed her heavy soft breasts between his fingers and thrust up and up into his daughter's wet-velvet heaven until she bent over him and he felt a metallic sting as of a razor blade beneath his jaw. Jessy fastened her lips there. He felt her throat working as she swallowed. Then a black and crimson mist began to drift into the edges of his vision.

He awoke tangled in Jessy's rumpled sheets that smelled of girl-skin. There was a nick on his throat, no worse than a bad shaving cut, smeared with dried blood and spit. He did not wash it. Jessy was gone.

After a few nights he began to look for her in all the places she had mentioned. All the nighttime haunts, the dark bars and clubs in the French Quarter. He did not know what he would say if he saw Jessy. He had begun to feel as if the thing that had happened were his fault, as if he had seduced her. As if he had forced himself into her. He did not know whether he would be able to meet his daughter's eyes. But that did not matter, for he never saw Jessy again.

More and more often during his search, he found himself drawn to the place called Christian's, the dark bar with the stained-glass windows that threw colored shadows onto the sidewalk. It was a little place way down Chartres, away from the life of the Quarter. He came here because he knew Jessy had liked the place, and he decided he might as well have a drink or two or three. He watched the bartender. Christian moved behind the bar, mixing drinks with detached expertise, answering his customers' chatter politely if rather coldly. Unless someone spoke to Christian, he was silent.

When Wallace watched Christian, studied the impossibly tall, gaunt, pale figure always dressed in black, the idea of Jessy's vampires no longer seemed quite so preposterous. Something about Christian frightened him. Wallace thought of himself as a religious man, but when he was in that chilly presence, God's warmth seemed to shrivel inside him. One night their eyes met across the bar, and Wallace felt his spine turn to ice. The coldness in Christian's eyes—that awful, empty coldness, like winds blowing across barren plains— was more convincing than all Jessy's talk, her books and movies, her fevered drinking of blood.

Wallace could not forget those eyes. When he'd seen them again tonight, he had felt the same icy hand, the same helpless fury. Wallace believed in vampires now.

Tonight, though, he would not be helpless. Fifteen years ago he had been afraid. His fear no longer mattered, not now. The finger of God had touched him, a fearful, excruciating touch that wrenched his insides and sometimes drew thin dirty blood from them, and soon he would be with Jessy. Tonight he would avenge her, and he would have his memories of her again, his memories of a child who danced and laughed, of a child who loved him, who was not a dark creature of sex and blood. He would eradicate his damnable sin. He would redeem himself.

The air sobered him. He drew himself up, refused to sway, refused to let his dizziness and fear overtake him. Tonight belonged to him, and to Jessy.

He walked toward the river.

8

Twig kept up a steady string of curses as they drove into DC. The streets seemed skewed to him, the signs indecipherable. Finally he turned the wrong way down a one-way street, screeched to a halt in front of a fancy hotel, and said, "That's where we're staying."

Molochai waved the parking valet over, and Twig presented him with the keys to the van. "Remember which one is ours," he told the valet. "We want this van back, not some pussy Volvo."

The lobby was all plush and marble opulence, red-carpet gaudy splendor. They appreciated it not a bit. As they checked in, Molochai gaped up at the three-tiered crystal chandelier, and Twig palmed the desk clerk's cigarettes.

Their room was not as gaudy as the public facade of the hotel. Here on the twentieth floor there was only pale carpeting as thick and rich as whipped cream. Zillah slipped his shoes off and wriggled his toes in its creamy depths. Here were only deep, cloud-soft beds and sofas that one might drown in, falling forever, never to be seen again. Oh yes, they could have fun here.

He drifted to the window and pulled aside heavy draperies. The city gleamed far below, green and white, immaculate. The crazy pattern of the streets was a puzzle that wanted deciphering. In the center of it all the Washington Monument soared up, as clean and stark as a bone. Zillah smiled a small secret smile. The city was delicious. All cities were delicious. They had only to wait until nightfall.

From behind him came a great howl of delight as Molochai and Twig saw the whirlpool bathtub. Zillah turned to see them ripping at each other's clothes, throwing shirts and sneakers and socks all over the room in their haste to get undressed. He watched them for a moment, still smiling, then untied the purple scarf that bound his ponytail and began combing his hair with his fingers, smoothing its silky length, untangling the snarls made by the wind on the road. Hair slipped between his fingers, tumbled down over his shoulders.

Molochai and Twig stood together by the whirlpool, naked as babes, waiting to see what Zillah would do. Zillah slipped out of his trousers and jacket, pulled his loose black T-shirt over his head. He wore no underwear; none of them did. Slim as a girl, he stood looking at Molochai and Twig, his skin creamy pale, his hair the color of coffee with milk.

They moved toward one another until their shoulders were almost touching. All three bodies bore the marks of various piercings, tattoos, and scarifications. Living so long in the same unchanging flesh made them restless; they were compelled to change it themselves. Age did its own decorating of human bodies—wrinkles, wattled flesh, random sproutings of coarse yellowish hair. Molochai, Twig, and Zillah were much more pleased with their own methods of decoration: silver rings, intricate patterns in ink or raised flesh.

Twig had twin strands of barbed wire tattooed on his wrists, twining up both arms, and two long thin pieces of metal that pierced the thin skin of his stomach just below the rib cage on either side, capped with nuggets of bone he had saved to have honed and fitted. Zillah wore silver hoops through his nipples; Molochai's were pierced with safety pins, from one of which dangled a polished fingerbone. All three had foreskin-rings (because of the circumstances surrounding their births, few of their race were circumcised as babies). They had linked these together to pose for a series of studies by a famous photographer of erotica, Zillah standing

on an inlaid-teak stool that brought his ring up to the level of
the others'.

Zillah put his hand on Molochai's shoulder and pushed
gently down. Molochai knelt before him and embraced Zillah's narrow hips. His mouth brushed soft skin and silky hair.
He put out his tongue and felt Zillah shiver. Then Zillah's
hand was under his chin, cupping his face and tilting it up.
Molochai looked up into Zillah's eyes. Green. Glowing, melting green.

"Molochai," said Zillah.

Molochai was lost in the luminescent sea of green; he
could not answer.

"Molochai."

He shook himself. "What?"

Zillah's face was calm. A small smile played about his lips.
"Do you want something from room service?"

Molochai stared up at Zillah for a few moments. Then he
hugged Zillah tighter, and it was as if two jagged edges fitted
together inside him. He turned and saw Twig standing jeal-
ously alone, watching them. They each put out an arm to
Twig, and he came to them.

"I want champagne," said Molochai. "And I want whipped
cream and kidneys and chocolate truffles and baby's-blood
ice cream."

They stood together, naked and embracing, the three of
them as much a family as anyone could be, anywhere, ever.

In the foamy waters of the whirlpool Zillah pulled Molochai and Twig to him and dipped his tongue into their
mouths, sweet with cake and cream, sharp and sour with
champagne. Once more they began their game of spit and
skin and passion, of slippery hands and soft bites, and sometimes harder bites. They played the game they knew so well,
the game they had played for such a long time, and when
they were done Molochai and Twig snuggled against Zillah in
the steamy swirling water, their heads on his shoulders, their
hands linked across his chest.

The three closed their eyes and dreamed their warm
bloody dreams. For a few hours they could rest, and then it
would be time to go out and party again.

* * *

When night folded like a deep blue cloak over the city, they roused themselves from their wet languor and began pulling on black shirts, black socks, dirty black sneakers. They favored black clothes because dark red stains would not show on them. Zillah put a tiny silver ankh through his earlobe. The other two wore large dangling crucifixes in their ears.

Twig, smearing on eyeliner in front of the bathroom mirror, found a raw red crescent on his chest. "You bit me," he complained to Molochai. "I'm bleeding."

Molochai, still half-naked, came closer and licked the blood from Twig's chest. When Twig's nipple puckered at the touch of the rough tongue, Molochai snapped at it. "I'm *hungry*," he said, and this time there was something in his voice that told them he would not be satisfied with sweets and chocolate.

When the sun set, Zillah sent the valet to get their van. They drove to Georgetown, taking wrong turns, being stopped by streets that suddenly turned one-way, weaving around and around traffic circles, swaying against each other every time the van navigated a curve. They had drunk more champagne back at the hotel, and by this time they were too blasted to care whether they got lost.

By persistence and luck they arrived in Georgetown before midnight. The sidewalks swarmed with people: tourists out for a big night, students wearing school sweatshirts, a group of black kids with roller skates and stocking caps spray-painting arcane graffiti on a wall. Molochai pressed his face to the window. " 'Fresh,' " he read before the van was past.

Twig licked his lips. "They better be."

"Trendies." Zillah waved his black-nailed hand in an elegant gesture of dismissal. "Trendies, all of them. We'll find better ones later, after these are home in bed."

They parked beside a fire hydrant. Zillah took a satchel full of empty wine bottles from the back of the van and gave them to Twig to carry.

Molochai looked at the block of shops. A lingerie boutique, a newsstand, a vegetarian café. It might have been a street in any city in America. "There's no magic in this town," he complained.

Zillah touched Molochai's lips with the tip of a sharp nail. "There's magic in every bloodstream."

Molochai nodded sullenly. He was hungry again. There might be magic in every bloodstream, but the bloodstreams in the French Quarter were tastier.

It was Twig who found the girl. He had a nose for Indian curry. The window was painted *CALCUTTA PALACE* in a flowing strange script. Below it a sign said *CLOSED*, but the door swung open when Twig pushed at it. The inside of the restaurant was decorated like some fantastic far eastern fairy tale: red silk drooping from the ceiling, purple velvet covering the walls, tables lacquered in black and gold.

Zillah looked around appreciatively, then sensed that Twig had gone quivering and taut beside him. He followed Twig's eyes and saw a lone dark-skinned girl at the back of the restaurant sweeping the carpet with an electric vacuum. She had not yet heard them over the noise of the machine.

As Twig watched, the girl raised her arm and pulled her heavy black hair back over one shoulder. The movement wafted a cloud of her scent to him. He could smell the oil of her hair, the sweat of her armpits, the odors of grease and spice and sandalwood that were a part of her being. And he could smell the dusky blood beneath the skin, hot and peppery, as exotic as all India. Her blood would taste of chili and almonds, of cardamom, of rosewater.

He motioned to the other two, and they slid forward, moving as one creature, fused in this act of killing. The girl turned and flung up her hands, but Twig's mouth stopped her cry, and they fell upon her. As Zillah grasped her head between his strong hands and twisted her neck to an impossible angle, as Molochai burrowed under her long cotton skirt and bit into his favorite spot, Twig cracked the bones of the girl's throat between his teeth and tasted spice.

* * *

They drove back to the hotel sometime in the hazy zone between very late and very early. Twig's eyes were glazed; with an effort he focused on the road. Molochai lay with his head in Zillah's lap nibbling a little sugared cake he had found in the kitchen of the restaurant.

Zillah's wine bottles were full now. He had topped them off with vodka from the restaurant's bar. The bar had been well stocked, and he had found a bottle of peppered Stolichnaya. It would blend well with the girl's spicy blood. This hot red cache would be a treat later on, during the long dry stretch between here and New Orleans.

They passed a nightclub. Children postured on the sidewalk, waving their spidery hands, tracking the van with their black-smudged eyes. A snatch of sepulchral song floated in their wake. Bauhaus.

Zillah tilted his head to one side and smiled. "Listen to them—the children of the night," he said. "What music they make!"

9

 When Christian turned away from the river, Wallace was there, several feet away, watching him. Wallace had seen him with the boy.

Christian's first emotion was not anger or fear but shame, terrible fiery shame. Wallace had caught him at his most secret, most vulnerable moment, and Christian wanted to sink to the ground and cover himself, to shut his eyes tight, to vanish. He pulled his cloak around him and stared at Wallace, feeling his eyes grow colder, knowing he must not panic.

The moonlight ravaged Wallace's face. The hollows beneath his eyes grew deeper, the lines bracketing his mouth more harsh. The silver cross at his throat gleamed, and his hand went to it. *"Vampire,"* he said, spitting the word out, making it ugly. "Filthy, cursed thing—"

"You knew," said Christian. "The story you told me—it was all made up. You didn't find her diary. You weren't suddenly seized with a desire to see her after such a long time. You knew."

Wallace's eyes glittered, dark, never leaving Christian's. "I did."

"Then why?" Christian spread his arms in a gesture of bewilderment; the cloak billowed around him, made him seem immensely tall. Wallace, perhaps misunderstanding the gesture, took a step backward. "Why now? If you knew then, why are you following me after fifteen years?"

"I knew then," Wallace told him. "After Jessy disappeared,

I began going to your bar, watching you, and I knew. I came to believe. And I knew what you had done to my daughter." He hadn't answered the question.

But Jessy wasn't even dead then, Christian thought, confused. *He is wrong. She must have been alive still, living upstairs, gazing out my window all day and pulling me into her body at night—*

"You look very much the proper vampire, Christian," Wallace went on, and Christian wondered whether he was supposed to take that as a compliment. "But I still could not quite believe. I was unsure. My religion does not acknowledge the supernatural. It considers such matters unholy, and consequently it ignores them. So one night I waited until you closed your bar down,.and when you went out, I followed you. I saw you speak to a boy near Jackson Square, a young boy with long hair who wore beads around his neck. I followed the two of you to the river, and here I saw you—I saw you do what you did to the other boy tonight. And I wondered how many other children you had put in the river, and I thought of Jessy's body sinking out of sight there, in that cold brown water—" Wallace's voice broke.

Yes, Jessy, thought Christian. *I put Jessy in the river. But that was later, after the baby came. And I didn't kill her, I wouldn't have killed her—* In an instant he realized who *had* killed Jessy. Zillah had, with the seduction of his hands and his lips, with his fertile seed. Or so Wallace would see it. Christian imagined himself trying to explain the events of that Mardi Gras to Wallace: *He planted his child in her womb, and by the time the baby tore her apart inside, he was far, far away. But that night was so bloody, and oh so green . . .*

No. Wallace would not understand the drunkenness that comes with blood or the light in the Mardi Gras sky. He would see only the image of Zillah's hands on Jessy's fragile body. He would picture Zillah writhing atop Jessy, stifling her screams with his tongue. The blame would be taken away from Christian, and Wallace would no longer want to kill him. He would want Zillah's blood.

Zillah, with those languid, graceful hands, with those

glowing green eyes, and the rest of that loud happy trio Christian had not seen for fifteen years, though he had looked for them every night of every Mardi Gras when the bright costumes staggered in and the laughter was high and drunken and the liquor flowed in the gutters. The only ones of his kind Christian had seen for so many years, more years than he wanted to remember, and the youngest, wildest, finest ones he had ever known.

No, Wallace could not be allowed to go after Molochai, Twig, and Zillah. He would never be able to find them—they might be anywhere in the world, anywhere they could find liquor, sweets, and blood—and if by some chance he did find them, they would laugh in his face as they killed him.

But Christian would not give Wallace even a wisp of a chance. He would deal with Wallace himself, and he would protect his kind. He did not love what he did, but for too long he had been alone in doing it. Wallace's blood would spill for Molochai's sticky smile, for the cleverness of Twig's foxlike face, for Zillah's luminescent green eyes.

"All right," he said. "You knew then. Why did you wait? Why have you come to me now?"

"I was afraid of you then."

Christian nodded and took a step toward Wallace. Wallace didn't back away this time.

"I have no reason to fear you anymore." Wallace shut his eyes, then opened them. "You are a godless thing, and you will die for that. Fifteen years ago I did not have the courage to avenge Jessy, but nothing else matters to me now." He unfastened the crucifix from his throat and stepped toward Christian, brandishing it at the end of its chain. "Begone from the face of God's earth, foul creature, thing of night, sucker at Death's teat—"

Christian shook his head sadly. He did not laugh, but there was a trace of amused contempt in his eyes. Wallace stopped chanting and lowered his arm. The crucifix swung from his hand, shimmering when the moonlight caught it.

"You are a fool," said Christian. "You are a fool, and your myths are wrong. If you touched me with that, it would not burn me. It would not blacken my skin. It would not poison my essence. I have nothing against your Christ. I am sure his blood tasted as sweet as anyone else's."

Christian imagined Wallace waving a crucifix in the faces of Molochai, Twig, and Zillah. *Those children,* he thought, *would laugh this silly old man into his grave.*

"Undead soul," said Wallace, not quite steadily.

"No. I am alive. I was born as you were born." *Well, not quite.* Christian thought of the mother he had never seen, wondered whether he had left her as torn and bloody as Jessy had been. "I am not the creature of your myths. I did not rise from the grave. I have *never* been one of your race, Wallace Creech—I am of a different one."

Now Christian was smiling, letting the sharp tips of his teeth show; it was an icy smile, masking his lust. Wallace, no matter how ineffective, was a danger, a threat. And that meant Christian should kill him now and let him follow his daughter into the river where their bones might drift together in the intimacy Wallace seemed to long for.

Still smiling, gazing steadily into the depths of Wallace's eyes, Christian stepped forward and rested his hands on the old man's stooped shoulders. Wallace stared back as if hypnotized, but Christian could feel the man's muscles pulled painfully tight, tense to the point of trembling.

Christian lowered his head and brushed his lips against Wallace's throat. And suddenly he found himself wishing that all the ancient human myths were true. He had seen no others of his kind in fifteen years, since Molochai, Twig, and Zillah appeared by some Mardi Gras magic and left again when the sun set on Ash Wednesday. Christian wished he had the power that the legends ascribed to him. He wished his victims could rise again and run with him, others of his kind to share the smell of the streets past midnight, the long hot days with the shades drawn, the taste of the sweet fresh blood. Even Wallace would do, even old tired Wallace with the pain in his eyes. He put his mouth against Wallace's throat. The skin there was dry, loose; it smelled of age. He bit down and tasted blood for the second time that night. . . .

But it was *bitter,* it was *foul,* and he spat it back against

Wallace's throat and gagged. Christian's nostrils flared. He had not detected it before, under the stinging mist of whiskey and sorrow, but now it was obvious, strong, and rank. The smell of sickness, deep rotting sickness that rioted through Wallace's body, as wet and brown as the smell of the river. Some virulent disease, probably a cancer. The taste was corruption in his mouth.

If that had been all, Christian could have fled or fought. He was very strong, surely stronger than Wallace. But a second later the nausea hit him, worse than the drunken sickness brought on by the Chartreuse, worse than the sharp immediacy of that pain. It knocked him down, and he lay as still as he could, languid with shock, trying not to move for fear of increasing the nausea. He felt his stomach convulsing, and he fought to keep the boy's blood down. He did not want to relinquish that.

Through the haze of sickness he was aware of Wallace pulling something from behind his back, something that had been tucked into the waistband of his trousers. The object caught the moon and became a thing of pure light, a slim pistol shining white and silver.

He saw Wallace taking aim and closed his eyes. Then the night exploded and pain slammed into Christian's chest. He could not breathe. He felt the hot pellet of lead tunnelling into him, through him. He kept his eyes closed so that he would not have to see the triumph on Wallace's face.

His last thought before the pain and the sickness washed his mind away was one of regret: *Three hundred and eighty-three years . . . such a very long time . . . he should have been beautiful . . . not this sad, old, tired man . . . he should have been lovely.*

10

Nothing hurried through the circle of brilliance made by a streetlight and slipped into the deserted darkness again. He pulled his raincoat around him (O sensuous black silk, as erotic as the touch of someone else's skin!) and hoisted his heavy backpack on his shoulder.

His passage was hidden by luxuriant hedges and the shadows they cast on verdant lawns, by sleek cars parked at the curb. Even if his parents missed him now, they'd never be able to find him. He had a sudden vision of them cruising the dark streets in his mother's Volvo, calling his name, waving a bottle of good whiskey to lure him home.

He was forcing himself to be absolutely silent, making a game of it so that he would not have to think too hard about what he had left behind. His room and all the things in it. Most of his tapes, most of his books, all his records and old toys and the stars on his ceiling. He thought of the stars still glowing there, lonely pinpoints of light above his empty bed, and he wondered if he would ever again sleep beneath a ceiling of painted yellow stars. Tears pressed against the backs of his eyes. He chewed his lower lip, hugged himself tight, and waited for the wave of loneliness to subside. Not even two blocks away and already homesick. This time tomorrow, alone on some Greyhound in the night, he might be a real mess.

He unzipped his backpack and felt around inside. He had brought only the bare essentials: his collection of Dylan

Thomas's poems, his notebook, the note stolen from his mother's drawer that would tell his family who he was when he found them, his Walkman, and as many tapes as he had been able to cram in. He would honor the backpack well; it would never have to lug schoolbooks again.

His fingers found the Walkman and the edge of a cassette tape. He didn't care what he listened to. He just wanted to hear something, something to carry him away, to blot out his thoughts for a while. He knew he didn't really have to watch for his parents. They'd never miss him. He had heard them come in sometime after ten, boozed up on expensive wine and stuffed with French food, arguing about him. "You want him to follow any asinine whim that catches his fancy," Father had said, and Mother replied, "He has to find himself," but she didn't sound as serene as usual. They'd gone into their bedroom and shut the door. Nothing lay in bed and thought about going south where he could follow his whims, asinine or not. Where no one would ever have to argue about him again.

He put on the Lost Souls? cassette. The music was soft and wailing, the singer's voice pulling him down south, down along the ways the trains travelled, down through the green land. Nothing wondered whether these musicians might be his family, his long-lost brothers. He thought again of the eerie-sounding town where they lived. Maybe he would go there.

What the hell, he decided, and lit a cigarette. Its red firefly glow would pick him out of the darkness if anyone was looking for him. But no one was. He knew that. Even if his parents missed him, they would figure he'd sneaked out to party with his friends. *We'll cancel his allowance for a week*, they'd say, and then they'd roll over and sleep their dreamless sleep. When he didn't come home the next day, they would call the police and set up a halfhearted search for him, but perhaps they would be secretly relieved. Now they could live their comfortable lives with no strange son to look at them and silently judge them. Now they need no longer wonder what they had raised, why their child had disappointed them so, whether they might have been happier if he had not been left on their doorstep that cold morning. Now he was on the road. He would smoke Lucky Strikes and wander, and he would find his home. He was on his way already.

Skittle's was almost empty when Nothing walked in. The cuffs of his jeans were wet with night-dew. The fresh cut on his wrist throbbed in time with his heartbeat. He saw Jack in a corner booth with four other kids, two boys and two girls. One of the boys was Laine. The table was littered with empty wax cups and half-eaten pizza, the ashtray choked with butts.

Nothing looked at Jack. "Can you still drive me to Columbia?"

"I said I would, dude. Since when do I go back on my word? I need the five dollars if you have it." Nothing handed him a bill, and Jack tucked it into his pack of Marlboros.

"I have to be at the bus station by one," Nothing said pointedly. "The bus leaves then."

Jack heaved a great sigh. "Okay. Okay. Let's peel out." He stood up, the chains on his boots jangling.

The others stood too. Laine slipped out of the booth and pressed up close to Nothing. His breath, sweet with cloves, tickled Nothing's ear. "Where are you gonna go?"

"I don't know. South."

"How come you didn't tell me?"

"I didn't know until tonight."

Laine took Nothing's hand between both of his, twined his fingers into Nothing's. "You should've called me. I would have gone with you. I hate it here too."

Nothing looked at Laine. Laine's lips were smeared with black lipstick; his feathery white-blond hair hid his eyes. Nothing wanted to brush the hair away, but he couldn't. He slid his hand out of Laine's and shoved it into the pocket of his jeans. "I thought you were going out with Julie," he said.

Laine shrugged, an unconcerned, eloquent gesture. "We broke up. She's such a damn poser."

"She's all right," said Nothing. "She gave me her Lost Souls? tape."

"Yeah, well, she never listened to it anyway. She doesn't

listen to anything but English *fashion bands*." Laine sneered. Nothing wondered whether Julie had dumped Laine this afternoon, or possibly even earlier tonight. The wounds seemed fresh.

If Laine wanted Nothing to lick them, though, he was out of luck. Laine wasn't getting an invitation to go south with him. No way. Nothing was leaving all this behind tonight—the school, the parents, and this goddamn pizza joint where the kids sat and smoked and talked about how great their lives would be if only they lived anywhere but here.

Jack and the others were heading for the parking lot. Laine grabbed Nothing's hand and pulled him along. "You don't want to get left, do you? You're getting the hell out of here!" Laine's voice was exalted, envious.

The ride to Columbia seemed to take no time at all. Guardrails, underpasses, dead orange sodium lights flashed past at a great speed. Skinny Puppy played on Jack's tape deck, so loud that the notes were mangled beyond recognition. Someone passed around a flask of cheap vodka, and Jack drank most of it in one long gurgling swallow—like the Irishman chauffeur in a story Nothing had read, Jack could not drive unless he was blind drunk.

Nothing was squeezed in the backseat between Laine and a diminutive purple-haired girl who called herself Sioux. Sioux pulled a little knife from her boot and passed it over to Laine. "See what Veronica traded me for that Cramps poster? It's fucking sharp!"

Laine fingered the tip of the knife and yelped as the blade pierced his skin. "Seriously! That hurt."

A spot of blood glistened on Laine's fingertip, wet and black in the orange light of the highway. Nothing bent and took Laine's finger into his mouth and licked the blood away. Laine lay back smiling. Nothing touched his tongue to the spot, questing for more, but Laine slid his other hand under Nothing's chin, tilted Nothing's face up, and kissed him deeply, wetly, hugging him close.

"I'll miss you," said Laine into Nothing's mouth, and pushed Nothing against the back of the seat and kissed him again.

Then Sioux leaned over and licked Nothing's throat, and Laine's hands were in his hair and Sioux's hands were on his thighs, sliding up under his shirt. Nothing closed his eyes and smiled into the darkness. His friends had disappointed him in every other way, but they certainly knew how to give a good send-off.

The others waited at the bus station with him until Jack put a nickel in the gum machine and kicked it over when no gum came out. Then the old man who sold tickets made them all leave, and Nothing sat alone in the dark waiting room, looking at the frosted glass of the ticket window, the dingy scrolled ceiling high above, the shiny pink bald spot on the back of the old man's head and the way his ivory-colored hair straggled over the buckle of his dirty visor.

Nothing took out his Dylan Thomas book, but there was no light to read by. He looked at his hands in his lap. Two weeks ago he'd put on some of Laine's black nail polish, but most of it was gone now. He examined the chips and flecks that were left. They looked like shapes on a map, like tiny states. Maybe like the places he was going. He cupped his hands over his face. They were scented with vodka and smoke, with Laine and Sioux. He felt his eyes closing.

The old man's bawling voice woke him a few minutes later. "Coach boarding for Silver Spring, Fairfax, Wash'ton DC, Fredericksburg . . ." Nothing felt for his backpack and stood up. Now he could get started.

The bus smelled of cigarettes and prickly upholstery and some heavy sweet disinfectant. Nothing decided he liked the odor. A few heads lifted to stare blearily at him, then drooped back against the dark windows. He took a seat in the back and lit a cigarette. The bus shuddered, heaved a sigh, and pulled away from the station.

Nothing smiled at himself in the window. He was on his way. His journey had begun. He was already a little closer to home.

11

Several hours after Nothing climbed the steps of a Greyhound bus in Maryland, Christian opened his eyes and saw dawn bleeding palely across the New Orleans sky. At first he could not remember why he was lying on the riverbank, why his clothes were wet with mist and his limbs so stiff and cold. He could not think why it seemed strange to see another dawn, why he had never expected to open his eyes again.

Then the whole night came rushing back, and he gave an involuntary shudder and let the relief and the fury wash over him. Relief because he had not wanted to die at the hands of one like Wallace, so clumsy and drained of passion; fury because Wallace should not have been able to defeat him, Wallace with his tired, ancient eyes. Christian's belly should be warm and heavy with Wallace's blood now; Wallace should be drifting away along the river bottom, the water filling his eyes, the creatures of the mud beginning to nibble at his hands.

Christian sat up and examined himself. There was a scorched hole in the fine black cloth of his shirt, its edges perfectly round. He undid the top two buttons. The bullet had shattered the third one. In the center of his chest was a shiny pink scar, the skin pulled tight and slightly rippled. There would be no matching scar on his back; Wallace's bullet was still in him, and there it would stay. It was not the first.

He had bled only a little. There was a crust of dried blood

on his skin, ringing the scar, and the ground where he had lain all night was stained dark red. But the spot was small, hardly worth noticing. *The fool,* he thought with a touch of incredulity. *He had to destroy my brain or my heart, and he had his chance at either one, and the old fool missed my heart by an inch.* With an intensity that he had not thought himself still capable of, Christian wished that Molochai, Twig, and Zillah had been there. They would have taken Wallace's silver cross away, thrown it in the river, and ripped Wallace's throat out, joking all the while.

But the fury faded even as he recognized it, and Christian sat quietly in the breaking light for several minutes, resting his head on his drawn-up knees, unable to identify his new emotion. As he pushed himself to his feet and gathered his cloak around him, he realized what this was, his reaction to waking healed and alive and still alone. It was disappointment.

Last night's trash lay tranquil in the gutter as he made his way home. The toe of his boot connected with a plastic Hurricane glass and sent it skittering across the pavement. The noise was too loud in this early-morning calm. Christian caught the odor of the sticky drops left in the bottom of the glass: rum and passion fruit gone sour, a rancid pink smell. The glass rolled into the arch of a courtyard where green and golden light was beginning to filter down through mimosa branches. The smell of the blossoms reached him, rosy-delicate, clear as the smell of water.

The Quarter was nearly quiet. Christian trailed his hand along the walls, along wrought-iron gates between high ornate pillars of brick and stone, along the doors and windows of the dark shops, the sleeping bars. He passed an all-night diner and caught a stew of breakfast odors: the savory, greasy smell of sausage and eggs and coffee for those on their way to early-morning jobs, hot fried oysters and the sliced ham and vinegar tang of po-boys for those who had been out drinking all night, who would soon head back to cheap hotel rooms and drab boardinghouses for sodden daytime slumber. He felt his stomach shift, last night's nausea raise its head, roll over, and settle back into uneasy sleep.

The sky was brightening more quickly now. As he turned east from Bienville onto Chartres, the nascent sunlight caught him full in the face. Again came pain that burned through his eyes and seared his brain. Christian flung up his arm and sagged back against the wall. The bricks were rough and cool. He pressed his face to them, resting for a moment. His eyes felt scorched. When he had to venture out into sunlight, he always wore dark glasses, a wide-brimmed black hat, gloves, and dark loose clothing that he could huddle into. This morning he had only the cloak to pull around him. Already he was beginning to be blinded by the new day, and he was so very tired. The sidewalk seemed to stretch endlessly before him, shimmering and baking in the sunlight.

Surely his bar was just ahead. He groped along the wall. He had to rely on his sense of smell, but the mélange of odors confused him; he could not tell where he was. Was the bar in this block, or the next? He couldn't have crossed Conti yet. *Idiot,* he told himself. *How long have you lived here? How many nights have you walked this street? You should carry a map of scents in your head, in your very being. . . .*

He forced himself to concentrate on separating the smells and identifying them. Here was the slimy sea-smell of the trashcans behind an oyster bar. Here was a sewer smell, brown and gassy. Here was the leather trade shop, black tanned hides and chrome and the dizzying chemical bite of butyl nitrate, and that meant his bar was only a few doors down.

He felt his way to it and let himself in. There was a separate street entrance that led straight up to the rooms, but Christian usually came in through the bar because that way he knew he would meet no one on the stairs. For a long time he stood in the lightening gloom of the bar, breathing the dark dust, the ghosts of liquor and beer and all the drinkers who had been here. If he breathed in deeply enough, he thought he could still catch the scent of Wallace Creech, the dry sick smell.

Wallace. Poor Wallace, who thought he had killed his nemesis, his daughter's supernatural defiler. What would he do when he discovered otherwise?

Christian closed his eyes. He would not think about Wallace now, would not plan. He looked around the room, saw the dark wood of the bar, the bottles gleaming softly on their shelves, the colored light filtering through the unbroken stained-glass window. In here the light could not hurt him.

But his eyes were sore, exhausted. He climbed the stairs to his room and burrowed into bed, into his own comforting, familiar smell. Cool dry skin and ancient spice and a hint of something darker, something thick and garnet-colored and faintly rotten. The smell from deep inside him, where the blood never quite washed clean. Borne away on the river of it, he slept.

When he awoke, the light seeping around the edges of the window shade was diffuse, milky, no longer bright and searing. Outside on the street, twilight must be drawing nigh. The streetlamps would blink on soon, softly illuminating each corner through opaque glass panes, and all the children of the French Quarter would come out to play.

Christian lay flat on his back, tangled in sheets that were not so very much paler than his skin. He pulled tendrils of his hair over his shoulder and twisted them as he daydreamed, and he stared at the delicate brown and cream pattern of water marks that had spread across the ceiling over the years, almost too dim to see in this fading light. He was not planning, not worrying, not even truly thinking. He was only waiting for full night to come, for he knew it was time to leave again.

This had happened so many times before. He might live in a place for five years or fifty before anyone became suspicious of him. But someone always became suspicious, and he always moved on. It was easier than trying to hide from them; it made him less heartsick than fighting them. When he was young he had fought them, and he had never lost. But he always had to kill so many. Eventually he realized that when he was not killing for lust and hunger, he hated it. Breaking the fragile span of their forty or fifty or eighty years made him feel vicious and cruel. He could outlast them; he could return long after they were dust and bones.

And it was most important to remain secretive, to remain a little afraid. For even if he killed them all, tore their throats out one by one, there were always more. This was the one thing he knew Molochai, Twig, and even Zillah would never recognize: no matter how invulnerable they thought they might be, their race was few, and the others were many.

Once he had been found out, they would rain down upon him. They would scream for his blood in return for the blood he had taken, and they would have it no matter what the cost.

Wallace might not be so dangerous. Not by himself. He was old and alone; perhaps he would have no friends to tell. But Wallace had God, and the godly. He belonged to a church. Christian knew the eagerness of the religious to believe in evil and their lust to crush it. To do something tangible in return for the intangible reward they spent their lives awaiting. Wallace by himself might not be so dangerous, but his faith could be deadly.

And so it was time to leave again. It was easier than being on his guard all the time, easier than slapping a hundred crucifixes out of a hundred hands, easier than ripping into a hundred terrified faces. Let Wallace die believing he had avenged his daughter.

Christian packed a very small bag. There was little to pack; for a long time now possessions had seemed fleeting and cumbersome, and his room was almost bare. He brought his day clothes, his hat and gloves and glasses, and he brought the money he had saved from the bar. He kept it in a box under the bed, but there wasn't very much of it. No one else would have been able to afford the rent and the upkeep—the bar was so far down Chartres, and no one ever came in until ten—but Christian had none of the expenses of a usual human life. He did not need food; he did not go out drinking. His enjoyments were more exotic and carried a potentially higher price. This money he would spend along the way, for gasoline. He could get more money when he needed it; there was always work for a good bartender. With a glimmer of hope, he put three bottles of Chartreuse in his bag. There was no telling whom he might meet on the road.

It had begun to rain, and the street was deserted. This was cold, grimy rain, rain that drifted down from the sky like broken spiderwebs and danced on the hood of Christian's car as if possessed by some mindless elemental joy. The golden cones of brightness beneath the streetlamps shimmered like spirits. Rain misted up from the sidewalks and rose back toward the sky. The clouds hung low and leaden, reflecting back the light of the French Quarter dull purple, like light seen through thick dirty glass.

Christian turned onto Bourbon Street. The rain hadn't stopped tonight's carnival. Crowds huddled on the sidewalks and made occasional mad dashes across the street, like fish darting between brightly lit riverbanks. The street was a riot of lights. Glittering gold ribbons, pink and green martini glasses, a giant red neon crawfish. He drove past Jean Lafitte's Old Absinthe House and remembered when it had first begun serving that bitter liqueur. The sign proclaimed *Since 1807*, and Christian had to trust it. His memory was good, but he had been in and out of the city in those years, more restless then. He had seen Lafitte, though, a handsome, sensual man who could hold forth on any subject and draw an audience whether he knew what he spoke of or not. Christian's eyes had met Lafitte's across a crowded barroom one night, and Lafitte had pulled a face at him, toothy and menacing, then winked.

The pirate had been drunk on absinthe, which produces visions. Molochai, Twig, and Zillah would have loved absinthe in its true form, before the poisonous wormwood was taken out of the recipe. But they had been mewling babes when it was banned in the United States in 1912.

Inside the strip clubs, spangles gyrated and flashed. Christian stopped his car for a crowd of people milling across the street. Soldiers, tourists, street-corner musicians—and the omnipresent children in black. He had seen those pale smudged faces before, in the clubs, in his arms . . . but no, those had been different faces.

Most of the crowd was drunk. Some turned and waved at Christian, and he lifted a gloved hand in return, half-smiling. Surely those could not be tears on his face. He had not cried in too many years. He could not remember what crying felt like. This was only leftover rain, dripping from his hair, pooling in his eyes.

Christian waved goodbye to the Bourbon Street crowd and wiped the rain from his cheeks. Then he turned north and drove out of town.

12

 As early afternoon light touched her eyelids, the sleeping girl moaned and buried her face in soft black oblivion.

Her sheets and pillowcases had been plain white cotton until last week, when she had run them all through the washing machine with six packages of black Rit dye. Now they were a flat bluish-ebony color that stained her skin on hot nights. She nestled deeper into her inky bed-clothes and flung an arm across the mattress. Empty space. No warmth or scent except her own, no reassuringly live flesh to press herself close to. The empty bed brought her awake with a jolt, and for a moment she panicked. Waking up alone robbed her of her frame of reference; she could barely remember who she *was*.

Then she saw the room around her, the posters on the walls, the paint-smeared easel, the clothes heaped on the floor of the big walk-in closet. Across the room she saw herself in the mirror of her vanity, eyes round and startled, pale face framed by tangles of long red-gold hair. She settled back with a sigh. She was Ann Bransby-Smith, and she was in her own room, safe in her own bed, and never mind the sick feeling it still gave her to wake up alone.

Not until she rolled over and hugged her pillow close to her did she realize that she had been thinking of waking up not with Eliot—even though she had spent most of last night with him—but with Steve.

Even the thought of his name made her heart twist. After

all that had happened between them, Ann still sometimes wished she could wake up with him, see his dark hair straggling across the pillow and his intense face softened in sleep, reach over and glide her fingers along the muscles of his back. God, but he had always felt good beside her, on top of her, inside her.

Well, almost always.

Well, except when he made her hurt like hell.

That was how she had started cheating on him in the first place: she'd wanted to have sex with someone who didn't leave her sore the next morning. Once she had loved the sureness and strength of Steve's touch, but drinking turned him rough and seemed to make his bones sharper. Ann woke with gnawed nipples, bruised hipbones, a throbbing ache in her crotch that turned to raw agony when she pissed. It was only good for an argument if she mentioned it, and she still desired him, so after a while she shut up.

And when she was honest with herself, she knew the rough sex wasn't the only thing that had driven her away. It was the music as well. Steve had already started playing guitar when she met him, and at the time she had liked the idea of having a musician for a boyfriend. She was happy for him when he started getting good and excited when he, Ghost, and R.J. decided to form a band. R.J. had never wanted it as badly as the other two—he'd always been a serious kid, and Ann thought music was just too frivolous a calling for him— and had dropped out early, but he still sat in with them sometimes.

All that had been fine. But when it got too heavy, when it started to appear that Steve and Ghost wanted to make Lost Souls? their life's work, Ann balked. She didn't want to be a musician's wife, spending months alone in Missing Mile while he toured, worrying about money during the lean years and groupies during the good ones. When they had started recording their tape, the final wedge was driven in. The all-night sessions, the hours upon hours Steve spent in Terry's home studio talking about levels, tracks, spillage, and other incomprehensible things he never bothered to explain to his lowly girlfriend. He had never felt so intensely about her, Ann was sure.

At any rate, she had known Eliot would make a gentler lover from the first time she met him.

At first Eliot had seemed exotic: twenty-nine to Ann's twenty-one, divorced, with a real job as a junior-college English teacher and half a novel sitting on his desk. He was a regular customer at the Spanish restaurant where she waited tables. He always sat in Ann's section and started leaving her giant tips. Eventually he asked her out. "You *disturb* me," he had told her, "but you *intrigue* me."

The line sounded stupid when Ann thought about it later, but by then she had already slept with him and had mistaken his tentativeness for tenderness. At least when Eliot went down on her, her clitoris didn't feel as if it were about to be sucked out by its roots. At least when Eliot's penis (she could not help noticing it was thinner and much pointier than she was used to) was inside her, it didn't feel like an angry fist battering her cervix. At least Eliot waited until she was wet. These days, such things were luxuries.

Also, Eliot had had a vasectomy. He was very proud of it and sometimes wore a bright orange button that said *I Got Mine!* If you asked him about it, he would launch into a speech about how None of Us Have the Right to Bring More Children into This Cruel, Overpopulated World. Ann didn't care for the button or the speech, but it was nice being able to go off the pill. Her sleep patterns and her depression patterns were so erratic that she had been forgetting as many as she remembered.

So it didn't matter when she read the half a novel and couldn't think of anything to say about it. It was a study of a rural family in Virginia. It was Tough and Gritty, but Sensitive. The hero turned out to be the youngest son, Edward, who went to the University and became a teacher of English. Edward was also the only character who didn't talk in dialect —Eliot had written his doctoral thesis on William Faulkner, and had never really gotten over it. It didn't matter that Eliot talked sneeringly of her "redneck boyfriend"—whom he had never met and never would—and derived a perverse glee from hearing that Steve was a college dropout. It didn't even matter that underneath all her self-righteousness she felt like the lowest kind of lying, betraying bitch. None of these things mattered to her in the slightest.

Until Steve found out.

Ghost knew about it first, of course. He had always been able to see inside her head, the way he could see inside Steve's head and almost anyone else's if he chose to. Ann had seen Ghost looking at her strangely, then looking away when she stared back at him. He would not question her or accuse her, but she knew he knew.

She had let herself into their house one day while Steve was at work. She stood in the doorway of Ghost's room, watching him write something in a spiral notebook. When he finally looked up, he didn't seem surprised to see her. His pale blue eyes had been calm but guarded.

"Are you going to tell him?" she said.

For a long moment Ghost only looked at her, and she didn't think he would answer at all. Then he lifted one shoulder in a tiny shrug and shook his head no—but in those small movements Ann saw what pain it was causing him to keep such an ugly secret from Steve. All the guilt and the sorrow washed over her then, and she fell on Ghost's bed, buried her face in his musty-rose-scented heap of blankets, and sobbed out the whole sordid tale. Ghost patted her back and stroked her sweaty hair, and all the time she knew she was telling him things he didn't want to hear. But he listened anyway, because he was Ghost. Because he was good.

And of course Steve found out anyway. Whether he sneaked into her room and found her carefully hidden journal, or whether the unspoken communication between him and Ghost was so strong that he picked it up without Ghost having to say anything, Ann never found out. Everything happened so fast. Steve came over one night when her father was out, and *he knew.* He didn't come right out with it, though. He talked around the edges of it; he was manic, almost raving, then sullen. She could see in his eyes that he hated her.

"*All right!*" she shrieked finally. "All right! I fucked somebody else and I liked it! He's a better lover than you. He's smarter than you. He's not a goddamn drunk—"

She was just getting warmed up when his hand flashed out and slapped her hard across the face.

The blow had enough force behind it to throw her backward onto her bed. She lay there for a moment, her heart and mind stunned. Steve had never hit her. No one but her father had ever hit her. Her cheek and jaw went numb, then began to tingle. Steve would beg her forgiveness, surely. But he stood over her, his dark eyes blazing, and when she tried to struggle up he planted the sole of his boot square in her crotch and shoved hard. A lick of pain shot through her.

"You cunt," Steve said. His voice was quiet, inflectionless. "I know how to make sure you won't do any more fucking around for a while."

And Steve's hands went to his belt buckle.

Ann threw herself back against the wall. Suddenly Steve was on the bed with her, pinning her there, trapping her. She thrashed against him and felt him getting hard. Seeing him excited by her terror scared her worse, made her limp. She kept trying to push him away, but she was weak now, and he was so strong.

He yanked her skirt up, thrust two guitar-callused fingers into her vagina. They were dry and felt as if they would tear her open. Now he had her hips pinned beneath his. His jeans were down around his knees. His cock was shoving at her, battering into her. She felt it thrusting through her dryness up into the unwilling heart of her womb, and most of her did not want it there—but it was Steve, and he had always fit inside her so damn well, and almost before she realized it she was coming. Coming against her will, coming in pain and humiliation, but coming hard nonetheless.

Steve mistook the throes of her orgasm for struggles and thrust her arms back against the mattress. His big hands were like vises around her wrists. Ann felt delicate bones grinding together; in a moment she thought they might snap. She threw her head to the side and sank her teeth into the ball of his thumb until she tasted blood. Now he was pounding into her so hard that he didn't seem to notice the pain—

but his grip loosened a little, and then he was shuddering to
his own violent orgasm, and the rape was over.

"There," he breathed, lifting his head to stare into her
stricken face. "There. See how you like fucking your new
boyfriend now."

After he had stormed out and roared away in his car, she
wondered why she felt so dirty.

That had happened more than a month ago, and it was the
last time she had seen Steve. She knew he had tried to call a
couple of times—or *someone* had called at 3:00 A.M. and hung
up when she answered—but she did not care, could not care.
She made Eliot her refuge, her sanctuary. He was so good to
her that she grew impatient with him, then completely sick
of him. But she could not let go. She was afraid of that empty
space in her life. She was afraid she might let Steve fill it
again, and that would kill her shaky self-respect forever.

She nestled deeper into her pillows and contemplated going back to sleep. These days it was not unusual for her to
sleep fourteen or fifteen hours at a stretch. She was just
drifting off again when the doorbell rang. She tried to ignore
it. The sound lingered in her ears, made her heart pound.
"Go away," she whispered.

The bell rang again. Ann swore, and as if in response it
rang a third time. She swung her legs over the side of the
bed, fought off a headrush that made the room spin giddily
around her, and went with great reluctance to see who was at
her door.

The boards of the old wooden porch shifted uneasily under Ghost's feet. The Bransby house was a Victorian mon-
strosity gone to seed, its paint peeling, its edges softening.
He had not called before riding his bike over here because
he was afraid Ann might refuse to see him, but he knew by
her beat-up little car in the driveway that she was home. He
also knew that her father was gone, probably to an AA meeting or to the library over in Corinth, the only places he ever
went that anyone knew about. That was good. Ghost had
always been a little scared of Simon Bransby.

He was trying to decide whether to leave or ring the bell

again when he heard steps inside the house—slow, dragging steps, in no hurry to reach the door. Eventually Ghost heard Ann fumbling with the chain. Then the tumblers of the lock slid back, and she stood in the doorway, leaning against the jamb, her face half obscured in the gloom of the foyer.

At first Ghost thought Ann had two black eyes. But as she blinked at him, he realized it was only her makeup, smeared around her eyes as if she had slept in it. In fact, though it was two in the afternoon, she looked as if she might have just woken up. Her long autumn-colored hair was tangled. Her black dress was rumpled and hastily buttoned.

For a long moment Ann stared at Ghost, his rainbow-painted bicycle beside him on the porch, the colored streamers tied to the brim of his old straw hat. She looked as if she might burst out crying or slam the door in his face. But at last she moved aside and said, "Come on in."

Without another word, she turned and walked back down the hall, away from him. Ghost shut the door behind him and followed. To the left was the dusty parlor, where several weeks' worth of newspapers were strewn about the floor and heavy draperies were closed against the day. Ghost wondered who had drawn them—Simon? Or had it been Ann, who used to keep the house sunny and clean?

To the right was the half-open door of Simon's laboratory. Ghost tried not to look, but the dull gleam of sunlight on glass caught his eye—the test tubes, the aquariums, the vials of weird fluid. He'd been in there a couple of times with Steve, though Ann's friends were not supposed to go in the room. The contents of the aquariums were innocuous enough —toads and mice—but the laboratory felt like a place of pain. And there was a big refrigerator with a chain and padlock on it. Even Ann didn't know what was in there.

Ann reached the kitchen table and propped herself against it for a moment, then collapsed into a chair. "Make some coffee, would you," she said. Ann's voice was hoarser than usual, nearly toneless. She curled her bare toes around the rung of her chair. Her red toenail polish was chipped and faded, as though she had not redone it for weeks.

Ghost found the coffee in the freezer and started making

it. He used only his grandmother's old Corningware drip pot
at home, and he had already put water on to boil before he
realized that the Bransby kitchen had an automatic coffee
maker. It took him several minutes to figure out where the
coffee went and where to pour the cold water in.

"You're not a part of the machine age, Ghost," said Ann.
She lit a Camel and narrowed her eyes at him through the
smoke. At last she asked, "Why did you come over?"

"I just wanted to see how you were doing."

"Oh? And how am I doing?"

"You look bad."

Ann gazed levelly at him. "Thanks. You look a little spooky
yourself."

"You know that's not what I mean." Ghost pulled the cof-
feepot out from under the drip-spout too soon. Hot coffee
hissed against the burner, and he hurriedly put the pot back.
"You're beautiful, Ann. But you look sad. Twitchy. You look
like those kids you used to make fun of at the Sacred Yew—
black clothes, black eyes, dead white skin. What are you
doing?"

"I'm in mourning," she said. "I'm mourning the death of a
relationship." She got up and pushed him away from the
coffee maker, expertly slid the pot out, and poured them
each a cup. Ghost put lots of milk and sugar in his. Ann left
hers black, which meant she was doing some kind of pen-
ance. Ghost knew she hated black coffee.

"Steve told me he hadn't seen you for over a month," he
said. She flinched at the name, but he made himself go on.
"Things must not be too good with your new guy if you're
still in mourning." It was out: he had crossed over into territory that was officially None of His Business.

"Look, Ghost." Ann swung around in her chair, faced him.
"I worked last night, okay? I was at that shitty restaurant
until midnight. Then I drove out to Corinth to see Eliot—
more precisely, to *fuck* Eliot. We fucked until four in the
morning because that's about all we can do together anymore. Then I had to drive back here because Simon usually
wakes up around six, and he gets crazy if I'm not home. So
I've spent the last twenty-four hours doing two things you

don't know much about—working and fucking. I'm tired. Now *lay off me.*"

"Okay," Ghost said quietly. The attack on his areas of ignorance didn't sting much, but the reference to fucking Eliot did, because he knew it would drive Steve up the wall. "I'll leave if that's what you want. I brought you something, though." He put a cassette on the table next to Ann's coffee cup. The words *LOST SOULS?* were printed in multicolored crayon on the liner.

Ann stared at the tape, then up at him. Her tough composure wavered. Her carefully arranged expression began to crumble. "Oh, Ghost . . ." She picked up the tape and pressed it to her lips. A couple of stray tears made crystal tracks through the smudged black makeup. "I miss you. I even miss Steve. But I can't go back."

"I know." He knew some of what had happened between them, not all. Steve hadn't told him everything, but most of it got through anyway. And the rest—well, he guessed he could see it now, in Ann's deathly pale face, in her smudgy, haunted eyes.

She and Steve had always been stormy together. Steve had blithely dated his way through high school, getting laid but never quite getting involved. His tastes were diverse. The only girls he couldn't stomach were the ones who seemed to make themselves up according to some redneck template, with the bleached-blond bubble hairdo, the feverish streak of blush across the cheeks, and the eyeshadow of colors never seen in nature. He had casual girlfriends of all other types: hippies who liked to get stoned with him, preppies who thought him wild and slightly dangerous, smart girls who appreciated his compulsive reading habit.

But Ann was the first one he had fallen for. In her way, Ann loved Steve as fiercely as she loved her weird father, and Steve wanted her more than he had wanted anything since he had learned to play the guitar. But one of the first things that had drawn them to each other was also one of the first things to start tearing them apart. They both pretended to be so tough and cynical that there was no room left to give each other the gentleness they both really needed. Steve had al-

ways been like that, and Ghost knew his way around it; there
was an honesty between them that surpassed any facade
Steve could put up. But Ann wouldn't play that game.

Ghost took a sip of his coffee. It was cold and too sweet
even for him. He drank more of it anyway, because he didn't
want to ask the question that had come into his head. But it
wouldn't go away; it had worried him ever since Steve had
come home that night, his shirt untucked and his eyes wild
and a bite mark on his hand. So finally he spoke again. "That
was a shitty thing Steve did to you. You could have called the
cops on him—or told your father. What stopped you?"

Ann laughed. It was a humorless sound. "Right, Ghost.
The cops. 'Officer, my boyfriend—the one I've been sleeping
with for four years—he raped me.'" She made her voice
deeper and spoke in an exaggerated redneck drawl. "'Sure,
little lady, we understand. You been givin' it away, and now
you want to take it back. Why don't you come on down to the
station and maybe you can show us *exackly* what he did to
you.' I don't think they would have been too sympathetic.
And Simon—well—" The bitter smoke from her cigarette
swirled around her head, obscuring her eyes. "Simon would
have killed him."

Ghost believed her. But she still hadn't told him what he
really wanted to know. "How come you did it, Ann? You
loved Steve. Maybe you still do. How come you wanted to go
running to that guy over in Corinth?"

For a moment Ann only looked at him with something
flickering far back in her eyes, and Ghost thought she might
throw her cup at his head. But then she looked at her burning cigarette as if she had just realized it was there in her
hand, and she sucked smoke deep into her lungs, coughed a
little, and answered him. Her voice was hoarser than usual.
"I believe in whatever gets you through the night," she said.
"Night is the hardest time to be alive. For me, anyway. It
lasts so long, and four A.M. knows all my secrets. And when I
was lying in bed next to Steve feeling like I was about to fly
apart and he wouldn't hold me because we'd been arguing
about some damn stupid thing—well, I went looking for
something to get me through the night a little bit better."

Ghost couldn't say much to that. Her point of view still bothered him, but he knew that was just because no matter how much he cared for Ann, he would always love Steve more. So he talked about mutual friends Ann hadn't seen for a while—she had been afraid of running into Steve, and Eliot was apparently a virtual hermit with no close friends of his own and no interest in meeting hers. Ann hadn't been getting out much.

Ghost gave her the news, such as it was. R.J. Miller's supposedly male cat had a litter of seven kittens, six solid black and one a sort of green. Terry, who owned the Whirling Disc record store in town, had gone on vacation and left the assistant manager in charge. The guy had filled out the form wrong when making an order, and they received a huge shipment of Ray Stevens albums. When he got back, Terry started playing the records all the time as punishment. Twenty times a day or more they were treated to the annoying country singer performing classic numbers like "The Mississippi Squirrel Revival" or "Everything Is Beautiful (In Its Own Way)."

He told Ann these things and made her laugh a little. He didn't tell her how much Steve was drinking, or that he had started robbing Coke machines again. She didn't ask how Steve was either. But when he hugged her goodbye on the porch and rode his bike away, he thought she looked a little happier, a little less pale and drawn. Not much, but a little.

A little worm of worry for her had already begun to gnaw in Ghost's heart. He didn't count it as a premonition. Sometimes it was hard to tell the difference between them and his ordinary feelings. But any friend of Ann's would be worried about her, seeing how she was now. If the worm kept gnawing, he would pay more attention to it.

He pointed his bike toward home. By the time he got there, the ugliest image he had picked up from Ann—Steve on top of her, shoving her down into the mattress—had almost faded from his mind.

13

Nothing fingered the colored glass bubbles in the partition between diner booths of torn maroon vinyl. The Greyhound had taken him down through Maryland and northern Virginia suburbs, down along anonymous highways flanked by chemical processing plants, cigarette mills, housing developments and the dull blue and green aluminum walls meant to protect them from the noise and smell of the highway.

The scenery was boring and oppressive at first. It made Nothing wonder whether he might be travelling deeper and deeper into the dead world populated by his parents and teachers and the sad, desperate friends he had left behind. Surely these couldn't be the roads that led to home.

But now, deep in Virginia, the roadsides were lush and green, even in the middle of September. He was sitting in a truck-stop diner somewhere south of nowhere, watching the afternoon light fade, staring at the ripped vinyl and the greasy tables and the flashy jukebox that didn't have the decency to play green and mournful country music, but played the pop top twenty over and over by the hour. Nothing held his backpack close to him. The place reeked of hamburger grease and cardboard-flavored coffee. But the colored glass bubbles in the divider were as beautiful as anything back home in his room. He wished he could somehow steal just one of them. By this time he wished he could have put his whole room in his backpack and carried it away with him.

He glanced through the window at the bus station across

the parking lot, lit a Lucky, tapped it, and rubbed ash absently into the thin torn cloth of his jeans. The jeans were soft and comforting, decorated with black ballpoint swirls, a chain of safety pins, artistic rips. His hightop sneakers chafed each other, tapped together impatiently, wanting to get back out on the road. There was a hole in one sneaker, over his little toe.

He found the Lost Souls? cassette in the pocket of his raincoat, opened the plastic case, and took out the paper liner. The liner was a grainy photocopy, a picture of an old gravestone dappled with shadow and sunlight, surrounded by pine needles and twining kudzu vines. Across the gravestone the words *LOST SOULS?* were printed in rainbow crayon. All five hundred copies were supposed to have been lettered by the band. He pictured the guitarist, hunched tall and awkward on the floor, pressing down too hard with the crayons and breaking them, cussing and turning the whole project over to the singer. The singer was surely in charge of the color yellow and with his fingers would have touched this paper, would have swirled in the question mark that kept the name from being stupid.

Nothing looked at the other side of the paper liner, at the photo of the two musicians. Steve Finn, sitting with his guitar between his knees, grinning with a certain easy cynicism, his messy dark hair shoved behind his ears and a can of Budweiser not quite concealed behind the pointy toe of his left boot. And the other one, the one who slid his eyes away from the camera, whose knobby wrists lay crossed in his lap. Whose patchwork clothes were too big and whose hair fell from under his straw hat as pale as tangled rain, half-hiding his face, obscuring him.

All Nothing knew about the duo came from this picture and the cryptic liner notes ("I like to drink my watercolor water"), those things and the long trainwhistle music and the spooky, wistful words of the songs. But he imagined personalities for them, felt as if he knew them. Lost Souls? belonged to the crowd of spirits inside his head, the ones he used to wish he was squeezed against on Saturday nights when Jack's car went too fast around a curve and the others

screamed for another hardcore tape. Those, his old friends—
with their leather jackets and their skull bongs, their Marlboro hard packs and their thwarted dreams—those were
teenagers. Nothing knew he was either a child or an ancient
soul; he had never been sure which.

He tugged at the drop of onyx and the tiny silver razor
blade that dangled from his earlobe. He fingered a ballpoint
pen in his pocket. Then he unzipped his backpack, dug for
his notebook, and pulled a postcard from between the scribbled, singed, softly ragged pages. It was the postcard he had
written while drinking his parents' whiskey, but he had not
yet mailed it. The gold leaf caught the light as he laid the
card on the table.

GHOST, he had addressed it, *c/o LOST SOULS? 14
BURNT CHURCH ROAD, MISSING MILE, NORTH CAR-
OLINA.* He wrote no zip code—they hadn't included one on
the tape case. Maybe Missing Mile was too small to have a
zip code. But, thank whatever gods watched over him, he
had remembered to put a stamp on it. He could hardly afford
to buy one now.

He finished his cigarette, lit another, tried to make out the
time through the layer of grease on the wall clock, glanced
over at the bus station again. But it was no good. He couldn't
get back on a bus even if he wanted to. The money from his
mother's jewelry box had run out two towns ago. His stomach hurt, and he had thought of spending his one remaining
dollar on a burger or some pancakes. But what if it was the
last dollar he ever got? He had to save it for something he
really wanted: a new notebook, a cup of expensive coffee, a
black slouch hat in a thrift shop somewhere. He could always
steal cigarettes. You had to spend your last dollar on something important.

He was going to have to start hitching. He'd never done it
before—he'd tried to catch rides to Skittle's or the record
store back home, but the young townie matrons only eyed his
long raincoat, his lank black hair, and stepped on the gas.
And hitching out on the highway, with the wide flat sky
stretching away overhead and the great trucks like dragons

screaming by—well, that was a different affair. Anyone might stop. Anything might happen.

He kissed the postcard and dropped it into a mailbox near the bus station, then crossed the parking lot and climbed a grassy embankment to the highway. Among the mosaic of dirty gravel and shattered glass on the shoulder of the road, he found a single long bone as dry and clean as a fossil. A chicken bone, probably, that somebody had tossed out a car window. But it might be raccoon or cat or even—Nothing shuddered pleasurably—a *human* bone. Maybe someone had been thrown from a wreck, or some hitchhiker like himself had been hit and killed here, and the policemen who cleaned up the mess had overlooked a finger or two. Nothing put the bone in his raincoat pocket and closed his hand around it. It nestled there, making a place for itself next to Lost Souls?

An hour's worth of cars went by, sleek and faceless, windows rolled up against the coming night. Colors melted across the sky; the sun died its bloody evening death. Out here, away from the lights of the diner and the bus station, the sky was a deep violet pricked with stars like glittering chips of ice. A night wind was freshening, and Nothing began to shiver. He had almost decided to go back and try to sleep in the bus station when the Lincoln Continental screeched to a stop beside him.

The car was unwieldy and enormous, salmon-pink splotched with great woundlike patches of rust. A rope trailed from the rear bumper, unravelling, its end stained dark. The car's interior, once white maybe, reeked of something rancid.

As he got in, Nothing saw the green plastic Jesus on the dashboard, but before he could reconsider the driver leaned across him and pulled the passenger door shut. Nothing realized suddenly what the rancid smell was: sour milk. It made him think of the Dumpsters behind the school cafeteria when they hadn't been dumped for a while.

"Where you headed?" After a moment's hesitation, the driver added, "Son?"

The green Jesus glowed faintly in the dimming light. Nothing dragged his gaze away from it and looked into the driver's face, but not before he had realized that the eyes of the Jesus were painted red. "Missing Mile," he said. It was the only place he could think of on a second's notice. "North Carolina."

The man nodded and turned back to the road. "Heard about the place. Maggot's nest of sin, nightclubs and bars, fast women." He scowled at the highway.

Nothing looked more closely at the driver. He seemed very white. His face was unlined and pale, with a kind of crazy exalted beauty to it, but the hair that hung in it was the color of flat, hard-packed ice. The man's hands were as spindly as two white spiders on the steering wheel, and the pale wrists disappeared into folds of cloth as white as milk. Was he wearing robes?

The white hands skittered on the wheel. "Have you been saved?"

"Shit," said Nothing softly.

"What was that?"

Nothing looked out the window at a graying landscape. Born-agains made him into a smartass. "Yeah. I was saved once, at a party. I was almost sober, and my friend gave me another drink."

One of the hands shot off the wheel. Nothing flinched, thinking he was about to get smacked, but the hand only crawled through the clutter on the front seat and came up with a smeary purple-inked tract clutched in its fingers. *Saved by the Blood of the Lamb.*

The man dropped the tract in Nothing's lap. A long white finger touched Nothing's leg through a rip in his jeans. "You read that," he said.

"Yeah, sure. I will." Nothing started to stuff the tract into his backpack.

"Now." The voice was ice-edged. Nothing thought of frozen milk, of shattering crystal. "You read me them words now. Sing it loud and clear."

"No way. Fuck that." Nothing pushed himself back against the door. "Let me out."

"I could tell you were a sinner from the minute you climbed in. Christ shows them to me, and it's my duty to

save them. I got to do it. I got to do it." The driver's voice
sounded almost frightened now. "You got to read, it's my
duty to make you."

The needle of the speedometer was jittering, climbing.
Sixty. Eighty. The Lincoln slipped on the shoulder, sprayed
gravel, righted itself.

Nothing unfolded the tract. The last fiery sliver of sun was
just slipping down behind the pines. The tiny violet letters
squirmed and blurred before his eyes. "I can't read it," he
said. "Too dark."

The driver touched a button. Dull light flooded the car.
The man glanced sideways at him, and Nothing saw that the
irises of his eyes were red. No, not red. Pink. Bright jewel-
pink. Nothing was so intrigued that he forgot to be afraid.
"Can you *see*?" he asked.

A kind of radiance suffused the man's face, lighting up that
crazy horrible beauty, making it glow. "My affliction," he
said. "They call me albino. I call it the hand of Jesus upon
me. I am stricken, and I walk with Him."

"They're *pretty*," said Nothing. "I wouldn't mind having
pink eyes."

The radiance disappeared. The speedometer trembled up
to ninety-five. "God-given affliction ain't *pretty*. You go on.
You got to read."

Nothing picked up the tract again. As he shifted in his
seat, his foot crushed something on the floor. Now he could
see where the sour smell came from: dozens of empty milk
cartons littered the floorboards, some fresh, some faded with
age. Missing children smiled sunnily up at him, refusing to
acknowledge that now they were probably just scattered
bones in a culvert somewhere.

Nothing took a deep breath and opened the tract. The
paper felt slick and cheap between his fingers. " 'What is
eternal life?' " he began.

"Go on," the driver told him. His breathing had begun to
quicken.

An hour later it was full dark outside the dusty windows.
The Lincoln was cruising at eighty. The albino had made him

read four more tracts, and between that and the sour-milk odor, Nothing's throat felt as if someone had poured hot sand down it.

" 'Don't let Satan deceive you, for he lies. BEING SAVED IS THE ONLY WAY INTO HEAVEN. . . .' " Nothing faltered. His voice was as hoarse as if he had just smoked a whole pack of Luckies. If the albino was going to kill him and dump him in a ditch somewhere, they might as well get it over with. If he stopped now, maybe he'd still be able to scream.

"I can't go any more," he said, afraid to look at the albino. Instead he stared out the window. The countryside was dark. Rain had begun to speckle the windshield, streaking down through a patina of dust and highway grit. There was no light anywhere, not by the side of the road, not on the horizon. Heavy clouds blotted out the moon.

The Lincoln's one working headlight picked out a line of bright orange cones by the side of the road. Highway work. The cones flashed by slower . . . slower. Gravel crunched beneath the wheels. The car came to a full stop.

The albino cut the ignition and turned to Nothing. The only light came from the glowing green Jesus on the dash, a ghostly light, faint and phosphorescent. The painted eyes stood out like holes in the tiny mournful face. The albino stared at Nothing, his face shadowed, his own eyes glittering flatly. When the craziness in his face was not showing, he looked like a sick child. One of the white spiders touched Nothing's leg.

Nothing glanced at the door. The button was pushed down. Locked. Would he be able to open it and jump out before the driver could grab him? The man was bigger, though his body looked sickly and loose-jointed under the white robe. Rain dashed against the window. Nothing peered out through streaks of dirt and swashes of clean black night. What was out there? If he made a dash for it, would anybody help him, or would the albino run him down? He stared at the milk cartons, saw again the eyes of the missing children. Little dark smudges in a sea of red and white, utterly help-less.

The white spider was crawling up his thigh, squeezing.

"Now we're gonna go over what you learned," the man said again. Suddenly Nothing wasn't scared anymore. This situation was familiar.

"Why didn't you just tell me what you wanted, instead of making me read all that crap?"

"It's my duty," the man said, but his voice shook, and his hand tightened on Nothing's leg.

Nothing didn't care what he had to do. Whatever it was, it would be worth it to get away from this sour-smelling car, those lonely cardboard smiles. The albino's jewel-pink eyes slipped shut as Nothing bent over his lap and pulled his robes aside. This was clumsy magic, but it was so easy; he had learned it in a hundred drunken backseats, in Laine's bedroom on lazy afternoons laying out from school. Sometimes older men in fancy cars would cruise past the schoolyard and park near the curb, out behind the cafeteria Dumpsters. Some of the boys, if they were saving up for a guitar or hurting for a bag of pot, would go out there and blow them for twenty dollars a throw. That was what the sour-milk odor reminded him of. Nothing had done it a couple of times back then, and he guessed he could manage now.

The albino had a huge erection that pulsed vivid red against all the whiteness. Even his pubic hair was like coarse cotton. Nothing had to stretch his mouth open until he thought his jaws would crack. The white spiders twined in Nothing's hair and stroked Nothing's throat and shoulders with a careful, psychotic tenderness. "I got to do it," he said as he came. "I got to do it."

His sperm was thin and milky, and burned Nothing's raw throat as it went down. But Nothing had never minded swallowing come. Something about it settled his stomach and made his whole body feel good.

The albino gave Nothing five dollars—five *lousy* dollars, Nothing amended silently. But the night air refreshed him as he pushed open the heavy door, and he got out fast, before the man could decide that he wasn't quite saved yet, that another round of tract-reading and blowjobbing might do the trick. The salmon-pink Continental rolled slowly away, the

stained rope trailing from its rear bumper, leaving Nothing
alone on the roadside. The albino had forgotten to turn his
single headlight back on, but as the car crested a hill and
disappeared, Nothing glimpsed a tiny green phosphorescence through the back window. The red-eyed plastic Jesus,
lighting the way through the night.

Nothing licked his lips. The taste of the man's sperm, still
fresh and raw, reminded him of something Laine had once
told him. *Did you know,* Laine had asked with innocent las-
civiousness, *that come has almost exactly the same chemical
makeup as human blood?*

The countryside was hilly, sodden, absolutely black. Nothing tore the back of his hand on a barbed-wire fence. Tears of
pain made his eyes glisten as he sucked at the blood. *I'm
alone now, all right,* he thought. *Nobody in the whole world
knows where I am.* His sneakers were soaked with cold rain,
and his toes ached to the bone. Long slick grass squeaked
under his feet. At last he staggered into an abandoned barn.
Great pronged shapes loomed around him—abandoned farm
machinery, heavy and rusted. It might fall on him in the
night, pin him to the musty floor, leave him to struggle and
die alone. He didn't care.

The rain raised dust and cobwebby chaff in the barn.
Nothing sneezed once, twice, three times—hard, choking
spasms that bent him double. The third sneeze turned into a
loud sob. He curled up beneath the loft and sucked at the
blood on his hand. His tears soaked into the dirty wooden
floor.

During the night, while Nothing dreamed uneasy dreams,
a small spider climbed delicately through his wet black hair.
It let itself down along the smooth line of his jawbone,
lingered briefly on his lips, and ran away over the damp red-
streaked fingers that Nothing pressed to his mouth, his
tongue darting out to lick the blood away as he slept.

14

It was still hot when Christian drove into Missing Mile.

He did not know he was in Missing Mile, not yet, for the road he came in on had no town limits sign. The sign, a splintered pine plank with its painted letters aged to translucence, had been knocked down twenty years ago by a man who decided to take two lovers that night; his head lay against Vodka's breast and his hand was on Whiskey's thigh when he lost control of his car. The sign lay several feet from the road, swathed in kudzu, stained brown with blood long dry.

So Christian did not know he was in the town, not yet. He knew only that he was almost out of money somewhere in North Carolina, that his fuel gauge was hovering on empty, and that all day the sun had threatened to emerge from low-hanging clouds. This, then, was where he would stop for a while.

He came in on Highway 42 and took a left, which brought him into town by way of Violin Road. He looked at the trailers and broken-backed shacks, the weed-choked family graveyards, the heaps of rusted scrap metal, as he drove slowly past. Christian felt no dread, no excitement; it did not really matter where he lived. *I might have gone all the way to San Francisco,* he thought, *and when I saw the Golden Gate Bridge and the glitter of Chinatown, I would feel this way still.* He could not go back to New Orleans, so any other place in the world would do for now.

A small child stood by the side of the road, a girl seven or eight years old but as thin as an old woman, dressed in a blue smock far too large for her. One sleeve dangled, half torn off. The child was swinging something in her hand. Christian drew the car up next to her and rolled his window down. The girl stared up at him. Her eyes were gray, as washed out as the sky.

"Can you tell me where I am?" he asked.

The girl lifted one knobby shoulder, then let it drop. From her hand the object still swung—a rat, its fur matted with the dust of the road, its head and forequarters mangled, dried.

Christian made himself look back at the girl's face. Her pale eyes seemed depthless; he could hardly tell where the irises faded into the whites. He caught the sour brown odor of death from the rat, the faint tang of dried blood. "What's the name of the town?"

The girl regarded him with her bottomless gaze. There was something wrong with the symmetry of her face. Her eyes were unevenly spaced, her forehead too low, the line of her brow crooked. Christian realized he was looking into the face of profound retardation. This was one of the few gazes that could meet his own: it did not fear, because it did not know.

He thought briefly of taking her into the car. The smell of roadkill, dry and fetid as it was, made him edgy with hunger. The nourishment from the boy at the river's edge was fading out of him. But he disliked the sight of her crooked mouth and the various knobs of her body. Christian had often gone hungry because of his weakness for beauties.

Wanting to leave the little girl behind, he touched the toe of his boot to the gas pedal. But in the rearview mirror he saw her empty eyes staring after him. The mangled rat swung from her hand.

The town was a few miles down the road. In comparison to the trailers and scrubby dirt yards of Violin Road, the buildings here looked square and sturdy. The shops on the main street were colorful in the lethargic heat of the day. A boarded-up storefront cast a baleful blind eye every few blocks, but such things did not bother Christian. He was looking for dark windows, for neon beer signs lit deep within shadowy interiors. There must be a bar. Somewhere in this town must be a place where the townspeople could drink, fight, pass all the long hot nights, spend their paydays away. Any redneck bar would do.

Christian was beginning to wonder whether he might not be in one of the dreaded dry counties of the South when a blue beer light caught his eye at last. The door of the place was a thick slab of pine carved with twisted letters: *THE SACRED YEW*. He eased the Bel Air over to the curb. There was always work for a good bartender.

Kinsey Hummingbird was an excellent bartender.

He was also the confidant of troubled youth from Missing Mile and surrounding counties. Bad kids, depressed and terrified kids, kids who found themselves adrift in the Bible Belt—all came to Kinsey as if he were some sort of benevolent Pied Piper. Before he opened the Sacred Yew, he had been a mechanic at the garage where his father had worked before him. It was not unusual to see Kinsey's long thin legs sticking out from under a car while some forlorn teenager sat nearby talking to Kinsey's sneakers. The metalheads, the hippies born decades too late, the sad ones swathed in black— all came. Kinsey Hummingbird was their guru; Kinsey Hummingbird was their oracle.

When his mother died in the terrible fire out at the mill, Kinsey received a substantial settlement and was able to open the Sacred Yew, or as the kids referred to it, "the Yew." Sometimes he looked at his club and felt a twinge of guilt that his mother's gruesome death had paid for it—she had fallen from a blazing catwalk and been impaled screaming on a row of spindles—but the truth was that Mrs. Hummingbird had always disliked her only son and had never troubled to hide it. Kinsey spent most of his own childhood trying to figure out what he had done to make her feel so mean. The Bible she spent all her free time reading said to love your neighbor. Seemed like it would say something about loving your own son too.

Kinsey was a whittled beanpole of a man, well over six feet

with that apologetic stoop so many tall thin men have. He always wore a cap with a feather in it pushed back over his stringy hair. The club was his private dream. Frequently he stared around at it in awe, expecting it to disappear before his eyes, hardly able to believe he had made it happen. The insurance money had paid for it, but *he* had built the stage, *he* had begun booking the bands, *he* had concocted the little menu of finger sandwiches and homemade soups so that the club would qualify as a "restaurant" and kids under eighteen would be able to come in without getting carded, though they had to show their IDs to buy beer.

The Sacred Yew was a place for Kinsey's children. After the first precarious year he made money, but that was not why he did it. He wanted the kids to have someplace to go. He wanted them to have someplace where they could be happy for a while.

But sometimes it was a backbreaking job. Long ago he had learned that to make it go smoothly, he had to attend to every detail himself—the booking, the ordering, even the decor. When there was no one else to do it, he also had to make the soup and sandwiches and tote all the kegs and cases of beer. A week ago he had fired his latest assistant bartender for serving beer to a fourteen-year-old, trying to put the make on her. The boy was astonished when mild-mannered Kinsey Hummingbird blessed him out, came within an inch of slugging him, then gave him his walking papers. But the Yew could lose its license for a thing like that. Nobody fucked with Kinsey where the Sacred Yew was concerned.

So he had been tending bar solo for a week. Steve and Ghost from Lost Souls? helped him out sometimes—Ghost, whose grandmother had left him her house and all the money he would ever require to live on, would do it gratis. But just now they were busy practicing a bunch of new songs. They played at the club once a week or more, and they were his biggest draw. People came from as far away as Raleigh and Chapel Hill to see them. They were getting good, and he *wanted* them to practice.

But Kinsey was tired. So when the guy walked in and said

he'd tended bar in New Orleans for twenty years, Kinsey hired him on the spot. He wasn't fazed by the funereal clothes and the cold pale face, or by the fact that the guy was even taller than him and maybe skinnier. When you ran a club, you met plenty of weirdos. This particular weirdo struck him as a good bartender.

"Christian, hm? Were your folks Holy Rollers?" That could drive anybody to a life of bartending.

The guy shook his head. "It's a family name."

"Whatever," said Kinsey amiably.

That same night, Christian fell back into the routine of popping bottle tops, tapping kegs and drawing foamy draft beer into plastic cups, replying to small talk without really hearing it. The bar seemed primitive: Kinsey served no liquor or even wine, only beer, and not many varieties of that. Without shots to set up, without Sazeracs and Hurricanes to mix, Christian felt he was hardly working.

Gradually and gratefully he came to realize that this was no redneck bar. He saw children in black, which he had not expected in a small southern town, and he watched them and began to know their faces. But he would wait. Some of these children might be drifters or flotsam from the state university in Raleigh, but he could not afford to be greedy too soon. He had waited before. Soon someone would come to town, alone and a stranger, someone he could take safely.

His wages from the bar would not be quite enough to pay for the trailer he rented—it was on Violin Road, but it was cheap—and the gasoline to drive to work each night. On his way north he had seen wooden stands by the side of the road. They sold flowers, fruit, trinkets. Behind his trailer was a scrap heap and a great thicket of roses rioting wild. Christian cut the huge blossoms and wrapped their stems in newspaper. In an overgrown patch of garden he found a few stunted pumpkins, a few gourds gone dry on the vine. He got some sixpenny nails and a hammer from the hardware shop in town, dragged several boards out of the scrap heap, put together a stand and painted a sign.

When the sun was not too bright, he drove around the

outskirts of Missing Mile and set up his stand on different corners. Sometimes people stopped to buy from him; he answered their chatter with the practiced glibness that came from a few centuries of bartending. From behind his dark glasses he watched their faces and their throats, wondering how long it would be until his mouth began to water at the smell of their blood.

Christian would stay in Missing Mile as long as he could, and when he had saved some money, he would fill the tank of his Bel Air and start driving north again. North was where Molochai, Twig, and Zillah might be, and he still thought of finding them. Sometimes at night he would take out the three bottles of Chartreuse he had brought from New Orleans. He read the legend on the green-and-gold foil label again and again, thinking of Wallace Creech and the children of the French Quarter and the dirty slow river, but he never cracked the seals on any of the bottles. He still remembered how the green fire had blazed through him on his last night in New Orleans.

15

By ten o'clock the next morning, Nothing was so hungry and lonely that he almost cried from sheer relief when the biker stopped and picked him up.

Sleeping in a barn hadn't been any fun. He'd gotten out of the rain for a few hours, but he woke up sore, hunger nibbling at his stomach and the taste of dust and rotten blood in his mouth. When he stumbled out of the barn, morning sunlight blinded him for a moment. Nothing squeezed his eyes shut, then opened them a crack, cautiously. The countryside glistened in green splendor around him. Tendrils of vine crept up the side of the barn, poked inquisitively through a hole in the roof. He closed his eyes again and breathed the smell of sunlight drying up last night's rain.

Back on the highway, not many cars went by. None stopped. He saw some men eating biscuits and drinking coffee in a pickup truck, and saliva rushed into his mouth. He spat on the side of the road; to swallow hunger-spit would only make him hungrier. Experimentally, he put his hand on his stomach. Through the damp cloth of his T-shirt, it already felt more hollow. Surely his hipbones were sharper than they had been two days ago. He lit a Lucky and sucked up the smoke as if it were orange juice.

The next half hour crawled by. Nothing walked slowly along the shoulder of the road sticking out his thumb whenever a car went by. Everyone in the cars stared at him, but no one stopped. Then he heard the growl of a motor around the bend he'd just passed. Something was coming down the highway fast—no car, no decrepit pickup. A motorcycle. A big one. He stared pleadingly as it approached, and when the driver saw him, the bike slowed and pulled up short beside him.

"Where you headed?" the biker asked. The question already seemed familiar.

"Missing Mile, North Carolina." Nothing wasn't sure if he was really going there, but the name had become a sort of talisman.

"Yeah? I'm going to Danville. That's almost over the Carolina border. Hop on."

Nothing had never been on a motorcycle before, though he had always wished he could drive one. This was a heavy bike, chopped and channelled, chrome winking through a layer of highway dirt. Nothing stood looking at the machine until the biker said, "You want a ride or not?"

"Yeah, sure." Nothing looked up into the biker's face. White-blond hair going dark at the roots, frazzled by wind. No crash helmet. Enormous hollow eyes, as round and glowing as a bushbaby's. Eyes like little moons, set back in gray hollows of bone. A young-old face, road-tough yet somehow melancholy, hanging over the turned-up collar of a black leather jacket. "What's your name?" Nothing asked.

"Spooky," the biker told him, and it seemed right.

Nothing climbed up behind Spooky and wrapped his arms around the biker's waist. Under the heavy jacket Spooky's body felt loose-jointed, thin as a whippet. The wide saddle thrummed; it was like climbing astride something living. Then Spooky let out the clutch, and the bike leaped forward. The wind pummelled Nothing's bare head, blew his hair straight back, stung his eyes. He wondered whether they were going very fast.

Around noon they stopped in a little town and got a bucket of fried chicken, which they ate in an old tumbledown graveyard some miles down the highway. Nothing wolfed the crisp flesh and sucked at the bones, but Spooky only picked at a drumstick, peeling off shreds of meat and shoving them listlessly into his mouth. Nothing licked the grease off his fingers and leaned back against the door of a crumbling family vault. The iron bars shifted beneath his weight, and Nothing waited to see whether he would spill in among the bones. The door held. A little disappointed, he looked back at Spooky. The biker's hands were shaking now.

"Shit," said Spooky. "Are you cool? I need to fix." He mimed jabbing something into the vein of his arm.

"Oh," said Nothing, understanding. "*Oh*. Sure I'm cool." He tried to look cool. "Who do you think I'd tell?"

"Just gotta be sure. You never know." Spooky dug through the pockets of his jacket and pulled out several objects. A tarnished silver spoon, a dirty shred of cheesecloth, a cheap plastic lighter. From the saddlebag of the bike he took a Thermos full of water. Last, he reached into some inner compartment of his jacket and removed a flat lacquered box inlaid with a bright scene of tropical birds. He opened it reverentially; Nothing half-expected silver light to spill out, bathing Spooky's face, engulfing him. But inside the box was only a plastic bag full of little foil packets, seemingly hundreds of them. And there, as innocuous as a dull gray viper, the syringe.

Nothing watched closely, trying to look as if he had seen it all before. Spooky removed his studded leather belt, shrugged off his jacket, and pulled the belt tight around his upper arm. His skin was faintly damp, mottled. He poured a little water into the spoon and shook a grainy white powder out of one of the foil packets. Then, as if remembering his manners, he glanced up at Nothing. "Oh, hey, you want to fix?"

"Yes," said Nothing without thinking. If he thought, he might panic. Dead rock stars flitted through his mind. William Burroughs chided him.

"I'll do you first. You're just a kid, you don't know how to do it. You might shoot an air bubble."

Nothing closed his eyes as Spooky unbuckled the belt from his own arm and drew it snug around Nothing's. He stroked the inside of Nothing's elbow, pressing down, smoothing out the skin. His touch was very gentle, but had

no sexual quality to it. All of Spooky's erotic energy seemed
to go into the handling of his drug.

"Okay, here's your vein. Keep your finger on it." Spooky
held the lighter under the spoon until the mixture started to
bubble. Then he laid the cheesecloth over the surface and
drew the solution into the syringe. Spooky's hands were
steady now.

"Still got that vein? Okay, hold it . . ." He held up the
syringe and flicked the needle's tip with his finger. "Don't
worry. I can *smell* you're scared, but this is good shit. There
goes the bubble. Safe as milk, like Nick Drake used to say.
Okay. Okay . . ." He bent over Nothing's arm and probed
the soft flesh with the needle. "*There* you go." Spooky drew
back the plunger. A diaphanous swirl of blood filled the syringe. Nothing realized he had been holding his breath.

"My turn." Spooky mixed the solution again and injected
himself with a cool eagerness. He shivered when the needle
went in. A moment later Spooky just seemed to start fading.
His eyelids fluttered, and his voice began to drag like a record played at low speed. As Nothing watched, those luminous bushbaby eyes slipped shut.

Nothing felt the junk spreading through him, tendrils ven-
turing into his hands and his legs, turning his blood as clear
and pure as water. He didn't feel sleepy at all. His mind was
sharp, cold. He felt as powerful as a god.

Spooky was completely gone now. He slumped against the
vault, his eyes closed, his breathing shallow, harsh. His
mouth was slightly open. Nothing saw the tip of his tongue
glistening.

Nothing moved closer to Spooky, moved so close that he
was almost on top of the biker. He encircled Spooky's shoulders with his arm. At the neck of Spooky's dirty white T-shirt
his skin was chill, sweaty, goosepimpled. With the tip of his
finger Nothing stroked Spooky's throat and found the spot
under the ear where the pulse beat. He left his finger there
for a moment, then shook his head. What was he thinking? If
you bit somebody there, you might kill him. Instead he
picked up Spooky's limp arm and bit at the soft skin of the
inner elbow, where Spooky had fixed.

The vein was already open, and the blood began to flow easily. From somewhere deep in his stupor, Spooky whimpered. A child's sound. Nothing sucked harder, trembling. He'd never really tasted anyone else's blood before. No more than a drop here and there, by accident, as when Laine had cut his finger in Jack's car. That night seemed long ago. Now Spooky's blood filled his mouth and ran down his chin mixed with spit, and the coppery sweetness of it mingled with the sweat from the biker's skin, and Nothing pressed closer and licked the last of the blood away. He couldn't take too much; he didn't know how much would be dangerous. Never mind that he wanted to *eat* Spooky, to swallow him whole. The junk-laced blood tasted so good, so pure.

It hadn't lasted long enough. He leaned against the vault looking at Spooky. Spooky's hair drifted across his face, stirred by the wind.

It might rain again. Nothing picked up the leather jacket and carefully covered Spooky with it. He knew he couldn't stay here until the biker came to. He might notice the fresh wound. And Spooky would probably beat the shit out of him. Nothing looked at the slack face one more time and touched his fingertip to Spooky's tired lips. Then he walked away from the graveyard and headed for the road again.

Maybe it was the effect of the heroin, but what he had done did not seem strange to him. Erotic, yes; sneaky and a little mean, yes—but not strange. He had wanted the blood. He had even been hungry for it. And it had made him feel better, had settled his stomach, just as the albino's sperm had.

The first spatters of rain started coming down ten minutes later. The cars still went implacably by. Nothing's wet hair fell in his face. The rain came down harder, colder. He was almost ready to turn around and go back to Spooky—the motorcycle wouldn't offer any shelter, but maybe they could hole up in the vault—when the black van came thundering down the road.

It was dingy and dusty, black going gray. The back window was covered with stickers and decals. As the van passed him, Nothing caught a glimpse of several legends half-obscured by mud and dirt: *PHOTUS/FETUS/VATOS*, in dripping red letters; *PARTY TILL YOU PUKE; BAUHAUS*, with the sketchy face that was the band's logo. And he thought he saw one that said *JESUS SAVES* and another that read *IF YOU DON'T LIKE MY DRIVING, DIAL 1-800-EAT-SHIT*.

Then the van jolted into reverse and pulled up next to him. Three heads swivelled to look at Nothing, three clumps of hair, three faces defined in blots of dark makeup. Their hands clawed at the windows, and their mouths opened, laughing, and for a moment Nothing thought they would drive away and leave him staring after the van, his foot already on the asphalt, his skin ready for warmth. But then the passenger door opened and one of the figures swayed toward him, spat hair out of its mouth, and said, "Hi. Want a ride?"

The air inside the van was as hot and wet as a kiss, and the sweet scent of cheap wine was so strong he could taste it. "I'm Twig," said the driver. His voice was low and amused, and his sidelong smile was as quick and sharp as a blade. "The bum here is Molochai. And the pretty one in the back, that's Zillah."

As the van started up again with a jolt, Nothing crouched next to the gearshift and studied his new companions. Twig was fox-faced, with eyes like chips of night. Molochai's features were more blunt, his smile more babyish. But there seemed to be some invisible bond between them. They laughed at the same time; their gestures mirrored each other.

Right now they were involved in some long meaningless argument about a drink they had invented—strawberry wine and chocolate milk, Nothing gathered after a moment. Twig steered the van with one hand and swatted at Molochai with the other. Molochai swiped back at Twig with grubby fists, then passed him a bottle of wine. Twig sucked at the bottle. Wine ran down his chin, and they giggled wildly as the van swerved across the center line.

Nothing crawled into the back of the van. The ceiling and walls were decorated with more stickers and decals and Magic Marker graffiti. Overlying it all was a pattern of large dark stains like some kind of cancer.

The third occupant of the van—Zillah—lay stretched out on a mattress where the dark stains were even more profuse. Zillah had an androgynous, perfect face and a ponytail tied back by a purple silk scarf. Wisps of hair escaped the ponytail, framing that astonishing face, those stunning eyes green as limes. From the sleeves of an oversized black jacket emerged strong graceful hands with long nails, nails filed sharp and painted glossy black. Nothing twined his own fingers together, trying to hide his chipped polish job.

Beneath the skin of Zillah's hands was a delicate purple tracery of veins. Nothing thought again of the heroin he had shot up, the drug still coursing through him. Then he looked away from the strong veined hands, up into Zillah's eyes. And Nothing felt himself falling into a green sea.

"Hello," said Zillah. The voice was soft, a little husky, razor-edged with amusement. Surely Zillah was used to being stared at, used to taking strangers' breath away.

"Hello," said Nothing. His voice wasn't working very well.

Zillah lit a tiny pipe carved in the shape of an ebony rose and passed it to Nothing. The substance in the bowl was dark, sticky.

When Nothing sucked at the pipe, a sweet strange taste came into his mouth. It was like smoking incense. "What is it?" he gasped, trying to hold the smoke in.

Zillah gave him an evil, heartstopping smile. "Opium."

Two new drugs in two hours. Nothing thought he could get to like hitchhiking. He lit the pipe again. With the next drag he became aware of Zillah's eyes still on him, felt that green light blazing along the lines of his body. But when he looked up, what he saw was Zillah's mouth: lips parted, the pink tip of a tongue caught between sharp teeth. And then Zillah's hands were on him, drawing him toward that mouth. He wondered whether he might fall in and lie on Zillah's tongue until Zillah swallowed him down.

"You are delicious," Zillah told him after they had kissed.

"So are you," Nothing answered, and his heart contracted. He had never felt so far away from home, or so glad to be there.

"You're bewitching."

"Bewitch me," Nothing managed to say, and then Zillah was sucking at his mouth again. Nothing slipped his hands inside the baggy black jacket, under the soft shirt. When he felt the rings through Zillah's nipples, his eyes widened a little—this was a wilder crowd than he was used to. Not that he was complaining.

Zillah's teeth were at his throat, biting hard enough to hurt, then seeming to hesitate and release his skin an instant before drawing blood. He had made out with virtual strangers before—among his friends back home this was almost as fashionable as bisexuality—but he had never done it with anyone half as beautiful as Zillah.

There was an explosion of loud laughter from the front seat. Zillah was whispering something in Nothing's ear. The words were jumbled, but Zillah's voice was as smooth as Kahlua with cream, and the junk in Nothing's blood made him passive. His body felt heavy and very warm. He lay back, not knowing what Zillah wanted to do to him, not caring.

Later, he could only remember trying to raise his hands, wanting to push Zillah's head away from his chest because Zillah was biting his nipples too hard. But he could not raise his hands, could not move them at all, so he lay back and concentrated on enjoying the pain. It was easy. He had been doing it for so long.

"I guess we could take you to Missing Mile," said Twig, trying to focus on Nothing's face. "We're headed for New Orleans. We're going to see our friend there."

New Orleans! That sounded good too. Nothing had never realized how many places there were to go. You could spend your whole life going from place to place, seeing everything and never getting sick of it. That was exactly how Zillah and the others seemed to spend their time. The piles of clothes and bottles and the heavy, almost meaty smell made him think they must live in the van. Again, he wasn't complaining. The smell did not seem unpleasant to him, and the idea of life in a travelling caravan was as glamorous as anything Nothing had ever dreamed of.

"Who's your friend in New Orleans?" Nothing asked. But Twig didn't answer at all, and Molochai only mumbled "Chrissy" through his mouthful of chocolate cupcake and washed down the sweet stickiness with a swig of strawberry wine. Nothing turned to Zillah, wanting to ask about New Orleans, but Zillah met Nothing's mouth with his own, his tongue flickering in and out like a snake's.

Nothing clung to the edge, teetering happily. He was laboring under the influence of more drugs than he'd ever had all at once before. He wasn't exactly drunk, and he wasn't exactly high; he simply floated. *Fucked up,* Jack would have said—in that other world, in that other life. *Just plain ol' fucked up.*

Zillah had claimed him immediately, which scared him a little and excited him a lot. Zillah was a rougher and more thorough lover than any of the inexperienced kids back home. He had a purple, gold, and green streak in his hair— he said they'd been in New Orleans for Mardi Gras a while back—and he teased the skin of Nothing's stomach with it, flicked it over the ridges of Nothing's hipbones. Molochai and Twig stared at them, then laughed and opened another bottle of wine.

An hour ago, sometime after midnight, Twig had slumped over the wheel, and Molochai had had to grab it and steer them away from the guardrail. Now they were parked in a field somewhere in southern Virginia, or maybe already in North Carolina.

Nothing sat up and cleared a spot on the foggy window with the sleeve of his raincoat. He saw rows and rows of stunted tobacco outside. The window was cold against his hand. He put his cheek on the glass and realized how hot his face was, how hot his whole body was.

Then his stomach convulsed, and he fumbled at the door handle. Molochai said, "Just puke on the floor," but Nothing fell out of the van and rolled over the crackling dead tobacco leaves and vomited copiously on the frosty earth. He choked, spat, felt steam from his vomit wash over his face. He tasted fried chicken, strawberry wine, bile. Dimly he became aware

that Zillah was holding him, that Zillah's hands were smoothing his hair back from his burning face.

Zillah bent to Nothing's lips and licked away the sour
sticky spit that webbed them, tenderly forced Nothing's
mouth open, kissed Nothing full and deep.

"I love you," Nothing told Zillah before he knew what he
was going to say. But Zillah only looked at him with those
glowing green eyes, and Nothing thought he saw a touch of
amusement there.

Back in the van, Nothing expected howls of derision; in
this crowd throwing up surely meant you were a pussy. But
Molochai and Twig didn't laugh at him. They were snuggled
down on the mattress, clutching each other like children.
Nothing lit a Lucky but wrinkled his nose and pitched the
cigarette out the window after two drags.

"Still sick?" said Molochai. "I bet we can make you better." A glance passed between the three of them. Molochai
dug under the mattress and pulled out a wine bottle half full
of a dark liquid, ruby-brown and thicker than wine. The outside of the bottle was covered with dried smears and fingerprints of the liquid. "Drink this. It'll fix you up."

"If it doesn't kill you," Twig added with his quick blade of
a smile.

Nothing took the bottle, uncapped it, lifted it to his mouth,
and sipped. There was some kind of liquor—vodka or gin,
something oily and stinging—but mingled with that was another taste, dark and sweet and a little decayed. Familiar. He
brought the bottle down, blinked, then lifted it again and
drank deep. Molochai, Twig, and Zillah watched him. All
three sat very still, seeming to hold their breath. Nothing
stopped drinking, licked his lips, and smiled.

"I don't think drinking blood is so weird," he said.

At first they only looked surprised. Molochai and Twig
were perhaps a little disappointed; Nothing thought he saw a
faint feral glow fading out of their eyes. Zillah raised his
eyebrows at them, lifted one shoulder in a slight shrug. The
air in the van was thick, tense; something seemed to be passing between them, something Nothing could not read. Then

Zillah laid his hand over Nothing's and pushed the bottle to Nothing's lips again.

They passed it around, drinking until the insides of their mouths were stained rotten red. Nothing no longer felt sick. He was giddy with joy, and when Zillah grabbed him again, he kissed back hard, then hooked his fingers through Zillah's nipple rings and tugged gently.

"Do that again, about three times as hard," sighed Zillah.

Nothing complied, dizzy with arousal. He could not have imagined a better lover if he had been given the blueprint.

He didn't know where the blood had come from, whether it was something they used to scare outsiders or a taste they genuinely cultivated, and right now he didn't care. Anyone who wanted to play vampire was all right by him.

Everyone passed out sometime before dawn. Nothing slept close by Zillah, his smooth cheek resting against Zillah's arm. Zillah watched him in the darkness, studied the lashes lying smudgily against the pale skin, the sweet lips parted in sleep, the breath from them rich with wine and blood. He brushed a strand of dirty black hair away from the boy's brow, traced the shape of the boy's face with his forefinger. It was a fine clear face, the delicate yet strong bone structure just beginning to emerge from the mask of childhood. He was perhaps the most attractive hitchhiker they had ever picked up. And what was so strange about him?

He had drunk from the bottle of blood without choking, without spitting or gagging. To the contrary—the blood had seemed to revive him, freshen his skin, brighten his eyes.

Most hitchhikers were glad enough to party with them, to share a pipe or a tab of acid or a tumble on the mattress. Then—always after these pleasures, for it made their blood sweeter—the wine bottle was brought out. Or the whiskey bottle, or whatever they had put the latest batch in. This was Molochai and Twig's favorite part: the hitchhiker, already drunk or high or fried on acid, would swig eagerly from the bottle. Then his eyes—or her eyes—would grow big and frightened, and his mouth—or her mouth—would twist in terror and disgust as the blood drooled back out of it, and

Molochai, Twig, and Zillah would be upon him. Or her. One rescuing the wine bottle, one holding the hitchhiker's panicked hands, and one at the throat. The sweet, rended, pulsing throat. Or the belly. Or the crotch. Anywhere would do, any spot that would bleed.

But none of that had happened with this boy—Nothing. Where had he come by such a name? And where had he come by a taste for blood? Again Zillah studied the clear sleeping face, the dark fringe of hair that fell across the eyes. This one could stay around for a few days. There was magic in his bloodstream, surely, but maybe a sort of magic that should be saved for a while. With the tip of his finger he touched Nothing's lips. And in his sleep, Nothing smiled.

The birth of morning found them all heaped on the mattress, tangled, hair across faces, hearts to backbones, hands clutching hands. Zillah stirred and muttered as the first light touched his eyelids—the last ancestral vestige of a reflex he scarcely remembered, even in his nightmares. He pressed his mouth against Nothing's throat. Then he came half-awake and, remembering that he had decided to keep this boy, did not bite but had to suck like a baby before he could sleep.

16

Steve had awakened with a hellacious hangover. This was no rare occurrence for him—usually he could sleep it off or chew Excedrin until he felt better—but today's was a real bulldog, tenacious and ugly, with pounds of power in its drooling jaws.

Now Ghost was trying to talk to him. The guy had some nerve. Steve glowered across the kitchen table. "You want to go *where?*"

"Miz Catlin's. You remember her, my grandmother's friend? She has her own store now. It's out on Forty-two toward Corinth. Just down the road, west."

"West," said Steve stupidly. He poked at his banana pancakes, then sipped the beer Ghost had given him. *Hair of the dog,* he told himself. *Hair of the dog that bit me. Who says there aren't nerves in the brain?* He pressed his hands to his temples, winced, lifted the beer again. That was all the exercise he planned on getting this morning. "What do you want to go out there for?"

"She makes herb remedies. I want to get some balm of angelica." Ghost shovelled in a forkful of pancake, licked honey off his lips. "I got a wisdom tooth coming in."

"I'll take you down to the 7-Eleven. You can get a bottle of Tylenol."

Ghost pulled his hair in front of his face and looked disdainful. "*That's* no good. I can't use any of that stuff—it makes me sick. Come on, you ought to get out of the house."

"Where is this place again?"

"West," said Ghost patiently. "You know. Like California, only not as far."

Steve lifted his middle finger, but the effort was too much for him, and he took another swig of beer. "I'm supposed to go to work at four."

"We'll be back by then. Come on, Steve. It might not be warm much longer."

Steve cast a suspicious look at Ghost. "You drank as much as I did. How come *you* don't have a hangover?"

Ghost smiled. "Miz Catlin gave me a potion. Want some?"

One of the four roads that led out of Missing Mile, Firehouse Street, crossed N.C. 42 a ways out of town. Steve turned the T-bird onto the highway and leaned out the window, letting the wind rush past his face. The air smelled of the long sweet death of summer and the gaudy return of autumn. Dandelions, creekwater, woodsmoke from an early bonfire. Steve breathed them all in.

He felt better now, had felt better ever since Ghost made him drink some bittersweet anise-flavored liquid from a tiny blue bottle. Steve had heard all the arguments against herbal medicine—it was dangerous, it was inaccurate, it was better left to real scientists with real Ph.D.'s—but growing up around Ghost and Miz Deliverance, he had seen folk remedies in action a hundred times over. They could be a damn sight more powerful than anything available at the local pharmacy.

Ghost had dug an old five-stringed guitar out of the T-bird's trunk. He sprawled in the backseat strumming random chords that sounded like crystal being smashed by a rusty hammer, singing as loud as he could over the wind and the hum of the tires on the road. "Sold in the market down in New Orleeeeens . . . I bet your momma was a voodoo queen . . . owhoooo, how come you dance so gooood?"

Ghost's voice always reminded Steve of Hank Williams before the speed and the whiskey got him, and in it Steve thought he could hear the beat of dusky blood and the roar of the Mississippi. But he only said, "That's not how that song goes."

Under Ghost's enthusiastic fingers, the guitar strings protested, then succumbed and sang their cacophonous song. The G-string pinged out a tiny death knell as it snapped. Ghost sang more softly, mourning it. In the front seat Steve grinned, shook his head, and pushed the speed up a notch. The sun was warm, and the road rose and fell smoothly away, and they almost drove past the place before Ghost stopped playing and said, "That's it!"

Steve slowed, looked around. "Where?"

Ghost pointed at a little house set back from the road. It was painted green and sat on a big lawn still speckled yellow and white with late dandelions. Out back, Steve thought he saw the gleam of a pond. Sure enough, as he watched, a fat white goose came around the house and marched up the porch steps. At the end of the driveway, a carefully stencilled sign read: *CATLIN'S COUNTRY STORE. PICKLES, PIES, PRESERVES. CLOSED SUNDAYS*

"No way," said Steve.

"Sure, this is it. Go on up the drive."

Steve twisted around to look at Ghost. "You're tryin' to tell me a *witch* owns this place?"

Ghost looked hurt. "Miz Catlin's not a witch. She was friends with my grandmother. You think my grandmother was a witch?"

Steve remained tactfully silent.

Ghost scowled. "Well, anyway. Miz Catlin just knows about medicine, that's all."

Steve maneuvered the T-bird into a wide circle of gravel at the top of the driveway, trying not to run over any of the chrysanthemums that nodded in the sun behind a tiny white picket fence. As he got out, another goose pecked at the toe of his boot, then flapped up onto the hood of the car and fixed him with a baleful eye.

"Stare at him," Ghost said. "They won't bite you if you keep staring at them."

Steve backed away. "They bite?"

"Not really. They hiss at you, mostly. The only time geese

are ever dangerous is when you happen to be standing on the edge of a cliff. I heard about a guy who almost got killed that way."

"By *geese*?"

"Yeah, there was a whole flock of them coming after him. All hissing and cackling and stabbing at his ankles with their big ol' beaks. He didn't know you had to stare them right in the eye, and he panicked. They backed him right over a fifty-foot cliff."

"So how come he didn't die?"

"This guy had wings," said Ghost. "He flew away."

Steve sighed with the air of one long-suffering but patient.

"Miz Catlin?" Ghost said, putting his head around the screen door. "You here, Miz Catlin?"

"GHOST-CHILD!"

A tiny old lady came barrelling out of the store's dimness and launched herself into Ghost's outstretched arms. Ghost lifted her off the floor and hugged her hard, knocking her big flowered hat off. Steve picked it up and held it awkwardly until Miz Catlin's little sneakered feet were on the floor again.

She adjusted the hat over her long gray hair, smiling up at Ghost. "How the hell did you ever get so big, child? You grow another inch every time I see you." She turned to Steve. "I was there when this kid saw his first light. My sister Lexy delivered him. I gave his mama a spoonful of mother-wort in wine, but there weren't no need. He was the easiest baby I ever seen. Once I pulled his caul off, he just laid there and watched us all with them holy blue eyes. I gave him a decoction of pomegranate rind for the runs once. Ate too many of my fresh green apples and couldn't stay off the pot for ten minutes at a time. He weren't but this high." Miz Catlin held her hand a couple of feet off the floor.

The little lady herself wasn't much taller; the top of her flowered hat reached about to Steve's rib cage. Steve thought he remembered hearing this story before, but he smiled at Miz Catlin. Ghost was studying the ceiling, the rose-and-vine-patterned wallpaper, the jars of bright penny candy on

the shelves. He saw Steve looking at him and scuffed his toe
on the wooden floor.

Miz Catlin disengaged herself from Ghost's arms. "You
and your good-looking friend just come out to brighten up an
old lady's day, or you need some medicine?"

"It's my wisdom teeth."

"O Lord. Let me see 'em." She peered into Ghost's mouth,
prodded his gums with a wrinkled forefinger. "You're lucky.
Got a big mouth. You won't have to get 'em pulled. I'll make
up that balm directly. You want to poke around in the back
room like you used to?"

A crazy light came into Ghost's eyes. "Shit, yeah! Steve,
wait till you see what's back there."

Miz Catlin's dried-apple face registered astonishment.
"This isn't *Steve*? That skinny kid who used to hang around
with you all the time? Well, age surely made *you* handsome,
Mister Steve Finn." The old lady stared at Steve with such
frankness that he wanted to look away, but he thought that
might be rude. Finally Miz Catlin giggled like a little girl and
waved her hand at them. "Listen to me—I never could give
up flirtin'. Anyway, you kids take a good look back there."
She indicated the contents of the front room: baskets of
hand-dipped candles, patchwork quilts, potpourris. "All this
stuff, it's for the tourists. Back in the back—that's my real
stock. Ghost'll show you. He knows."

After the white-painted, sun-dappled walls of the front
room, the back of the store seemed dark, the air heavy and
oppressive. There was a scent of dry antiseptic dust, of
strange oily spirits. Of herbs. As Steve's eyes got used to the
light, he realized that he and Ghost were standing in a room
lined with thousands of small boxes and bottles. There were
shelves crammed with them, tall glass-fronted cabinets dis-
playing them, open drawers stuffed with them.

"It's all medicine," Ghost said with reverence. "Antique
patent medicine. New ones, too. Herb remedies. The stock
of a hundred old-time pharmacies. Miz Catlin's got it all right
here." He stood in the middle of the room swaying gently
from side to side, seeming to take in the essence of the place.
His hands hung limp at his sides.

Soon Ghost's eyes seemed to go transparent. Steve thought that if he looked close enough he could see all the way through to the whorls of Ghost's brain, to the vaulted chamber of Ghost's skull. The first time Steve had seen his friend go into this state, when they were kids, it had alarmed him. He thought he was either watching the start of an epileptic fit or Ghost was about to die on him. Now he was used to it. Ghost was just getting real heavy into some mind-groove, as their friend Terry might have put it. Other people thought hard, sometimes, but Ghost tranced out. Steve watched him for a moment, then shrugged and started exploring the room.

He found big brown bottles with murky contents gone to powder, little bottles of heavy blue and green glass, cardboard boxes whose corners had gone softly ragged with age, their colors sifting down to the dusty wooden floor to mingle with the cobwebs. Tucked into odd corners of the shelves were all manner of pharmaceutical curios: brass weights and measures, stained mortars and pestles, a glass globe full of brightly colored pills that looked like candy, a scale whose sign, *YOUR WEIGHT AND FORTUNE*, was almost obscured by dust. A row of large amber bottles, all marked in a flowing black script: *ELIXIR MALTO-PEPSIN, AQ. ROSAE AND GLYC., HEXATONE*. A drawer full of patent medicine bearing once-bright labels of yellow and red and green, fabulous claims, long arcane lists of ingredients. In a blue box stained with what must be rusty water marks, *DOCTOR DeBARR'S MANDRAKE BLOOD AND LIVER PILLS*. In a big bottle of pure white glass, *NOAH'S LINIMENT—FOR ALL CREATION—MAN OR BEAST*.

"Come and look at this stuff," Steve told Ghost. "It's got something in it called uva ursi. What the hell is uva ursi?"

Ghost didn't answer. He was still in the middle of the room swaying. "Aloes," he said softly. "Bear's-foot root, elm bark, gentian, Jamaican ginger root . . ."

"Look at *this* shit," Steve said. " 'Powdered Nutgall Suppositories.' Nice, huh?"

"Indian rhubarb, nux vomica, quassia chips, asafoetida, peppermint . . ."

Steve saw a little brown bottle on a high shelf. " 'Extract of *Cannabis*'!" He reached for the bottle.

"Leave it alone . . . mullein leaf, boneset leaf, senna pods, anise, snakeroot . . . liverwort." Ghost shook himself and opened his eyes. "Sorry. I was smelling."

"Balm's ready!" Miz Catlin called a few minutes later.

Ghost took a final sniff of the room's delicate crumbling scent. As they turned to leave, Steve stepped onto the *YOUR WEIGHT AND FORTUNE* scale and dug in his pocket for a penny. "It doesn't work," said Ghost. "It broke a long time ago." But Steve had already put the coin in. The scale clattered, clanked, ratcheted. A yellowed card fell out of the slot.

"It never did that before," Ghost said.

Steve handed him the card. Ghost read it twice, first silently, then aloud: " 'Pain lies ahead for you and your beloved.' " Ghost's eyes were dark and troubled.

"Big fuckin' deal," said Steve. "I don't *have* a beloved." He crumpled the card.

Miz Catlin eyed them suspiciously as they came out of the back room. "Somethin' the matter?"

"Your scale gave Steve a bad fortune," Ghost said. He told her what had been printed on the card.

She shook her head. "Well, I wouldn't pay it too much mind. That old thing usually stays broke, but once in a while it gets temperamental. You can predict a passel of woe in anyone's life if you've the inclination." She stared at Steve, and her eyes sharpened. "You, though—I remember what Deliverance said about you. I don't have the gift like her and Ghost, but I can see it too. You're hotheaded, and you let your temper lead you. Don't listen to your good heart as much as you ought to. Deliverance said you'd hurt somebody someday, no doubt about it—but that you'd end up hurtin' yourself worst of all."

The drive back to town was subdued. The day had clouded over, grown muggy and stifling. Steve's hangover was starting to come back. Ghost let the guitar lie on the floor. From time to time he hung his head out the window and checked the sky, his nostrils flaring anxiously, trying to scent rain.

Ghost knew the next rain would bring on a cold spell; soon after that it would be time to batten down for the winter.

"What the fuck is *that*?" said Steve when they were halfway home.

Ghost looked. They were past the spot and over the swell of the road before he registered what he had seen: a lone angular figure huddled behind a flower stand. *ROSES*, said the painted wooden sign. The figure was tall, pale, wrapped entirely in black. Black cloak, black hat, big dark sunglasses. Even his hands were sheathed in black gloves.

"Some fun, huh," said Steve, and nervously cranked up his window. The air in the T-bird grew thick, smothering. Ghost didn't know why the figure at the flower stand gave him a sick feeling, but he did know that such feelings seldom came to him without a reason. The worm of worry for Ann was still gnawing away in him too. And until he knew the reason, there was nothing he could do about it. Ghost put his forehead against the window and didn't think again until they were home.

17

Morning on a sunny road with the music
cranked up and the wine flowing free. Morning
in this new world without long days at school
and wasted evenings spent smoking too many
cigarettes at Skittle's. Morning, and someone to wake up
with, three someones with their warm friendly bodies and
their interesting, meaty smell. Nothing realized now that
they smelled of blood, both old and fresh, and he found himself getting used to it, liking it. And at last he was in the
South, with its green cathedrals of kudzu and its railroad
tracks to clatter over at eighty miles an hour.

Around lunchtime Zillah passed out tiny squares of paper
—blotter, he said. "Crucifix" from New York. Molochai and
Twig gulped theirs down. Nothing looked thoughtfully at his.
He had only taken acid twice, weak stuff called Yin/Yang,
bought off Jack for three dollars a hit. Then he shrugged. The
tempo of his days would be different from now on; he might
as well enjoy what came with them. He touched the square
of paper to his tongue and let it dissolve there.

Soon afterward they stopped at a Waffle House. Molochai
wanted pie, and Twig requested a burger cooked very rare,
but Zillah ordered only a glass of water and Nothing did not
dare eat anything. Already he could feel the acid beginning
to tickle inside him.

Molochai and Twig spread their fingers on the greasy ta-
bletop, laughing over some obscure private joke. Molochai
started opening packets of sugar. Zillah was quiet, but Noth-

ing could feel his gaze, green and hot and somehow demanding. Nothing toyed with the cream pitcher, shredded the corner of a paper napkin. What should he do? What did Zillah want him to do?

He looked at Molochai and Twig, hoping for some kind of clue, but they were tussling. Arguing over who had more room in the plastic booth, it seemed. "I only have *one inch—*"

"I know you only have *one inch,* stupid, why are you telling me about your *dick*?"

Nothing's stomach tightened and his head swam. This was going to make the other times he'd tripped look like children's games, like dreams of dreams. Thousands of tiny fingers came alive inside him, crawling. He rubbed his hands over his face. His skin felt numb, tight, rubbery. His throat was closing. He breathed deep and with an effort was able to swallow. The spit ran down his throat, syrupy, slicking its way along the passages of his body. He started wondering about something he'd never thought of before: where did spit go when he swallowed? Did it all go to his stomach, and did that mean his stomach was full of spit?

He wanted to stop thinking.

He stared across the table at Molochai and Twig, who appeared to be primping. Twig took out an eyeliner pencil, pried Molochai's left eye open, and drew a shaky line along the tender edge of the lower lid. Molochai sat through it without a protest. Despite their squabbling, the two seemed to trust each other unquestioningly.

Nothing's gaze dropped to the table. At some point the others had gotten their food and devoured it; the remains of their meal lay there, mangled. Bits of Twig's hamburger, fragments of meat and onion stuck to bread stained pink. The ruins of Molochai's pie, smears of strawberry bleeding into smudges of whipped cream, gory as a roadkill. In the midst of the carnage rose Zillah's glass, immaculate, free from fingerprints, half full of cold clear water.

Molochai put his fingers into the pie and licked them. He smiled across the table at Nothing. His eyes seemed all pupil, black-ringed and enormous, hectically shiny. There was red goo in the spaces between Molochai's teeth: pie filling. It reminded Nothing of the bottle hidden under the mattress in the back of the van, still half full. That taste rose again in his mouth. Sharing their weird blood cocktail somehow made him feel closer to them than any drug or kinky sex act could. It made him more a part of their psychedelic nighttime world.

For the blood was the life—

He frowned. Where had that thought come from, out of what acid-swirled corner of his brain? A feathery touch slid up his thigh. Zillah was smiling at him too, a smile like the Mona Lisa's, if the Mona Lisa had crazy green eyes and was blasted out of her mind on Crucifix acid.

"Are you having fun?" asked Zillah.

"Sure," said Nothing, and realized that he was. He marvelled at how the world could shift in an instant. A moment ago he'd been getting tied up in mind knots, half-afraid of his new friends. His friends who were more exciting than anyone he had known before, their company more intoxicating because somehow they were like *him*. They accepted him. This was what he had wished for on nights alone in his room, rubbing the ash of incense between his fingers, drifting among the stars on the ceiling, bleeding from the wrist or from somewhere deep inside. What was there to be afraid of?

They got back in the van, cranked the music up again, and drove. Later in the evening they took another round of Crucifix, and sometime after midnight Nothing was just coming into the thick of his trip. He lay curled up on the mattress, his hands pressed to his eyes, watching the brilliant checkered patterns that swirled in the darkness behind his eyelids. His insides shifted; he thought he felt the ends of his intestines twitching. His mind plummeted, raced, soared. He wanted to raise his head and talk to Zillah, but just then a new design swirled up from the depths of blindness all black and silver and crimson, and he could only lie there and watch it.

"Cool," said Molochai happily, as if he too could see Nothing's designs. But Molochai was out of his head. He and Twig had taken *two* doses of Crucifix each, and they were tripping hard. Molochai might have been talking about the luminous colored stars in the sky or the moth that had just smeared itself stickily across the windshield or the sweet taste in his mouth.

Twig snorted. "There's no room for another hitchhiker. Anyway, we've already *got* one."

"I want that one too," said Molochai, enraptured. "His hair was full of flowers."

"We don't know quite *what* we've got, do we?" Zillah mused. "This would be a good chance to find out. If not—then more for us."

Nothing didn't know what they were talking about, but he felt the van lurch to a stop. Zillah's warm breath touched Nothing's ear. "Wake up. We have a surprise for you. We're taking on a passenger."

Nothing looked up. Molochai was opening the side door. The hitchhiker climbed in, staring at the colored stickers, the graffiti, the dark stains all over the walls and the mattress, as scared and eager as Nothing must have looked yesterday. He was a boy of thirteen or fourteen, a boy too small and thin for his years, a pale child whose feathery white-blond hair hung in his eyes, escaping in wisps from a blue bandanna. As Nothing watched, the boy lifted a delicate hand and took a long drag on his cigarette. His clove cigarette. His mouth would taste of ash and spice, and surely of his tears, as it used to. If it was him . . . if it was impossibly, magically him.

"Laine?" said Nothing.

"Omigod," breathed the boy, and then they were hugging each other fiercely. Nothing was brushing Laine's hair from his eyes, forgetting how Laine had annoyed him, how he had risen above the futility of his friends' lives, how he had felt such scorn for their complacent desperation. He had not thought he was homesick, but now seeing Laine was almost like being back in his room. The damp salty taste of Laine's mouth made him remember the stars on his ceiling. Tears. Laine's mouth always tasted of tears.

"I found you," Laine said. "I can't believe I found you. I knew I would."

"What happened to you?"

"I left the day after you did. When we dropped you off at the bus station, I realized you were the only thing in my life that wasn't bullshit. You were the only one of that whole crowd I ever cared about. I had to get out of there too. I didn't know if I'd ever find you, but I had to try." Laine kissed him again, timidly touching Nothing's lips with the wet tip of his tongue.

Nothing looked up. The other three were watching him avidly. Twig looked on with a mild predatory interest. Molochai's mouth hung open; his teeth glistened with spit, and his cheeks were flushed pink. He looked almost healthy. But Zillah . . . Nothing tried to disentangle himself from Laine. Zillah was sitting up very straight, his black-nailed hands clenched on his knees, his eyes full of that cold green fire again.

"He's my friend," Nothing managed to say. "From back home."

"How nice," said Zillah; his voice was like a bonbon of creamy white chocolate filled with some green corrosive poison. The fire in his eyes snapped, spat. It seemed about to burn a line through the air to Nothing, crisp Nothing's eyes with its luminescence.

"He's cool," said Nothing without much conviction. "Maybe he could ride with us." Surely Zillah wouldn't make Twig stop the van and put Laine out in the chill September night just because Nothing knew him from back home. But worse than that—what if Zillah put them both out? What if they put him out on some glittering 2:00 A.M. stretch of nowhere, tripping his brains out, with only Laine's cold little hand to hold?

He wouldn't be able to stand looking at Laine's face again, the sulky mouth and the eyes shadowed with wispy white-blond hair, not if Laine lost him his new family. Not if he was banished from this drugged dreamland of wine and song, where the graffiti writhed on the ceiling and the stars sped by all night long. Not if he was banished from Zillah's arms, from the half-painful sorcery of Zillah's lips. From the only place where he had ever felt truly accepted.

In an instant he made the choice that would fashion the rest of his life. Hating himself, but feeling something dark and fathomless begin to open within him, he slid out of Laine's embrace and pushed him away.

"Nothing? What's going on?" Laine stared around at the circle of eyes: Molochai's and Twig's tripped-out and hungry, Zillah's still spitting green fire. He tried to crawl back across the mattress to Nothing, but Zillah hooked a finger through the string of beads around Laine's neck and pulled back hard. Laine made a low choking sound as the beads tightened across his throat. Then the strand snapped, and bits of sparkling bright plastic were everywhere—rattling under the mattress, landing in the folds of Nothing's raincoat, catching the moonlight and all the colored glints from the dashboard. Molochai grabbed at them as if they were candy, put one in his mouth.

Then Molochai and Twig were on either side of Laine, flanking him, pushing him down onto the stained mattress. Their hands encircled Laine's arms just above the elbow. Their sharp fingers dug into the soft meat there.

Laine's eyes, terrified but still trusting, found Nothing's. "Make them stop," he pleaded. "Don't let them hurt me."

Zillah grabbed Laine's kicking feet and forced them to the mattress with one hand. Zillah's grip seemed to span both of Laine's ankles; on the back of the hand, veins stood out darkly purple. Laine was wearing pink hightop sneakers with laces of the kind that had been popular with trendy girls a couple of years ago, white patterned with small rainbow figures. Laine's seemed to be striped, but looking closely, Nothing made out tiny letters. *BULLSHITBULLSHITBULLSHIT*, said Laine's shoelaces.

Laine bucked on the mattress. His eyes never left Nothing's. They had an accusing look now, and Nothing felt a flash of anger. *I didn't ask you to follow me,* he thought, *I didn't tell them to hurt you.* And he didn't think they would hurt Laine, not really. Not yet. But why did Zillah look so expectant and yet so scornful? Why was Molochai drooling out of the corners of his mouth?

"He looks sweet," said Molochai. "You'll share, won't you?"

"You can use this if you like." Zillah held up a little pearl-handled straight razor, a lethal-looking thing he had produced from his pocket or some fold of the mattress. "But you really should do it with your teeth. That's the best way. The most . . . *intimate.*"

Laine made a small sound deep in his throat, something between a laugh and a moan.

He's talking about it like it was a drug, Nothing thought. *Like he had some hash and he was talking about whether he should smoke it in a pipe or chop it up and roll it in a joint . . .* Then, with a clarity that nauseated him, he realized just what Zillah *was* talking about. It all came together then, with no jagged edges and no loose threads. It all meshed like the strands of a rich and crimson tapestry, the time he had spent with these three, the eternity that had comprised a day and a half on the road. Their sharpened teeth, the bite marks Zillah left all over him. The blood in the wine bottle, which he had thought an exotic, delicious affectation.

It was not an affectation. It was their life.

For the blood was the life . . .

They were vampires. The cynical thought that they might be just a bunch of blood-drinking psychopaths never crossed Nothing's mind. He had always believed implicitly in things supernatural, things beyond the ken of the world he woke to every day. He believed in them because they had to be there; otherwise there was no hope for him, because he had always known he could not live his whole life in the real world. He had had faith that someday he would find them . . . or they would find *him.* And now they had. They had seemed to recognize him from the first, and was that not sign enough?

Suddenly Laine cried out. But it was not a sound of mortal pain. Twig had grabbed Laine's chin and forced his head back, and Zillah's razor had flashed out to nick the exposed throat. Zillah dipped his finger in the blood and rubbed it over Nothing's lips, painting his mouth, slicking it with Laine's blood.

Nothing's head had begun to clear a little, but the taste of the blood sent his brain swirling back down into acid-madness. Laine was sobbing, long hopeless sounds that seemed wrenched out of his guts. Molochai and Twig sat up straight, their eyes flickering from Zillah's bloody finger to Nothing's bloody mouth to Laine's bloody throat. The blood glistened black in the moonlight.

Tears coursed down Laine's face, silver in the night, dampening the hair at his temples. Nothing knew how they would taste, mild and salty like Laine's mouth. But now he found himself wondering how they would taste mingled with Laine's blood. He saw himself licking a sheet of wetness off Laine's cheeks, a sheet of blood streaked through with crystal tears.

That was when he realized that he could do it. He could tear Laine's pulse open and drink from it. Not because Zillah wanted him to—not even that—but because *he* wanted to. Somewhere in his mind was the knowledge that they would probably kill him along with Laine if he refused, but that hardly mattered anymore. The fresh blood had given him a hunger of his own.

"I'll help you," Nothing told Laine. "Don't be scared." He lay down beside Laine, spread himself on top of Laine. His arms stretched along the length of Laine's arms, up to Laine's wrists, which Molochai and Twig still held pinned. His hips met Laine's hips, his legs locked with Laine's legs. Laine's body was shaking violently. It vibrated through Nothing, turned him electric. Faintly he was aware of music. Someone had put a tape on. Ziggy Stardust.

He kissed Laine deeply. His mouth moved down to Laine's throat, to his pulse. He thought of the biker, Spooky. He thought of cutting his own wrist and suckling from it, thought of how unsatisfying that had been.

"Please," Laine sobbed, and some small dim part of Nothing, some part untouched by acid or the night, realized what he was about to do. Laine had once held Nothing's head over the toilet at a party, after too many screwdrivers. Laine had whispered meaningless words of comfort and kissed the sick-

sweat away from Nothing's face. Laine had been his friend, in another life.

Nothing twisted to look at Zillah. Zillah smiled a dark smile and said, "Come and be one of us," and Nothing knew he was being told to make his choice. *Come and be one of us* —or suffer the consequences of your refusal: die, or be alone, and never drink from the bottle of life again. *For the blood was the life*—

So he opened his mouth as wide as it would go and bit into the soft flesh of Laine's throat. Zillah had marked the spot right over the pulse, and there was no cartilage or bone in his way. But the skin was hard to tear; his teeth would not go all the way through it. He had thought they would sink smoothly in, like needles, like fangs. Instead it was like trying to chew through tough raw steak. He ground his teeth into the skin and pulled at it and felt it begin to come away in a wet chunk, peeling away from the great vein. Then he felt the vein itself throbbing against his lips. *What am I doing,* that last sane part of his mind screamed, *o god what am I doing WHAT AM I DOING,* and it kept screaming even as his teeth tore out Laine's jugular.

The torrent of blood washed over Nothing's face and bubbled into his mouth. It was as different from his previous small tastes as whiskey from water. This was the taste of life, its very essence. More than that—he was actually *drinking* a life, swallowing it whole. He felt himself borne up by the mindless, agonized convulsions of the thin body beneath him and the churning guitar of the spiders from Mars.

The taste of blood meant the end of aloneness.

As Laine's movements became weaker, the others fell upon him. Molochai and Twig nestled into the crooks of Laine's elbows; there was the sound of their mouths churning, then a long wet sound like the last drops of soda being sucked from a glass. Zillah had pulled Laine's pants off and buried his face in Laine's crotch. He fed with delicate licks instead of noisy sucking, but when he looked up at Nothing, his smile was red, and a pulpy shred of flesh was caught in the corner of his mouth.

Soon Laine no longer struggled, but he was still alive. A

long continuous sound came from his open throat, a keening beyond pain or hope. He had come away from home because Nothing had; he had followed Nothing, trusting him. But Laine should have learned by now that when you have too much faith in something, it is bound to hurt you. Too much faith in anything will suck you dry. In this way, all the world is a vampire.

Nothing held Laine close and drank his life, lost in the slowing pulse, in the taste of blood and salt. He never realized that most of the tears he tasted were his own.

18

Heavy rains came to Missing Mile during the night and turned the weather cold, turned the sky leaden. The last sprays of goldenrod withered and died under a coat of rime, and people shovelled last year's ash from their fireplaces. It would stay cold now.

Sometime in the dull gray afternoon, somnolent and weary of silence, Ghost put down the map he was drawing with crayons and said, "I'm gonna bike to town. I want some wine."

Steve looked up from his book. "Shit, Ghost, it's freezing. I have to go to work in half an hour. I'll drive you in."

"I don't need a ride. I'm dressed warm." Ghost pulled his drab layers of clothing around him. "I like the wind in my eyes."

"Suit yourself." Steve unfolded himself from the couch and pushed the straw hat more firmly down over Ghost's head. "Call me if you get icicles on your balls. I'll come pick you up."

As Ghost rode, the wind sluiced over his face, froze the winter-tears in his eyelashes, whistled through the spokes of his bicycle wheels like a lonely song. His hair whipped across his face, pale and cold.

The grocery store was painfully bright after the dark day. Ghost wandered among the shelves, studied candy bars and magazines, finally chose a bottle of scuppernong wine. It took most of the change in his pocket—Ghost hated to carry cash, hated buying things at all—but the wine was forty proof, good and high. Wino wine, the kind he always drank, even though Steve ragged him to hell and back for it.

He put the bottle in his saddlebag and walked his bike down Firehouse Street, looking into dusty shop windows, stepping over the cracks in the sidewalk. Outside the hardware store he stopped to talk to the old men who congregated there, playing checkers with orange and grape Nehi bottle caps and a beat-up checkerboard. The men were as dry and tough as hard nuts and would not move their gatherings inside until snow flew. The grape team was winning today.

Ghost greeted the old men by name. "Hey, Mr. Galvin, Mr. Berry, Mr. Joe."

"Hey there, Ghost. How you?"

"I feel bad times coming on," he told them. He hoped one of them would know something about it.

But the old men just laughed at him. "You and your long-haired friend been smokin' that dope out at your place, Ghost?"

"Naw, he's Miz Deliverance's grandkid. If he says bad times comin', then there's bad times comin'. Mebbe we'll be dead by the time they get here."

The oldest, most wrinkled man shot a stream of brown spit into the gutter. "Shit-fire, save matches."

Ghost took the long way home. It was twilight now, and the streets of Missing Mile were deserted. The hills were checkered with the yellow light of faraway houses. Steve would have gone to work by now, but Ghost hoped he had left a light burning. He rode past the town-limits sign. The fields that stretched away on either side of the road were bare and dry, already stripped of their harvest. Across the furrows a window glimmered on the dusk.

He thought of the twins he had seen up at the hill, the twins who should have been shrivelling in their graves but were instead vibrant and alive. He hoped the bad times that were coming didn't have anything to do with them. He was pretty sure they had been nothing but shades, things only he could see, maybe even brought to brief life by the dream he had had about them. But they had terrified him for no good reason. And they had known about the little boy dead on the road, had even implied in the sly manner of spirits that they had killed the boy.

At the corner where Burnt Church Road met the highway, a tall figure sat hunched behind a sign that said *ROSES*. *The flower-seller*—the same one he had seen on the way back from Miz Catlin's. He was sure of it. A few huge frothy bouquets shivered in the wind. Some stunted pumpkins and gourds were piled around the base of the stand.

Ghost tried to ride past without seeming to notice the flower-seller, but as he drew close, the figure got to its feet and spread its arms wide . . . wider . . . immensely wide, stretching. The sleeves of its long dark cloak billowed. Ghost slowed his bike. Everything in him screamed *danger*, but he had never been one for turning away from things that scared him, or running from them. He would talk to this person, try to figure out what the sick feeling and the worry were about.

"Roses?" asked the flower-seller. "Or a jack-o'-lantern to light your path?"

Ghost pulled his hair in front of his face. He had seen people who looked a little like this, their pale gauntness and loose black clothes vaguely similar. Such people had sometimes visited his grandmother, bringing her mysterious powders and oils in murky bottles or buying herbs from her. They had scared him; sometimes he saw the skulls beneath their faces, long pale orbs, or the bones of their hands as clear and luminous as an X ray. Sometimes he felt their thoughts focusing on him for an instant with a flicker of cold interest like a flame in a dark tunnel of wind. But none of those had worn sunglasses and gloves in hot September weather; none had sold roses and pumpkins at the side of the road. And none had had eyes quite so cold . . . or so desolate.

"I don't have any money," he said, "or I'd buy a pumpkin. But you ought to pack up for tonight. It's too cold to sit out here." Even as he spoke, a night wind seemed to be whipping up, carrying the russet smell of autumn in from the fields.

"Pity? For pity you may have a rose. And I was just packing up." The figure stepped closer and tucked a deep red
bud into the lapel of Ghost's army jacket. When one of those
long thin hands brushed the bare triangle of skin at the base
of his throat, Ghost shivered. Even through his gloves the
flower-seller's fingers were as cold as bone, as loneliness.
Ghost looked up into the flower-seller's face. Those cold eyes
glittered somewhere deep in shadowed sockets. Ghost
looked quickly down at his own torn white sneakers.

But it was too late: all at once he caught a rush of images,
not words but feelings. The first thing he sensed was age and
dark wisdom beyond his ability to measure; he knew this was
no man. The second was a terrible, resigned loneliness, a
longing for someone he thought might never come. The
flower-seller's mind was like a sentient void, too empty even
to be sad, colder than the night. Without thinking, Ghost
said, "You'll be warm when your friends get here."

The pale face snapped up. "What friends? Have you news
of Zillah?"

Ghost stumbled backward. "No—I mean, I only know
somebody's coming—I mean, somebody must be coming to
pick you up. Or I guess maybe you live around here—" He
shut his mouth before his words could get any more tangled.
Ghost seldom had to make excuses for the things he knew.
Not everybody wants his heart looked into, his grandmother
had told him when he was very young. *So look if you have to,
but learn to keep your mouth shut.* Since her death six years
ago, he spoke of such things only to Steve, or to no one at all.
But sometimes things just materialized in his head, and he
said them out loud before he could stop himself. As soon as
he felt that emptiness pouring out of the flower-seller, he had
known that *friends were coming, already on the way.* And as
much as he feared to wonder what sort of friends they might
be—the resurrected dream-twins, or worse?—he had had to
say it. Comfort might warm those cold eyes.

But the eagerness glittering in those eyes put a stupid
panic into Ghost, panic like a moth beating itself against a
window, panic that made him want to hide anything he

might know, hide his own head. *This is the bad times coming,*
he realized. *The start of it, anyway.*

"You don't know them," the flower-seller said flatly.

Now Ghost was no longer afraid. Now he felt only a terrible empathetic loneliness. He might have been as hollow as a
gourd. *What if nobody in the whole world loved you? What if
you were alone?*

"I'm sorry, I'm sorry," Ghost said wildly.

The flower-seller leaned across his wooden stand. His eyes
met Ghost's, and his tongue darted out over his pale lips. The
long thin hands trembled. Then that cold gaze darted toward
the moon, and the flower-seller drew himself up and knotted
his fingers together. "Get away from here," he said.

"What—"

"Go." Now there was a light of desperation in the deep-set
eyes. Hungry desperation, it looked like. "Go now if you
want to live."

The last light of day disappeared from the sky. The flower-
seller's face was partially obscured by the growing dark, making it look pointed, feral. He made a half-despairing, half-
starved sound deep in his throat, and seemed about to lunge
right over the stand. But Ghost was already straddling his
bike, shoving at the kickstand, reaching up with one hand to
steady his hat and pedaling as hard as he could. After a few
minutes he stopped and looked back over his shoulder. But
the flower stand and the lone figure, if there, were hidden in
shadow.

The T-bird was still parked in the driveway when Ghost
rode up, though the house was unlit. He leaned the bike
against the side of the house, where the paint was flaking
away. By now it was almost too dark to see, though weak
moonlight limned the edges of the clouds. On the porch
Ghost almost fell over a crate of beer bottles that Steve had
dragged out of the house. Then he pushed the door open and
was inside, throwing the deadbolt lock, turning on lamps.
There must be light. Light to keep him from thinking about
the flower-seller out there in the deepening night.

Steve lay on the couch, blearily rubbing his eyes against

the sudden brightness, several empty beer bottles on the floor beside him. He had been using a pile of dirty sweatshirts for a pillow, and his face still bore the faint pattern of seams and creases. Ghost felt something under his foot—Steve's keyring lay by the door as if Steve had hurled it across the room. He picked it up, rubbed his thumb over the plastic tab that said *Budweiser,* held it in his hand. The keys jingled faintly against one another—the house key, the keys to the T-bird and the Whirling Disc record store where Steve worked, other keys obsolete and useless but too venerable to be thrown away or tossed into a drawer. There was a feeling on the keyring like the object's aura, Steve's emotion as he had last touched it. Disgust and nausea. It gave the metal a cold, faintly slimy feel. "Did you call in sick?" he asked.

Steve nodded. "Was just gonna have a beer before I went to work. Next time I looked down, four of 'em were gone, so I just kept on drinking. Might as well call in *drunk* for all the difference it makes."

"What happened?"

"I fell asleep and had this dream . . . about Ann. I dreamed her face was all bloody and some of her teeth were knocked out. I reached out to touch her and saw my hand was bloody too. I'd done it to her. You know what I really did to her? Do you know about it, Ghost?"

Ghost looked at the floor. "I guess you raped her."

"I guess I raped her too. I guess she didn't mind. I guess she liked it pretty good."

"Come on, Steve. That's a shitty thing to say. She didn't *like* it."

"Whose side are you on?"

"Yours."

"How do you know she didn't *like* it? You read her sick little mind or something?"

"No. I went over to see her the other day."

All at once Steve was up off the couch, grabbing handfuls of Ghost's sweatshirt, pushing his face up close to Ghost's. *"What the fuck you mean you went to see her?* You went over there without telling me?"

"I wanted to see how she was."

Steve stared into Ghost's placid face. He knew he wasn't scaring Ghost, not in the slightest; he was only making a fool of himself. But the alcohol in his brain refused to let him shut up. "You stay away from that lying cunt," he snarled, "or else you decide whose friend you really are."

Ghost's wide blue eyes met Steve's, forgiving but unrelenting. Ghost would not soothe Steve this time, would not capitulate. What the fuck did Ghost know? Ghost hadn't gone through Ann's mind-games, hadn't been betrayed by her. But here he stood, oh so self-righteous. It would be easy enough to slap that obstinate look off Ghost's face, shake the visions out of that thin body . . .

What was he thinking? Hit *Ghost*? What the hell was he turning into? "Jesus," he whispered. "Jesus Christ."

"He's not here," said Ghost sullenly. "You gonna put me down?"

"Shit, no," said Steve. He pulled Ghost down on the couch with him, hugged him tight. "I'm sorry. I'm so sorry. Don't hate me."

Ghost didn't say anything, but his hands found Steve's face, touched Steve's aching temples and smoothed back his messy dark hair. Steve let his head droop onto Ghost's shoulder. Holding any other guy this way would have made him feel like a fag; with Ghost it wasn't an issue, it never seemed to matter.

After a few minutes he tried to speak. The words came like slow drops of blood from a ragged wound. "I . . . I tried to call her a couple of times. Hung up when she answered, real cool. Then I got Simon, and he wouldn't let me talk to her. She asked him to screen her calls, I guess. I guess I fucked up pretty good."

"I know," said Ghost. "I know how things were."

And you probably do, too, Steve thought. *You probably know everything that ever happened to us, the hot nights and the sodden-silk texture inside her, the weeks when things were starting to go bad, the ether of betrayal, the look on her face, and the moment of absolute shock, like falling into deep*

icy water, when I realized I had really for chrissake raped
her.

He pulled away from Ghost. He felt his face contorting,
but he would not cry; he *would* not cry.

For a long time they sat in companionable silence. Steve
felt his drunkenness receding to a comfortable buzz, and
Ghost opened his bottle of scuppernong wine to catch up.
They were booked at the Sacred Yew the following night, so
Steve dragged out his guitar and they ran haphazardly
through their set, knowing it didn't matter. They had played
the Yew hundreds of times. They might play there a hundred
times more, and their little group of fans would come to
drink and dance, and nothing would matter except the exuberance of playing.

"Let's listen to the tape," Steve suggested. He thought he
ought to remind himself what the songs really sounded like.
Ghost stumbled to the stereo, and soon Lost Souls? filled the
little house, the guitar hard-edged and gloriously mad,
Ghost's words bittersweet, with a visionary longing. "We
need the roots but you can't dig up the tree . . ." Ghost
sang along with his own golden-gravel voice. "So walk the
mountain roads with me and drink some clear water . . ."

Steve sang along too, strumming the guitar. Those were
the words of a visionary, weren't they? Those were the words
of somebody who remembered what magic was. There was
magic left in the world; there had to be. Steve banged at the
strings. Beneath the noise he heard a fiery, chiming melody.

Ghost lifted his head and sang louder. His voice soared
high and found its way through cracks in the windows and
walls, out into the sparkling night, down to the road that led
past the house.

At the sound of that voice, an old passing drifter looked up
and remembered a train track he had hiked along down to
Georgia some thirty years ago. A train track flanked with
rioting kudzu and towering pines and the bewitching scent of
honeysuckle, a train track that made a two-bit bottle of wine
taste of nectar and cool shade. The drifter, whose name was
Rudy, lifted his face to the chill cloudy sky. A mile down the
road he would find himself in the arms of Christian, whose

hunger by now overshadowed his taste for thin children in black. But the last few minutes of Rudy's life were spent in sweet memory.

Back in the house, Steve stopped playing and smacked his forehead. "I forgot. Some mail came for you. Our first fan letter, I guess." Steve dug through the clutter on the floor and found a postcard, creased and dog-eared, its colors muted with the grime of small-town post offices.

Ghost read it: " 'You don't know me, but Dylan Thomas drank eighteen straight whiskeys on November ninth, 1953, and I am drinking one for you.' " He looked up at Steve. "It's signed 'Nothing.' "

"What's it about?"

"Who knows?"

"Why don't you hold it to your forehead and find out? Go on, tell me to fuck myself."

"Suck my aura," said Ghost, and swigged the last sweet drops of his wine.

19

"WAKE UP!" said a loud voice that seemed to reverberate from the center of Nothing's brain. "WE'RE HERE!"

Nothing opened and shut his eyes several times. "I wasn't asleep," he said. "How could I sleep?"

Zillah had placed another hit of Crucifix on his tongue sometime between midnight and dawn, and since then Nothing had not known where he was, or who he was with, or why he had ever bothered to wonder. He roamed the corridors of his mind, hopelessly lost, unable to find his way back to the familiar voices he could hear—faintly, faintly—arguing and laughing outside his skull, and his body jittered like a skeleton on a string.

Yet maybe he had slept, for he thought he had dreamed strange dreams. Dreamed of sucking at a hot torn pulse, splashing in blood that still pumped in weak spurts from the vein with each beat of the dying heart. Dreamed of rubbing his gory hands over Zillah's face, licking blood off Zillah's eyelashes, drinking it from Zillah's lips where it tasted sweeter yet. He had dreamed of Molochai and Twig wallowing in blood, sudsing it into each other's hair, rolling in it half-naked, their pallid skin streaked sticky red. Why was there so much blood?

Because your teeth weren't sharp enough, a voice in his mind answered. *There was nothing neat about it. Don't you remember how you had to tear chunks of his throat away before you could lap up that sweet blood? Don't you remem-*

*ber Zillah's face buried in the ruin of his crotch like a sadistic
lover?*

Nothing shied away from that voice. But he could not forget the music of screams that died away to a tired confused
whimper of pain, then to silence. He had dreamed of standing in front of a culvert somewhere, a dank concrete pipe
choked with weeds, kudzu, highway trash. It was dark, soul-
dark in this hour long past midnight and far from dawn, but
Nothing could see. He could see clearly in the dark: the acid,
or some new vision refining itself? Slung over his shoulder
he held a limp little bundle, a bundle of stained rags and skin
gone paler than before.

"Put it in there," Zillah had said, and Nothing stuffed the
bundle deep into the culvert. Looking back, he caught a last
glimpse of feathery white-blond hair straggling from a blue
bandanna. Wet threads of scarlet ran through that hair . . .
and for a moment Nothing stopped, struck by the enormity
of what had happened. *Of what you did,* his mind amended.
The blood would never get washed out of that hair, except by
rainwater and runoff from the highway. No one was going to
shampoo that hair or give it a fresh blond dye job ever again.
Perhaps for a while it would keep growing, dark roots pushing slowly up through the cold waxy scalp. Then it would
loosen and separate and scatter, washed away strand by
strand, stolen even as Laine's bones would soon be.

But he had dreamed, surely he had dreamed. He must
have dreamed. "Oh God," he said, and shuddered.

"Who?" Molochai, hovering over him, looked honestly
puzzled: *Do you remember how we slaughtered your friend
and half-tore him apart, or are you just hung over?* Molochai's eyes glittered through enormous smudges of black
eyeliner. Nothing smelled something sweet on Molochai's
breath, some buried childhood odor. Twinkies.

"What's wrong, kiddo?" Twig asked from the front seat.

Nothing didn't answer. Instead he sat up, put his arms
around Molochai's neck, and buried his face in the dirty
black cloth of Molochai's jacket, cloth that smelled of sweat
and sweets, of sex and . . . blood. Laine's blood. Nothing
knew it was probably on his own clothes too, on his skin and

greased into his hair. Because he had not dreamed. Last night had really happened. He had killed Laine, killed him with bare teeth and hands and only a little help from his friends.

They really are vampires, he thought. *You've consigned yourself to a life of blood and murder, you can never rejoin the daytime world.* And he answered himself: *Fine. As long as I don't have to be alone again.*

"We're here," Molochai said, dropping Nothing back onto the mattress. "This is it, right, Twig?"

"Yup," said Twig. "Fourteen Burnt Church Road, Missing Mile, Enn Cee. Curb service, kiddo."

The roof of the van billowed and rippled. With an effort, Nothing focused his eyes. The streaky faces of Molochai and Twig hung over him, haggard and grinning, waiting to see what he would do.

Where was Zillah? Asleep on the mattress nearby, his warmth close enough to touch, his head pillowed on a fold of Nothing's raincoat. Wisps of his dry Mardi Gras hair trailed away over the black silk.

"We could come with you," Molochai offered generously. "We like musicians."

"We like *you,*" Twig said, the sharp tip of his tongue flickering over his lips. "It's not often we meet a drinking man such as yourself."

Nothing struggled to his knees, cupped his hands to the window. He saw a small wooden house nestled among trees far off at the end of a gravel driveway. Was Ghost in that house right now, awake or dreaming? His vision seemed to shift again, and he realized that even the watery light of the early afternoon hurt his eyes. His pupils felt distended.

Molochai turned on the tape player. As Bauhaus began blasting a live cut of "Stigmata Martyr," Zillah came slowly and luxuriously awake. He opened first one brilliant eye, then the other, ran his hands through his silky hair, yawned and stretched his catlike body. When his eyes lit upon Nothing's, he sat up and took Nothing into his arms and kissed him.

Zillah's mouth was as sour and sweet as wine, and his spit

had a rich red corrupt taste. Nothing let it flow into him, drank it, took strength from it as if it were the potion in the wine bottle. That taste was everything. The taste of blood and Zillah's spit and come and the roughplay and the drinking and all the long enchanted days and nights. Everything. Nothing still wanted to talk to Lost Souls?—he had come all this way—but he no longer ached for a family. He no longer wanted to pretend that Steve and Ghost were his long-lost brothers. He had his family now; he had chosen them and their nighttime world.

"Come on," he said. "You're all going in with me." He had asserted himself for the first time, he was becoming their equal, and he thought he saw approval in the slant of Zillah's smile.

He felt so good, so strong and confident, that he never stopped to think what might happen once they got into the house.

They left the van parked near the road and made their way unsteadily up the driveway. Gravel crunched under Nothing's feet. The house was thirty steps away. Twenty. Molochai and Twig clutched each other, trying to stay upright. Zillah's hand brushed the back of Nothing's neck. Nothing shivered at the touch. It made him want to be back in the van, on the mattress with Zillah, tangled, sweaty, biting again.

But now he was so close to Ghost, he thought he felt the tendril of a golden aura touching him. The house loomed up, if such a scruffy little house could be said to loom. One shutter hung askew like the half-cynical tilt of an eyebrow. The windows were lidded, deeply humorous eyes. This house was good.

The porch steps sagged a little under their weight. Not much; the house was old but sturdy. Someone had painted a hex sign at the threshold of the door: a red triangle and a blue one interlocking to form a six-pointed star, and in the center a small ankh traced in silver. Molochai and Twig drew back from it, still clutching each other uneasily, but Zillah cast them a look of contempt. "That thing won't hurt you. Just step over it."

The door sported an incongruously fancy knocker: the face of a gargoyle wrought in silver, with a heavy ring through its nostrils and eyes that seemed about to bulge out of their sockets. Nothing used the ring to knock, first gently and then loudly, but no one stirred inside the house. He looked doubtfully at the old brown car in the driveway. Someone must be here. "Maybe they don't want company," he said, not sure whether the sinking inside him was disappointment or relief.

"Try the door," Twig suggested. Before Nothing could respond, Twig stepped up and rattled the knob himself. It would turn no more than a quarter inch in either direction. The door was locked.

"I guess that's it," said Nothing. His hand, deep in the pocket of his raincoat, touched the single long bone he had found on the shoulder of the highway. Four days ago—a lifetime ago—he had set out thinking he might come here. Had he hoped to find his home in Missing Mile, at an address he had found on the liner of a tape put out by an obscure band? Now that he was here, it hardly seemed real.

Molochai had been peering through the window next to the front door. Now he gave it a shove. It slid up with only a small groaning protest. "*I* found a way in," Molochai said proudly.

And before Nothing quite knew what was happening, the other three had climbed through the window—even Zillah, who stepped delicately over the sill and was received on the other side by the outstretched hands of Molochai and Twig. Nothing stared in at them. They grinned and waved back, daring him. But he couldn't follow. The car was here; someone must be home. He couldn't just let himself in, no matter how much he wanted to see the inside of the house. He couldn't go through the window. He mustn't.

A splinter from the windowsill snagged his jeans as he went in.

The jumble of decor—obscure, lovely jazz and acid rock posters, religious samplers, a bookshelf with volume after volume of herbal lore cheek by jowl with things like Kerouac, Ellison, Bradbury (the Bradbury books surely belonged to Ghost; Steve would never choose anything so romantic)—

caught Nothing's attention at first. Then he realized what the others were doing. Molochai and Twig were in the kitchen, ransacking the refrigerator. He heard pop-tops cracking open as they helped themselves to cans of beer. Zillah fell dramatically onto the couch and began unbuttoning his shirt with dreamy fascination, his long hair draped over the arm of the couch, streaming down.

The passage down the hall, pale and wavering and tantalizing, held Nothing's attention for a long time before he noticed the smell. When it finally breached his awareness, he did not recognize it at once. It was so faint—there, on a breath of air, and gone again. He licked his lips, took a shallow breath through his mouth. Although he did not realize it, he was testing the air, beginning to use sensitive scent organs that had lain dormant all his fifteen years. The scent was familiar, he had smelled it just last night, but now there was something different about it. Something foreign, more ethereal, more delicate . . .

The dark metallic smell of blood. And beneath that, the bittersweet scent of rose petals.

Now Zillah was beckoning to him from the couch. Nothing could tell from the tiny smirk on his lips what Zillah wanted, and he had to quash a tiny flare of irritation. Didn't Zillah know how wrong it would be for them to make love in this house? Nothing could not go to him, not this time. At the end of that hall, drowning in that scent, might be Ghost. And Nothing thought that somehow the smell might be his fault. He should not have brought his new family here. He lived in a different world now, and could not cross back and forth.

He started down that white passage.

The hall was long. Light filtered into it from the open rooms. Someone had left the bathroom light on. Nothing reached in and turned it off as he passed, looking at the ivoried tub squatting on gryphons' feet, the lone beer can on the edge of the sink. He was seeing things very lucidly now, aware of each detail. The air in the house was as clear as cool still water.

Then he was at the door of someone's bedroom. Ghost's, it had to be. Delicate colored leaves and dead flowers were pinned to the ceiling. On the walls, in crayon and ink, pencil and Magic Marker, was a fabulous twisted riot of color—maps of real lands, maps of strange lands, faces that seemed about to speak. And words. Hundreds of words. There were words strung together in sentences and quotations and lyrics. There were words alone, written there because of their individual bright or dark glory. And there on the ceiling—above the bed, showing through a nest of brittle foliage—there were stars. A universe of stars and planets painted there, a thousand tiny heavenly bodies, yellow, glowing faintly.

My god, I'm home, thought Nothing, and stepped into the room. And in that instant, the figure on the bed—the figure that Nothing had not seen because it lay so still, swathed in a great heap of bedclothes, because its pale hair fell so transparent across the pillow—sat bolt upright and shrieked, "NOTHING!"

In the living room, three heads swivelled toward the sound. Molochai's throat stopped working in midswig, and beer cascaded over his chin. "Nothing?" he sputtered.

"Nothing," said Twig, nodding.

Zillah's eyes narrowed. "We'll see about Nothing," he hissed. With one fluid movement he was off the couch, disappearing into the recesses of the house. For a moment Molochai and Twig gaped after him. Then they looked at each other, shrugged, and followed Zillah down the hall.

Steve was dreaming. Somewhere in his head Ann struggled, beat her fists against the inside of his skull, trying to force her way out. Fuck her. She could rot in there. (*What the hell do you* think *she's doing*? his mind asked nastily, but he ignored it.) Why was she complaining? She liked to play with his mind.

But suddenly there were teeth.

At first he thought he had imagined the gnawing. But pain flared inside his skull, razor-sharp, ripping, and he knew. She was trying to chew her way out of his head. She was trying to *eat* her way out. He felt her teeth tearing at the soft meat of his brain. He clawed at his forehead, trying to stop her, trying to wrench her out before she made wounds that would never heal—

"Jesus fuckin' Christ," he gasped, jerking himself awake. A *Penthouse* centerfold grinned at him from the wall above his bed, pulling her anatomy open like pink bubble gum. Steve snarled and tore it down, crumpled it, threw it into the corner.

Ghost shrieked from the next room, his voice clear and terrified. *Nothing,* it sounded like he'd said.

Nightmares for everybody this morning. Or this afternoon, more likely. What time had they finally gone to bed? No idea. A hangover began its stealthy gnawing inside Steve's head, no dream this time, and he almost rolled over and let Ghost sleep through it. But Ghost's dreams were always just a little too real to ignore.

He rolled out of bed, dragged on semiclean underwear and a T-shirt that didn't even approach a state of cleanliness. Got to do some laundry, he chided himself. Yeah, laundry, and maybe haul some whiskey bottles and beer cans out to the recycling dump, and maybe make some apologies and get his life back together while he was at it.

That was when he heard the voices in the living room and the footsteps coming down the hall.

Having his privacy or his belongings invaded anywhere, at any time, was enough to piss Steve off mightily. Someone had stolen the radio out of his T-bird right after he'd gotten it back in high school, and Steve had sat outside for three nights waiting for the asshole to show himself again. The asshole never had, of course. But the idea of *this* house, Miz Deliverance's house, being broken into was almost unbearable. White magic had happened here. This place had *sanctity,* dammit.

He had never expected anything bad to happen in this house, had vaguely thought it had a magic circle around it or something. But he hadn't been willing to stake his life on it, so he kept a taped-up Louisville Slugger next to his bed. It reassured him, along with the claw hammer under the driver's seat of the T-bird and the sock full of pennies he kept behind the cash register at the record store. Steve was hyperaware of the possibility that violence could erupt anywhere at any time; he supposed that meant *he* was really the one with the violent nature. But he was glad of it now.

He grabbed the bat, hefted it, and stepped out into the hall.

Right into the path of Zillah.

"Who the fuck are *you*?" he had time to get out, and then the crazy green-eyed apparition was lunging at him, all bared teeth and hooked claw-hands, so Steve pulled the Slugger back and swung it straight into the fucker's face. The crunch of bone and cartilage reverberated through the wood into Steve's hands. It wasn't a bad feeling.

Green-eyes staggered back and hit the wall hard, but didn't go down even with the fountain of blood pouring between his cupped hands. His mouth and nose were erupting blood; Steve had felt the bat take several teeth out. Two taller, bulkier figures were coming down the hall.

Steve was afraid somebody might be in Ghost's room too; he had to get in there first. He grabbed the bleeding figure by its long hair and one shoulder and with all his strength shoved it down the hall toward the approaching strangers. It crashed into them, spraying blood, and all three staggered and nearly went down.

Steve ran into Ghost's room, slammed the door behind him, and locked it.

As Nothing approached the bed, Ghost went limp and collapsed back into the tangle of bedclothes. Reality did another slow giddy roll as Nothing stood looking down at the fair dreaming face, gone tranquil now. This was Ghost, the lost soul of all lost souls. This was his secret brother—some part of Nothing's mind still clung dimly to that wish, though he knew now that it was not true. There was a deep scarlet rose in the lapel of Ghost's rumpled army jacket, full blown and fragrant.

Then he noticed the stain at the corner of Ghost's mouth. Not much blood, not much at all. Just a drop. Ghost must have bitten his lip or his tongue. Nothing bent without thinking to lick the blood away, and Ghost's eyes flew open and stared straight up into Nothing's.

"Born in blood," Ghost whispered. "Born in blood and pain—"

Then the door burst open and slammed shut again, and strong hands seized the back of Nothing's raincoat and yanked him up. All at once he was flying toward the wall. His forehead caught the edge of something sharp. Tiny colored stars exploded through blackness. Blue, red, silver. All the stars from Ghost's ceiling were showering down on him. He closed his eyes and let them land on his eyelids, tingling.

Steve's adrenaline rose another notch at the sight of the strange kid bending over Ghost's bed. But he couldn't bring himself to bash the kid's skull in, not from behind. Instead he grabbed the kid by the back of his coat and threw him across the room. He did not know that he was screaming Ghost's name, but later his throat would be sore.

He turned, weighing the bat in both hands, keeping it between him and the kid, keeping himself between the kid and the bed. "What did he do to you?" he asked Ghost, who was looking dazed, not quite awake.

"I didn't do anything," the kid said. "I wouldn't hurt him, honest. Or you either, Steve."

"How do you know my name?"

"I like your music and—"

"Yeah? This how you usually show your appreciation for art? Breaking into people's houses?"

The kid looked so sad and shamefaced that Steve almost felt sorry for him. Not quite, though. The kid didn't seem dangerous, didn't seem to have any fight in him, and he was locked in here with Steve and the baseball bat. This kid might be the only weapon he had against those three creeps in the hall if Steve handled it right.

"Ghost. Wake up, Ghost, WAKE UP, YOU DUMB-FUCK." Ghost would be worse than useless in your typical barroom brawl, but in mortal danger Steve suspected he could hold his own if he was fully awake.

Ghost blinked and rubbed his eyes, trying to shake off the

last shreds of nightmare. Steve edged closer to the kid, who was still sprawled on the floor staring miserably up at him. He had enormous street-orphan eyes and that phony dyed black hair that so many kids wore and Steve hated.

"What's your name, kid?"

"Nothing. I—"

"Nothing?" said Ghost. "Did you send a—"

Something crashed against the door. It shuddered in its frame. The kid looked toward the source of the sudden noise. Steve reached down, hauled him up by his coat collar, and pinned his arms behind his back. It must have hurt, but he didn't cry out; he was a tough little kid. Steve didn't really want to hurt him. But he would if he had to. He got a good grip on the baseball bat and pulled Nothing back toward the bed.

The object crashed against the door again—they must be using the big piece of quartz that sat in the hall; nothing else could make that much noise—and Steve saw the doorknob splinter loose from its moorings. Another crash and the door swung halfway open. From the corner of his eye Steve saw Ghost scrambling up in bed, pressing his back against the headboard.

The two larger figures appeared in the doorway, supporting the smaller one between them. The entire lower half of the small one's face was a mask of bruise and blood. His hands dangled at his sides, bloodied, the fingers clenching and unclenching. When he opened his mouth to speak, Steve saw with grim satisfaction that he had taken out most of the bastard's front teeth.

"You hurt my face," said Green-eyes. Through the mush of blood and ruined tissue, his voice was low and smooth, smoother than it should have been considering how much he must be hurting. "I don't like it when people hurt my face. We're going to tear you up."

"Try it if you want your ugly face smashed in worse," Steve said. He hoped he sounded more confident than he felt. To pull this off, he could not show an iota of fear in the presence of these creeps, even though they smelled as if they'd been eating roadkill for breakfast. Steve jerked his arm tight across the kid's throat. He saw the light-colored roots of the kid's hair and the tender scalp beneath, and knew that he could bring the Slugger down on it if he had to.

Green-eyes stared at him for a moment, considering. "Let him go," he said. "If you do, we'll just settle our score with you. But if I have to take him away from you, I'll rip open your pretty friend and have his intestines for breakfast."

"Yeah, fucker. I'm real eager to make deals with a bag of pus like you." Steve throttled the kid a little harder and heard him choke, though he had not struggled or cried out.

"Not 'fucker,'" said Green-eyes. "*Zillah.* Remember the name. Remember it when you feel my teeth sink into your heart."

"Well, if you're gonna sink 'em into my heart, you better go pick 'em out of the hall runner first." Steve thought he felt the kid stifle a helpless laugh, of all things. He eased up on the boy's throat a little.

Zillah glanced right and left at his cohorts. They were poised like springs, like big cats on the prowl. "Molochai— Twig—take him down," he said. "Save the boy if you can."

Steve knew his shaky bargaining chip was gone. He thrust Nothing as far away from him as he could and started swinging the bat as Molochai and Twig closed in.

One came at him high, one low. He brought the bat down on a shaggy head and felt it thunk against a cushion of hair. The owner of the hair staggered but recovered fast. Then one long pair of arms was wrapped around his legs and one slobbering feral face was pushed up close to his, and he lost his balance and went back onto the bed with both of them crushing him.

Sharp nails raked across his chest, drawing beads of blood. Sharper teeth sank deep into the meat of his hand, and he screamed and lost his grip on the bat. It clattered to the floor and rolled under the bed. In an instant Zillah had darted across the room and retrieved it.

A snorting, snuffling head burrowed in between Steve's neck and shoulder. The filthy dishevelled hair tickled horribly. Steve whipped his head around, tried to bring his chin down tight against his chest. He felt hot drool on his neck. Teeth found his skin and nipped.

"Don't do him just yet," said Zillah mildly, and the teeth went away. One creep had Steve pinned on the bed, sitting on his chest and trapping his arms. Molochai and Twig were heavy and bulky and amazingly strong, and Steve couldn't catch his breath with the full weight of whichever one it was on top of him. Ghost hadn't even had time to struggle before the other creep had pinned him. Steve aimed a useless kick at Zillah, who stepped gracefully away.

Nothing pushed himself away from the wall, flung his arms out in a pleading gesture. "Don't hurt them."

Zillah snorted and hawked a bright pink gob of blood to the floor. "Why not?" he said, dangerously quiet.

"Because they know me. Ghost knows who I am. He said so."

"Yesss?" Zillah's smashed face convulsed in what might have been a smile. "I know who you are too. You're a pretty little boy who hasn't learned his place yet. You're a pest who is going to have his throat ripped out in about two minutes if he doesn't SHUT THE FUCK UP!" Zillah rounded on Nothing, jabbed him hard in the stomach with the baseball bat. The boy staggered backward, the wind knocked out of him.

"I want *him* to watch," Zillah continued. He held the bat up, waved its broad end in front of Steve's face. "I don't need this, you know. I could kill both of you with one hand while I jerked off with the other. But since you used it on me . . ."

Zillah moved to the head of the bed, stood over Ghost's prone form. By craning his head back, Steve could just see him. Zillah shoved the bat into Ghost's face, and Steve's mouth went dry. "Such a fine, straight, *hard* piece of wood. But so *plain.* It needs brightening up, don't you think? . . . with some pretty red GORE? . . . and some silky blond HAIR? . . . and some MAGIC BRAAAINS?"

Zillah's voice rose to a shriek on the last word, and he raised the bat high above his head. Steve brought his knees up hard, bucked and arced and thrashed. But the creep's grip on him did not slacken and the bat was falling, *falling* . . .

"NOOOOOO!" A black blur was in the air, raincoat billowing like great wings, arrowing straight across the bed and slamming into Zillah. The bat flew out of Zillah's hands and sailed across the room. It connected with the window and punched through the glass, and then the Slugger was gone, no longer a factor in the equation.

Nothing's momentum carried him and Zillah straight into the opposite wall. Zillah took most of the impact. He slid down the wall and lay against it, dazed, his head bracketed by words in pencil and paint and crayon. There was a comma-shaped smear of blood on the wall where Zillah's head had hit. Minute cracks in the plaster radiated from it.

Nothing crouched astride Zillah, still gasping for breath. "I'm sorry," he sobbed. "You made me kill Laine and I did it. But not Ghost. Not Ghost."

Molochai and Twig were so surprised by the whole spectacle that they let go of Steve and Ghost. Steve scrambled up, expecting them to go for him at once. Instead they bounded across the room to Zillah.

Twig grabbed Nothing and pulled him up by the front of his coat. Molochai raised his hand to his face. After a moment Steve saw that he was biting through the skin of his own wrist. When Molochai's blood began flowing freely, he pressed his wrist to Zillah's mouth.

Steve's hands ached. He supposed it was an aftereffect of the adrenaline rush. Later he would realize he had been gripping the bat so tightly that his fingers were still curled in the shape of its handle.

Nothing's teeth clacked together when Twig hauled him up, and he tasted blood again. The taste reminded him of the potion in the wine bottle, the feast of Laine's blood they had shared. More than anything he wanted to be back in the van, singing, drinking, on his way to New Orleans. Going away from here. Something had gone terribly wrong.

At least Zillah wasn't dead, though he looked as if he ought to be. He had taken a baseball bat in the face without going down, and Nothing thought he could have taken the blow against the wall too, though it had been hard enough to break someone's neck. But the two blows so close upon each other had stunned him. Maybe Molochai's blood would bring him around. If it did, Nothing didn't know what Zillah would do to him, or to Steve and Ghost. He had to get them out of here before Zillah came all the way back.

He reached up, grasped Twig's hands, and removed them from the lapels of his coat. "You want to waste time fucking with me?" he asked. "Zillah didn't tell you to fuck with me. And he's hurt bad."

"Because of *you*," Twig growled.

Nothing could feel Twig's hands trembling in his grasp, aching to go for his throat. He knew Twig could kill him in a heartbeat. "Then save me for him. Let him punish me for getting him hurt. He'll be pissed if he comes round and you've already sucked me dry, won't he?"

Now Nothing was sure Twig wanted to rip his throat open. Molochai would do it if Twig did. They would kill him and then tear into Steve and Ghost. Nothing met Twig's eyes and held them. Twig was wilder and meaner, oh yes; Twig was the badass here.

But Nothing was smarter.

"Zillah's lying there bleeding," he said. "If you won't help me, I'll carry him out myself. But he'll know what happened."

He jerked away from Twig and tensed, ready to fight if Twig lunged at him.

Twig's eyes blazed feral light.

Nothing blazed right back at him.

And Twig's eyes dropped.

Later, Steve would be unable to find the right words to tell Ghost how he had felt in the next few moments. Ghost got it anyway, of course, but not because of Steve's attempt to describe it.

The atmosphere in the room changed subtly. It had been electric, dangerous, full of blood and the possibility of murder. But then something happened.

Steve considered himself much less perceptive than he really was. What he would say to Ghost later was "If even *I* could feel it, it *must* have been there." It was as if the kid were putting out pheromones or something. Something that felt (he would shake his head and laugh a little, saying these words) like the essence of childhood lost. This was baby powder and cigarette smoke, forgotten toys and eyeliner and torn black lace, nursery rhymes and dank nightclub restrooms haunted by a breath of vomit. This was the distilled essence of all that was lost forever and all that came to replace it.

I'm twenty-three years old, thought Steve, though he didn't know why. *I'm supposed to be a grown-up. This game is for keeps. No one is ever going to come along and make everything all right for me again, because no one* can.

Then all at once the strangeness was gone from the room, and there was only the electric tension again. But it did not feel quite so murderous now.

"You help me carry him," Nothing told Molochai. Then he glanced back at Twig. "You go on out and start the van."

Twig's eyes flared again, and for a moment Steve thought the kid had pushed it too far. But Twig just exhaled noisily—Steve smelled rotten blood—and left the room.

Nothing and Molochai got Zillah's arms around their necks and helped him up. Nothing looked at Steve with wide brimming eyes, trying to smile. Sadness and pride warred in his face. "I didn't let them hurt you," he said. "Now maybe you'll believe me. I never meant for any of this to happen."

Now that the fight was ebbing out of him, Steve felt weaker by the minute. "I just want you out of here," he said. "*All* of you."

"We're going. Don't worry." Nothing glanced at Ghost, and his carefully composed expression seemed to crumble a little, but he caught it quickly.

Steve's anger lessened as he looked at the kid. Scruffy and none too clean, in ragged clothes and that damn phony-looking black dye job, looking as if he hadn't had a good night's sleep or a decent meal in weeks, there was nonetheless a strange, innocent dignity to him. His features were clear and heartbreakingly young, and when he'd stood up with Zillah leaning against him, a kind of holiness had broken over his face. A sense of *rightness,* of arriving at a place he had been seeking for a long time.

Next to him, the creeps looked worse than ever.

Ghost stared at Nothing. As he had come awake, he had known something about Nothing, about his past. A baby—a jumble of bright festive streets—a spreading pool of blood on a hardwood floor. He had known that somehow Nothing was connected to the bad times that were coming, maybe already here. Most of it was gone now, though he knew he could get it back if he tried.

Instead Ghost did something he could not remember doing before, not ever. He tried to block Nothing out. He tried to keep his mind from touching Nothing's, from sharing Nothing's secrets. He did not want to know who Nothing really was, or where he had come from, or where he was going. He did not want to feel this boy's pain because he could not lessen it. Nothing was lost. He might not know it yet—but, what frightened Ghost still more, he *might* know it. He might know it very well. He might have chosen it.

Zillah swayed against his two supporters, nearly unconscious. Beneath the blood and the swelling his face was androgynous and achingly beautiful in the way that a statue or a mask might be beautiful—smooth and symmetrical, but cold. Bloomless. His lips, purple with lipstick and gore, stretched tight across his broken teeth. His slitted eyes burned bitter, the color of poison.

"Is he okay?" asked Ghost. "Is he—" He stopped, his eyes widening. A low sexless voice had begun to speak within his head.

No, I'm not okay, it said. *I am in terrible pain because your idiot friend surprised me with his baseball bat and my own lover betrayed me for the sake of your worthless songs. So what? I can take pain. It will pass. And if I choose to return and take my pain out of your hide, I will, my pretty seer. Or, if you like, I'll shove my tongue down your throat and corrupt you with my spit. Or, if you prefer, I'll unzip your skin and kiss you with your own heart-blood on my lips. Are you tempted yet?*

"No," said Ghost. "Get out of my head." He was not sure if he had spoken aloud; it didn't matter. He knew Zillah could hear him. The voice crested into laughter, lewd and savage. Ghost thought of a blank soul, a being with no morals and no passions except those that could be gratified at a moment's notice, a mad child allowed to rage out of control.

Now Ghost could only see Zillah and the others through a veil of tears. Tears not for the awful feeling of having his thoughts raped by such a being, but for Nothing. For that quiet little boy with the thin haunted face, with the dyed black hair. For that boy who loved Zillah with all his soul.

"Stop it," said Nothing. "Please. Everyone just stop it. We're leaving right now." He pulled Molochai and Zillah toward the door.

He hadn't meant to cause all this pain. How could he have known what would happen? No one had told him much of anything yet. They had taught him how to rip through resisting flesh, how to coax the last drop of blood from a limp cold body that had once been warm and alive. But no one had sat him down and told him how quickly and inexorably the other world—the day world, he supposed—would begin to slip away. Zillah hadn't said to him, *We are your whole world now; we and others of our kind. We are the only friends you can have now.* Or as Molochai and Twig might have put it, *Everyone else is just cocktails.*

He glanced back at Ghost one last time. He wished he could crawl into bed with Ghost, pull the pile of patchwork quilts and scruffy blankets around him, and sleep in Ghost's arms. Ghost would be a friend, not a wild and predatory master like Zillah. If Ghost would love him, he might still have some choice as to what his life would be.

But Ghost did not want him. And why think such thoughts anyway? He had made his choice. Not even a choice, really. He had simply come home.

Steve got up to make sure the creeps were leaving. The kid's big dark eyes were smeared with makeup and tears. Steve felt a touch of pity for him. He couldn't be much older than thirteen; right about now he ought to be cadging his first joint or his first feel, not breaking into people's houses with assholes like these. But that was the kid's choice. Pity wouldn't help him. Steve looked back at Ghost on the bed, but Ghost was facing the window, avoiding everyone's eyes.

Steve followed them down the hall into the living room. "Don't go out the way you came in, huh?" he said. "Use the door this time."

The kid—Nothing, what a weird name, what a *shitty* name when you thought about it—turned as he went through the door and looked at Steve. In those dark eyes Steve saw again the essence of childhood lost. The dark innocence, the doomed sadness. And the shame.

"I'm sorry," Nothing said again.

Inanely, Steve wanted to tell him it was okay. But just then Zillah lifted his head and looked at Steve. His eyes were dull, and the wreckage of his nose and mouth still oozed thick blood. Steve hoped he was fucked up for good. Brain-damaged, maybe. But he managed to unglue his swollen lips and shape his mouth around four bitter words. "You'll pay for this," he said.

Steve lunged at him. "GET THE FUCK OUT OF HERE!" Broken nose and busted lip or not—

But Molochai and Nothing moved quickly, hauling Zillah out to the porch and down the steps. Steve saw a dingy black van parked at the end of the driveway, its tailpipe already belching exhaust. He thought of trying to get the license number, but knew he wouldn't call the cops: they were happy to bust you for underage drinking or possession of weed, but not too thrilled when you wanted anything else done.

Steve slammed the front door. Three shadows—one large and unkempt, two small and slim and bowed—slid across the window. Then they were gone.

He went back to Ghost's room. Ghost was lying flat on his back, looking at the stars on the ceiling. His hands lay limp on the blanket. Steve sat on the edge of the bed. "Shit," he said. "We still have a show to do tonight."

"They'll be there," Ghost told him with absolute certainty.

20

The black van cruised Missing Mile for an hour. The town was so small that they passed the same places four or five times. Nothing sat with his face pressed to the window. Zillah lay on the mattress for a while, still dazed from the blows he had taken.

Nothing thought guiltily of how he had hurled himself across the room and thrown Zillah against the wall, how it must have hurt. He hadn't even thought about doing it; he had just seen the bat in Zillah's hands, about to come down on Ghost's skull, and he had known that Ghost's death would be lodged in his heart forever if he didn't do something fast.

Now maybe Zillah would abandon him on the highway somewhere, or maybe all three of them would kill him, their teeth and tongues burrowing into the soft parts of his body as he had done to Laine. Nothing found that he didn't much care. He had fucked up. He had tried to have everything he wanted, all at once, and now it was all swirling down the drain.

After a while Zillah propped himself up and stared moodily out at the dusty storefronts, the gas station with its wooden facade and old-fashioned pumps, the psychedelic red-and-blue whirligig in the window of the Whirling Disc record store. Soon Zillah's head drooped forward onto his knees. When Nothing tried to hug him, Zillah pulled away.

Nothing had seen his friends back home use such behavior on one another. When one of Julie's previous boyfriends got her twentieth-row Cure tickets for her birthday instead of the tenth-row ones she had wanted, Julie appeared to undergo a grieving process of major proportions. She sat in her room reading the poetry of Sylvia Plath and Anne Sexton. Six pounds melted from her already skinny frame. When anyone at school tried to talk to her, she would stand dramatically silent for several seconds, then slowly shake her head and walk away. In short, she sulked for a week.

Now Zillah was doing the same thing. Nothing was only a little angry at being manipulated; he deserved it for getting Zillah hurt. What made him angrier was that it worked. He was responsible for the pall that had been cast over the day. Zillah's beautiful face was all torn up, and that alone made Nothing feel as if he'd pissed on the Mona Lisa or something. No one was tripping anymore, and no one had started drinking yet. The van's usual air of carnival was gone, and the mood that replaced it was flat, subdued. Nothing wondered, not for the first time, how old the others were. He had thought them older and more sophisticated than he, but right now they were acting like a bunch of teenagers who are mad at each other but aren't sure why.

The third time they drove past the record store, Twig slowed the van and pointed out a sign taped to the window. "Hey kiddo. Look at that."

Nothing looked. The sign was a grainy photocopy like the gravestone on the Lost Souls? tape. Only this was a picture of a stone angel, wings spread, hand raised in warning or benediction, idiot gaze downcast. Written across the picture in large curly letters was *LOST SOULS? TONIGHT AT SA-CRED YEW.*

"Where's the sacred yew?" Molochai wanted to know. "Is it in the graveyard?"

"It must be a club," Nothing said. All at once he made up his mind. Zillah might be glad to get rid of him; if not, then they could kill him here, right in the middle of Missing Mile. "You can let me out anywhere," he told Twig. "I'm going to see that show."

Twig slowed the van. "You're *leaving*? Just when things were starting to get interesting?"

"Let's at least eat him," said Molochai in a loud sotto voce.

Zillah seemed to wake up. He raised his head and looked at Nothing. Nothing stared back at him for a long moment, trying to register just what he was seeing. The torn skin of Zillah's mouth was knitting itself back together; its appearance was already closer to fresh pink scar tissue than raw wound. The smashed cartilage of his nose was straightening, rebuilding itself. And his gums were still bleeding—but not from the teeth he had lost. They bled because new teeth were coming in, poking white and shiny through the tender pink flesh.

"This is a goddamn pain in the ass," said Zillah.

Nothing lowered his eyes. "I know."

"Every second it's growing back is agony. I can feel each cell stretching itself toward the next one, each nerve end screaming. And do you know when was the last time I had to be *carried* out of a place? DO YOU?"

"When?"

"1910. I was about your age. I'd been picked up by a pretty young artillery officer in Savannah, Georgia. I made him take me to a company party—posed as his little brother —where they served a punch you could have embalmed corpses with. It was made of wine, rum, gin, brandy, whiskey, champagne . . ."

Nothing thought of a concoction he and Laine had mixed in a Mason jar when they'd been learning to drink—an inch from every bottle in their parents' liquor cabinets. They had dry-heaved for *days*.

"I lost control of myself. Broke a gentle lady's arm, bit through her left nipple, and put out one of her eyes. It took five men to knock me out and carry me away. They hanged me from a live oak, and I cut myself down. And that was the *last time it happened,* do you understand? THE LAST TIME UNTIL TODAY!"

Zillah's face was an inch from Nothing's now; he could actually see particles of skin forming on Zillah's lips, forming a thin web, then meshing.

"I understand," he told Zillah. "I'm getting out here."

Zillah stared at him. "No," he whispered. "No. You

mustn't." A strange smile played upon his half-healed features. "Your friends weren't hurt, were they? And you've learned your lesson. Why don't we stay and see the show *with* you?"

Then, at last, Zillah stretched out his hands. The palms were turned up and the fingers were trembling slightly. Nothing was almost sure the tremor was genuine. Almost. He took Zillah's hands in his own and kissed them.

All through the remainder of the afternoon Steve was bored and restless. Ghost watched him do the Steve Finn equivalent of pacing the floor. He folded his long body into a hundred positions on the couch. He pulled the ratty coverlet around him and tried to read. He picked up his guitar, then his banjo, but put them down without touching the strings. He got out an old shoebox full of stuff Ann had sent him, letters and notes and postcards with weird little messages on them. With one finger Steve poked at an envelope, prying at the stamp with his fingernail, slowly peeling it away from the paper. Then he did the same thing to a second stamp. When he started on a third, Ghost got up and went to his room.

He took off his clothes and curled up in bed. For an hour he lay listening to the syrupy dark voices on the gospel radio station, trying not to think about the strangers who had broken into his house. He was sure he had dreamed about Nothing—for Ghost, having a dream about something he was going to do or somebody he was going to meet was as common as getting a call from a friend.

A recollection came to him. Something about the name *Zillah*. The flower-seller had mentioned that name, his pale face snapping up eagerly: "Have you news of Zillah?" That was the connection. But Ghost still didn't know who they were or what they wanted in Missing Mile. And three of today's visitors had a look that reminded Ghost of the twins on the hill: a sleek gloss, a well fed but somehow unhealthy look.

Nothing did not have that look, not yet. But the others were obviously old hands at—at whatever sort of pain and death they dealt. Ghost only knew that they didn't feel hu-

man, though judging from the new bite mark on Steve's hand
and the bruises on his wrists and legs where Molochai and
Twig had held him down, they were more corporeal than the
twins on the hill.

Well, he was doing a great job of not thinking about them.
He was glad toward early evening when Steve stuck his head
in and said, "Let's head on over and do the sound check. We
can grab a couple of beers before the show."

Ghost got dressed fast, pulling on a pair of jeans torn out at
the knees, a baggy T-shirt and sweater, his army jacket, his
hat with the colored streamers. When he went out, Steve was
standing by the front door rattling the knob, jiggling his guitar case, glancing toward the window every few seconds.
Ghost decided not to talk about the visitors. Not yet. Steve
would bring it up if he wanted to.

Ghost was relieved to get into the T-bird and sit back,
watching the cold empty roads slip by, letting Steve vent his
frustration on the steering wheel, the gas pedal, the radio
whose knob he twisted as if wreaking vengeance on the music. The roads were nearly empty tonight. Ghost saw a rusty
blue pickup, its bed piled high with pumpkins that mirrored
the pale orange light of the moon. He saw a Greyhound bus
going north. The air inside the T-bird was heavy with Steve's
restlessness. Ghost knew Steve would get very drunk tonight.

Well, what the hell. So would he. Maybe.

But after the music was over.

At the Sacred Yew, they did their sound check. Ghost sat
on the edge of the stage, swinging his legs, listening to Steve
curse the club's shitty PA, occasionally singing a few lines
into the microphone. When the check was over, Steve
headed for the bar, a separate room at the back of the club.
Ghost followed, trailing his fingers along the hand-painted,
crayoned, and Magic Markered mural on the wall. He had
drawn part of the mural himself. Anyone who wanted to add
to it could—Kinsey kept pens and finger paints behind the
bar.

Ghost knew every corner of the Yew, every one of the
fancy antique-gold ceiling tiles Kinsey had put in, every graf-

fito in the restrooms. When you played at a club forty weeks out of a year, it got to be home.

As soon as Ghost came into the bar, Steve handed him a can of Budweiser. Kinsey Hummingbird was serving at the bar, smiling his awkwardly amiable smile, already setting up a second beer for Steve. Steve finished his first one and started on the next.

Ghost sipped his beer—he didn't need it, not tonight; he would drink music—and watched the kids come in. Soon the club was full of them. College students from Raleigh, and dropouts like Steve and Ghost. High school students from Windy Hill, the hippie Quaker place, but hardly any from the county school; they were all metalheads over there. Younger kids too—junior high kids smoking Marlboros and Camels, kids trying to look jaded and managing only to look bored. Kids with wide-open innocent faces and easy smiles, kids with long dark hair and eyeliner, kids with razor scars on their wrists, kids already sick of life, kids happy to be alive and drunk and younger than they would ever feel again.

They were so very young, Ghost thought as he stood among them, feeling their pain and their exuberance, their stupidity and terror and beauty brush his mind. They were so young, and they wore their thrift-shop jewelry, their ragged jeans, their black clothes like badges of membership to some arcane club. Some club that required drunkenness—on cheap liquor, on rainy midnights, on poetry or sex. Some club that required love of obscure bands and learning to lie awake at 4:00 A.M., bursting with terrors and wide-awake dreams.

None of these kids was Nothing. Ghost looked for the long silk coat, the lank black hair, the three lurking figures that would surround the boy. But he was not here, though many of these kids looked like him—the same big, black-rimmed, blasted eyes, the same pale flickering hands. Ghost hoped Nothing wouldn't come. Not with those three. But he knew they would be there.

Something in him ached for that boy. For the sadness in his face, for his eyes yearning to stay young. He wanted to grab Nothing away from his companions and tell him that sometimes everything *could* be all right, that pain did not have to come with magic, that childhood never had to end. And yet he wondered whether Nothing had not known all those things when he made his choice. Whatever that was.

The right choice was not always clear. Nevertheless, Nothing had had to make one. Ghost had felt him do it, right there in the bedroom as he woke up, and he had felt the boy grow a little older. He felt his mind straining at something it could not quite grasp, and the feeling was odd; there wasn't much Ghost could not empathize with. He reminded himself that he had not really tried, had not wanted to try.

Then Steve grabbed Ghost's arm and dragged him through the crowd toward the stage. It was time to play. Ghost felt the small shiver of something like stage fright and something like wild intoxication, when the room swims, when you can no longer stand up straight or trust your eyes.

Hands plucked at Ghost's clothes, at the streamers on his hat. He was greeted by a multitude of young voices. He felt the brush of their fingers and their minds; he breathed their cigarette smoke. Then they were stumbling onstage, Steve and Ghost, Lost Souls? come back again.

Steve clawed at his guitar, letting loose the night's first jangling scream. Ghost glanced at the set list taped to the floor, scrawled in Steve's illegible handwriting, and the words of the first song rose to his lips. He stepped up to the microphone and, gripping it with both hands, whispered those words: *"Don't go on the beach. . . . Realize the lions have come in . . ."*

The audience swayed at the touch of his voice. He looked into those upturned young faces bathed in dim stagelight, the fresh faces, the pale hollow-boned faces with their darkly lined eyes.

And there in the middle of the crowd was Nothing, not swaying but standing very still, his face tilted up with the rest, his eyes wide and shadowed. His three friends were there too, clustered around him. Zillah stared at the floor, his face in darkness. One of the two bigger ones poked Nothing and shouted something into his ear, but Nothing only shook his head and kept staring at Ghost.

Then, as the first song ended, Zillah looked up at the stage. Even from behind the lights, from fifteen feet away, Ghost could see that Zillah's face was perfect as a mask again. His nose was straight, his lips full and lustrous. There were no bruises. There was no swelling.

Zillah caught him staring and smiled.

Smiled with a complete mouthful of sharpened, shining teeth.

Ghost faltered. He forgot the words of the next song. Steve was trying to give him the cue, but Ghost couldn't look at him, couldn't turn his head away from that perfect mouthful of teeth. What was he dealing with here? What the hell had decided to visit itself on Missing Mile?

The moment of silence stretched, became unbearable. Now Steve was at the back of the stage fucking with the equipment, trying to cover for him. They did a couple of songs that required a prerecorded bass and drum track, and Steve was turning knobs that didn't need turning, adjusting levels that were already set. But how long could that stretch out? Where were his words?

Then Ghost tore his gaze away from Zillah's shining smile and looked out over the sea of faces again, and the spell was broken. So Zillah had new teeth, new skin. So what? He and Steve had a show to do. The fragile faces could not be turned away; the burning hearts could not be quenched by disappointment. Ghost felt a righteous anger fill him. Hypnotized by a smile? Oldest trick in the book! It couldn't trick him, though, not now. He had to sing.

Steve was staring at him, half pissed off, half scared. He tapped his foot three times and gave Steve the nod. And when Ghost started singing again, the words poured from him like a river of gold.

They played "Mandrake Sky," an odd chiming melody, the first song Ghost had more or less composed on his own, then an assortment of their older songs, rocking numbers. Ghost began to be drunk on the music. When he felt himself swaying, he clung harder to the microphone.

The audience was a sea. The music pulled like the Mississippi; he could be swept away, he could drown. But drowning might be sweet. In his throat, his voice was thick wine. The pale hands snatched it and bore it up on a cloud of clove smoke. For those children Ghost sang harder, letting his voice soar, pushing it down deep and gravelly, stringing it out in a howl like a shimmering gold wire.

Between him and Steve the electricity crackled. Ghost clenched his hands in front of him, raised his face to the gilded tiles of the ceiling. Steve shook his head madly. His hair stood out like a scribbled black cloud. Sparkling drops of sweat landed sizzling on his guitar, on the audience, on Ghost's upturned face. Ghost licked the sweat off his lips and tried to breathe. There was no breath left in him. The audience had taken it all. In him there was only song, endlessly swelling. If he did not let it out his heart would burst.

He had forgotten all about Zillah's perfect new face.

At the end, Steve joined Ghost at the microphone to sing backup on the last song. It was "World," the song they always closed with. Steve's fingers stroked the strings, lingering on them, making them chime. "World out of balance," Ghost sang. Steve gave the accompanying line, "World without end," in his usual off-key tenor. But Steve's singing was better tonight than ever before. It was still pretty bad, but there was an element of rawness to it, a hoarseness born of beer and sorrow. The audience rose on tiptoe. "WE ARE NOT AFRAID," Ghost chanted, throwing his shoulders back, pushing his voice harder. "WE ARE NOT AFRAID."

Behind him, Steve sang, "Let the night come, let the night come . . ." That wetness on his face was only sweat, or so he would claim. And Ghost wouldn't say different, not for anything. *"We are not afraid,"* he whispered, and the audience whispered back, "Let the night come . . ."

Steve shoved his guitar into its case, snapped the catches shut, and headed for the bar. He was already half-drunk, and he registered that this was not Kinsey Hummingbird handing him his beer. This bartender was even taller and paler, and a hell of a lot weirder-looking, but Steve didn't remember seeing the guy before. A vague impression of a black hat and sunglasses flashed into his mind. It didn't mean anything to him, and he forgot it.

Ghost had wandered off into the crowd. At the bar Steve saw a curly head wrapped in a tie-dyed bandanna: Terry Buckett, who owned the Whirling Disc record store where Steve worked, who played drums on their tape and sat in on their shows sometimes. Terry had been out of town recently. When he saw Steve, he signalled the bartender for two more beers. The bartender took two bottles of National Bohemian out of the cooler. Natty Bohos, Terry called them. Steve called them possum piss, himself, but Terry was buying.

"What's up?" Steve asked after a long and companionable swig.

"Been tripping for two weeks, man. Hey, no shit—*bike* tripping. You know I rode down to New Orleans?" Steve knew, had in fact discussed it with Terry at work, but Terry talked to so many people that he often forgot who had heard what. "They got a bar in the French Quarter"—Terry was just about drooling at the memory—"serves twenty-five-cent draft every Thursday night. And they play these same two Tom Waits albums over and over all night. *Blue Valentine* and *Heart Attack and Vine* . . ."

Steve imagined the place. The floor would be sticky, the walls slicked with blue light from an old beer sign. The records would get scratchier every Thursday night, as if Tom had progressive cancer of the larynx. He wished he were there, sucking the foam off his fifth or sixth draft, forgetting all about Missing Mile and the Sacred Yew. (*Those aren't the things you really want to forget,* said a small demon-voice in his head. It was quiet enough to be ignored, but a couple more beers would drown it for sure.) Terry's bar sounded pretty good. Maybe he and Ghost could take the T-bird on a road trip one of these days.

"Man, you can get some heavy shit down there in the Quarter," Terry said. The new bartender was turned away, filling plastic cups, but his back had an attitude of listening. "I got an ounce of this stuff called Popacatepetl Purple. Couple bong hits of that'll give you some heavy mind groove—"

"Did somebody mention bong hits?" R.J. Miller boosted

himself onto a bar stool on Terry's other side. He had grown up from a skinny hyperspace-machine-building kid into a skinny young man who could play a bass line like the thunder of God, but right now he was having trouble holding onto his beer. He swayed against the bar, then managed to prop himself up on his elbows. His glasses were crooked. He pushed them up with his forefinger. "Hey, Steve. Awesome show, man."

Terry considered him gravely. "How many beers have you had?"

"Three," said R.J., and burst into sudden laughter. "Seriously, you guys, what about those bong hits? You wanna go outside or what?"

"You're not old enough to smoke," Terry told him. Under the bar, Terry nudged Steve's knee. Steve looked down. Terry was holding a pack of Camels. From the pack protruded the end of a joint, fat and twisted. Steve palmed the joint and slipped it into the pocket of his jeans.

"Popacatepetl Purple," Terry said softly. "You look like you could use some heavy mind groove."

Absurdly, Steve felt tears start in his eyes. His friends loved him. Girls might fuck you over, but you could always count on your friends. "I gotta find Ghost," he told Terry. "I want to smoke this with him."

"Sure," said Terry. "Enjoy it, huh?" He turned to R.J. and started talking about the strip clubs on Bourbon Street. R.J. had gone to sleep on the bar, his head cradled in his arms, his face smooth and blameless as a child's. His fourth Natty Boho sat in front of him, untouched.

Steve pushed his way through the crowd, still carrying his half-finished beer, smelling clove smoke and the dusty musk of thrift-shop clothes, searching for the streamered beacon of Ghost's hat. He saw black berets, bright dyed hair, pale scalp showing through buzz cuts. Ghost was nowhere to be found. "Fuck it," Steve muttered finally, heading for the men's room. He couldn't carry the joint around all night. He guessed he would just have to smoke the whole thing himself. Life was rough.

He locked the door behind him and dug in his pocket for

matches. *FINISH HIGH SCHOOL FOR $50!* the matchbook cover exhorted him. His first drag filled his lungs with bitter, delicious smoke.

By the time half the joint was gone, Steve had decided he was in dire need of a tattoo. It would be a grinning skull with black bat wings veined bloodred, and it would have a rose clenched in its teeth, and in the center of the petals the name ANN would be etched in flaming letters. He would show it to the bitch next time he ran into her. Then she would know how he really felt about her, and she would die of guilt.

Maybe there was time to drive to Fayetteville tonight. That was where the tattoo parlors were. Steve stashed the joint in his pocket and started out of the restroom. He raised his beer to his mouth and scanned the crowd, looking for Ghost, meaning to get their equipment loaded up and start for Fayetteville. Instead he saw a girl standing at the bar talking to Terry, a girl with long gold-red hair beneath her vintage 1940s mourning hat, with a tough, pretty face. A girl who shaped her words with her hands, whose hands were paint-stained and delicately ugly. Between the forefinger and middle finger of her right hand, a Camel cigarette burned.

On the third finger of that same hand Steve saw the dull gleam of a ring. He couldn't make out the design, but he knew what it was. A pair of hearts, wrought in silver and turquoise, interlocked. He had given her that ring, and she still wore it.

Ann had come to see him play tonight.

Steve started to duck back into the men's room in case she turned around. But then she lifted her arm in a gesture he remembered well, lifting her heavy hank of hair off the back of her neck for a moment. The lapel of her black suit jacket folded back. Beneath it she wore a lace tank top, also black. Steve saw the sideswell of her breast, and above that the dark auburn tuft of her armpit hair.

That had surprised him when he'd first started going out with her, back in their senior year of high school when she was still just Ann Bransby-Smith, the cute redhead in his psychology class. He had never before gotten laid with a girl who had armpit hair. It was sort of weird, but it seemed somehow to go with the black turtleneck sweaters she wore and the beret she pulled down over her ears sometimes.

"Artsy chicks who paint aren't allowed to shave their pits," she'd told him that night. Steve had only looked up at her—she was half-straddling him on the couch, her jeans still zipped up but her shirt off and her hair hanging in her face. He wasn't sure whether she was kidding, and he didn't especially care, since his hand had slipped inside the filmy cup of her bra and her nipple was as hard as a piece of candy beneath his fingers. A few minutes later he discovered that she *perfumed* the hair under her arms, and from that moment on, those tufts had not disturbed him in the slightest.

Until now. That fleeting sight filled him with such a miserable surge of desire and loneliness that he almost spit out his mouthful of beer. He thought about how fucked up the past month had seemed without her. Playing wasn't fun anymore; she got into all the songs somehow. Even *drinking* wasn't fun —often as not he got hung up in a jag of self-pity, cursing her name, crying in his beer, hurling things she had given him against the walls of his room. He was sick of working at the Whirling Disc, sick of reading, sick of his dreams. Only spending time with Ghost seemed to help, but even Ghost couldn't be there all the time, though Ghost often came padding into Steve's room and sat in the dark with him when Steve couldn't sleep at two in the morning. Ghost did that, but he couldn't do everything. He couldn't be Ann, with her smell of paint and tea-rose perfume and Camel smoke, with her welcoming body.

Steve circled around the bar and approached Ann from behind (*From behind,* the demon in his mind said wickedly, *yeah, I remember that one pretty good, but there were lots of other positions too,* and he told it to shut up). She was saying something to Terry, who nodded sagely and glanced past her at Steve. Terry raised one quizzical eyebrow. Steve shrugged and reached out to touch Ann's shoulder.

At the same moment, R.J. raised his head and regarded them all with bleary good humor. "Hey, Ann!" he exclaimed. "Hey, Steve! You guys getting back together or what?"

Ann's back stiffened. Her head whipped around, and a

red-gold strand lashed across Steve's face. Her eyes met Steve's and seemed to crack a little. Out of that fault line spilled all the nights, all *their* nights. The wild sweat-slicked ones when nothing short of devouring each other would satiate their hunger. The quiet beery nights on the front porch of the house, sitting with Ghost, who always knew when to stay up talking past midnight and when to go to bed early. The nights lying across Steve's bed in the half-darkness of the moonlit window, before the *Penthouse* centerfold went up, watching life go by and not needing to chase it because they were together and that was enough.

Those nights, and the psychobloody ones when they said things that could not be taken back, when they didn't care what they said. "I just can't compete with alcohol, can I?" she had asked one bitter night, and he had responded, "Fuck, no—you're not *that* good."

But that was nothing.

That was nothing compared to *the* night, the one he couldn't bear to remember, the one he couldn't help remembering in every gory detail.

When he had thrown Ann on the bed and unzipped his pants, he had ceased to be Steve Finn. Maybe that was a cop-out, but that was how it had felt. His sense of selfness had deserted him. The feeling of Ann's body beneath him, bucking and struggling against him, was remote as a figure on a movie screen. In fact, the whole thing was like a movie; watching a badly faked snuff film might have given him the same sense of mild, free-floating disgust.

The shame and horror at what he had done hadn't hit him until, driving home, he had looked at his hand on the steering wheel and seen the mark of Ann's teeth. Tiny beads of blood were welling up from the imprint, which circled the base of his thumb. What had he done to make her bite him that hard?

Get home, his mind had chanted. *Get home, to Ghost. Just get there and you'll be okay.* He had. They hadn't talked much, but Ghost had sat up with him until he could sleep.

The next few weeks had dragged by. He missed her, he ached for her; he hated her; he pictured her making wild sweet love with her schoolteacher boyfriend. He called her house and hung up twice. Then one time her father answered, and he worked up his courage and asked to talk to her. Surely she wouldn't have told her *father* what he had done. But Simon only informed him in accents more clipped than usual that Steve was not to try to see Ann, telephone her, or communicate in any way. This was the only warning, Simon told him. On his second attempt Steve would be disposed of.

Arguing with Simon Bransby was like smoking a big joint of killer grass and then trying to take an exam in Nietzschean philosophy or organic chemistry. You had no idea what made sense and what was bullshit; Simon bombarded you with words faster than you could sort them out. Steve had hung up again.

He had not seen Ann since then. Until now. He was very high and more than a little drunk, and here she stood before him, come to see him and Ghost play at the Sacred Yew. A few minutes ago he had been thinking about getting her name tattooed on his arm.

The crack in her eyes closed, and she smiled what Steve recognized as her most guarded smile. "Hey, Steve. How've you been?"

Steve wanted to grab her, to bury his face between her breasts and sob for all those lost nights, even the ones that had ripped both their souls open. He wanted to wipe that fake glossy smile off her face. He couldn't stand to see that smile on the lips he knew so well, the lips he had nudged open with his tongue, the lips that had brought him to the forbidden zone between pleasure and madness. The betraying lips. Were they printed with the kisses of the teacher from Corinth? He wanted them for himself, wanted to reclaim them.

But even as drunk as he was, he could not. To do that, he would have to show his desperation. He would have to apologize or cry or something. Such raw openness, with its possibility of scorn, was not in Steve. Ghost had it, but Steve's dark eyes hid his soul as Ghost's pale ones never could. So he only smiled back, as easily as he was able, and offered her his half-full bottle. "Wanna beer?"

"Natty Boho, huh?" she said. Steve winced. She liked Rolling Rock, he knew that. But her voice was the same as ever, that tender voice roughened by too many Camels, with the hoarse little catch in it, like a fingernail on a jagged piece of tin.

"Uh, yeah," he said. Jesus. Brilliant repartee.

"Oh well." She took a swallow and managed not to grimace. "Ghost brought me a copy of the tape. Oh, wait, did he tell you he came over?" Her hands played nervously with the tattered veil of her hat. Obviously she didn't want to get Ghost in trouble.

"Yeah, he told me." *And it was no big deal, not like I yelled at him or nearly decked him or anything . . .*

"It made me want to come see you play again. I'm glad I did. That was a damn good show, Steve. You two are getting too good for this town."

Terry slid off his bar stool and hauled R.J. down by the back of his collar. After testing his balance, R.J. managed to remain precariously upright. "We'll catch you later, man," said Terry. "Hey, here—you want these?" He put a fresh beer in Steve's hand, and another in Ann's. A Rolling Rock and a Bud. Before Steve had a chance to thank him, Terry had dragged R.J. off through the crowd.

"You think we're too good for Missing Mile?" Steve said. Another scintillating reply. Jeeesus . . .

"Yeah. I mean, Kinsey's great, but how much farther can you go playing at the Sacred Yew? You ought to take it on the road. You could get as big as R.E.M. or somebody like that. You could travel. You could get to be famous."

Steve looked at the beer in his hand. He popped it open and drained a third of it in one swallow. Then he opened his mouth to answer Ann, and what came out was "You really want me out of town, huh? I guess your boyfriend over in Corinth can still get it up for you."

OH, JESUS. He hadn't meant to say that. It was the demon. He should have stuck with sparkling wit like "yeah" and "uh-huh."

But it was too late. Ann's face had snapped shut, her eyes hardened. "You bastard," she said. "You couldn't wait, you couldn't even talk to me—"

"Listen—Ann—"

"*Shut up!* You had to get a jab in right away, didn't you? Like you were the one who should be pissed at me. *Like I raped you, not the other way around!*"

"Dammit, shut up for a minute—"

"Shut up? Keep my voice down maybe? That's real good, Steve. That's so good you can shove it up your ass." Now she was turning away. She thought she was so tough, but she was turning away to hide her tears. Before he could reach out and stop her, she was pushing her way through the bar crowd, her head down, making for the door. Steve started to follow, but the demon spoke up again: *Wait a second. She started all this, she fucked around on me. What the hell is she pissed off about? Let her shove it up her own ass.*

He turned back to the bar and met the cold eyes of the new bartender, who must have seen the sordid little melodrama from the beginning. But under the coldness in those eyes was a strange sympathy, a look of solitude and wisdom. The bartender raised one shoulder in a tiny shrug: *Such is life, friend.* And in his long thin hand was another can of Budweiser, cold and frosty and waiting for Steve to grab it.

Ghost prowled around the club for maybe fifteen minutes, staying in the shadows, saying hello to people he knew but not stopping to talk to them. Instead, he watched Nothing. Right after the show he had found himself wanting to talk to Nothing, though he wasn't sure what he wished to say. Maybe only to offer a word of kinship. To say *I can't heal your pain, but I can see it. And you don't have to be lost. Not forever.* So he waited and hoped that Nothing would move away from his three friends, if only to go to the restroom or something. But they huddled in a tight little knot passing a flask with a Grateful Dead sticker on its side—Ghost could just make out the roses and the grinning skull.

The two larger friends laughed a lot and sloshed the liquor in their mouths before they swallowed it. But Nothing and

Zillah were quiet. Zillah always seemed to have his hands on
Nothing, touching the sleeve of Nothing's raincoat, speaking
occasionally (with his soft, untorn lips—but Ghost would not
think about that, not now) into Nothing's ear. Leaning in
close, protective or predatory or both. Zillah probably would
have followed Nothing into the restroom. Nothing stood silently, looking very young and a little nervous, his face lit
orange by the glowing eye of his cigarette.

After a while the air inside the club began to press on
Ghost's face. It was heavy with smoke and the neon-bright
energy of the kids. A girl in black silk shimmied to the music
piping over the PA system. A boy with long unruly hair
played air-guitar furiously, miming a Steve Finn lick for his
friends. Other kids shouted back and forth, fluttering hands
stamped in ink with the many-boughed Yggdrasilian logo of
the club. Ghost passed them on his way to the door. His head
swarmed with their conversation and their stray thoughts.

Outside, in the night, the air felt as clear and hard-edged
as slivers of ice. Ghost breathed it in deep and blew it out.
Pale steam plumed from his mouth and his nostrils. For a
minute he stood on the sidewalk in front of the club, his
hands deep in the pockets of his army jacket fumbling with
the objects he found there. Rose petals. An old ace of spades
he had found in the dead grass at the end of their driveway,
water-marked and crusted with dirt. A guitar pick, the lucky
one Steve had given him. Then, his hands still in his pockets,
he crossed the street and stood in the middle of the empty
block.

Missing Mile was not a large town, but it was big enough
to have a couple of run-down areas. The Sacred Yew was
right in the middle of one. The kids didn't care, and Kinsey
liked the cheap rent. Some of the shop windows were
boarded up or broken. Ghost stood in front of a building that
had last been a dress shop. Magic Marker signs in the display
window still announced *GOING OUT OF BUSINESS!* and
ALL STOCK 75% OFF! and, optimistically, *BEAT XMAS
RUSH!*

But between the signs the window was soaped in great
cakey swashes. Looking through one of the gaps, Ghost saw a

pink torso splashed with moonlight and shadow. Above it, a smooth, featureless oval of a head gazed back into the dark recesses of the building. A mannequin, left behind to preside over ruin.

He did not turn when Ann came silently out of the club, her hair flying like a banner behind her, cold tears dripping off her chin. He stood looking through the window of the abandoned dress shop for a long time. The only voice in his head was his own, and his thoughts drifted like the clouds up by the moon. Then, sometime later, he sensed a presence behind him.

When he turned, Zillah and Nothing were across the street, standing by the club door. Zillah was still for a moment, seeming to scent the cold night air. Then he started down the street, walking fast, not looking back at Nothing. Nothing hurried to catch up.

After a moment, Ghost followed too.

Christian turned away from the rangy guitarist without asking him to pay for his beer. He had learned to know when a customer needed a drink on the house. The boy nodded his thanks and walked away, already raising the beer to his lips.

As Christian pulled the Michelob tap forward and began drawing another beer, he glanced up at the bar clock—and his breath caught in his throat. The glass clockface was reflecting three lights at once: the purple glow of the ancient TV set that flickered all night up in the corner; the green luminescence of a beer sign across the room; and the yellow of someone's striking a match. That was all, but for a second those three colors flared together, and in that circle of glass Christian saw the tawdry splendor of a hundred Mardi Gras nights—the fire, the liquor, the beads, the burning glow of Chartreuse—all up there in the dusty clockface.

A wave of homesickness such as he had never known shuddered through him. It did not matter that his bar had been way down Chartres, far from the heart of the Quarter. In that moment he saw only Bourbon Street, the neon carnival going on all night, the glitter that lit up the dawn. And he thought suddenly that New Orleans was his home as no place had ever been—not in all his years. He must go back. Better to face the dry danger of Wallace Creech than to stay in this dark little town serving endless cups of bad draft beer through every endless night.

Then, with an effort, he stilled his thoughts. Of course he could not go back. He had abandoned his bar. When no rent check was sent to the owner, the bar and supplies would be seized, would no longer belong to him. And did he wish to die at the hands of one such as Wallace, to die for the dogged obsessions of a sick old man, or to have to kill him and his endless string of true believers?

No. He would stay here, where fate and the highways had brought him. He would serve beer and sell roses as long as they grew. He would put away money. Someday, when he knew Wallace had to be dead, he could return to New Orleans. But for the present, as soon as he had enough money, he would go north to look for the others.

He drew another beer. Above the noise in the bar a loud voice said, "Hey, Count Dracula, can we get a drink?"

Christian turned, his shoulders stiff, his eyes frigid. But the two faces before him were familiar and as comically surprised as he must look. The ridiculous smudges of kohl around the eyes. The masses of ratted hair framing pallid cheeks. One of them held a sticky red lollipop in his hand. They had let their hair grow longer and wilder, and their style of dress was now tinged with punk. One wore a studded leather collar around his neck; the other's black denim jacket seemed to be held together chiefly by hundreds of safety pins. Otherwise Molochai and Twig had changed not at all since Christian last saw them, waving goodbye from the windows of their van on that Ash Wednesday night fifteen years ago.

His first clear thought was *What happened to Zillah? beautiful green-eyed Zillah? he must be safe.* He blocked that thought, and his second one was *They are here, they are really here; the time passed as if I were asleep and they have found me again.*

Then Christian did something he had never done before, not once during a long, long bartending career. He dropped

the cup of beer he was holding. It foamed around his boots
and made a huge puddle on the floor. Kinsey came out from
the back and saw it and glared at him, and Christian could
not have cared less.

Nothing gazed around at the kids in the club. They were
all so beautiful. He loved their choppy hairstyles, their cos-
tume jewelry, their ragged black or multicolored clothes. He
loved the way they all somehow looked like *him,* and he
wished he could make friends with every one of them. Most
of them smiled at him, and a few said "hey"—they all
seemed to say that instead of "hi" or "hello"—but he didn't
dare talk to any of them. He couldn't make friends now. Not
when they might end up like Laine, alone in a culvert with
rainwater washing through their hair.

Not yet.

He was content just to be among them, watching them
talk, smoke, dance. Zillah was beside him, and the others, so
he wasn't alone. And he had the show to remember. The
songs. Ghost swaying at the microphone, bathed in golden
light. Steve bounding across the stage, playing guitar like the
devil was chasing him. Ghost's hands like pale birds shaping
the music. Nothing stood still, trying to absorb every detail of
the club—the smells of clove-smoke and sweaty perfume; the
mural sprawling across the walls, some of it faded or rubbed
away, some bright as the fresh blood on the walls of the van.

Then Molochai and Twig stumbled off to the bar in search
of some drink called a Suffering Bastard. Zillah disappeared
with them, but a few minutes later he was back. He gripped
Nothing's arm and nodded meaningfully toward the exit.

Outside, Zillah turned without a word and stalked away
from the club. Nothing stared after him for a moment, then
ran along the sidewalk to catch up.

All day it had been like this. Ever since slinking away from
Steve and Ghost's house—that was how Nothing thought of
it. In broad daylight they had slunk away. Now Zillah's face
was completely healed, and Zillah had managed to be nice to
him all night. But now Zillah was acting as if he had been
disgusted with the show. Had the music bored him? Was the

club too small, too unglamorous? Or did Zillah just harbor an
unshakable hatred for Steve and Ghost?

If that was the case, Nothing wanted to retrieve Molochai
and Twig and get out of town. He'd seen Missing Mile; he'd
seen his show. There was no place for him here, not with his
new family. Nothing caught up with Zillah and walked along-
side him. On their right was a block of abandoned stores. On
their left was a line of parked cars, windshields reflecting the
moonlight back at Nothing. Up ahead he could make out a
figure hunched on the hood of one of the cars. As they
walked closer, he saw that it was a girl. Her long hair spilled
down over the back of her sweatshirt. Closer still, and he saw
that she was crying.

Zillah pulled him toward the girl. Surely he couldn't be
hungry again, not after last night—but Nothing put that out
of his mind. He couldn't do that again, not yet. And Molochai
and Twig weren't here. When Zillah touched the girl's shoulder and asked, "Can we help you, my dear?" Nothing
thought he understood. He had crossed Zillah, and his punishment wasn't over.

But Nothing didn't care. Zillah could have this girl if he
wanted her. Or any girl, any*one*. Because now Nothing knew
something he hadn't known before: Zillah wasn't just angry
because Nothing had gone against him, or even because
Nothing had hurt him. Zillah was jealous too, jealous of
Steve and Ghost, of Nothing's love for them and their music.
The new knowledge coursed through him, making him feel
weirdly powerful, like the time he had shot heroin with
Spooky. He could make someone jealous, even someone as
beautiful and charismatic as Zillah. It was a heady feeling.

He could get used to feeling like that.

Ann's head jerked up when the man touched her shoulder.
She hadn't heard him approaching, probably wouldn't have
heard the march of Sherman coming up the street. At a better moment she might have welcomed a stranger's attention,
but right now she knew her bangs were plastered to her
forehead, her eye makeup smeared across her cheeks, the
pale complexion she cultivated flushed and blotchy from cry-

ing. *Damn* Steve Finn, she thought, damn him to death. But
then she saw the man who had spoken to her, and she forgot
about Steve; she even forgot that she probably looked like a
bag lady on crack.

She was transfixed. Her stare flicked over the boy beside
him, dismissed him as a high school trendy, and went back to
Zillah. The eyes were amazing, the first thing anyone would
notice. The rest of him wasn't bad either. He was shorter
than she usually liked her guys, and a little more muscular—
Steve and Eliot rivalled each other for the Ichabod Crane
Bodybuilding Award. But the bones of his face were like a
mask carved out of moonstone, perfect and faintly cruel, the
face of an aristocrat. His skin was smooth and flawless.

As he reached out and took one of her hands, dwarfing it
in both of his, Ann noticed the dark tracery of veins beneath
his silken skin. After a moment she realized that these were
noticeable because the man had almost no hair on the visible
parts of his body—none on the knuckles or the back of his
hand, none at the open collar of his shirt. She wondered if he
was so smooth elsewhere, if she was about to find out. Those
green eyes gave her a reckless feeling. How could you turn
down a man who looked at you with those eyes?

"We were going back to our car to smoke a touch of
opium," Zillah told the girl. "Would you care to join us?"

For a moment Ann was almost afraid. If he had said "pot"
or even "hash," she would have thought nothing of it, but
who had opium in Missing Mile? She thought of serial killers, of girls found rolled up in rugs with their arms and legs
sawed off, of toolboxes and power drills.

Then she straightened her back, thrust out her chest, and
smiled. None of that could happen to *her*. And if it did—
well, then Simon couldn't practice his emotional torture on
her any more, and Steve would feel so bad that it would
almost be worth it. "Why not?" she said. "I haven't gotten
stoned in three weeks."

She slid off the hood of the car, and Zillah took her arm
and led her toward the van. Ann kept her arm squeezed
against her body so that his fingers would come into contact
with the sideswell of her breast. He didn't move his hand

away. Soon she felt his fingers begin to move, subtly caressing her, a forefinger darting out to graze her nipple. The nipple shivered erect, and he toyed with it a second longer. Ann felt something happening in her lower pelvis, a warm throbbing tension. If this man really got her stoned on opium, he might get more than the quickie he seemed to be looking for.

Neither Ann nor Zillah looked back to see whether Nothing was following, but after a moment Nothing did.

Ghost tailed Zillah and Nothing, keeping to the shadows, staying a good ways behind. They were well into the rundown section now. All the windows here were boarded up or broken. Ghost saw a milky swath of stars reflected in a long splinter of glass. The stars were cold in the sky. This part of town was always cold. Even in the middle of summer, nightwalkers might shiver and pull their light clothes more tightly around them. The glinting spears of glass, the crust of dirt in the gutter, the cloud of steam that boiled like some graywhite phantom from a sewer grate cast a chill over everything.

Ghost walked with his hands in his pockets and his hat pulled down low. Once Zillah turned his head, and Ghost thought he could see hot green light spilling from those eyes. He ducked into a dark doorway, his heart beating faster.

Zillah and Nothing melted into the cold shadows without a glance at the desolation around them. They moved silently and did not speak or touch, though their hands sometimes brushed together. Ghost stayed in the doorway and watched them. Down the sidewalk he saw a girl sitting on the hood of a car. She looked as if she might be crying. Her long hair could have been any color; the flat illumination of the few unbroken streetlights turned it black. But Zillah approached her and spoke to her, and when she looked up at him, Ghost saw her face. The girl was Ann Bransby-Smith.

After talking to them for a minute, she slid down from the hood of the car. Frantically, Ghost reached out for Ann's mind. If he could feel her, maybe he could warn her . . . of what? This kind, urbane man raising a baseball bat above his

head, ready to split Ghost's skull? Of Zillah's smashed face
that had magically repaired itself, of Zillah's smooth voice
murmuring cold lewd words in Ghost's head?

Ann would never believe it. And at any rate she wasn't out
there tonight, or if she was, he couldn't find her. There was
only the cold void of the dark. The ether, his grandmother
had called that empty-feeling place. The ether was alone, and
Ghost left it so. He watched as Ann walked away with Zillah,
and when they had gone several paces, he started following
again.

When they got into the black van, Zillah helping Ann up
and motioning Nothing in after her, Ghost thought it was all
over. Up Shit Creek, Steve would have said, without a pad-
dle. Now they would drive away, and Ghost would have to
go back to the club and try to decide whether to tell Steve
that his ex-girlfriend had just taken off with two of their
mysterious visitors.

But the headlights never came on; the motor didn't start.
The van didn't move. A few times the back window lit up
with the red flare of matches. Then the van stayed dark and
still. Ghost walked closer, scared and confused. He didn't
know what to do. He wanted to go hammer on the windows,
break the glass, rescue Nothing and Ann from that beautiful,
awful creature with the bright green eyes.

But Nothing had cast his lot already, and Ann was old
enough to take care of herself. If Ghost tried to rescue her,
she would probably punch him in the nose. So he prowled,
and shivered, and wished for X-ray vision to see through the
sides of the van. He closed his eyes and stood very still with
his hands at his sides, swaying, but the van might have been
a million miles away, might have been empty. He couldn't
feel anything.

Ghost turned away, thinking he would go back to the club.
He would keep his mouth shut if Steve was still conscious.
He would take Steve home and give him a lot of coffee and
maybe one of Miz Catlin's potions. Maybe everything
wouldn't be so weird tomorrow. He turned away, and then
he heard the door of the van slam.

Nothing was standing on the sidewalk, half in the streetlights' glare, half in the shadow of the storefronts. He stood as if he might be very tired or very drunk, but he held his head up, and there was strength in his face, strength and stubbornness and a resignation that should never have marked a face so young.

"Hey," said Ghost softly.

Nothing's eyes sharpened, and his lips parted a little. For a moment he stared into the darkness, but he didn't look as if he cared much what came out of it. Then he saw Ghost and stepped forward, and they stood facing each other on the cold sidewalk.

"That's Steve's girlfriend in the van there," said Ghost.

"That's my lover in there with her," Nothing said. "She's on top now. He was on top before, when they started, and the sweat on his back was shining, and she *screamed* when he spread her legs and rammed it in . . ." His voice trailed away, and he stared at Ghost. His eyes were dark and huge, all pupil. His face was naked, exquisitely shadowed, desperate. "Be my brother," he said. "Zillah loves me. He'll let me stay now. I can stand it if you'll be my brother just for one minute."

So Ghost put his arms around Nothing and hugged him tight, as he had wanted to do ever since he first saw the pain in those dark child-eyes. Nothing sagged against him as if never wanting to let go again, and Ghost felt all the exhaustion in that thin little body. There was strength in this boy, a lot of strength, but he was just a kid and God only knew what had been happening to him. He must have had about all he could stand for today.

"Hold me," said Nothing into the folds of Ghost's jacket. "Please don't let me go. Not yet."

"No," Ghost told him. "Not yet. It's all right."

He felt so damn helpless. It wasn't all right. It would never be all right. If Nothing stayed with those three, with *that one*, he was lost. "Listen," he said into the boy's lank damp-smelling hair. "Do you want to come stay with me and Steve? I mean, he'll cuss about it, but he won't kick you out. Not if you need us."

Nothing looked up at Ghost for a second. Then he let his

head fall back onto Ghost's shoulder. The touch of his lips against Ghost's throat was light, shivery. "I can't," he said. "If I went home with you, they'd come for me. Zillah would. And I have to go with them."

"Why? What are they to you?" Ghost knew his voice was getting louder, but he couldn't stop it. "What the hell *are* they, Nothing? Steve's pretty strong, but when that guy held him down, he couldn't move. And I dreamed about you—or *someone*—and there was so much blood. *What are they?*"

"Never mind," said Nothing. "Never mind what they are. This is all you need to know: whatever they are, so am I."

"What are you, then?"

"I wish you could tell me," Nothing said. "I wish you remembered your dreams." He let go of Ghost and turned toward the club.

But in Nothing's path was a shape that stood tall and awry, blocking the sidewalk. A scarecrow with hair wild and tangled, shirttails flapping, feet planted wide apart in a half-crouch, knees bent at crazy angles, arms outstretched, fingers clawing at the night. A shape that moved in a cloud of beer and murder-lust. Steve.

His eyes found Ghost, wavered, shone. "Where the fuck is she? She's with a guy. I know she's with a guy. I'll kill 'em both. Where the fuck—"

The door of the van slammed again. Ann was there, steadying herself with one hand against the side of the van. Her hair was rumpled, her face flushed. Behind her, Zillah stepped out, placing his feet carefully on the sidewalk.

Zillah was wearing pink sneakers, Ghost saw. The laces were printed with some kind of bright pattern—it looked like letters, but Ghost couldn't make them out. Zillah looked at Nothing and smiled darkly. Nothing gave him a shaky smile in return, a smile that made Ghost want to cry, a smile that proved better than anything else that Nothing was lost.

Steve looked from Zillah to Ann. His eyes gleamed; his mouth worked soundlessly. "Ann?" he managed at last. "You didn' . . . you cou'n' . . ."

Ann walked right up to Steve. She held her head high and her back very straight, smiled sweetly into his stricken face.

"I could and I did," she said, "and you don't have a goddamn thing to say about it."

"But he . . . but he . . ." Wordlessly, Steve gestured at Zillah, who turned away smiling. Ghost couldn't tell whether Steve had noticed Zillah's unmarked face.

"*He* was the best lover I've ever had. *He* made you look pretty sorry. But you don't need anyone to make you look sorry, do you? You do just fine on your own—or maybe with a little help from your bottle. Why don't you just get out of my life, Steve? Why don't you just drink yourself into an early grave?"

"Shut up, Ann." Ghost spoke mildly, but his face was pale, and his hands were clenched into tight fists. He wondered how events had managed to fall into place this way, the worst way anyone could imagine.

Bad times coming, said a voice in his head. But they were already here.

Ann's eyes flickered to Ghost. "I'm sorry you have to see this," she told him. "You're good, Ghost, you really are. You better get away from this loser before he fucks up your life the way he fucked up mine." She turned and walked away, back to Zillah, who was leaning against the van. Steve watched her go, terrible emotions warring in his face.

Ann reached Zillah and tried to link her arm with his. For a moment it seemed that he would embrace her. But then Zillah's hands closed on her shoulders, and he gave her a hard shove away from him. Ann staggered, almost lost her balance on the curb. Her head snapped back and hit the side of the van, and she barely managed to keep her balance.

Zillah gazed at Steve. His eyes were triumphant. "So sorry," he said. "I didn't know the slut belonged to you."

With a low, desperate cry, Steve threw himself at Zillah. Ghost grabbed for him, trying to catch Steve's arm or the back of his shirt, anything. He was afraid of what Zillah might do to Steve, who was hurting worse than ever before, who was too drunk to know what he was doing. But Ghost's hands closed on air.

Steve lurched forward. Zillah's arm shot out, something

pearly and silver glittering in his hand, and Ghost caught a glimpse of Zillah's expression—amused boredom.

Then Steve staggered back, blood dripping down his face, making dark flowers on his shirt. The razor had opened his forehead just above the eyebrows, and blood was pouring into his eyes, blinding him. He stumbled toward where he had last seen Zillah, taking wild swings at the air.

Horrified, Ghost tried again to grab him. Surely now the razor would take out one of Steve's eyes or slice straight across his throat.

But Zillah had other things in mind. He sidestepped neatly, then stuck a pink-sneakered foot into Steve's path. Before Ghost could get to him, Steve tripped over it and went down on the sidewalk.

Ghost knelt beside Steve and shoved the messy hair back from his face. The cut across his forehead looked shallow, but it had to hurt like hell. Through some reflex not quite drowned in beer he had managed to get his hands in front of him as he hit the pavement, and his palms were scraped raw.

Ghost searched for Steve's mind with his own, wanting to soothe it. No good. Steve's mind was inflamed, walled off, and Ghost could only feel around the edges of it. Its heat hurt him. He drew his own mind back, but held Steve tighter.

"What the hell do you mean?" Ann asked. But there was little anger in her voice. She was edging toward Zillah. Her eyes never left his face; she didn't seem to notice Steve bleeding on the sidewalk. "How can you call me a slut? That was magic. No one ever made me feel so good. Your cock— your *tongue*—" She shuddered.

Ghost shut his eyes and pressed his face to Steve's. Steve growled deep in his throat, low and feral, and tried to struggle back up. Ghost held him down. If Steve got loose now, he would kill someone or get killed, and the latter seemed a lot more likely.

"My apologies," said Zillah. "That was an unkind word. But you mustn't love me. I have a lover already, if he has learned his lesson." He held out his arms to Nothing. After the barest hesitation Nothing went to him, huddled into the curve of Zillah's arm, laid his head on Zillah's shoulder.

"No," said Ann. There was dull desperation in her voice. "No. I've never fucked anyone else like that. You can't leave me."

Steve made a low choking sound, twisted his head, buried his face in Ghost's lap. His raw hands scraped weakly at the sidewalk. Ghost caught them and held them tight.

Nothing looked at Ann. His expression was pitying, a little disdainful. "Go away," he told her. "Go find somebody else. *I* belong here—not you."

Ann's face twisted. She stared around wildly, as if the night and the broken glass and the boarded-up storefronts were suddenly strange to her. Ghost ached to go to her, even after all she had said and done, but he couldn't let go of Steve. Ann's mouth opened, and for seconds it seemed as if her scream must split the night wide open.

But then, from far down the sidewalk, another voice came. A loud voice, full of drunken cheer. "Hey! Zillah! Look who we found—it's Chrissy!"

Christian could barely stand up straight. This was what it must be like to be drunk. Of course, Twig's arm was looped tight around Christian's neck and Molochai seemed to be leaning his full weight against Christian, but it was not the burden of Molochai and Twig that made him unsteady on his feet. It was a combination of relief and giddiness, their warm coppery smell and the touch of skin that would not soon be dead and cold.

They had waited for him until his shift at the bar was over, chattering about cities they had seen over the past years, rare new drugs they had taken, impossible scenes of carnage through which they had come unscathed. They assured him that Zillah was with them, still very much alive.

After the bar closed, they dragged him out of the club before Kinsey could give him his cash pay. Their van was parked a few blocks away. Christian saw an assortment of figures on the sidewalk near it. One of them was Zillah, and something in Christian loosened at the sight of those brilliant green eyes, that face still so insouciant and smooth. For fifteen years he had waited to see that face again. Zillah greeted him with a raised eyebrow and a small evil smile.

But who were these others? Two of them he had seen before. The girl with the smudged face, she had been at the club tonight. And the fair boy, the one whose pale eyes widened when he saw Christian—well, he was the singer for Lost Souls? But there was something else about him . . . Seeing him up close, Christian remembered. This was the boy who had come riding his bicycle at twilight, when Christian was about to close up his flower stand and go hunting. He had been so hungry, barely able to wait, but for reasons he could not explain to himself he had not wanted to take that boy.

Another boy—the guitarist, Christian thought—lay on the sidewalk, his face buried in the fair one's lap, his long legs sprawled at an uncomfortable angle. Christian smelled his blood, but it was of secondary interest to him. For there was another figure here, an unfamiliar one.

Huddled beside Zillah, standing in Zillah's shadow so that Christian had not noticed him at once . . .

This must surely be the true child of night, the soul of all the thin children who wore black, who traced their eyes in kohl and stared out their windows waiting for the sun to set. This boy looked as if he had been raised in the back room of some hole-in-the-wall nightclub, fed on bread soaked in milk and whiskey, the bones of his face shaped fine by hunger. That was the word for this child: *hungry.* For what?—for drunkenness, for salvation or damnation, for the night itself. The shadows beneath his eyes might have been painted in watercolor. The wrists protruding from the cuffs of his raincoat were thin, delicately knobby.

Christian disengaged himself from Molochai and Twig, took a step closer. He did not know that he licked his lips. "Who are you?" he asked.

"This is Nothing," Zillah told him.

The name took a moment to register. But Christian had never forgotten Jessy or her beautiful sugar-candy baby. All through the years he had wondered whether he might have

kept the baby and cared for it himself; time after time he had
reminded himself that he had abandoned it to give it a
chance at a life untainted by blood. But he had never forgotten.
Now he knew that he might as well have kept the baby
after all. Blood calls to blood; curses and blessings find the
ones they were meant for.

"Nothing?" he asked, and took another step toward the
boy. Shyly, the child nodded.

Christian closed his eyes, and the words of his note pinned
to a blanket on some long-ago cold dawn came back to him.
" 'His name is Nothing,' " he quoted. " 'Care for him and he
will bring you luck.' "

He was not at all prepared for the boy's reaction. Nothing
tore himself away from Zillah and launched himself at Christian,
threw his arms around Christian's waist. Christian felt
the boy's body pressing against him, warm and vital.

"Yes!" Nothing cried. "Yes! Yes! They changed my name!
They called me Jason but I hated them and I'm still Nothing
and now I'm home and *you know who I am*! Tell me! *Tell me
who I am!*"

"Why, you're Zillah's son," said Christian. He had assumed
they knew. But there was silence. Absolute silence.
Even Molochai and Twig were quiet.

Nothing only stared up at Christian. The shadows beneath
his eyes were suddenly deeper; his mouth was limp, half-open.
He had the look of an ill-used child, a child kept out
too late. "Oh," he said. That seemed to be all he could say.
"Ohhh."

Zillah gently pried Nothing away from Christian. Nothing
shut his eyes tight and curled into Zillah's arms. His head lay
heavily against Zillah's chest. In an instant he seemed to
have fallen into deep shock.

Zillah caressed him absently. "Mardi Gras?" he asked
Christian. "That little girl at your bar?"

Christian nodded.

"Well," said Zillah. He was paler than usual, but he held
himself straight, and his eyes were fiercely happy. More than
that, Christian realized. Zillah's eyes were proud. "Well. That

changes things, doesn't it? That makes things even better. Lovely."

Molochai and Twig began whispering to each other. Christian heard a smothered giggle. The singer had been listening to the exchange, but he was more concerned with his friend. The girl seemed to be in a world of her own, slumped against the side of the van, her arms wrapped around herself, her chin tucked into her chest. The streetlight was very bright on her hair.

Christian looked up at the moon. It hung gravid in the sky, nearly full. Its light was strong enough to hurt his eyes, and he closed them, but still the moon shone through. It shone down upon them all there on the sidewalk—Steve, his head in Ghost's lap, furious, wounded, defeated; Zillah, with his sleeping child in his arms; Molochai and Twig, clutching each other, still whispering.

And Ann alone. Ann alone under the moon. Some of Zillah's seed was trickling out of her, seeping slow and creamy down her thighs.

Some—but not all. Inside Ann, two specks of life had glued themselves together, and deep inside her where all was raw and red and wet, something came alive. A microdot of meat, part human, part strange. Nothing's half-brother, or his half-sister.

Steve shuddered and lay still again. Ghost stroked his hair helplessly. Nothing moaned, beginning to surface from his shock, burrowing into his father's arms. The moon shone down, and Christian stared back at it. And inside Ann, the infinitesimal blob of meat stretched and began to grow.

PART TWO

PART TWO

21

Night.

Heavy green night, pine branches bending low to sweep the gravel road, the dying grass, the trash in the ditches. Snaky night, riotous with the last October kudzu. The kudzu would be dead in another month, like a dry brown blanket thrown over the trees and the roadsides. But now it still writhed under the moon, succulent, shifting, green.

Green night.

Violin Road.

A trailer up on cinderblocks, a silver Bel Air and a sagging black van parked in the scrubby dirt yard, behind the trailer a tangled thicket of rosebushes that would bear great lacy blossoms on into November. The roses had gone wild.

Nothing knew that if he turned his head, he would be able to look through the bedroom window and see the spiny etchwork of the rosebushes against the night sky. But he didn't really want to turn his head. Instead he lay very still, stretched out flat on his back in Christian's bed. His hands moved through Christian's glittering black hair, stroked the long curve of Christian's back.

Christian sighed and moved closer, nestling his head under Nothing's chin, and Nothing felt a tiny sweet flare of pain as Christian's teeth slid a little deeper beneath the skin of his throat.

He knew Christian was being careful. He knew Christian wouldn't hurt him, would take only a taste of his blood. This was not feeding; this was lovemaking. Weren't Christian's long fingers moving over him, tracing patterns on his ribs and his thighs, seeming to worship the texture of his skin? Still, Nothing had seen those teeth. They were beautiful; he envied them and wished he might have been born hundreds of years ago, before the adaptations of life among humans caught up with his race—but having to stay sober every night of his life would be too great a price even for fangs that curved down over his lips like hooks of ivory.

At first the teeth had only pricked Christian's lower lip. They lengthened imperceptibly. Nothing looked into Christian's mouth, but he could not see how it happened. They were simply longer all of a sudden, like hooked needles, silver-white and glistening. Nothing felt those teeth hard against his lips when Christian kissed him, and when he drew back he tasted blood.

Christian bit into Nothing's throat as gently as a junkie sliding a hypo into a sore vein, but Nothing still caught his breath and shivered at the cold exquisite pain. Then Christian's tongue was there, licking the blood away. Christian stroked him, a different touch from Zillah's: slower, gentler, less sure. They strained against each other.

At last Christian's mouth unfastened from Nothing's throat, and blood flowed between them, trickling over Nothing's chest, staining the sheets a little more. Nothing realized he had been holding his breath. He let it out in a great rush. What had he been afraid of? Christian wouldn't hurt him. He was of Christian's kind.

Still, he hadn't wanted to turn his head.

"Nothing," moaned Christian: a breath of fading ecstasy, borne on the scent of blood. "O Nothing. I would like to rip your throat open."

"Thank you," said Nothing. He knew this was a compliment. Then, after a moment: "Tell me about Jessy again."

Christian sighed. "She looked like you. The same great dark eyes. The same pointed chin. The same listening silence."

"You, um, you fucked her."

A pause, then: "Yes. Many times over a hot New Orleans summer."

"She was sixteen," Nothing said thoughtfully.

"Something like that."

"A year older than me."

"Yes."

"How old were *you*?"

A pause. "Three hundred and sixty-eight."

Nothing wanted to laugh, but he could not. The thought of all those years stored up in the being who lay beside him, belly warm with his blood, mouth slick with his spit . . . no, he could not laugh. The sheer weight of those years overwhelmed him. He wondered how it was for Christian. Surely three hundred and sixty-eight years of feeling could not be borne. Had Christian stopped feeling? Did he simply look upon the world, watchful, shutting out joy to keep back the pain of all the years?

Nothing pressed his face into the pillow. His eyes had gone hot and wet. He kissed Christian's throat, his mouth. It was just a mouth again, a rather cold mouth now, with a dark sweet taste on the tongue. Two of the top front teeth were unusually sharp . . . but Christian didn't smile much. Probably no one ever noticed those teeth.

"Will I live that long?" Nothing asked.

"Perhaps. If you're smarter than Molochai and Twig, and more cautious than Zillah." Christian stroked Nothing's head. "I can see the true color of your hair at the roots. Golden-brown. It was that color when you were a baby."

"I need a dye job." Absently he twirled a piece of his hair, put it in his mouth. Then he took a deep breath and asked, "What's it like to live such a long time?"

Christian didn't reply. He glanced at the window and said, "I have to leave. I'm to be at the club at eleven."

Nothing wanted to hold Christian, to take away those years, to do something for him. "I could come with you," he said.

"Thank you, but no. I'll lose my job if I keep slipping you drinks. You stay here with the others. When they wake up they'll want to go out." Christian stepped into a pair of impossibly long black trousers, buttoned a black shirt up to his chin. He turned to go. At the bedroom door he paused.

"Christian?" said Nothing.

"I would not wish it upon anyone," Christian told him. He disappeared into the dark recesses of the trailer. A moment later Nothing heard the front door close. Then the Bel Air was grinding out of the driveway, heading down Violin Road toward town.

Nothing lay among the cool tangled sheets, staring at the rags of mist that drifted past the window and obscured the rosebushes. For a while he played with his damp pubic hair, uncurling strands of it, gently tugging at them, letting them spring back. It wasn't often he had a bed to himself anymore. Usually he slept in a sweaty knot of blankets, hair, limbs. He would wake to find Molochai's fingers in his mouth or Twig drooling on his pillow. Often he woke to the perverse, sometimes scatological endearments that Zillah liked to murmur in his ear. So he relished this bit of privacy. He lay and let his mind drift where it would.

How old was Christian now? He calculated and came up with three hundred and eighty-three years. Nothing's mind tried to balk at the thought of all those years, but he would not let it. *No,* he told himself. *You might be that old yourself someday, so think about it.*

That was so much time. Unless you found others of your kind, others who lived as long, you were bound to spend a lot of that time alone. Others—he made himself think it: *humans* —would just die on you. Steve and Ghost would die, and he would still be young and roaring—but he would not think about Steve and Ghost.

Still, he had Zillah, his father, his lover. And he had Molochai and Twig and Christian. They would be there with him, alive. But there must be others of their race who were alone. Christian had been. Maybe that was why Christian seemed so reserved, yet so hungry for love when someone offered it. Just because you got used to being alone didn't mean you had to like it.

Maybe time passed differently in New Orleans. Maybe a sort of dream-time existed there, a time that could stretch a single day or compress three hundred and eighty-three years. In New Orleans he had been conceived by the bright sperm of Zillah. In New Orleans Christian had made love to Jessy. His mother. That thin, dark-haired girl of sixteen. That girl who had died giving bloody birth to him.

Nothing tried to imagine that summer in the French Quarter. The endless sweltering days above the bar. Christian's long bony hands moving over Jessy's slick breasts, her distended belly. Her belly that cradled *him*, unborn. He wished he could be Christian's hands. He wished he could feel Jessy's weight above him, her skin slick as if with oil. He imagined Christian thrusting up into her, parting her womb, nudging up against the fetus there. Me, he thought. In the womb, had he been bathed with Christian's semen? Had it nourished him along with the blood of Jessy?

And there in the womb, half-formed, had something in him known even then whose child he was? Had he longed to be nourished by Zillah's sperm instead of Christian's? Had something in him wanted his father? Was that why he had spent the first fifteen years of his life alone, always alone, always searching for a place he might belong—for a perfect love?

Well, he had it now. Body and soul and all the realm between.

He remembered the night outside the Sacred Yew, now a month past, and all that had transpired on the cold sidewalk. The night of punishment and revelation. He had awakened sometime past sunset the next evening—even then he was beginning to get used to the hours his new family kept, sleeping most of the day and howling all night. He woke back at the trailer, in Christian's bed. Zillah lay beside him, his head turned slightly away, his hair making colored stripes on the pillow. In slumber, Zillah's face was almost innocent. When you could not see those eyes.

Father, Nothing thought.

He had slipped quietly out of bed, not wanting to wake Zillah yet. He had looked at himself in the bathroom mirror, still able to meet his own eyes, and he had told himself: *For a week now you have been fucking your own father. His tongue has been in your mouth more times than you could count. You've sucked him off . . . you've swallowed stuff that could have been your brothers and sisters!*

But he could not disgust himself. He could not make himself ashamed. He knew these were things he was supposed to feel, things the rational daylight world would expect him to feel. But he could not force himself to feel them. In a world of night, in a world of blood, what did such pallid rules matter?

He wasn't sure he could ever have felt the things expected of him in the normal world, not even when he had been an unwilling part of it. Its morals had never been his; its baubles of status had never hypnotized him with their false glitter. He tried to imagine his friends back home making love with their fathers: Julie humping her fastidious attorney dad, Laine sucking off his hippie-throwback old man who grew stunted pot plants in his study and was supposed to be a genius at computer language. The idea did not offend him; it was sort of gross, because most of the fathers were not what Nothing would call hot-looking, but he could not label it with words like *wrong* or *bad.* He wondered if he had ever known what those words meant. Were members of his race born with some sort of amoral instinct that shielded them from the guilt of killing to stay alive? If he had not been born with such an instinct, could he have taken that first bite out of Laine's throat?

Nothing tried to imagine the circumstances that would lead, purely by coincidence, to a half-breed vampire leaving home, hitchhiking more than two hundred miles, and being picked up by the very member of his race who had fathered him fifteen years before. He could not do it. This was not coincidence; this had all been meant to happen. A map of his life was printed somewhere, and for a long time he had been wandering its boundaries, hopelessly lost. Now he had found its pattern. That the map might be printed all over with the legend *Here There Be Monsters* did not bother him in the least.

His bond to Zillah was also his bond to this world of blood and night. He knew that now Zillah would not leave him, would not abandon him. He had faced Zillah down once, and he could do it again. In a weird way, it seemed to make Zillah proud of him.

Zillah had wanted him from the beginning. There must have been some biological pull between them. The seed returning to the sower. But Zillah hadn't known why. The sentiment might still have been revocable. The pull might have weakened, even dissolved, when the next bottle of cheap wine was gone. But when Christian spoke those words outside the club—those terrifying, magical words, *You're Zillah's son*—the bond had become flesh.

No, not just flesh. *Blood.* The bond was forged in blood, of course, his and Zillah's, and Jessy's that had poured out of her. Nothing was of Zillah's blood, and Zillah would not let him go now, not in a thousand years. They might live that long, might live a thousand years or more, and still they would be together. He would ride the highways with Molochai, Twig, Zillah, and now Christian, forever. They would drink and make wild love and never grow old. And he would never have to be alone.

Nothing smiled at the ceiling. Though he did not know it, there was a wantonness to his smile that had not been there a month ago.

A soft footfall made him look toward the bedroom door. A figure stood in the doorway, a black shadow haloed by a thin line of silver light. Long wavy hair, straight shoulders. A small slight figure that stood as if it might be seven feet tall, massive and regal. Zillah.

"Come here," said Nothing. Zillah came to him and slipped under the cold sheets with him. As Zillah's arms tightened around him, Nothing heard himself say, *"Daddy."*

Zillah kissed his eyelids, his forehead, his lips. "Yes. That's lovely. Call me that."

"Daddy," Nothing whispered as Zillah unwound the sheets, kissed his throat, his chest, the tender concave stretch of skin below his ribs.

"My baby," said Zillah, and bit him gently. Nothing felt the last tattered shreds of his old life—the town, the desperately apathetic crowd at Skittle's, the two well-intentioned fools who had pretended to be his parents—tear loose and drift away on the warm river of Zillah's tongue. On the scent of blood, of herbs, of altars.

A night for reflecting.

A night for thinking of matters ordinarily left untouched, left half-buried in the sludge of the unconscious. Some nights seem shaped by an unseen dark hand. Some nights seem made for lying awake, eyes following the cracks and flyspecks on the ceiling, or the dead leaves and flowers pinned there, or the painted stars. Some nights seem made for plodding through the mind-sludge, poking at swollen and corrupted things, then ruthlessly heaving them over and staring them full in the face.

Some nights are made for torture, or reflection, or the savoring of loneliness.

Zillah lay draped around Nothing. To someone who lifted the tin roof off the trailer and looked upon the two small figures tangled in the sheets, Zillah's position would have appeared both protective and possessive. He lay with his cheek against Nothing's smooth hair, and he thought, *Mine. More than anything was before, more than anything will ever be again, this is mine. My seed, my blood, my soul.*

In town, a bad country-and-western band took the stage at the Sacred Yew. Christian wiped down the bar and tried not to listen to the mournful strains of the Rickenbacker, tried to blot out lyrics like "This heart was made for drinkin', not for thinkin'." His mind turned to Zillah and Nothing, to their obsessive incestuous passion for each other. *Well,* he asked himself, *what difference can it make? Who can it hurt? There are so few of us, and if it stops two souls from being alone, then where is the harm?*

He worried for Nothing because he knew Zillah was mad. Madder even than he had been fifteen years ago at Mardi Gras. The green light in his eyes was crazier, his passion for violence and pain more evident. But perhaps the whole race was mad in one way or another. Surely years upon years of living on the fringes of the world would drive anyone to madness. Zillah and the others—their madness was that they had grown to love living as nomads, outlaws, murderers. Their madness made them happy. And as for Nothing, perhaps being loved by his mad, beautiful father was better than being alone.

In another part of town, out where the pines hung heavy and green, where the October colors of the other trees flamed darkly in the night, where the kudzu marked the passage of the road, Ghost lay curled in bed. He was aware of Steve in the next room, sleeping the sleep of alcohol, sodden and dreamless. Steve wasn't drinking so much beer lately. He had started on Jim Beam instead. Tonight he had begun by drinking it with tap water and ended up taking straight slugs from the bottle, and by the time Ghost helped him stagger to bed, he had put away a fifth of the stuff.

Steve talked and talked. Laying blame. That bitch, he said. That fucking betraying bitch. And that green-eyed motherfucker, I wonder how he'd smirk if somebody cut off his balls . . .

Ghost listened, saying "yeah" and "uh-huh" at the appropriate places. But where was the point in laying blame? Zillah had bewitched Ann. Ghost knew from his grandmother that love-spells don't work on people who don't want them, and they are surely the hardest kind of spells to undo once they are done. And as for Nothing . . . well, Nothing was home after all, wasn't he? Blood calls to blood. If Nothing wanted to sleep every night in his father's arms, then Ghost guessed that was what he must do.

He wrapped his arms around his pillow and wondered, *What will come of all this? Where will all these lost souls go?* But that was not the question he wanted to ask. What would come, would come. He reached out with his mind and found Ann in the dark somewhere, wandering by herself, searching for something that would only hurt her if she found it. Bewitched. She could not feel his mind brushing hers, would not answer him. He closed his eyes and tried to will himself to sleep. He'd been crying a lot lately. But he didn't want to cry alone in the dark.

As Ghost began to dream, the inhabitants of the trailer on Violin Road congregated in the tiny kitchen and greeted the new night with plastic cups of wine. At the Sacred Yew, Christian watched the bar clock and counted off the hours until closing time.

Night.

22

(Scratch)
(Pop!)
A yellow-orange explosion in the dark. Steve lit a fat joint that had been rolled from more of Terry's Popacatepetl Purple. Sparks showered down, flared like tiny nighttime suns among the damp pine needles, and died.

It was Halloween night, and they were sitting in the tiny Civil War graveyard in the woods behind their house. Ghost liked to come out here to smoke, to be among the trees and lie on the thick carpet of pine needles. He liked the gravestones that seemed to sprout like mushrooms from the forest floor, the weathered crosses of wood and granite, the white lambs and winged death's-heads so worn away that they might have been natural outcroppings.

When Steve sucked at the twisted cigarette, its light made his eyes into deep dark pools, threw his sharp nose and chin into spooky shadowed relief. Ghost took the joint and dragged deeply. The glow turned his hanging pale hair fiery, suffused his eyes. He held his breath for a long time, sighed out a great plume of smoke, and leaned back against his favorite gravestone: that of Miles Hummingbird, 1846–1865. Kinsey's great-great-great-uncle. A private in the Confederate army, shot somewhere in the Virginia woods on a rainy day near the end of the war, trundled home to North Carolina and buried in the springtime mud. Miles's gravestone was rough and gray and moldering, and Miles's bones fell

softly away to dust below. In the drifts of his body lay a shell
with creamy pink insides, a shell he had carried home from
his family's one trip to the shore when he was twelve, a shell
his sister had laid in his hands, over his torn chest, a shell
with dry tears inside a hundred and twenty years old.

Ghost put his cheek against the cool granite and thought,
Is it cold in the shell tonight, Miles?, and Miles's rusty Carolina voice, so very far away, said, *It's warm, Ghost. It's warm
and yellow as the sand, and the ocean is the color my sister's
eyes once were.*

"Blue-green?" said Ghost. "Like the calm ocean? Or blue-
gray, like before a storm?" He didn't realize he had spoken
aloud until Steve glared at him.

"Shit. What a way to spend Halloween, in the graveyard
listening to you talk to the spooks. I ought to be over at R.J.'s
party with five or six brews already down and another one
ready to go. Not in the damn graveyard getting stoned."
Steve lay back in the pine needles with his hands behind his
head and regarded the smeary glittering stars that were beginning to appear. He looked as if he would like to snuff
them out.

"You don't need any beer," Ghost told him. "You've been
drinking too much. Weed clears out your brain."

"You think Ann will be at that party?"

"Not if she thinks *you* will."

"No, I guess not. I guess she's still hanging around that
trailer on Violin Road. Out where those creeps moved in."
Steve was silent for a moment. "You know, they never let her
in. I drove past there one day and saw her in their yard.
Thought maybe her car had broken down, so I stopped and
asked her if she wanted a ride into town, but she told me to
get lost. Said she was waiting for her true love." He sucked at
the joint. "I hope they tell her to fuck off."

Ghost lay down next to Steve. "What did you do?"

"I sprayed gravel. Peeled out of there. I figured if I hung
around, I'd either kill her or that little green-eyed fucker."

Ghost heard Steve's knuckles cracking. "You don't want to
mess with them," he said.

"Yeah, I know what you told me. His face was all healed

up, and that means he must be Count Dracula or something.
I don't remember, Ghost. I don't know."

"Trust me, then."

"Guess I better. What else have I got to trust?" There was
no anger in Steve's voice now. He only sounded sad, and
very tired. A man who wanted to stop thinking.

Ghost would have done anything to make Steve happier.
But what could he do? Unbewitch Ann? Tell Zillah and his
crew to get out of town before sunrise? He propped himself
on his elbows and shook a few pine needles out of his hair.
The sweet orange smell of singeing pumpkin flesh drifted in
from the houses at the edge of the woods.

Ghost wondered if the one-eyed jack-o'-lantern he had
carved was still burning on their front porch. He felt desperate to talk about something, anything else. "The lost souls get
to come out tonight," he said.

"Huh? You mean us?" The joint had gone out. Steve lit it
again.

"Uh-uh." Ghost sucked spicy smoke, felt his lungs expand
and his brain swirl. "All the dark things. All the sad things
and the minds left over from the bodies, the minds who don't
know they're dead, the ones with no place to go." He felt his
pupils grow larger against the dark. "And the evil things,
too."

"Now you're trying to give me the creeps. Well, I can play
that game too. Want me to tell you the story of the Hook
again? Huh?" The joint had burned down to a quarter inch.
Steve snuffed it and dropped it in the pine needles, then
began to cough. "Fuck it. I want a beer. Let's go over to
R.J.'s."

"Shhh." Ghost's head came up. His hair fell over his eyes,
and he brushed it away. After a second Steve sat up and
stared into the woods too. Something flickered through the
pines and kudzu, a bright orange smudge on the night. A
jack-o'-lantern, Ghost guessed, burning on someone's porch.
But he thought he heard a rustle, a noise just slightly too
loud to be made by a squirrel or a night bird—a crunch.
Footsteps. Soft footsteps, coming through the woods.

"Something's out there," he told Steve.

Steve opened his mouth and shut it again. He was going to say something about smoking too much weed, Ghost supposed, but had thought better of it. Good. "Okay," Steve managed in a whisper. "What do we do?"

"Get up quiet. Stay behind me."

Steve grabbed Ghost's arm. Ghost felt electricity flowing between them, white and crackling and pure. "Like hell I will. I'm not letting you—"

"Stay behind me," Ghost said again, and looked straight into the woods, trying to feel out whatever might be coming.

Then branches broke, dead leaves rattled down like dry brown bones. Something round and fiery hurtled toward them. Steve went down fast, pulling Ghost with him. Ghost fell as limply as a rag doll. The savage orb exploded against Miles's gravestone. Ripe orange pulp splattered them.

Ghost shielded his face with one hand and felt wildly for Steve with the other, then heard an unhappy young voice wail, "*Shit*—I tripped—my shoelace came untied—"

Ghost lifted his head. "Nothing?" Chunks of pumpkin and pulp slimed the ground, shiny black in the moonlight. In the middle of the mess, the boy struggled to his knees and swiped futilely at his raincoat. He wouldn't meet Ghost's eyes. "Shit! I tripped over my own goddamn shoelace—I'm sorry—"

"It's okay. Don't worry about it." Ghost crawled over and put his hand on Nothing's shoulder. Nothing's face tilted up to Ghost's. His eyes were shadowed, his cheekbones more prominent than they had been outside the Sacred Yew a month ago, his lips drawn tight across his teeth. For no good reason, Ghost thought suddenly of certain strange happenings in Missing Mile lately. The bodies of two railroad bums, mutilated and decayed, found half-buried in the dead kudzu near the train tracks. The disappearance of a little boy out on Violin Road. But those things did not bear thinking about right now. "What happened?" he asked Nothing. "They didn't kick you out, did they?"

At the thought, a breath of cold wind seemed to pass through Nothing. He shuddered. "No. Oh no. Christian gave

me the jack-o'-lantern. I was bringing it to you. I walked over
here—"

"You walked all the way from Violin Road?" Steve interrupted. "Shit, kid, that's three or four miles."

"Yeah," said Nothing. "I didn't want the others to know I
was coming. I told them I was just going out for a—for a
walk. And you weren't home, but I heard your voices back
here, and I saw you lighting matches."

"So what do you want?" said Steve. He seemed to have
remembered that Nothing was on the wrong side. "Does
your green-eyed buddy want me to send Ghost on over? He
already took my girlfriend. He might as well have my best
friend too." Ghost poked him, but he kept talking. His voice
was unsteady. "Maybe he wants my car. Or my bag of pot.
I'll just go home and pack it all up for him."

Nothing stared at the ground. "No. I just—I came to tell
you that we're leaving. All of us. Tonight. We're going to New
Orleans."

"Even Christian?" asked Ghost. "He's from New Orleans.
He's going home?"

"The new barkeep?" said Steve. "How the fuck do you
know that?"

"Yeah," said Nothing. "He's scared to go back. Somebody
there is after him. But he can't let us leave without him. And
I was born in New Orleans. So this time I really am going
home."

"I'm happy for you. I guess." Ghost was surprised to find
that he would miss Nothing. He hadn't seen the boy since
that night at the club, that horrible night, but now he realized he had been hoping that Nothing would show up on the
doorstep one day. Forsaking his family, or forsaken by them.
Saving himself.

But that was impossible. Blood calls to blood. Nothing had
to go home.

"Wait a sec," said Steve. "How come you walked all the
way over here to tell us you were leaving? This doesn't have
anything to do with Ann, does it?"

Nothing studied the ground some more, stirring the pine
needles with the toe of his sneaker. "I was kind of hoping

you knew. I'm afraid she'll try to follow us. She came and told Christian yesterday—" Nothing swallowed, glanced at Steve, blinked several times. His eyes looked huge in the half-light. "Forget it," he said. "Mostly I just came to tell you goodbye. I'm sorry things turned out like they did. I wish they could have been different. But I'm with my family now." He slipped his arms around Ghost's neck and quickly kissed Ghost's cheek with cold chapped lips. Then he turned away.

"Wait!" Ghost snatched at a thin black-clad arm. Nothing looked back, his face wary, half-hidden in shadow.

"It scares me, Nothing." Ghost pulled his hair over his face. "But I need to know. What are they? *What are you?*"

"I think you know." Nothing stepped back and gave them a wide smile. On any other face so young it would have been a sunny, angelic smile. But on Nothing's face it was wrong, so wrong that at first Ghost could not grasp why. Then he knew. Most of Nothing's front teeth had been filed to sharp points.

"What did Ann say to Christian?" Ghost whispered.

"I didn't want to tell you," said Nothing. "She's going to have a baby. She says it's Zillah's baby."

Ghost could not speak. After a moment he had to close his eyes. When he opened them, Nothing had faded back into the woods. Without the glow of the jack-o'-lantern to mark his path, he disappeared quickly, melting like a black wraith into the shadows between the trees.

Ghost turned to look at Steve. Steve had pulled a plant out of the ground and was using its leaves to wipe pumpkin pulp off his face.

"Are you okay?" Ghost asked.

"Huh? Yeah. Why shouldn't I be?" Steve looked at the leaves he'd been wiping his face with, held them up to the moonlight. "Poison oak. It figures. Shit."

"You won't get it," Ghost told him.

"How do you—" Steve slapped his knees. "Okay. Okay. I won't get it. Do we have to wait till somebody slings a rotting corpse at us, or can we go over to R.J.'s now?"

"Sure. We can go to R.J.'s." If Steve wanted to pretend he

hadn't heard Nothing's parting words, if Steve had refused to
notice that mouthful of sharpened teeth, Ghost wasn't going
to force it. It would catch up to Steve sooner or later, and
then all hell would break loose.

The lights were bright at the party. Terry Buckett answered the door wearing a pair of long johns with psychedelic peace signs painted all over them. He took one look at
Steve, pointed over his shoulder, and said, "The keg's that
way."

They found it out on the back porch in a garbage can full
of ice. As Ghost was pumping it, R.J. caught up with them.
His Dracula makeup was smudged on his nose where he
kept pushing his glasses up. "We're having a vampire film
festival," he explained, supporting himself against the porch
railing. "They're just finishing up *Near Dark*, that one's real
cool. You missed *The Lost Boys*."

"Fuckin' shame," said Steve darkly, draining half of his
first beer.

R.J. put a dripping cup into Ghost's hand. He sipped it,
tasting the tingling foam and the barley funk and something
metallic. Something metallic and red— No. The beer was
clear, white and golden, pure. He swallowed that mouthful
in a hurry. Then he drank off the rest of the cup.

Ghost sat on the floor and drank two more cups of beer.
Vamp was on now. All the vampires seemed to be aged, running a honky-tonk joint, the remainders of a glorious race.
He tried to talk to Monica when she walked by, but she was
dressed as the Raven and would only say "Nevermore."

He was about to go in search of some fruit juice when
Steve loomed in front of him, swaying slightly, reeking of
beer, his T-shirt stained with it. Steve grabbed Ghost's hands
and pulled him up. "Let's go."

They staggered out to the T-bird, Steve leaning most of his
weight on Ghost. When Steve tried to get behind the wheel,
Ghost said, "Uh-uh. I'm driving."

Steve put the keys in his hand without argument. Ghost
slid in and cranked up the engine. Beside him, Steve lay
against the passenger door, eyes slitted, staring up at the
night sky.

Ghost reached over and touched Steve's shoulder. "Steve. Hey, Steve. Where we going?"

"New Orleans," said Steve without looking away from the stars. "Drive."

23

"She's going to *what*?" said Molochai when Christian told them.

"*Again*?" said Twig. "What would we do with a baby?"

"We could eat it," Molochai offered.

Zillah grimaced. "Eat my baby! Are you mad?" After a moment's reflection he added, "Nothing and I might eat it, but you couldn't have any."

"Zillllaaaah . . ."

"*Pleeeeeezzze*? . . ."

"Not one drop. Not one pink sugar drop."

They might eat it, too, thought Christian. *They just might, even if it was Nothing's half-brother or -sister*. The idea did not strike Christian as particularly immoral, but it made him sad. He stood silently before them, considering Zillah. Those eyes, and the perfect pink lips twisted in amusement or disgust, and his entourage clustered around him.

For a moment Christian almost disliked them. Not Nothing, but the other three. He hated their insouciance, their cheerful cruelty. They didn't care about the girl. Their time in Missing Mile was done. They would go on to New Orleans and carry on their never-ending party without a backward glance. It did not matter to them that another girl's belly would swell with a malignant child, a child that would eventually rip her open and bleed her dry.

"You must get rid of it," he had told her. He'd been out behind the trailer cutting the last roses of the season. The bushes were dry now, brown and gnarled. Somehow he would have to stretch his income from the bartending job to pay the rent on the trailer and buy the sweets and liquor that the others throve upon.

Nothing had already offered to look for a job; he was good-hearted, but what place would hire a boy who looked so young and so strange? And Molochai, Twig, and Zillah were used to their luxurious nomadic life, travelling from city to city, living off the blood and money of their kills. But in Missing Mile there were no wealthy victims. There were only drifters and bastard children and travellers who had lost their way.

As he was cutting the last rose, a great frothy pink-orange thing whose veined petals curled delicately into red at the edges, the girl Ann came up behind him and touched his sleeve. Christian had seen her near the trailer before, trying to look through the windows, tugging at the doors of the black van. He had not known precisely what had happened between her and Zillah. When she told him, Christian's heart sank. Had Zillah grown up not at all in fifteen years? Had he never heard of *condoms*?

"I'll have a beautiful baby," she said. "With green, green eyes."

"It will kill you," he told her. "They'll leave you and you'll be alone, and it will kill you." He turned to face her, the huge rose in one hand, a rusty pair of scissors in the other. "Listen to me. You have to get rid of it. You *must*."

"Why?"

Christian met her eyes. Ann's eyes danced like spiders; they gleamed, empty of reason. She had not looked that way a month ago at the Sacred Yew. Already Zillah's essence was infecting her as it had infected Jessy.

He could tell her the truth. That Zillah was of another race, a race whose seed was bloody poison. That Zillah's baby would rip her apart inside and she would die as Jessy had died fifteen years ago, her thighs sticky with blood, her eyes rolled back silver-rimmed in her head. Yes, he might tell her all that. She was already mad enough to believe it. But if she knew what danger she was in, she might tell someone else. She might convince someone. And that would endanger Nothing, would endanger Zillah and the others. The young, the fine, the fire of a dying race. No. He could not betray them.

"You must get rid of it because he will leave you," Christian said lamely. "You'll be alone."

"I'll follow them wherever they go," Ann said. "I'll follow Zillah."

Her hair hung loose about her face, straggling, bright as flames. She was just a girl. A girl like Jessy, a human girl who should have a life without fear or pain caused by the whims of others. A girl who should have healthy children that she could live to care for. Babies she could nurse at her breast; babies that would not feed upon the tissue of her innards.

Christian knew he could not let the others leave him a second time. He could not watch that black van disappear down the road and wonder whether he would ever see it again. If they left Missing Mile, he would follow them. They would protect him from Wallace Creech. And if Ann followed too, perhaps he could convince her. Perhaps there would be some way to keep her from giving birth to another of Zillah's beautiful, deadly children.

"They'll go to New Orleans," he told her. "To the French Quarter." There; it was done. She might follow them; she might find them. She might not.

Christian turned away toward the trailer. He did not look back at the girl who stood by the rosebushes, the girl with funereal black lace tied in her bright hair. The girl who even though there was no physical resemblance, none at all, reminded him so strongly of Jessy fifteen years ago.

The same bewitched light shone in her eyes.

24

After they left the Halloween party, Ghost drove to Ann's house. Her Datsun was not parked in the driveway, but her father's red Buick was. Ghost didn't want to talk to Simon Bransby, not tonight, not about all this. And he could see that there was no light on in Ann's corner room.

Ghost swung past the Greyhound station over by the old Farmer's Hardware store. Ann's car was in the parking lot, but it already looked abandoned. The bus station was dark; no one sat on the lone bench out back. The southbound night bus came through Missing Mile every night at 10:05. It was long gone.

Ghost drove back to Burnt Church Road, grabbed their toothbrushes and Steve's bag of pot, and pointed the car out of town. He could think of nothing better to do. New Orleans, Steve had said, and Ann was probably headed there too.

Steve slumped against the passenger door, his breathing deep, heavy, exhausted. He was in no shape to answer questions. So Ghost took N.C. 42 south out of Missing Mile without looking over his shoulder. He knew he would be back. He and Steve could travel anywhere, but they always came back to Missing Mile.

The road made him as nervous as a racehorse. He wasn't good at driving, not like Steve. Driving was in Steve's blood. But the highway billowed and writhed before Ghost's eyes; stars glittered in the rearview mirror; the moon dodged shreds of pale cloud. The night was dark, then bright, then dark again.

Halloween night. A bad time to travel. What might be keeping pace with the T-bird? What strange eyes might mark the car's passage? Ghost kept the windows cranked tight shut, kept his nostrils flared for trouble.

As he drove past Miz Catlin's place, Ghost saw a lone candle flickering in the front window. Miz Catlin knew enough to stay inside tonight, her small fire warming the good spirits and keeping the bad ones away.

With a longing that ached in his bones, Ghost wished he were asleep between the crisp faded sheets of Miz Catlin's guest bed. He had spent so many childhood nights in that bed, napping, waking and tossing, twining his fingers in his hair and trying to hear the quiet conversations of Miz Catlin and his grandmother in the next room. Sometimes they spoke of things he couldn't understand, things that frightened him, names he could never recall when clear sunlight spilled through the windowpanes the next morning. Astaroth. He thought he remembered that. Or was it asafoetida? Sometimes, as old women will, they spoke of recipes and grown children and husbands strayed or buried. Still Ghost had listened rapt, turning over each word he could hear, keeping it like a jewel-colored pebble or a broken blue eggshell somewhere in his mind.

And sometimes . . . sometimes they spoke of him. At those times he thought his ears would pull loose from his head and fly away, so hard did they stretch to listen.

"He won't ever have it easy, Deliverance. The boy's gift is just too damn strong." That was Miz Catlin. She meant him, Ghost. The gift was the things he knew, or felt, without having any way to know. The things he couldn't tell just anybody, the things his grandmother always understood.

"I know it, Catlin. Nobody with the gift ever has an easy time, 'specially not when they're as open-hearted as my Ghost. Let that boy try to tell a lie and his forehead turns to glass." That was his grandmother, her voice softer than Miz Catlin's, her words softer too. "But I trust him to use it well. He'll never hurt anybody with his gift." Her voice had low-

ered then. "The only thing I worry about is, his gift might
hurt *him*. He'll spend his life feeling everybody else's pain.
Takes a lot of strength not to lay down and be crushed under
that weight."

Ghost jerked awake and tossed his head. He was being
lulled to sleep by voices from the past, by the night road, by
the spirits drifting between midnight and dawn. As he drove
past the graveyard outside Corinth, Ghost saw the humped
stones palely gleaming, the rags of mist that rose from the
cold ground.

He felt the hair at the back of his neck trying to stand up.
Lie down and be quiet, he told it. Those graves weren't dangerous. Even if spirits roamed there, they were just people.
Frightened, maybe, because their bodies were rotting and
drying and dusting away. Frightened and maybe even angry.
But still people. They couldn't hurt him or Steve. Not like
some things. Some of the monsters were alive.

Ghost thought of Miles Hummingbird. Did Miles roam
tonight? Did his spirit soar on the night winds like the roar of
the ocean? And would Miles have to return to his grave at
dawn, summoned back by some rooster crowing, some train
whistle blasting far away in the cold morning? Ghost tried to
send his mind into the night, out where Miles or Miz Deliverance might hear him. *Help me, my dear dead,* he thought.
*Help me stay awake. Help Steve wake up without a really bad
hangover. Let him want to drive because I don't know how
much longer I can keep this steamboat on the road. Help me if
you can.*

It didn't work, not right then. But an hour later, as U.S. 1
took them down into South Carolina, Steve unfolded himself,
groaned, and said, "What the fuck are you doing driving my
car?"

Thank you, thought Ghost as he went to sleep, his head
leaning against the window, his eyes blessedly shut. *Thanks.
And good night.*

Speeding away from midnight, Steve felt good. Good because they had found a truck stop where four cups of bitter
black coffee had sent his hangover to headache heaven. Good

because he'd tuned in to an FM station that played classic rock all night long. He sang along with the old tunes loud enough to keep himself awake, soft enough to let Ghost sleep.

But good most of all because they were on the road again. He was not thinking about Ann, or green-eyed Zillah (that little jerkoff, Steve's mind automatically subtitled him), or even New Orleans. He was not brooding over the way the last few months had turned to shit. He was not thinking at all. He was only singing along with the radio, letting the cold wind whip his hair across his eyes, letting the road wash his soul clean. Heaviness fell away with each mile he left behind. He felt weightless. God, he could road-trip forever. He knew what lay at the end of the road: more of Ann's bullshit, more fury, more pain. But the highway was home.

After a while something began to nibble at his happiness. *I've got maybe thirty-five bucks on me,* he figured. *My last paycheck from Whirling Disc, less beer money. And Ghost never carries any cash. We're gonna need money soon.*

Okay, but there was a way to solve that problem. Dangerous. Fuckin' renegade business. But so easy, if he could pull it off.

Steve started scanning the roadside. Used-car dealerships, orange sodium lights glinting on rows and rows of souped-up wrecks, making them look like cars in an old black-and-white movie. A railyard, tracks crossing and diverging like some tangled puzzle of wood and iron, boxcars casting long square shadows. There, up ahead—that was what he wanted. A ramshackle little gas station, closed down for the night. And outside, the dim glow of a Coke machine. The old-fashioned kind. The kind you could jimmy. Steve pulled up in front of the store and killed the lights.

"Don't," Ghost said thickly.

"Go back to sleep," Steve told him. "It'll buy our beer in the French Quarter."

He fished through the mess in the backseat and found his trusty coat hanger, knelt, and fed it into the coin-return slot. It was about to catch . . . there . . . he could feel it nearly catch. If the Coke machine had been a girl, Steve would have been getting ready to make it come like a banshee.

"That's it, baby," he muttered, and then something with a lot of weight behind it slammed into his back. Pain flared deep in his kidneys. Steve lost his balance and spilled backward into the dust of the parking lot.

"Looks like we got us a trick-or-treater."

Steve twisted to meet the two most emptily gleeful pairs of eyes he had ever seen. These two made Zillah's thug friends look like geniuses . . . or at least subgeniuses. They had sloping foreheads and tattoos that wound down ropy-muscled arms and spread dark tendrils over the backs of grimy hands. One of them was broad-chested with features that seemed too large and sensual for his face—a redneck Dionysus. The other was scrawny; his colorless hair fell straight and fine from under a mesh baseball cap stitched with the Coors logo, a trusty asshole indicator if there ever was one. In one knuckly fist he gripped a hammer.

He grinned at Steve, showing crooked little teeth. "We got anything for trick-or-treaters, Willy?"

Willy laughed. The sound made up in malice what it lacked in humor. "Shit, I didn't save no candy. You got any candy, Charlie?"

"Yeah." Charlie swung the hammer. It whistled past Steve's head, inches away. "I got me a big jawbreaker right here."

"Fuck off," he said, struggling to his knees. "I wasn't bothering you." His voice sounded thin and scared. He cursed it.

"Now will you listen to this?" Willy's face was suddenly the picture of shocked innocence. "Asshole was fixin' to rip off my daddy's Coke machine in the parking lot of my daddy's store. And he thinks we ought fuck off and leave him be. What you say, Charlie?"

"*Uh*-uh." Charlie let loose a high, toneless giggle. "I think we better beat the shit out of him."

The gas station didn't belong to Willy's daddy. With a sudden helpless fury, Steve was sure of that. They were carrying a *hammer*, for fuck's sake. Why would you carry a hammer around a deserted gas station in the middle of the night? To bash in the skull of some punk city kid you caught ripping off the Coke machine? Not likely. To bust a window, maybe? To pound hell out of the cash register? *Bingo,* Steve congratulated himself. *You win the prize. Willy's gonna give you the Golden Ticket.*

Steve sputtered laughter. It came with no warning, hysterical and beyond control. He leaned against the Coke machine and tried to catch his breath, but he couldn't help it. Willy was going to give him the Golden Ticket, and bang-bang, Charlie's silver hammer was going to come down upon his head. Then maybe they could make him *sqeeeeeeal* like a pig.

Steve knew he'd better stop laughing, knew things might get real unpleasant around here if he kept laughing, but he couldn't quit. Not until Charlie's fist smashed into his cheekbone and the sole of Willy's boot came down on his ribs. Or maybe it was Willy punching him in the face and Charlie stomping his ribs. It didn't matter.

He grabbed a thick jeans-clad ankle and yanked. Charlie went down. The hammer flew out of his hand and thunked into the dust six feet away. Steve smelled shit. It was masked under the smell of cheap beer and redneck sweat, but it was shit all right. He thought of saying *Pardon me, but which one of you stepped in shit?* and snorted more laughter, crazy laughter, through the pain in his face and his ribs.

Willy was coming for him again. He brought his legs up and pistoned both boot heels into the greasy crotch of Willy's jeans. Willy doubled up with only a loud grunt; apparently he was more of a man than Charlie. But here came good old Charlie again, and he'd got his silver hammer back, could you say amen and hallelujah, and he was raising it high above his head. Steve wondered briefly whether maybe he should have had his soul saved after all.

And then Ghost shot into the fray, screaming like a mad thing and swinging his own hammer, the one Steve always kept under the front seat of the car. Ghost's hammer connected with Charlie's elbow, and Steve heard something crack. He just managed to get out from under Charlie's hammer as Charlie dropped it, howling and clutching his elbow.

Steve grabbed the stray hammer, rolled, and came up on his feet. Now he and Ghost both had hammers. They faced the rednecks, keeping each other covered.

The rednecks didn't seem like much of a threat now, cringing back against the wall of the building. Willy's hands were still cupped tenderly around his crotch. Charlie's right arm dangled uselessly; his face had gone the color of bad cheese. They stared at Steve and Ghost like cornered possums, too stupid to be really scared, but wary.

"We ought to bash your cracker brains in," Steve told them.

"But we're not," Ghost said hurriedly. "We're just gonna get back in our car and leave. Don't make any fast moves." He brandished his hammer at them.

Steve waved his too, but he was beginning to feel he had lost control of the situation. He edged around the front end of the car and pulled his door open. Out of the corner of his eye he saw Ghost doing the same. They threw themselves in and both doors slammed at once. Steve thumbed the lock button. Ghost was ranting at him. "Hurry, *hurry*, let's get the hell out of here before they stomp both our asses—"

The engine started on the first try. Steve gunned the car across the parking lot and had the satisfaction of seeing Willy and Charlie scrabble out of his way like crabs in boiling water. He thought he might have clipped one of them, hoped so. Then the gas station was dwindling in the red glow of the taillights. He glanced at Ghost, who was sprawled backward in his seat, half-grinning. He thought he could see Ghost's heart pounding through the thin cloth of his T-shirt. "You just saved my ass," Steve told him. It was a rare moment of awkwardness between them. "I owe you one."

"Wait till we get to New Orleans," Ghost said. "You can buy me a bottle of Night Train." His hand crept across the seat, found Steve's hand and held it tight. Steve thought he could feel a message flowing into him through Ghost's warm fingers: *You get yourself killed, Steve, and that's it. That's the end of the game for me too. I know you're bummed out and you think I'm the only person in the world you can trust, but I need you too. So you better keep your ass safe. I need you too.*

* * *

Sometime closer to dawn—but not too close, not dangerously so—a battered silver car drove along the same road
that Steve and Ghost had left behind an hour ago. A Bel Air.
Zillah hadn't wanted to wait for Christian to gas up his car
and give Kinsey Hummingbird his notice, so they had all
arranged to meet in the French Quarter the following night.

Christian had forgotten to turn his headlights on. For him
the road was lit well enough by moonlight and the faint glitter of the stars. And there were no other cars on the highway,
not this late at night.

At least there had been none. But as he rounded a sharp
curve, a pickup truck screeched out of a side road onto the
highway behind him. Its headlights burned a blinding bar
into his rearview mirror. Its horn blared as the driver saw
Christian's car too late, and braked too hard. Then the
pickup was skidding off the road, smashing down a short
embankment, rolling over and over. At last the truck came to
rest against the trunk of a massive pine. The windshield was
cracked, blood-smeared.

Christian pulled off the road and left his car. He picked his
way carefully down the embankment. The passengers in the
pickup were dead, or nearly so; he could smell that. There
was no oily tang of gasoline, no smell of heat; the truck would
not catch fire. There was only the heavy scent of blood, rich
and laced with alcohol.

Christian knew the accident had been his fault. After all,
he had left his lights off. But he had not meant to. And the
truck had been going much too fast.

And he was hungry.

The truck's passenger must have died instantly. His features were smeared across his face in a blur of blood and
bone studded with broken glass. The driver was still alive.
His body lay twisted across the seat, his scrawny legs pinned
somewhere beneath the dashboard, but he was conscious.
Blood soaked from under his mesh cap, beaded his colorless
hair. The driver moaned when he saw Christian, and when
Christian bent to the passenger's torn throat, he tried to
scream. But he could not open his mouth. His chin had

struck the steering wheel with crushing force, and his jaw-
bones ground together, pulverized.

As Christian lapped the dying-blood off Charlie's lips and
chin and throat, Willy could only watch.

25

Everybody else had a car to drive, or a bunch of loud companions, or at least, like Christian, a radio to play all night, brave rock and roll occasionally exploding into bursts of static, whispering in voices that almost formed words.

Ann's decrepit Datsun would never make it all the way to New Orleans; she had no car, no companion, and she had sold her Walkman to another girl at work so she could see R.E.M. play at Duke University last month. She couldn't even listen to her Cocteau Twins tapes on her way to meet her love.

By the time she got home that night, she knew she was going to New Orleans. It had been easy enough to stand there in the trailer yard talking to the tall bartender, telling him she would follow Zillah anywhere. But when it came right down to going—well, that had to be thought out for a while.

At work, waiting tables in the Spanish restaurant whose gold flocked wallpaper and red pile carpet passed for elegance in the North Carolina sticks, she thought it out. By the time she left, she was able to phrase a note to the kitchen manager explaining that there was a sudden illness in her family and could the balance of her pay please be forwarded to Ann Bransby-Smith, General Delivery, New Orleans, Louisiana. She didn't really expect to see that money. Maybe when Zillah saw how she truly loved him, he would provide for her; the purple silk lining of his coat spoke of wealth.

She had thought it out carefully, but she was still scared by her decision. Leave Missing Mile? She had never done that, not even to go to college. After high school graduation she hadn't applied to any schools, telling herself she was taking a year off to concentrate on painting. Steve and Ghost were going to State. If they thought college was worth anything, then she might go. But the year turned into two. Steve and Ghost got disillusioned and came back home, fell back into their dream of being rock stars.

She couldn't talk to Steve now, didn't think she ever would again. But there was still Eliot, only ten miles down the highway, who knew nothing about her night with Zillah outside the Sacred Yew. She could see him any day after work. She admitted to herself that she hadn't wanted to see him much lately. He wouldn't smoke pot and was a little shocked that she did. He even wanted her to quit smoking her unfiltered Camels: "Can't you at least switch to one of the low-tar brands?" he'd asked, and hadn't understood why Ann burst out laughing. Eliot couldn't even outdrink her. What kind of man got sleepy after drinking three Lite beers? The only thing Eliot really liked to drink was his loathsome gin-and-Cokes.

She couldn't pretend that Eliot mattered anymore. He had tried to make Ann jealous last weekend, telling her his ex-wife was coming to town. "She's got no place to stay," Eliot had said innocently, "Do you think I should offer to put her up here?" Ann didn't give a shit. She had not stayed in Missing Mile for Eliot. She had not stayed for Steve. She had stayed because of her father. Simon's strangeness had kept her here, kept her worried enough to postpone her life. Now it was the final thing that drove her away. If Simon found out she was pregnant . . . well, he would think she was stupid. And Simon did not suffer fools gladly.

But none of those men mattered now. Steve, Eliot, Simon —they were just names receding into her past, names with none of the susurrant magic of *Zillah*. She whispered his name to herself constantly. It was like the smooth taste of whipped cream, like a deep tongue kiss.

She drove out to Violin Road, but the trailer was dark. The

black van and the silver Bel Air were gone, and there was an air of emptiness about the trailer: already it looked as if no one had lived there for a long time. They were on their way to New Orleans, then. Soon she would be too.

Simon's car wasn't there either, when she drove home. She wanted to see him one more time, but she was afraid to. This was how it had to be. She began to pack. What should she put in the one small bag she would be able to carry? She wished she could take the new series of paintings she had begun. All of them were unfinished; all were of faces with sly pink smiles and iridescent green eyes. But those would have to stay. She wouldn't need them in New Orleans. Instead she packed her black lace underwear and two pairs of old pink cotton panties. Her toothbrush, her cigarettes, her little wooden pipe and her film can, which contained three pinches of marijuana she'd cadged off Terry. She might need to sneak a toke in some bus station bathroom between here and New Orleans. Somewhere in the swamps.

There were a few crumbly leaves left in the bottom of her bowl, so she sneaked a toke now. It put her at loose ends. She stood staring around at her possessions, suddenly feeling unable to leave anything behind. Her mourning hat with the little black veil, her record collection. The R.E.M. poster on the wall stared down at her. Stipe's eyes were like loss. Peter Buck's were like dark fire. How could she leave her posters, her clothes, her canvases and paint box?

Frenziedly she snatched at a black lace scarf and tied it around her throat. That, at least, would go with her. She put on a string of ebony beads, a gray sweatshirt, a skirt with a torn silk lining. She was caught in the mirror, adding lipstick and silver eyeshadow (in just eighteen hours or so she might see her true love again; she must look beautiful), when she heard Simon at the front door. She snatched off her beret and with the side of her foot shoved the suitcase under the bed.

Ann heard him stepping carefully through the mess in the living room. Picking his way through the piles of books and newspapers, emphasizing how untidy the room was. *He* dragged the books off the shelves, *he* read the newspapers, but she was supposed to keep the house picked up. That was one of her duties. Simon was very big on duties. Sometimes she wondered whether he didn't strew his things around just to make the absence of liquor bottles more obvious. He said he had not taken a drink for five years, six months, and twenty days, and Simon was never wrong.

Here he was at the doorway, small and spare. His hair, uncombed for days, flared wildly about his head. It was thick and snow-white; his skin was almost phosphorescent in the gloom of the hallway. In the summer Ann worried about her father's health. He had come over from Dorchester twenty years ago, but the hot, humid summers here still made him droop. He was like some glacial plant whose fragile structure was supported by ice crystals; his hair went limp, he perspired from the dark bags beneath his eyes. But in the winter he exuded a kind of mad vitality.

Suddenly she was sure he would be able to read her mind, or look through the mattress and see the suitcase beneath it. He would begin to argue with her, calmly, reasonably. But his argument would be slippery. There would be no tail end she could grab onto so that she might argue back. In ten minutes she would feel as if she were trying to wind up earthworms on a spoon. In half an hour she would feel as if she were trying to drive a nail through a blob of mercury. In an hour or two or three, he would have her talked out of the whole stupid notion. She would not go to the Greyhound station, would not catch the all-night express to New Orleans. She would never see Zillah again.

Simon had talked her out of so many things.

But all he said now was "Good evening, daughter."

As always, the form of address half-annoyed her and half-warmed her. "Hi, Simon," she said.

"Your day was . . . ?"

"Rawther shitty."

He nodded and allowed himself the slant of a smile. Ann's voice had as much of a Carolina twang as her mother's had had, but she knew it amused him when she imitated his accent. "As was mine. I dissected three toads today. There was no change in any of them."

Simon had taught once, so the story went, at one of the
Great Universities of the World. Ann wasn't sure where. He
hinted at Germany, France, the United Kingdom. Now re-
tired, he spent the days in his study trying to change the
chemical composition of various types of blood. Until recently he had used his own, and sometimes hers; once Steve,
drunk off his ass, had offered a sample.

But lately Simon had been getting into animals. Ann had
pitched a crying fit the day she found him cutting up the
lusterless carcass of Sarah Jane, a black-and-white kitten
she'd been feeding on the back steps. Since then, as far as
she knew, he had stuck to using mice from the Woolworth's
in Corinth and toads he caught in the vacant lot next door.
He injected the toads with varying amounts of his own blood
and sometimes with liquid LSD. Mostly they jumped around
a lot.

Over the rims of his glasses Simon looked at her oddly.
"Were you thinking of going out tonight, Ann?"

Involuntarily she glanced at the space beneath her bed.
The bed skirt hid the suitcase, but again she felt sure that her
father could see through mere cloth, that he knew her inten-
tions. "I might go down to the Yew," she said.

"You aren't going to see Steve, are you? After the way he
dishonored you?" She had told her father only that Steve had
slapped her. For once, with rare sensitivity, he had not
pressed the issue.

"No, Simon," she said. "I'm not going to see Steve."

"Or his peculiar friend?"

"Simon, Ghost isn't—" She stopped. There was no point
saying Ghost wasn't peculiar; that wasn't what she meant
anyway. "Ghost never did anything to me," she finished.

"I wish you wouldn't go out tonight, daughter."

She looked at him. "Are you requesting or ordering?"

"I have your best interests in mind," he said frostily.

Ann rubbed her wrists. At sixteen she had come home
roaring drunk one night. Simon was still drinking then too,
but that didn't make him any more compassionate. He
trussed her to her own bedposts with rope and kept her tied
there for seven hours, until she pissed herself and begged

him to forgive her stupidity. The memory of the chafing had never quite gone away.

"So I'm not supposed to go out tonight," she said. "I'm supposed to stay home and wait on you." Defeat welled in her. Why did Simon have to get his way every damn time?

Maybe he didn't.

She looked up at him again, this time trying to make her eyes submissive, to wipe away the frigid hurt from his face. "I'm sorry, Daddy." That would get him for sure. "Had a long day at work. Why don't you go read the paper? Or your library books? I'll fix us a pot of coffee."

Simon was touched. He came across the room to kiss her forehead. She had to stop herself from flinching back, sure he would know what was up when he tasted the sweat at her hairline. But he straightened and gave her another slanted smile. "You may rest," he said. "I will make the coffee."

No, dammit! That wouldn't work. She put on her sweetest smile. The taste of vomit rose in her throat. "Let me do it," she said. "I know you want to see the paper. There's another article about the disappearances."

That got him. Simon had followed the disappearances with a weird avidity, considering it was only a Violin Road rug-rat and a couple of bums that had been killed. Maybe he had been dissecting them, too.

As soon as Simon left the room, Ann dug through the top drawer of her dresser until she found a little plastic bottle. She opened it and shook the contents into her cupped hand. Several tiny pills, wafer-thin, each with a V-shaped cutout in the center. The Valium dated back to her mother's last nervous illness. Ann had stolen it out of the medicine cabinet a year ago. She had taken almost all the pills on various sleepless nights; only these were left. She hoped there was still some decaf in the freezer.

"There you go," she said a few minutes later, setting a yellow ceramic mug on the arm of Simon's chair. "It came out a little strong, so I put in a lot of sugar. I hope it's not too sweet."

"I'm sure it will be lovely," he said.

She held her breath as he took the first sip, but through

the steam his face registered only tired contentment. He might have been any father letting his daughter bring him a cup of coffee after a hard day's work. She still felt a little sad.

An hour later she kissed his lips lightly and locked the front door behind her. His breathing was a little irregular, and she tasted the sourness of coffee and tranquilizers on his mouth, but she would save a prayer and a curse for him when she got on the bus. No one could stop her from going to meet her true love now.

The Greyhound took her south, frosting her to the bone with its air-conditioning adjusted for the middle of August, not for this November night. As the bus lumbered away from the dark depot, Ann half-rose out of her seat, one hand on her suitcase, the other raised to stop the driver. *Wait,* she almost said. *Wait, I went a little crazy, let me out and I'll trade in my ticket and go back home, maybe Steve will take me back, maybe my father will welcome me home.*

But the bus lurched and toppled her back into her seat. Then they were bumping across the railroad tracks that led out of Missing Mile, and she saw an omen: far down the line, at some other junction, a pair of signal lights gleaming in the night.

They were green.

Bright green.

Like the color of her lover's eyes.

26

"This is the best goddamn food I ever ate," said Steve, digging a spoon into his third bowl of gumbo. They hadn't had much to eat on the road.

"Better than my cooking?" asked Ghost, hurt.

"Shit, Ghost, you can't eat mung bean sprouts and tofu *all* the time."

"That's good stuff," said Ghost. But the waitress put another bowl of gumbo in front of him, and he hunched over it, breathing the savory steam, his eyelids fluttering with pleasure. He stirred it and spooned up a mouthful. The flavors melted together on his tongue. He tasted the delicate meatiness of crab and shrimp, the green sassafras tang of filé, the soft blandness of okra. "This might be even better than soybean-mushroom loaf," he admitted when he had swallowed.

Back outside, agreeably full of gumbo and strong chicory coffee, they dodged the tourists on Bourbon Street and turned down a shady side street whose iron balconies were festooned with lush green hanging ferns and thousands of colored Mardi Gras beads. Soon the street turned into a narrow alley, and Ghost thought they'd gotten lost. Instead they suddenly found themselves in the cacophony of Jackson Square, with the silvery spires of St. Louis Cathedral looming up behind them and a panorama of portrait painters and street musicians spread before. In the middle of it all Andrew Jackson reared up on his horse, sour-faced and pigeon-spotted, challenging the giant magnolias that surrounded the square.

Ghost couldn't recall ever seeing a map of New Orleans, but he knew the Mississippi River curved around the city in a giant crescent shape, like a cradling hand. He could smell the water and feel its throbbing current in his nerves. But he knew about the miasma that could sometimes hang over such a powerful body of water, especially in such lush, humid weather. It was as if the water vapor created a palpable feeling of despair. His grandmother had told him of a man she'd known who stood on a spot in England by the sea and heard a voice urging him to jump to his death on the rocks a hundred feet below. Later the man found out that several suicides had occurred from that spot. Considering the state he and Steve were in after driving all night, if they saw a large expanse of water, they might be tempted to take a swim.

They crossed the square and were soon deep in the Quarter again. The side street they were on did not look as well travelled as some of the others. The long shutters on either side of the doorway stoops hung crooked, their bright paint fading, and some of the cobblestones in the sidewalk were smashed to pieces. Steve's pace slowed as they passed a dark little bar, and he stared in longingly at the rows of bottles reflected in the mirror. "So what do we do now?" he asked Ghost. "You think they're here yet?"

Ghost closed his eyes and tried to send his mind out, tried to find something familiar, something young and lonely, something green-eyed and frightening. At last he opened his eyes and shook his head. "I can't tell. There's too much magic here. This place is too haunted. I can't separate it all."

Steve clawed at his hair. "Well *fuck it*, then! Let's just go back to that bar! Jesus, I thought you'd know what to do once we got here."

"Calm down," said Ghost. "I'm working on it. First we need a place to stay, I guess." Steve shrugged. *Okay,* thought Ghost, *if that's how it is, then that's how it is. Steve's tired and disgusted, I don't blame him. And maybe when we find Ann, she'll tell us to fuck off. But I'm not giving up yet.* "Come on," he said. "We'll ask around for a cheap place. Then maybe we can get a drink and decide what we're gonna do next."

They asked at several hotels and guest houses, starting with the modest ones and progressing to the seedy-looking dumps. There was nothing under fifty dollars a night, which would take just about all the cash they had. "Let's just stay up all night drinking," Steve suggested. Ghost was almost ready to agree with him when he saw a small wooden sign at the mouth of an alley: *MAGICK SHOPPE.* Below that, in smaller letters: *Arkady Raventon, Proprietor.*

Had he found his way here on purpose? Were such places like a magnet to that part of his mind? Ghost was too tired to care much; at any rate he would inquire here. He felt comfortable among practitioners of the occult; he had grown up around them. Maybe Arkady Raventon, Proprietor, would know of a cheap place to stay.

The shop was far back at the end of an alley, its door hidden behind shadows and garbage cans. "Creepy place," said Steve.

"You never know," Ghost told him. "There might be somebody here who can help us. You got a better idea?"

The alley was dim, and the inside of the shop seemed fully black. Steve and Ghost stood just inside the door for a moment, waiting for their eyes to adjust to the sudden absence of light. Slowly, pinpoints of fire began to appear in the darkness. They were candles, Ghost realized, scented votive candles, the only source of light in the shop. He smelled cinnamon, orange blossoms, nutmeg. And under the perfume of the candles, a smell like the back room of Miz Catlin's store. Spices and ancient dust, herbs and medicines, rust and wood and bone. He breathed in deep. His nose prickled. He sneezed once, twice, three times.

"Bless you," said a voice from within the darkness. "If your spirit has escaped your body, I promise not to capture it."

Only now did the darkness in the shop begin to soften. Ghost made out a figure standing behind a long glass counter, a small emaciated figure draped in white. The proprietor. Ghost saw sharp jutting cheekbones and hollow eyes, thin dark hair, spidery hands resting flat on the glass, bony fingers splayed.

"We just got into town," said Ghost. "We're looking for a place to stay a few days." He stepped forward. His feet felt too big, his arms long and awkward. The shop seemed too full of stuff, the walls leaning in toward the center of the room. There were shelves crammed with tiny bottles and boxes. There were books—at a glance he saw the *I Ching*, titles by Aleister Crowley and Robert Anton Wilson, crudely printed booklets promising charms for love and luck and revenge. He saw a rack of bejewelled metal daggers, jars full of herbs, candles, sticks of incense. At the back of the shop hung a curtain of colored plastic beads, and beyond that, more blackness.

"I am Arkady Raventon," said the proprietor. Ghost could see his face more clearly now, but could discern no hint of age. The skin was smooth, the eyes depthless dark pools. He took the hand Arkady offered, a hand whose bones would surely crumble if Ghost squeezed too hard, a hand with bones like the bones of lizards. The hand was dry, cool, the grip surprisingly strong. Ghost opened his mouth to introduce himself and Steve, who was lounging near the door looking skeptical.

But before he could speak, Arkady Raventon said, "You must be Miz Deliverance's son. Or is it grandson? Yes, grandson surely. Miz Deliverance's grandson."

Ghost heard Steve's sharp intake of breath. He met Arkady's limpid dark gaze. "How did you know?"

Arkady smiled. Was that a youthful smile, open and easy? Or was it the wise, humorless grin of an old, old man? "Everyone knows of Miz Deliverance," he said. "Everyone who has dealings with magick." Ghost could hear the *k*. "You may be too young to know it, child, but your grandmother is a legend from here to the mountains of West Virginia."

"I knew it," said Steve. "She *was* a witch."

"A white witch," Arkady told him. "A benign conjurer. And a fabled beauty too, in her youth. My own mother told me tales of her hair like yellow spun glass, her lips bowed

like the lips of the infant Christ, her clear unlying blue eyes.
I saw a silvery old photograph of Miz Deliverance once,
taken when she was about your age. Yes, she was a fabled
beauty. And you are her image, Ghost. Her very image."

"I didn't tell you my name," said Ghost.

Arkady smiled again. "Poor child! Did your grandmother
let you think you were the only sensitive in the world? I have
been to the other side, Ghost. I know things too. I know
you."

Steve came forward and stood next to Ghost, positioning
himself so that he shielded Ghost a little. "Wait a minute.
What the fuck are you talking about? What do you mean,
you've been to the other side?"

"I brought myself back from the dead," said Arkady
Raventon.

They went through the front room of Arkady's shop,
through the dimness, the smell of dust, cobwebs, herbs. They
went through the back room, where flowers and plaster
saints and bones (chicken bones, Ghost thought, though
Steve eyed them warily) were arranged on a small altar covered with a velvet dropcloth. On either side of the altar, pink
and black candles burned.

In a torrent of dust, Arkady swept aside a heavy velvet
curtain and led them up a narrow dark staircase. They
climbed, climbed, turned a corner. The staircase grew even
darker. Ghost had to feel for the stairs, placing his sneaker
carefully each time. He raised his hand to his face and wiggled his fingers. Before his eyes, five pale wavering sticks
danced; they might have been a trick of the darkness, an
afterimage of light. Still Arkady led them upward.

They went around another corner and now Ghost could
see a dim rectangle of light far above them. At last they came
to another velvet curtain; beyond that was daylight. Arkady
pulled the curtain aside. At the top of the stairs was a cozy
suite of rooms with clean white walls, large windows that let
in dazzling sunshine, hardwood floors gleaming golden.

Arkady showed them the rooms one after another. "That
one is mine. The small one belongs to two of my brother's

friends. And this"—indicating it with a grand sweep of his arm—"is the room where you may stay. If you so wish. I would not think of turning Miz Deliverance's grandson away from my door."

The room was simple. A clean mattress. A window high up on the rear wall. A square room. Four walls of equal length, four sensible walls to contain Ghost's thoughts, to keep out green-eyed wraiths and voices that might invade his mind at night. A place for Steve and him to whisper the nights away, snatch a few troubled hours of sleep, then go out and do whatever it was they had come to New Orleans to do.

"It looks okay to me," he said, and waited for Steve to argue. Steve wouldn't want to stay here in a room above a voodoo shop given to them like a gift by a creepy little proprietor who claimed to have known Ghost's grandmother, or to have heard of her. Steve would be suspicious, cynical, probably spooked, though he wouldn't want to admit that last one. But maybe Steve was exhausted from being on the road, or maybe he wanted a drink so badly that he would agree to anything, or maybe he just didn't give a damn anymore.

He only sighed and let his long body sag against the doorframe as he said, "Whatever you think. We'll take it."

"You said you brought yourself back from the dead," Ghost reminded Arkady as they finished descending the stairs. Behind him, Ghost heard Steve mutter something, but he ignored it.

Arkady drew himself up to his full spare height. "Perhaps I spoke too soon." The hem of his white robe shushed against the floor, raised a cloud of dust around his bony ankles.

"No, Mr. Raventon. I'd really like to hear about it."

"Arkady," said Arkady absently. His eyes had gone distant. He led them into the back room of the shop and stood beside the altar, stroking its corner.

Ghost's gaze wandered over the wooden framework, the dropcloth of dark sapphire velvet. He saw things he had not noticed before: intricate enamel charms, little scrolls of parchment, an inverted wooden cross bristling with nails.

Arkady's dry, faintly foreign voice brought him back to

attention. "It was cold in Paris that winter. As cold as the moon. As cold as loneliness. As cold as the kiss that killed me."

His eyes flicked to Ghost's, to Steve's. Ghost's were wide open, a little scared; he was picking up a barrage of feelings from Arkady, sorrow and fear and pain, but all of them were overlaid with the facile pleasure of a gifted actor performing a cherished role. Ghost didn't know what to make of it. Steve's eyes were hooded, wary, waiting for lies.

"Yes, my young friends. My poor young friends with your beautiful faces and your innocent dreams. You think love is sweet, that it can never hurt. But it was not the Parisian cold that killed me, not the wind in my bones, not the ice that rimed my heart. It was the kiss of a lover."

"The *kiss*?" Steve's voice was heavy with cynicism.

"Well, perhaps a bit more than just the kiss. But you must allow me my bit of romance." Sarcasm sharpened Arkady's voice, and Ghost shot Steve a warning look. Steve stared at the altar.

"So," Arkady went on, "this, ah, *kiss*—and the rest of my lover's body as well—was ripe with death. Ripe, and sweet as rotten fruit. Have you ever bitten into a rotten peach, either of you? A plum? A melon, perhaps? There is one moment of absolute, blissful, delicious sweetness before the taste of decay oozes over your tongue. That is how it was with my lover. And then the sickness rotted my lover away, and I had caught it too by that time, and I was alone. In Paris, in the winter. I was alone." A faint smile played about Arkady's lips.

"Have I mentioned my brother Ashley? No? Ashley was my younger brother. The beauty of the Raventons." Arkady laughed, a sound like wind among chips of crystal. "When I went to Paris, he stayed here, and I vowed that I would come back. I had to teach him, you see. I had to tell him all I knew of magick, of death and love and pain. Ashley was to be my apprentice. And I went to Paris, and the sickness took me. But I had vowed to Ashley that I would return. I had given him my word. And I would not break that."

Arkady's fingers strayed to the altar, toyed with the dark velvet dropcloth. "So before I died, I prepared. I had just enough time to find the things I needed. I sent for powders from Haiti, for potions from Guatemala. I procured the blood of an ancient man in the Rue aux Fers, the bones of a child in the catacombs of Montmartre.

"But at last I could search no longer. The sickness came and smiled its final soft dark smile at me, and my blood dried in my veins, and my eyeballs shrivelled. One morning before dawn I swallowed the concoction I had made, and I let the sickness take me. I felt its lips upon mine, its tongue lapping the last sour drop of spit from my mouth. I felt my life leave me. I felt my very selfness slip away; there was one instant in which I thought, *My God, now I am dead.*

"And then I was. And I awoke in the morgue of a Paris hospital, and when I stretched myself and smiled, one of the morgue attendants suffered a heart attack. Fortunately it was not fatal."

This time Arkady's laughter was like the clanging of a heavy door, a door of stone or steel, a door that would not be opened again for a very long time. "Then I made my way home to New Orleans, to keep my vow to Ashley. But, as any sad story should end, Ashley too had died, and had not come back. He would never be my apprentice. He would learn none of my secrets."

Ghost licked his lips nervously. His tongue was as dry as Arkady's must have been all through that long winter in Paris. "What happened to Ashley?" he asked.

Arkady knelt and flipped up the velvet dropcloth. His hands disappeared into the blackness beneath the altar. Shadows lapped at his knuckles, his wrists. Then he withdrew his hands.

Steve cursed and took a step backward. Ghost's eyes widened. Arkady was holding a perfect human skull, smooth and narrow, bleached to the golden-white of old ivory.

"Ghost and Steven," Arkady said, "meet my brother Ashley."

Later, Steve thought that if he hadn't known Ghost so well, he would have suspected Ghost of trying to win Arkady Raventon's heart at that moment. But of course Ghost was Ghost, the most uncalculating of all people, and what he did

next was just his nature—the pure crazy chemistry that
flowed between his brain and his heart and his soul. Never
mind how Arkady Raventon's eyes melted when Ghost
reached out his hands and said, "Can I hold him?"

Arkady put the skull into Ghost's hands. Ghost cradled it
carefully. Its surface was somehow devoid of temperature,
neither warm nor cold. He looked into the sockets of its eyes.
It was the only skull he had ever seen that didn't look as if it
were grinning. It just stared, and the arch of its teeth was
impassive, perhaps sad. He hoped Steve wouldn't make a
joke (Why can't Ashley Raventon go to parties anymore? Because he doesn't have any body to go with).

Ghost was very aware that here had once rested a brain, a
mind, an identity. A soul? Here had once been the cradle of a
life. He felt as if he were holding something alive and vulnerable. Something that depended on him not to drop it. If he
dropped it, it would surely crack. It might shatter. So Ghost
held the skull carefully, and then the feelings began to come,
as he had known they would. The essence of Ashley washed
over Ghost, and he lost himself in the depths of the skull's
empty eyes and let the impressions come.

A great loneliness. That was the first thing. Loneliness for
Arkady, wanting him, wanting his arrogance, his self-assur-
ance. Misgivings in spite of the desire to trust, and then the
conviction that Arkady was never coming back from Paris. A
void. A slew of things to fill the void—alcohol and opium,
lovers and new leather boots—but still the late nights crept
in, and Arkady was never coming back, never could,
never . . .

Then two familiar faces rose up before him, two pairs of
silvery eyes, a tangle of scarlet and yellow hair. They were
smiling at Ghost as they had the last time he'd seen them,
sitting astride the branch of the old oak in the clearing, on
that first night of strangeness. But this time their ripe mouths
were smeared with blood and other juices, with shreds of
tissue.

Ghost felt sick. A stupid panic welled up in his throat. But
he put the skull back in Arkady's hands and said only, "Your
brother was very handsome, wasn't he?"

"Not handsome. Beautiful. Did I mention that Ashley was the beauty of the Raventons?" Arkady pressed his lips to the top of the ivory cranium before continuing. "His hair was the color of burgundy, and he wore it long down his back, and it sparkled when he walked in the rain. His cheekbones were like razors—I always thought that I might cut my finger on one of them, but I never did." With the tip of one forefinger, Arkady touched the skull gently. "And those *eyes*—I used to say to him, 'O Ashley, those eyes, those *eyes*'—so dark and lost when they tilted up to me—like holes through time." He ran his finger around the edge of one of the empty eye sockets. "Those eyes—how they could slay me.

"But he died. Yes, I came back home and he had died. My Ashley. My brother. And now I am alone."

"Wait a second." Ghost's voice was halting; there was no doubt in it, only wonder. "You came home. You were there. Why didn't you bring *Ashley* back from the dead, too?"

Arkady held the skull a moment longer. Then he knelt and slid it back under the altar. He spent some time rearranging the velvet, brushing away dust, picking up some black feathers that had fallen from the altartop to the floor. When he stood, the joints of his knees cracked as loudly as shots in the silent room.

He met Ghost's eyes, and when he spoke, his voice was soft and even.

"Ashley didn't want to come back," he said.

"So was it vampires that killed your brother?" Ghost asked Arkady a little later. He figured it couldn't hurt to find out just what the twins were. Allowing for the existence of one kind of vampire, it seemed to follow that there might be other kinds, feeding on things other than blood. The existence of the first type scared him but didn't really surprise him. All his life he had been accepting as normal things that most people didn't even believe in.

They were sitting in the front room, talking over a decanter of sherry that Arkady had brought out from some recess of the shop. At least Ghost hoped it was sherry. It tasted funny, musty and a little sour, but Steve was putting it away with no problem. Ghost sipped from his first glass as Arkady poured Steve's third.

"Vampires?" Arkady's hand twitched; he almost dropped the bottle of sherry. He crossed himself twice, first upside down, then right side up. "Lord, child. Why do you want to know about vampires?"

"Jesus, Ghost," Steve muttered. Ghost glanced at him, but Steve was bent over the counter examining things in the glass case. Ball canning jars full of pale rubbery orbs, the lids labelled *CATS' EYES* and *TOADS' HEARTS* in a faded flowing script that must be Arkady's. Jewelry in the shape of silver pentagrams, ankhs, razor blades. A bowl of tiny, carefully molded clay skulls marked *50 CENTS APIECE*.

"I just wondered," Ghost said lamely.

Arkady looked hard at him. "Ghost. My child. It is difficult to imagine you 'just wondering' about anything." He clasped Ghost's hand between both of his. Ghost resisted the urge to pull his hand from the confines of that cool parched skin, all those tiny crackling bones. "You are a far more powerful sensitive than I could ever be. I pick up bits and pieces. I can hear thoughts when they are as pure and lucid as yours. And I can do little more than that. But *you*—you have an eye in your heart, Ghost. An eye that shines. An eye that feels."

"What the fuck is he babbling about?" Steve asked thickly.

I'm the only person in this room who isn't at least half-drunk, Ghost thought. He made himself drink more of his sherry, though the rancid taste lay upon his tongue like a sour old blanket. Sherry got worse with every sip, it seemed.

"I should never, never like to lose your favor," Arkady slurred. His hand was on Ghost's knee now. His fingers brushed skin through a hole in Ghost's sweatpants, and Ghost shivered at that dry touch. "But vampires, Ghost . . . vampires! They are not to be mentioned lightly. Not as in the cheap novels, the Hollywood legends. You think vampires are the Undead, the children of the night. You believe they rise from their graves when the moon hangs high, sucking the blood of virgins, melting into misty wraiths at sunrise, turning into bats and swooping away . . ."

"I don't think they turn into *bats*," said Ghost, and Steve surprised him by saying, "Me neither."

Arkady ignored them. "You see, Ghost child, the myths are wrong. And that very wrongness makes the creatures all the more dangerous. They are not undead. They have never died. Some of them never do, or not for hundreds upon hundreds of years. They are a separate race—or races. There are those who suck blood, those who suck souls, those who feed on the pain of others. Some of them can walk among us, free in the sunlight. Some of them are able to live as human beings from day to day, from year to year. Of course, they must move about like nomads, because after a point they do not age. They are beautiful, and they stay beautiful. And no one must notice. So they move, and they live among us, and then one day—"

"One day—BOOM," Steve said.

Arkady and Ghost turned to look at him. He grinned rather humorlessly at them and filled his glass again, slopping sherry onto the counter.

"Then one day," Arkady continued smoothly, "they discover their particular hunger. Some may live for ten, twenty, even thirty years before the lust comes upon them. Some can digest nothing but blood, and must be fed upon it from the time of their birth. But the hunger always comes."

Timidly, Ghost interrupted. "How come you know so much about them?"

"I have known vampires of all sorts," said Arkady. "On my first visit to Paris I met a most charming one. A blood drinker. She was elegant, well-mannered, cultured. Most of them are."

Ghost thought of the wine-swilling, Twinkie-gobbling occupants of the black van. He tried to stretch his imagination to picture Molochai and Twig as elegant, well-mannered, or cultured. Then he shook his head. Either those two were aberrations, or Arkady Raventon didn't know as much about vampires as he thought he did.

"We were never lovers," Arkady went on, "though how badly I wanted her . . . Richelle. Violet-eyed, though she always wore dark glasses. Even at night. Hair as black as a thousand midnights, as eyeless sockets—with tips dyed white and fuchsia. She had lived two hundred years or more, and she knew where all the underground clubs in Paris were. I could never count the nights we danced away on dark smoky floors below the level of the street—"

"How come you didn't fuck her?" Steve interrupted.

Arkady lowered his eyelids at Steve and gazed coldly from beneath them. Steve glared back. Arkady poured himself more sherry. He topped off Ghost's glass too, though it was still half full. Ghost eyed it bleakly.

"Richelle was celibate. She had a terror of becoming pregnant. She insisted that no precautions were reliable enough. Should she conceive, she told me, it would mean the end of her.

"We occupied ourselves in other ways. We spent whole nights driving each other mad. She tasted lovely, hot and rich and always faintly bloody. Once—only once—she took me out on a kill. She found a child begging for milk money in some gutter far from the lights of the city, and she bent as if to whisper something to the child and sank her teeth into that soft face. When she had drunk, she undressed me and smeared the child's blood over my body. She lathered me with it. And then . . . then her exquisite tongue lapped me clean. . . ."

"Wait a second," said Ghost. He was afraid that soon Arkady would start panting and clutching at himself. "How come she was so scared of getting pregnant? What would have happened?"

"*Did* happen," said Arkady. "Poor Richelle; her worst fear came true. One night she went to her favorite club, the Café Zeitgeist, without me. She met a boy . . . just a boy, she told me. Perhaps sixteen or seventeen. She took him behind the club, into an alley. I don't know whether she meant to feed upon him or only to engage him in her usual sort of love. She needed blood, but semen would do in a pinch.

"For a snack, you might say.

"At any rate, he was a randy boy. He became too excited by Richelle's beauty. Perhaps by the smell of bloody lust she exuded. Richelle should have been able to overpower him;

she was very strong, but she had drunk too much vodka—
that was easy to do at the Café Zeitgeist, where they flavored
the vodka with essence of rosewater. The boy ripped her
dress open . . . and he took her by force."

"Fucker," said Steve. He let his head thump down on the
glass counter. "But some girls don't hafta be raped, huh,
Ghost? Some girls just . . ." He mumbled and subsided.

"What would happen if she got pregnant?" asked Ghost.

"It would have eaten its way out of her," Arkady told him
with relish. "It was half vampire. Even in the womb they are
killers. *Our babies are born without teeth,* Richelle told me,
*but even so they manage to chew their way out. Perhaps they
have a set of womb-teeth. Perhaps they claw their way out
with their tiny fingers. But they kill, always they kill. Just as I
ripped my mother apart.*

"I begged her to see one of the back-alley surgeons, to
have the child removed as one would excise a cancer, but she
refused. By that time she was half-mad with fear. *It would
know,* she insisted. *It is too late. It has already started eating
me—I can feel it churning inside me, shredding my
womb. . . .*

"So Richelle took a little stiletto that she sometimes wore
in her boot—to slit her lovers' veins, of course, though she
could use her teeth when she wanted to. She had very sharp
teeth. Teeth that could give pleasure as well as pain.

"She tried to cut the child out of her body. I found it in the
ruins of her belly, half-hidden behind coils of entrails; it was
shrivelled, bloody, long dead. It was still tiny, as large as a
red bean. But I found it because her fingers were cupped
around it. She had been trying to pull it out. She did not
want to die with it still inside her."

Ghost's mind was rocketing in too many directions, re-
bounding off the walls of his skull. A voice in his head was
saying, *Wait a second, wait a second. Maybe we need to think
some more about this business of killer vampire babies that
eat their way out of their mothers' wombs. Maybe we need to
think a whole LOT about it.* That voice was still faint, but
getting louder.

At last Ghost was about half-drunk on the sherry too. Ap-

parently it was strong stuff if you could keep it down. So he
was able to keep his voice steady when he said, "I don't get
it. Richelle was your friend. How come you're afraid of them
now?"

Arkady lowered his eyelids. "You might say I have a bone
to pick with them now. You guessed right, Ghost. Ashley's
lovers were vampires. A different sort of vampire. They ap-
preciate the taste of blood but do not need it. They feed on
willing souls; they come into your dreams and try to find a
niche in your brain; but they are real, and if you let them in,
they will destroy you as surely as any bloodsucker. These
were Ashley's lovers. The lovers who killed him."

"Where are they now?" asked Ghost.

"They took no blood from Ashley, but they sucked from
him something just as vital," Arkady went on, apparently
unhearing. "They sucked his youth, his beauty. That is what
they live upon; they only feed on the lovely. They left him a
husk. Ashley could never have lived without his beauty; the
nerves of his skin ran to his soul—"

He stopped, sighed, shook his head. "They are beautiful
too," he said. "They took all of Ashley's beauty, and their
own beauty remains. They rejuvenate it often. And I cannot
tell you why I let them live upstairs. Perhaps I hope that one
day I will have my chance for revenge. Perhaps I am simply
too afraid of them to refuse them anything."

Ghost's thoughts still ricocheted. His skull felt too fragile;
his mind might burst it. He put a hand to his forehead, and
his palm came away damp with sweat. It was the sherry, the
stuffy room. But more than anything it was the tales Arkady
had told. Terrible love that sucked away beauty, that could
invade your dreams; babies that could only be born in blood
and agony. *What can we do?* he wanted to ask Arkady. *How
can we help our friend* now, *before the vampires tear her
apart inside and out?*

But he couldn't say that. Not in front of Steve.

And he was pretty sure he already knew the answer.

27

Nothing awoke to bright afternoon sunlight filtered through dirty glass and dusty window shades. He could see only a pair of indistinct humps beside him, and for a moment reality did another of those slow giddy rolls: he recognized no part of this place. He had never seen it before. There were no stars on the ceiling as in his old room, no thrumming of wheels and rich smell of old bloodstains as in the van.

He hitched himself up on his elbows and blew a limp sheaf of hair away from his eyes. To his left curled Zillah, deep in his catlike sleep. On his right slept Christian, laid out straight, narrow, immensely long, his eyes and mouth shut tight. Molochai and Twig must be on the floor, cuddled in some corner. Nothing couldn't see them, but he thought he heard their breathing, deep and moist.

He yawned, licked his lips. What was that taste in his mouth? Fuzzy and rancid and somehow *green* . . .

Nothing's eyes had begun to slip shut. Now they flew open again. He pushed the covers away, scrambled over Zillah, ran to the window. He stood for a moment with the shade-pull in his hand, wondering what he would see outside, hoping it hadn't all been a drunken dream.

The shade clattered up. No one else in the room stirred. Nothing pressed his face to the window. Below him lay a narrow alley strewn with broken glass that sparkled in the sunlight, and beyond that stretched a vista of bright streets. Royal? Bourbon? Dimly he remembered names from last

night, magic talismanic names, names of streets where anything might happen. He saw tiny dark shops that beckoned
to him, and he knew how they would smell—cool and dank
and spicy, full of weird treasures. He saw wrought-iron balconies hung with colored flags that fluttered and winked like
some silken sea. He saw gleaming whitewashed retaining
walls spotted with soft brick-red where the paint had peeled
away, and behind them, crumbling buildings that must
surely house spiral staircases, palely lit ballrooms, secret
chambers whose walls were stained with the leavings of
blood sacrifice.

It was real, it was there, it was *his*. New Orleans. He had
made it all the way from the false home of his childhood to
the true city of his birth, to the wondrous glittering French
Quarter, to the very room where he had emerged between
Jessy's blood-slicked thighs.

Christian had arrived before them and secured their lodg-
ing. The bar—the legendary bar where Zillah had met Jessy,
had made love to her among the dusty cases of wine and
liquor—was closed, its windows boarded up, but Christian's
room was still empty and he had no trouble renting it again.
The landlady showed it to a prospective taker or two, Christian said with a glimmer of amusement, *but they told her it
smelled funny.*

The room of his birth. The thought made Nothing turn
away from the window and stare into the dimness of the
room. His eyes flicked from shadow to shadow. He wondered if the wraith of his mother would drift out of a corner,
whispering to him: *You killed me, my baby. In this room you
killed me. On this very floor.*

But whatever wraiths lived here were silent. Nothing
crouched to examine the threadbare carpet, but if the stains
of his gory birth remained, he could not see them in this half-
light.

He decided not to wake the others. He wanted to explore
the strange but somehow familiar maze of streets by himself.
A small thrill of anarchy went through him as he tore a page
out of his notebook and wrote a message to Zillah: *Back by
tonight* was all it said. He signed it, the point of his *t* a

dagger, the tail of his *g* an extravagant loop. This was the name Christian had given him, the name that undeniably belonged to him now. He would write it every chance he got. He signed the note again, then a third time, making the letters sprawl wildly across the page: *Nothing, Nothing, Nothing.* In this room Christian had held him all blood-slimed, had given him his name. Now he would go out and discover the streets that were his home.

When his sneakers hit the cement, it was as if the whole of the French Quarter jarred through his bones. Last night in the hazy hours after their arrival, he had been dazzled by the carnival of Bourbon Street, drunk on Chartreuse. Now, sober and clear-headed in watery afternoon sunlight, he wanted to bound through these old streets shouting *I'm here, I'm here!* He wanted to embrace each ornate lamppost and street sign, to fly from every balcony. The French Quarter was his, every ancient brick, every heady drop of it.

He pulled a pair of cheap sunglasses from his coat pocket and put them on. He'd taken to swiping them from convenience stores and gas stations in lieu of Lucky Strikes, which he'd almost stopped smoking. The cigarettes just didn't taste good anymore. His newest pair of shades had small round frames with rainbow-mirrored lenses; they made him feel like John Lennon in his trippier days. It was good to keep a couple of pairs of sunglasses on you all the time. Daylight didn't hurt him and the others as it did Christian, but it could give them a headache that pulsed red and maddening behind the eyes.

Nothing wandered the streets and the sidewalks for hours. A string of purple Mardi Gras beads was draped over a wrought-iron gatepost, left over from the carnival in the spring, a garland to welcome him home. He fastened it around his throat.

He visited St. Louis Cathedral with its dizzy vaulted ceilings and its thousand votive candles flickering in stained-glass light. In the cathedral's gift shop he palmed a rosary and added it to the beads around his neck; the two strands jangled against each other, then nestled together in an uneasy camaraderie of sacred and profane.

He sat at the Café du Monde and sipped a cup of coffee shot through with hot steaming milk. He wandered to the top of the levee and looked down upon the surging brown river. *My mother's bones lie there,* he told himself. *And they do not rest, they drift and break apart and come back together year by year, and they never rest.*

When shadows began to stretch across the sidewalks and tired eyes watched his progress past the doorways of the bars, Nothing retraced his steps toward Christian's room. The others would be ready to wake by now. Christian might accompany them on their rounds tonight, or might find some other way to amuse himself, since he no longer needed a job. "We get money in other ways," Zillah had told him coolly when he proposed going back to work at some bar.

They would descend upon the French Quarter, reeling from bar to bar, singing down Bourbon Street with their arms around one another's shoulders. In the company of Molochai, Twig, and Zillah, Nothing was served drinks without a second glance. The taste of Chartreuse was magical, fragrant and heady beyond imagining; yet somehow it also tasted natural to him, as if he had been weaned on the blazing green liqueur. Already it felt as if they had been here forever.

And all the bloodstreams here were sure to be sweet. With a shock, Nothing realized how hungry he was. The memory of Laine's blood gave him no guilt now. He remembered only how rich it had tasted, its heat, the way it had pumped into his mouth with the beat of life itself. But now Laine's death felt like something that had happened a long time ago. Too long ago.

Since then, there had been those drifters in Missing Mile, and the child. They had been easier. When he found out how Molochai, Twig, and Zillah filed their teeth to make them sharp, Nothing had sharpened his too. Now he liked to run his tongue over them, teasing the small points. But not even the kid from Violin Road had tasted as sweet as Laine. In the French Quarter all blood would taste alcoholic, purple. . . .

Yes, tonight they would surely go out for blood.

Now he was almost home. Some small rational part of his mind wondered how he was able to walk these streets so easily. But he could not really think it strange. He had dreamed of this city, of roaming these streets. A glittering map of the French Quarter seemed to unfold in his head, half-imagined and half-remembered, as clear as the burn of Chartreuse. He swung around a lamppost, and his coat floated out in an undulating circle of black silk.

Not until he was half a block from the room did Nothing notice the man following slowly behind him. The man walked bent slightly at the waist, one arm clamped across his stomach as if it hurt him to move. He was only a shape in the fading light, neither large nor small, featureless. Nothing slowed his steps. The man slowed too. Nothing walked faster. So did the man, doubling up even more.

Instead of stopping at the boarded-up bar, Nothing turned right. He would lead the man into the alley that ran beneath Christian's window. The alley was fenced off at the other end and blocked by a heap of garbage—he might be trapping himself. But he could face the man there, find out what he wanted and deal with him however necessary. He didn't look like much of a threat.

Nothing heard the man follow him into the alley, shoes crunching over broken glass. He stopped and swung around, his hands on his hips and his sneakers planted firmly on the pavement, trying to look dangerous.

The man stopped a few feet away, badly hunched now. His breathing sounded harsh and painful. His face was a wavering pale blotch on the dusk. Below it, a silver cross on a chain gleamed. He stared at Nothing for a long moment, his lips working silently, his eyes disbelieving. Then he took two unsteady steps forward.

"Jessy . . ." he whispered.

Nothing felt his heart cannon against his ribs, bounce crazily off his breastbone. *Hush,* he willed it, *hush, heart, no one can hurt me. Zillah is close by, and I have no fear.*

The man came closer. With dry fingertips he touched Nothing's face. Nothing thought, *He's old. He is much older than I thought. And he looks so sick. He cannot hurt me.* He caught the man's hand in his and pulled it easily away from his face. The fingers were like bones wrapped in parchment.

"Jessy," the man said again, more evenly this time.

Nothing tried to make his voice calm. It came out husky, as if he'd smoked a whole pack of Luckies that day. "That's not my name," he said.

"You are so like her—" The old man pulled himself upright. His face contorted. Nothing imagined tissue pulling loose inside him, bleeding bad blood. He gripped the man's arm, trying to give what support he could. The man breathed deeply and was able to continue. "My daughter died many years ago. But you are so very like her . . ."

It's Wallace, Nothing realized wildly. *The sick old man who nearly killed Christian and drove him away from here. He is my grandfather. He shot Christian in the chest . . . but he is my grandfather.* His heart caromed again. Should he tell Wallace his name, or should he lie? Something in him rebelled at denying his name. It was truly his now, and he would claim it. "My name is Nothing," he said.

"Who are you?" The man grabbed Nothing's shoulders and gave him a feeble shake. *"Who are you, child?"*

Nothing half-wanted to fall into Wallace's arms and sob out the whole confusing story. After all, this man was his grandfather. He had almost killed Christian, but he hadn't known the truth then. He thought Christian had lured Jessy to her death. Nothing could explain the truth.

But then he realized he couldn't. Even if Nothing was Wallace's only grandson, even if Nothing looked so much like his dear dead Jessy. Because if Wallace heard the whole story, he would know who had really killed his daughter.

Zillah. Zillah had caused Jessy's death, hadn't he? *He didn't mean to, it was my fault—I tore her apart inside before I was ever born,* Nothing thought hysterically. But Wallace would not blame him. Wallace would love him because he was Jessy's offspring, because he looked like Jessy and was just the age she had been when Wallace had lost her. And Wallace would want to take him away from Zillah, away from his family.

Besides, Wallace was in pain. Suffering.

Maybe Nothing could do one small mercy for his grandfather.

"My mother's name was Jessy," he said.

Doubt flickered in Wallace's eyes, brighter than the pain and weariness. If Nothing wanted Wallace to trust him, he had to think of some kind of proof. At once it came to him.

"She disappeared fifteen years ago, at Mardi Gras," he told Wallace. "That was when she met my father."

Not until the words were out, hanging in the cool still air of the dusk, did Nothing realize his mistake.

"Then you are one of the unholy creatures too," Wallace whispered. "The city has become riddled with them." With a convulsive motion he tore the crucifix from his neck and thrust it at Nothing, trying to drive him toward the end of the alley. "Repent—while you are still young—in the name of the Father, the Son, and the Holy Ghost, tear the bloodlust from your heart—"

Nothing could not bring himself to laugh. He caught Wallace's hand and took the cross away. "I'm sorry, Grandfather," he said. "That doesn't work on all of us."

"Then it's lucky that the Lord told me to carry other protection," said Wallace. In one jerky movement he whipped a small pistol from the waistband of his trousers and aimed it at Nothing's forehead.

"Bless you, my grandson," he said. "When you look upon the face of God, you will thank me."

Nothing was never sure how long he stood there staring down the round black barrel of the gun, wondering whether he would see the flash of fire or hear the explosion before the bullet smashed into his face. *The brain or the heart,* Christian had told him. He had time to think of all he had found, all he was about to lose, all the miles he would not travel.

A mist seemed to surround Wallace's head, suffusing his face with dim light. Nothing saw Wallace's finger tightening on the trigger: actually saw that.

Then something was plummeting toward them. Nothing saw the large dark shape hit Wallace dead-on, saw Wallace's body jerk forward and his arm fly up. The shot went wild. Brick splintered far overhead.

Zillah crouched atop Wallace's prone form. He must have

launched himself from the second-story window, but he was not even breathing hard. The other man's body had stopped his fall.

Wallace lay on the pavement in the shards of glass. He groped weakly for the pistol. Zillah stamped on Wallace's hand, and Nothing heard a sound like strands of raw spaghetti breaking. Wallace screamed once, a shrill, despairing sound. Then he began to mumble softly. Nothing realized he was praying. Did he still think his God was going to pull him out of this one?

"Some fine messes you get yourself into," said Zillah. "What if I hadn't seen you from up there?" His eyes gleamed; his lips were purple with fury. "You little fool"— the pointed tip of his shoe met Wallace's cheekbone; black blood sprayed—"do you think you're too smart to die? Do you think I can always watch out for you?"

Zillah knelt above Wallace, pulled Wallace's head up by a handful of bloodied gray hair, and smashed Wallace's face into the pavement. The sound made Nothing think of eggs being dropped onto broken glass. Gore began to pool beneath Wallace's head. "I won't lose you now, Nothing." Zillah rolled Wallace over and began to slap him across the face, over and over, glaring up at Nothing. "Don't you know"— *slap*—"I love you?" *Slap.* "I LOVE YOU." *Slap.*

Zillah's long nails dug into the loose flesh of Wallace's face. He wrenched Wallace's head back, exposing his throat. Incredibly, Wallace was still praying: ". . . the flesh of the Son," Nothing heard him mumble.

For a moment Zillah seemed ready to sink his fingernails into the old man's throat. But he only ground Wallace's face down again, then leaped off him and came for Nothing. He grabbed Nothing by the front of his coat, nearly choking him. With his other hand he cupped Nothing's chin. The gesture was almost tender, except that Zillah dug his long nails into the flesh of Nothing's cheeks. Zillah was hurting him on purpose. Nothing felt a clear, icy fury begin to rise within him.

"Get your hands off me," he said.

Zillah's eyes flared brighter. "What?"

"I said get them off me." Nothing shoved Zillah's hand

away from his face and twisted out of Zillah's grasp. They faced each other in the darkening alley. Nothing's heart beat painfully fast, but he was pleased to realize he wasn't trembling. "I'm sorry I get myself into stupid messes, okay? I haven't been doing this very long. I don't know what's right and what's wrong. Nobody except Christian ever tells me anything." With each word he grew angrier. "You don't treat me like your son—you treat me like I'm half sex slave and half lapdog. When I'm good, you pat me on the head, and when I fuck up you yell at me and hurt me. But you never explain anything to me. What kind of a father are you, anyway?"

Nothing gasped for breath. He could see only two bright green spots on the darkness. "All I have to say is this," he continued. "Don't ever hurt me again. I love you. I want to stay with you. But don't you hurt me. I'm not Molochai or Twig. I won't take it. I'm sick of it."

Zillah stared at him. Slowly the blaze in his eyes died down; they became cool, appraising. "Wait here," he said.

Then Zillah did an odd thing. He knelt beside Wallace again and yanked Wallace's trouser legs up past his ankles. When Zillah reached into the purple silk lining of his jacket, Nothing knew what he was going to do. He wanted to look away; instead, he watched helplessly as Zillah unfolded his pearl-handled razor and carefully sliced through the back of each ankle. He drew the blade through the old man's threadbare socks, through the thin skin, through the big tendon as if it were butter. Nothing saw the razor falter as it grated on bone. Wallace was now beyond sound; only a long shudder ran through his body.

"Wait here," Zillah said again. Nothing half-expected him to skitter up the brick wall and climb back through the window. But Zillah just walked to the mouth of the alley, glanced over his shoulder at Nothing, and turned toward the staircase that led up to the room.

Nothing could not look at Wallace now. He stared at the ground, at the broken glass and the pile of garbage. Something gleamed near his foot. The crucifix. Nothing looked at

it for a long moment, then picked it up and thrust it deep
into his pocket. Zillah wouldn't like him keeping it.

Too bad.

In a few minutes Zillah came back down with Molochai
and Twig. They had left Christian sleeping, they said. They
could tell him about Wallace later. It would be a surprise.
Nothing suspected they were just greedy.

Wallace was already bleeding from several places. The
wounds in his ankles pumped with his heartbeat. Molochai
and Twig latched onto them. Nothing imagined that the big
veins of the legs must be like soda straws.

Zillah picked up one of Wallace's limp hands, the one he
had stomped. The palm was smeared with blood where it
had been crushed against the broken glass and rough brick.
Zillah opened his razor again. He slid it smoothly in, and the
flesh of the palm parted cleanly. A sheet of thin blood mixed
with saliva ran down Zillah's chin as he began to suck at the
wound.

Nothing's stomach growled.

He crawled forward and knelt beside Wallace. His grandfather's cheek rested on a broken bottle. His eyes were open,
still aware, brimming with rage and pain. *At least I can end
the pain for you,* Nothing thought. He put his mouth against
the slow pulse of Wallace's throat. The skin there was dry
and soft; it felt very old. He choked back a sob and sank in
his new filed teeth.

His grandfather's blood was bitter.

But he and his family drank every drop.

28

Late that night Ghost opened his eyes and blinked up at an unfamiliar ceiling. There were no dead leaves up there, no painted stars. There were only shifting patches of moonlight like a white and silver sea.

For a moment he felt the floating giddiness that always came when he woke in a strange bed. Then, slowly, the world fell into place around him. There was the softness of a mattress under his back, the weight of blankets. There was the deep regular breathing of Steve beside him, and the warmth of Steve's skin, and Steve's smell that had gone strange in the past couple of days. It made Ghost wonder whether Steve's insides had been thrown off balance somehow.

Steve usually smelled of beer, but now, often as not, the harsh odor of whiskey was on him instead. And dirty hair, but that was normal because Steve's hair was getting long and he said it was a royal pain in the ass to wash. But now Steve's clothes were dirty too, and there was some strange secret smell that made Ghost lift his head and flare his nostrils, trying to scent it out, to pin it down. It was the smell of exhaustion, the smell of frying brains, the smell of despair.

It might mean that Steve was only clinging to some remote edge of sanity. It might mean Steve was about ready to say *Fuck this shit, man,* and give up altogether. Steve still loved Ann, but it was a wretched kind of love, a love that made him hate himself for feeling it. Steve was just blaming himself now. He had reason to blame himself.

But Ghost knew guilt could be traced back forever, blame could be laid every which way, and what good would it do? Whose pain would be lessened by it? Steve had done what he had done, and because he was Steve, he could not have done it any other way.

Steve had always been like that: he would go through the fire, would never shy away no matter how hellish it was. When the pain burned off him, he seemed stronger, more pure. But sometimes it nearly killed him. And sometimes he tried to quench it by drinking, which only made the flames burn higher and hotter.

Why couldn't Ann understand how Steve was? The rocker with a hundred midnights stored in his heart for nobody to find; sure, he was tough, but he *did* hurt, and somehow you had to soothe that pain while pretending you couldn't see it. Ghost stared into the dark. Sometimes he thought he was the only person who understood Steve at all. They had been together so long. But what good did that do Steve?

He remembered what Ann had said the day he went over to her house. *The night is the hardest time to be alive,* she had told him. *And four A.M. knows all my secrets.* She had wanted something, or someone, to get her through the night.

Zillah with his green eyes had gotten her through part of one night, anyway. But what saved her from four A.M. now? What had she thought about on those nights when she prowled around the trailer on Violin Road, maybe knocking and not being let in, maybe afraid even to knock? What was she thinking now, as she rode a southbound bus, as she roamed the dark streets of the French Quarter, breathing the mist of beer and the essence of time? Did she know yet where Zillah lived; was she staring up at his window, whispering words he would not hear?

What was getting her through this night? And what would get her through all the nights yet to come, as the poison fetus grew inside her?

Ghost sat up and swung his legs over the side of the bed. He caught a whiff of himself. His clothes were as dirty as

Steve's, though not as beer-stained; they had only the things
they'd been wearing when they took off for New Orleans.
Tomorrow they would have to go and buy a couple of fresh
T-shirts. Something classy, like the oyster bar shirts that said
SHUCK ME, SUCK ME, EAT ME RAW.

The wooden floor was cold. Moonlight dappled Ghost's
feet. He stood up slowly, easing his weight off the mattress,
trying not to wake Steve. There wasn't much chance of Steve
waking up, though. Earlier tonight Steve had declared his
intention to drink a pitcher of Dixie beer in every bar on
Bourbon Street. When they didn't have Dixie, he settled for
Bud. As far as Ghost could recall, they had gotten about
halfway before he was able to drag Steve back to the room
and dump him into bed.

Ghost had had his share of those pitchers too. He was still
swaying a little. He steadied himself against the doorjamb
and crossed the threshold into the hall.

He and Steve had the first room at the top of the stairs.
Next to that was the room belonging to Arkady's mysterious
guests; beyond that was the bathroom, where Ghost was
headed, and at the end of the hall was Arkady's bedroom.

As Ghost passed the open door of the second room, he saw
moonlight filtering in through a dirty window. The cold glow
spilled over the rumpled sheets and blankets on the bed,
made the floorboards gleam, threw the closet door into
shadow so that Ghost couldn't tell whether it was open or
shut. At the foot of the bed, drooping halfway to the floor, a
small twisted shape hung.

Ghost's breath caught in his throat. As he stared at the
shape, it seemed to twitch. Ghost took two quick steps backward. Were the occupants of this room really the ones who
had killed Ashley? Could Arkady be that perverse? Was the
twisted shape another of their victims, a child with all the life
sucked out of it, hanging bonelessly? Or was it some voodoo
creation of Arkady's, some dried effigy that would come to
life and jerk toward him in a horrible parody of dance?

Ghost stood in the doorway a moment longer, pulling his
hair over his face, staring through its pale curtain into the
room. He didn't want to know what the shape was. He

wanted to pull the door shut, go on down the hall to the bathroom, and get back to bed. With Steve asleep beside him, he would not be afraid.

But he had to know what was going on here, whether this was a safe place or not. Before he could think about it any more, he made himself walk to the foot of the bed and prod the shape with one finger.

A pillow, wadded into a hard little knot. That was all it was. For a second he was glad Steve was in the other room passed out, not here to see him getting spooked over a pillow. Then he wished Steve were here, even though he knew Steve would call him a pussy. Steve hadn't been laughing at much of anything these days. Even tonight. Usually when they went on a real bender, they would start remembering stuff they had done when they were kids, making stupid jokes, imitating each other. "Fuckin' shit, Steve, you sure are sucking down that fuckin' brew," Ghost would say, and Steve would reply imperturbably, "Yeah, but I can feel the spirit of the beer inside me."

But tonight Steve had swilled his beer silently, staring into its golden depths, at the mirror behind the bar, at the colored lights out on Bourbon Street. When he met Ghost's eyes, he would not hold the gaze. But before Steve looked away, Ghost had seen stark terror in his eyes.

Ghost picked up the pillow and smoothed it out. As he was about to toss it back onto the bed, he saw the strands of hair clinging to the linen. He picked a few of them off—they were brittle, translucent—and held them up to the moonlight, trying to see their color. Some of the strands were clear ruby-red. Some were bright bleachy yellow. Neither color looked natural.

Over to his right, the closet door creaked and swung halfway open.

Ghost looked at it, his head lifted high, his nostrils flaring a little. The door was tauntingly still, trying to pretend it had been halfway open all the time. Trying to pretend a sudden gust from nowhere had swept through the room. Trying to pretend the floor wasn't level and it had just happened to swing open while Ghost was standing there alone in the middle of the night.

Ghost wasn't fooled. He moved toward the closet and put his hand on the knob. When no one twisted it from the other side, he yanked the door wide open.

For one terrible second he thought something was drifting toward him, some bright many-armed wraith. Then he saw that the closet was haunted only by clothes, strange, beautiful clothes of colored silk. Were they dresses? Shirts? Ghost took a sea-green sleeve between his thumb and his forefinger, rubbing the slippery sensuous cloth, wondering. Loose hangers kissed softly against each other.

Who wore these rich clothes? He pulled a swath of rose-colored silk toward him and buried his nose in its cool depths. The cloth was saturated with the smells of strawberry incense, of clove cigarettes, of wine, of tangy sweat.

The smells drew him in.

And as he breathed the heady mélange, a voice whispered to him from the depths of the closet: "Ghost . . . easy . . ."

He was never sure how he got out of the room and made a wrong turn down the hall. Maybe he meant to go racing back to his room; maybe he meant to lock himself in the bathroom and stay there all night. He never meant to barge into Arkady's bedroom—that much was certain. But all at once there he was, and there was Arkady burning a candle on his nightstand, playing with several little heaps of colored powder on a white plate, pushing them into intricate convoluted patterns of arrows, curlicues, lines, and crosses.

When Ghost slammed into the room and leaned panting against the door, Arkady looked up and smiled. All the colored powders fell back in a bright spray across the plate. "What a lovely surprise," said Arkady. "Well. Not precisely a surprise, since I heard you coming down the hall. But I am ever so pleased to see you nonetheless."

First, Arkady made Ghost swallow a tranquilizing powder. Ghost didn't want it, but in the end it was easy to make him swallow it: Arkady just slipped inside Ghost's mind and *pushed.* Usually he would not have tried such a thing on a sensitive as powerful as Ghost, but the boy was terrified and exhausted. It was easy.

Then he made Ghost tell his tale: the whole thing, vampires and all. It was more convoluted and full of pain than Arkady could have guessed. Ghost's hands twitched all the way through the telling; he tugged his pale hair over his eyes, and more than once Arkady heard a sob catch in his throat.

At last Ghost fell silent. He tried to remain sitting, but his head kept drooping and his eyes threatened to slip shut. Arkady saw Ghost's hands clenching into loose fists: the poor boy was trying to *will* himself to stay awake.

With a light finger Arkady touched Ghost's lips, those lovely lips so pale, so delicately lined, tucked in at the corners with worry and fear. Under his touch he felt Ghost's lips tighten. Ghost was exhausted, nearly asleep; most likely he did not know who touched him. Nevertheless, Arkady imagined how it would be to slide his finger between those lips, to stroke the pink rag of a tongue, to be surrounded by the wet warmth of Ghost's mouth. He wondered how it would be to taste Ghost's sweet spit. *Poor boy,* he thought again. *Poor lost boys, both of them. One trying to drown his fear in a bottle, and the other—this beautiful child—trying to confront it all alone.*

"Poor boy," murmured Arkady. "You are very brave, Ghost. Dreadfully, achingly brave." He stroked the smooth curve of Ghost's throat, feeling the flesh shudder beneath his touch, then let his fingers stray between the neckband of the voluminous tie-dyed shirt Ghost wore. When Ghost had come slamming into the room, Arkady's heart melted for the child standing there trembling in that enormous shirt that made him look so terribly young. He had wanted to hold out his arms to Ghost. . . .

Why deceive himself? He had wanted to bewitch Ghost and lure him into bed, to drive him pleasure-mad, to drown him in a sea of silk sheets and feather pillows. It wasn't as if he meant to *seduce* the boy—but might they not offer each other a night of creature comfort, a night of companionship?

Ghost would not have to lie awake beside his poor drunken friend, pondering fate, bloody births, lost souls. Arkady would not have to sit up all night tracing useless vévés by candlelight, hoping for things he might never attain. Hoping to look up and see the beautiful proud face of his brother Ashley floating outside the window, begging admission with those eyes. Hoping to discover a way to hurt Ashley's lovers, those two lovely dangerous creatures who would surely destroy him someday.

Arkady thought of what those creatures had done to Ashley. Might that story not win Ghost's sympathy at least? The tranquilizing powder had made Ghost's body somnolent, sapped the strength from his muscles, but his mind would still be alert. Absently caressing Ghost's rigid shoulder, Arkady began to tell the tale.

"They gave you a bad scare, Ghost, did they not? In the guest room. In the closet. Ah, but you were snooping. You should never have looked in there—not with your gift. Not with that shining eye in your heart. They are far too strong, far too heady for one who feels things as you do. They are not even in that room, Ghost. Not tonight, though they will be back in the morning, or the next morning, or the one after that. Who knows? The Lord—" Arkady crossed himself with his free hand, upside down then right side up—"the Lord alone knows where they are tonight. What strange new substances they have swallowed or sniffed or shot into their perfect ruby veins, or whom they have found to love.

"Whom they have found to love.

"They leave their essence everywhere they go. It must be dreadfully strong in that closet where they throw their dirty clothes, the clothes full of their sweat, their smoke, their sweet clove-scented ectoplasm. Did that drift out at you, Ghost? Do they know you, perchance? Have you met? Or did they just speak to you as one lost soul to another? Ah, but you must not be afraid of them. To you they are as harmless as a forgotten song on an antique record. To you they are as harmless as a rotting old gravestone. It is me they can hurt. It was Ashley they could hurt, and whoever they have found to share their deadly ecstasy tonight.

"That is what they want, Ghost. Nay—that is what they *need*, for they feed upon your pleasure and your terror and your pain. They must terrify you, as they do the children who are their victims; they must enter your dreams and give you a nightmare so horrible that you never awaken from it. But their greatest pleasure is not to terrify—it is to bewitch. They want you to love them; it makes the final moment of betrayal sweeter. They must come to you in the flesh and make love with you. They must lure you down onto some ancient stained mattress, or beneath a silken coverlet, or into an alley where they will kneel before you in the filth. You must become addicted to their spit; you must breathe their scent until you are intoxicated.

"Only then will they consummate their love for you as they did for Ashley—by sucking you dry. By taking every drop of your beauty, your youth, the fire that drives you. By leaving you a husk, a dry, living shell. As they did to my brother Ashley.

"I found him when I returned home from Paris at the end of that long dying winter. We had been living in a church down by Bayou St. John, an abandoned place. Ashley hanged himself in the bell tower. He had no choice, truly; Ashley was born with a healthy dose of the Raventon dramatic flair. He hung there for a week before I came home. He knew I would be back—I never broke a promise to Ashley—but he could not wait.

"When I cut his body down, I saw why. It was as dry and twisted as a mandrake root. Ashley had been dead seven days, but nothing in him had rotted except his eyes and his tongue. There was nothing else left to rot—they had sucked all his juices out. He rustled in my arms as I cut the rope, and when I lifted him down and laid him on the floor of the bell tower, he rattled like a sack full of bones. His mouth was stretched open; his lips were bloodless, pulled away from his teeth. Teeth that had gone the color of old ivory. Far back in his head, his tongue lay withered. His hair was colorless, drifting. And his eyes—the eyes I wanted to die for when they tilted up to meet mine—those *eyes* . . . they were gone. Those eyes were gone, and Ashley looked at me out of

the darkness of his shrivelled brain, and his face flaked away
when I touched it.

"His lovers were still there, living on the top floor of the
church, burning incense to mask the faint smell of Ashley's
decay. For seven days they had let him hang with his face
sifting to dust and his eyes moldering. When I descended
from the bell tower cradling Ashley's skull—the flesh fell
away from it as easily as old crumbling parchment—they
were making love on a dirty mattress they had dragged in.
Biting throats, clutching hands, laughing and sobbing with
their pleasure. I sat with Ashley in my arms and waited for
them to finish. At last one of them looked up at me and said
It was easy for him, Arkady. As easy as breathing. And the
other one told me, *Death is easy. You should know that,
Arkady. Death is easy.*"

Ghost had been drifting back to sleep, his head pillowed
on his arms; dreaming the story more than hearing it, his
mind filling with pictures of the boy's withered body on the
long-ago roadside, the giant oak tree up on the hill, the final
image of his dream in the car that had frightened him so
badly—the twins lying side by side on the stained mattress,
their skin drying and cracking, their beauty spent. Now he
looked up and said sleepily, "Death is easy?"

Somehow, Arkady sensed, those words were familiar to
Ghost. But he smoothed pale strands of hair from Ghost's
brow, and Ghost let his head sink back down.

Perhaps Ghost really would stay with him tonight. Perhaps
Ghost wanted to drown in this bed. Surely such a thing was
possible. Ashley was the beauty of the Raventons, to be sure,
but Arkady too possessed the high clear forehead and the
sharp proud cheekbones, if not the sparkling burgundy hair
or the unbelievable eyes, those depthless eyes. Perhaps
Ghost wanted to sigh in Arkady's arms, to writhe and moan
beneath the ministration of Arkady's lips. It had been so very
long.

The twins could still lure Arkady into their bed on occa-
sion, because they were beautiful and he was alone. But he
hated them for what they had done to Ashley, and he was
afraid of the hold they already had upon him. And there was

no one else. Not until now, not until this nervous magical Ghost-child with the pale blue eyes, the ragged clothes from some fantastic thrift shop, the translucent hair that fell across his eyes as he slept.

"Asleep, Ghost?" Arkady whispered. "Perhaps not yet." He bent and kissed the corner of Ghost's eye as lightly as he would have plucked a spider from its web to dry and grind for *gris-gris*. His tongue flickered across the silken scrap of Ghost's eyelashes, then slid down Ghost's cheek and sought passage between those exquisite lips.

Every nerve in Ghost's body seemed to come instantly alive, tensing, uncoiling. He flew off the bed backward and landed in front of the door, back pressed flat against the wood, chin lifted and nostrils flared wide. Even his eyelids seemed to tremble. His eyes met Arkady's and locked there, large and scared, aglow with pale blue fire.

Arkady held the look for a long moment. Then he let his gaze flick to the window, and he lifted one bony shoulder in a tiny, unconcerned shrug.

"She'll die, Ghost. Unless that foetus comes out soon, its growth will be too far gone. This is no vulnerable morsel of meat to be scraped out by any back-alley abortionist with a curette and a roll of dirty cotton. Try that, and it will rip open her womb even sooner.

"No. You must poison it. Otherwise it will grow, and Ann will die, and perhaps your precious Steve will die too. Guilt twists a man, Ghost. You cannot protect him forever. He may bleed his life away in a car crash, or pick a fight with someone who carries a razor in his boot—the Vieux Carré is full of them. Or perhaps a slower death. A pickling of the liver? An insult to the brain? Death can come in a bottle, Ghost. And I think Steve has already opened that bottle and taken the first swallow.

"You must poison it, Ghost. To save Ann. To save Steve." Arkady paused, then delivered the bitter coup de grace. "I know the recipe. I developed it after Richelle died. I can help you . . . if I wish."

Arkady twitched the sheets back. They made a tiny dry rustling sound, like long linen wrappings falling away from a

mummy's face, like dead moth wings dusting down. Ghost
jumped a little at the sound. With both hands he raked his
hair, pulling it in front of his face. Arkady saw him shudder.

Then his back straightened, and his shoulders squared,
and his eyes flared dark once and then were as pale as before.

"Okay," he said.

Those few steps back to the bed were the worst Ghost had
ever taken. He felt the floorboards under his bare feet,
coated with a dry and silken dust. Arkady's skin would feel
that way against his own. Arkady's hands would caress his
soul; Arkady's tongue would explore his brain. . . .

He would not think about it. He would think about singing
at the Sacred Yew, with Steve going wild on guitar. Back
when things were simple. That was what he would do.
"Okay," he said, refusing to hear his own words. "I'll do
whatever you want."

He was onstage now, clutching at the microphone, ready
to let his voice flow. But Arkady's papery lips clamped over
his mouth, sealing it. Arkady's tongue cleaved to his, tasting
of bitter herbs. Arkady's dry touch spidered down his chest,
under his T-shirt. He felt that touch in the depths of him,
razoring along his backbone, turning his intestines shuddery.
He began to choke.

"*No,*" said a voice from the dark doorway. A weary voice, a
voice for speaking long after midnight, a voice to be used
when all paths are blocked, when castles have fallen to ruin,
when morning will not come again.

Ghost's eyes swept the darkness. "Steve?" For the voice
was Steve's, and the smell was Steve's too, the clothes stiff
with drinking-sweat. But the smell of lonely desperation was
gone. There was exhaustion, and fear, and the damp secret
scent of sorrow. But beneath those was something new,
something Ghost hadn't caught from Steve for a long time. A
vibration more than a scent. A tremor that thrummed the air
between them, turned it electric, webbed it with white
crackling lines of energy.

It was anger. Good old pissed-off Steve Finn anger.

Arkady hissed air in through his teeth. "You."

"Get your hands off him," said Steve. He gripped either side of the doorjamb, holding himself up. His hair stood up in crazy dark tufts and wings, shoved messily behind his ears, a week dirty. "Let him *go*, motherfucker," he told Arkady again. "I don't care what kind of badass juju guy you are. Right now I could reach down your throat and tear your foul black heart out. *With pleasure*."

Arkady let go of Ghost.

"Come on," said Steve. He jerked a thumb toward the staircase. "We're leaving. We're getting in the goddamn T-bird and going home. Ann can get torn apart from inside out if that's what has to happen. If that's what she wants. You're not gonna make yourself into a whore for her.

"Or for me.

"Or for anybody. You're too good for that, Ghost. You're too goddamn fine."

Steve's eyes shone crystal-bright in the dark. Two wet lines glistened their way down his cheeks. Tear-tracks. But he stood straight, and though his hands still gripped the doorjamb and his clothes hung from him like rags on a scarecrow, he was strong. Strength vibrated from him. He had made a decision, and he would abide by it. But not alone.

Ghost went to him. After a moment Steve let his arms drop onto Ghost's shoulders, and Steve's tears fell into Ghost's hair and were lost there, palely tangled. They stood leaning on each other, strength passing between them.

"Let's go," Steve said at last.

"Wait!" called Arkady when they were halfway down the hall.

Steve stopped but did not turn. His grip on Ghost's arm tightened. Ghost looked back over his shoulder, drawing closer to Steve, afraid to meet Arkady's eyes.

"*You are too fine, Ghost,*" said Arkady, and though his voice was only a moth-whisper in the dusty hallway, they heard him. "I did not lie when I said you were brave—dreadfully, achingly brave. You shared none of my lust, but to save your friends you would have given yourself to me. And I would have let you.

"Indeed, you are too fine. We must band together against the eternal night. The vampires took my brother, and I will not let them take another beautiful young life. I will help you. Lord help me, I will help you."

And Arkady Raventon crossed himself twice. First upside down, then right side up.

"Fern," said Arkady, holding a packet of dried leaves up to the light.

They had come downstairs and lit the candles in the shop, calling up the spirits of cinnamon, nutmeg, licorice. Arkady had arranged his materials on the glass countertop: vials and encrusted bottles, a mortar and pestle, a bundle of crumbling envelopes. Now he picked through them, sifting, pinching, sniffing and muttering.

Steve slouched against the opposite wall, scowling but surreptitiously interested. Ghost watched with his chin propped in his hands, horribly rapt. He did not want to watch the making of the poison that would scour Ann's womb, but he had to. This was too familiar. This awakened memories of his grandmother and Miz Catlin, or his grandmother alone, hunched over some candlelit table with an assortment of packets and tiny shining bottles close at hand. Ghost would creep out and hide in the shadow of the bookcase or the doorway, and sometimes his grandmother would sense his presence and call him over to watch. Then she would tell him what fragrant oils and leaves she was mixing. *This will bring luck to someone's door,* she would explain, or *This will ease a woman's monthly pains.* But sometimes the concoctions did not smell sweet at all. Sometimes they smelled brown and fetid, and vapors curled up from her mortar. When his grandmother was mixing that kind of concoction, Ghost always got sent back to bed.

"Basil," said Arkady. "Bay leaf."

Steve shifted, slumped further. "Shit, we could have gone to the A&P for this."

"Pennyroyal," said Arkady, lowering his eyelids at Steve. "Yarrow, brooklime. And *garlic.*" A small secret smile crooked his lips. "It won't like all this garlic." With a flourish he uncorked a small blue bottle and poured a few drops of cloudy liquid into the mortar. Herbs hissed coldly. A twist of vapor wafted up.

Steve pushed himself up. "What the fuck was *that*?"

Arkady smiled. "The crucial ingredient. Without it, this would be a mere salad." Steve scowled; Arkady might as well have said *Wouldn't you like to know*?

Ghost watched Arkady scrape the paste from the mortar onto a square of waxed paper. It was a bright organic green, and it seemed to seethe on the paper. *Made from a thousand herbs, made from altars,* Ghost thought; this stuff would surely burn Ann's throat when they forced her to swallow it.

At least, he hoped she only had to swallow it.

Arkady folded the square of paper in half and twisted the ends. "That," he said, "is that. Now you must find the girl and bring her to me."

Steve and Ghost started speaking at once:

"How the fuck are we supposed to do that?" said Steve.

"I can do that," said Ghost.

Back upstairs, Ghost looked out the window at the landscape of wedding-cake buildings iced with intricate scrolls of wrought iron. Far to his left, beyond his line of vision, the lights of Bourbon Street glittered; the crowds still staggered; the very stars in the sky swam—bright round stars, great glowing ones, hallucinatory stars.

At the end of the hall Arkady slipped into bed, and Ghost caught one dry lonely thought: *He is too pale, too fragile; my love would surely have shattered him.*

Above it all, above Ghost and Steve and Arkady and the rest of the gaudy town, a small cold moon hung. A moon like a sliver of frosted bone, a moon to bring down winter.

Ghost turned away from the window.

Steve was already in bed, his arms wrapped around his pillow. The moonlight smudged crescents of shadow beneath his eyes. With his fingers he had combed most of the tangles out of his hair, and now it lay along his cheeks and forehead, limp with the dirt of the French Quarter, with the sweat of a long road trip. He looked terribly young, younger than the first time Ghost had laid eyes on him, walking through those sun-dappled autumn woods. Back when things were simple.

"Come on to bed," Steve said. "It's almost morning. Tomorrow we'll figure out how to find Ann and make her swallow that shit. It'll probably kill her."

Ghost sensed unsaid words hanging in the air like rivermist. He slid under the covers, into the comforting pool of Steve's warmth, and waited.

At last Steve said, "But I guess that's better than letting the vampires kill her."

"You believe it," said Ghost, softly enough that Steve could pretend not to have heard.

But Steve rolled onto his back and answered. "Yeah. I guess I do. I saw Zillah's face that night, outside the club—I know that now. I saw it, and it was all healed up. I'm sick of lying to myself. You don't lie to yourself. You're not scared of what your heart knows.

"I believe something bad is going to happen to Ann. I believe it because *you* believe it so much. You think Ann will die if nobody helps her. You believe it so hard that you were ready to sell yourself to Arkady. To save her, if you could. And I guess to save me, too.

"And anything that you believe in that strongly, Ghost, I'm not gonna argue with. Not in a million years." Under the covers, Steve's hand found Ghost's and gripped it hard, almost painfully. Ghost heard the rest of the thought: *Because I trust you, Ghost. You and nobody else—and if you believe it, then damn, I guess I believe it too. The Easter Bunny didn't come through; neither did God or the Haircut Fairy, but you're still magic.*

"Steve . . ." Ghost whispered the name. His heart was swelling in his chest, wanting to join somehow with Steve's heart and become one live pulsing thing. Siamese twins joined at the heart, all the beats of their lives measured out together, their blood running through the same miles of veins.

Ghost rested his hand on Steve's chest and found Steve's heartbeat, even and strong. Under the touch Steve seemed to loosen a little, to uncoil. Did the shadows beneath his eyes grow paler? Ghost put his fingers out to touch those shadows, to try to capture them under his fingernails, maybe put them in his mouth and swallow them. Steve's eyelashes flickered, but at the last moment his eyes stayed open. He trusted Ghost that much. *You are my oldest friend, you are my only brother. . . .*

Ghost touched the raw-silk skin beneath Steve's eyes, the roughness of Steve's cheeks with their four-day stubble, the slowly melting tightness of Steve's mouth. He laid his head against that steady heartbeat. He felt Steve's lips shape a word: "Ghost . . ."

He managed to make a small sound in his throat.

"Don't you ever leave me. Don't you *ever* go, man—" Steve stopped, but Ghost heard the sudden hoarseness in his voice.

"No," said Ghost. "It won't be me who goes." He could say no more. Instead he would swallow those shadows smudging Steve's eyes; he would lick them away. He bent, and instead of finding Steve's eyes, his mouth met Steve's mouth in a clumsy kiss.

They both grew tense. Ghost thought, *No, oh no, that wasn't what I meant to do,* and Steve's hands came up to push Ghost away.

But somehow his hands were treacherous; instead of shoving Ghost away they slid over Ghost's shoulders and locked behind his back. Steve was pulling him closer, Ghost realized. Maybe he could help Steve now, tonight. Maybe he could overcome that terrible loneliness for a while. He nudged Steve's mouth open just a little at first, then wide, and their tongues met like two beating hearts.

Molasses, he heard from somewhere. *You still taste like molasses.*

"Mmmm?" said Ghost. "What?" Their mouths untangled briefly, then met again.

Stray thoughts weren't important. These minutes had to stretch and stretch; this one kiss had to last for a long, long time. In a moment Steve would pull away. That golden flavor on Steve's tongue, that was not Dixie beer. It was the taste of childhood summers long gone, and laced through it was the dark taste of fear. Already Steve was scared of how much he trusted Ghost; he had said so. This one kiss would end, and there would not be another, because anything beyond this would be too much for Steve to deal with. It was already freaking him out a little, Ghost could feel that. But he needed it so bad.

They slept clutching each other as if they might drown in the blankets and pillows. Ghost stayed awake for a long time. Steve's head burrowed fiercely into his shoulder; Steve's breathing stirred the fine hair on his neck; Steve's long legs entangled with his. Ghost knew full well that in the morning Steve would wake, narrow his eyes against the sunlight, and mutter, "Shit, man, I was so drunk last night, I don't remember *what* happened."

But tonight Ghost could dream Steve's nightmares for him. And so he did.

29

Ghost walked the streets of old New Orleans looking for Ann.

When he started out from Arkady's shop, he thought he would never be able to do it. Better they should have hired a private detective, like the guy in *Angel Heart*. At least Harry Angel might've had a chance of finding Ann by logic and luck. But what chance did Ghost have, who knew these streets not at all, who had only his intuition and blind faith to guide him?

At first it seemed that there was too much magic here, that it could only cloud intuition and distract faith. On every street corner was another story, in the elegant shade of each courtyard another hovering spirit. Some of them were greedy and reached out to his sensitive mind, whispering *come in, come into me, listen to my tale.* The buildings and sidewalks themselves seemed to have a susurrant, subliminal voice.

But soon Ghost realized that he was trying too hard. If he relaxed, he could listen to these sounds with only part of his mind, like a radio playing far away. If he didn't think about it so hard, his feet would lead him the right way.

He passed a group of kids wearing black clothes, black lipstick and eyeliner. Silver crosses, daggers, razor blades dangled from their wrists and earlobes. They passed a joint among themselves, from hand to thin hand. Deathers: kids who loved the night, loved the bands whose music spoke of dark beauty and fragile mortality. Vampires were their dream come true, their ideal to aspire to. Bela Lugosi might be dead, but the deathers would keep him alive in their hearts forever. At the Sacred Yew one night, Ghost had seen a boy showing off his new tattoo: two tiny scarlet fang marks on the white flesh of his throat.

The kids could dream of vampires all they liked, but their faces bore the undeniable stamp of humanity. It was in their imperfections: pimples, scars, the beginnings of laugh-lines. The real vampires had a uniform sort of beauty, ageless and cold. Ghost thought of Zillah's face, only imperceptibly older than Nothing's, and then only because of the smirking mouth and the dramatic, wanton eyes.

Would Nothing catch up with Zillah and the others? Would he reach that same indefinable age and just stop? Ghost wondered how it would feel to know that you weren't going to age anymore, weren't going to *change* anymore, that your skin would never grow creased and delicate, your hair would not turn brittle white, your hands would stay smooth and strong. He shivered. He wouldn't like it, looking in the mirror every day and seeing the same face, with none of the sorrow and laughter of life reflected there.

Ghost's heart twitched at the thought of Nothing becoming one of those blanks. The other three had faces like stylized masks, smooth and white, with only drunken madness blazing out of their eyes. Even Christian's face was blank, though a faint frigid sorrow gleamed in his eyes. But Nothing . . . Nothing's face was so young, the corners of his mouth so tender, his eyes full of wondrous pain. All that should not be wiped away by immortality.

But Ghost was here to save Ann, not Nothing. Still, he could not stop hurting for Nothing, no more than he could stop his heart beating. But . . . *Help the ones you love,* his grandmother had told him, *help them when you can, and after that, mind your business. Your gift doesn't give you the right to go rearranging other people's lives for them. You might see their souls, but they won't always want you to be their mirror.*

Yes, he could see Nothing's soul. It was in those haunted eyes, and in the shadows under them—fatigue, drink and chemicals, yesterday's makeup. Nothing was a lost soul because he wanted to be. It was what he had always wanted; it was his birthright.

But Ann had been bewitched. Done in by the light of chartreuse eyes, by loneliness, by the opium of Zillah's spit and the poison juices of whatever grew inside her.

And what was that? All along, Ghost had been thinking of the baby as a dark lump of blood, the seed of Ann's death. And it was. But it was also Nothing's brother or sister, and Nothing was not evil. Only lost, as surely lost as Ann's child would soon be.

Ghost imagined himself trapped in the womb, his soft bones crumbling, the poison searing his raw new skin away. The poison he and Steve had asked Arkady to make. Had ended up giving Arkady twenty dollars to make.

Ghost leaned against a wall and closed his eyes. There were a million sides to everything. Most people were able to block out some of them. Ghost sometimes thought he saw them all—not that it helped.

"Come in and kiss me . . ." whispered a voice that seemed to emanate from within the wall.

He jumped and opened his eyes. Voices from nowhere made him more nervous than usual these days, but this hadn't sounded like the voice in the closet: it was faint and dry, almost too tiny to hear, like the voice of an insect.

When the voice didn't speak again, Ghost looked around and found himself lost. He didn't even seem to be in the French Quarter anymore. To his back were forbidding, scorched-looking apartment towers. A wide, busy avenue stretched in front of him; a small gate opened in the wall to his left. He slipped through the gate and entered the city of the dead.

Ghost had heard about the cemeteries of New Orleans. The groundwater here was so high that the coffins had to be entombed above ground. There was no real earth to bury them in; if you tried to dig a hole, it would quickly turn into a pit of oozing mud. A heavy rain could float coffins and corpses to the surface. But nothing he'd heard had prepared him for the blinding whitewashed landscape of Saint Louis

Number One, possibly the oldest cemetery in the city, certainly the gaudiest and most haphazardly arranged.

There were coffins bricked into the walls, layer upon layer. That was the first thing Ghost noticed. Some of the brickwork had collapsed, and he could see ashy shadows within the wall, the occasional glint of sunlight on bone, brick, or broken glass. No wonder there were voices in these walls. At his feet a maze of narrow pathways stretched away into the necropolis.

Farther in, he was amazed at how tightly packed together the tombs were. In some places he had to turn sideways and squeeze between them. High peaked vaults loomed over the path. Tall iron crosses jabbed into the sky, bristled along the tops of the intricate ironwork fences that bordered several plots. Almost all the tombs were white—made of moon-pale marble, silvery granite, or whitewashed brick—and the sunlight upon them dazzled Ghost's eyes.

Against all the whiteness a thousand bits of color swarmed. There were flowers everywhere, plaster Virgins and saints with gaily painted robes, colored-glass tumblers full of rainwater, copper and silver coins embedded in cement. Some of the ironwork fences around the graves fluttered with ribbons; others were hung with rosaries or Mardi Gras beads.

Ghost passed a tomb chalked with hundreds of red *X*'s in groups of three. He stopped and looked at it for a long moment. At first it gave him no feeling at all; it might have been empty. Then suddenly he knew what he was supposed to do. Chips of brick and nubs of red chalk were scattered near the base of the tomb. Ghost picked one up, turned three times around, and carefully inscribed his own three *X*'s on the door of the tomb. "I wish I knew where Ann was," he said. His lips barely moved, but even the softest whisper seemed to bounce off the tombs and echo along the empty paths.

Then he closed his eyes and listened with all his heart. When the presence came into his head, he was ready for it.

It was a greedy spirit, and an arrogant one. In fact, it reminded him of no one so much as Arkady Raventon—but without Arkady's weak flesh, without his craven lust. This was a spirit like a flaming ebony arrow. *Look behind you,* it

said. That was all. Then it was gone. Ghost stepped backward
and almost hit his head on the overhanging doorway of another tomb.

Then, very slowly, he turned his head and looked behind
him.

Nothing there but gleaming white walls and flowers trembling in the breeze.

Feeling stupid, obscurely tricked, Ghost headed back the
way he had come. But after a couple of minutes he realized
he was no longer on the same path. That made him feel even
more stupid, because the tomb with the red X's had been
less than twenty feet inside the gate. He was sure of it. How
could he have gotten turned around? This path led deeper
into the cemetery.

Soon there were tombs on all sides of him, and he had no
idea which path led toward the gate. The tombs in the center
of the cemetery must be taller; that was why they seemed to
tower above him, soaring up into the bright cloudless sky.
Over the edge of the far wall reared the dark mass of the
apartment blocks . . . the projects, he realized. It was probably dangerous to be in here alone. The night before, when
they were walking down the dark street that led back to
Arkady's, Steve had talked morosely about the crime in New
Orleans. Little kids would run up and shoot you in the head,
then rifle through your pockets. At least that was what Steve
said.

The path twisted deeper in. Now the sky was a bristling
forest of iron crosses. Granite peaks wavered overhead,
seemed to bow over the path. The tombs pressed closer.
Ghost wedged himself between two of them. For one horrible moment he was stuck. Soft brick crumbled away. Something wriggled against his back. He felt his shirt rip.

Then he pulled free. He half-ran, half-stumbled into an
open area where the tombs were lower and squarer, the tall-
est ones only shoulder-high.

In the center of the open area a girl lay supine on a low
marble slab. Bunches of dried long-stemmed roses were arranged around the slab, crimson gone to black, white to
ivory, yellow and pink to dusty echoes of themselves. The

girl's long red-gold hair hung down over the edge of the slab, and some of the roses had become ensnarled in it. She was not visibly breathing, but Ghost felt a weak tremor of life as he approached.

Then the girl raised her head, and Ghost saw what he had known all along. It was Ann. And she was sick.

"Ghost." Her red-rimmed eyes tried to bring him into focus. "What are you doing here?"

"Did you sleep out here all night?"

She thought about it, then nodded slowly. "Nowhere else to go. I don't have any money, and . . . I didn't find . . ." She coughed, spat out a mouthful of phlegm. It glistened faintly iridescent against all the whiteness. Ghost heard the breath rasping in her chest.

"What are you doing here?" Ann asked again. "Do you know where they are? Where Zillah's staying?"

Ghost swallowed. He wasn't sure he could do this. He hadn't counted on Ann being sick; it was too easy, she had no chance of resisting. But the fact that she had asked for Zillah instead of Steve—that helped. As did the emptiness he saw when he met her eyes.

"Yeah," he said. "I know where they are. I can take you to him."

He found the path that led to the gate on his first try.

"What's that?" asked Ann. She was staring blearily at the altar in the back room of Arkady's shop. The shop was dark and empty, but Arkady had left the door unlocked.

Ghost fumbled the velvet curtain back and ushered her ahead of him. "Careful on the stairs," he said. "It's dark up there."

Ann stared up into the blackness, then slowly began to climb. Up one flight, around the bend, up another flight to the wavering rectangle of light that was the door. Ann went through it, took two unsteady steps into the hall. "Zillah?" she said.

And Steve stepped out from behind the door and plastered a wet cloth over her face. They couldn't imagine why Arkady kept a bottle of ether in his back room, but he had said it would work.

Ghost saw Steve's eyes clench shut as Ann struggled against the sick-smelling cloth. When she went limp in his arms, Steve's face slackened too. For a moment he looked as if he would collapse with her. But he held Ann upright and steadied her drooping head against his shoulder, then slid his other arm under her knees, cradling her.

Ghost couldn't remember the last time he had seen Steve hold Ann so tenderly.

Arkady pulled his fingers out of Ann's mouth and wiped them on her gray sweatshirt. He patted her cheek, then pushed her limp jaw shut. "Excellent," he muttered.

Ghost leaned his head back against the wall and closed his eyes. Beside him, Steve shifted, crossed and uncrossed his long legs. "So what do we do now?"

"Wait," Arkady told him. "It is all you can do."

"Wait!" Steve spat out the word. He hauled himself up and began to pace, the heels of his battered boots clocking against the floor, his hands clawing at his hair. "I can't wait. I'll go crazy."

Ghost stood, steadying himself against the wall. He realized neither of them had eaten all day. "Look. Why don't we go out for a while? Over to Bourbon Street or—"

Arkady clapped his hands. The sudden sharp sound brought all movement in the room to an end: Steve stopped pacing; Ghost shut his mouth without finishing his sentence; even the dust seemed to stop sifting down. Arkady glanced at the window. Twilight had begun to filter through the glass, sending long gray fingers of shadow into the room. Below, on the street corners, Ghost could see lamps lighting one by one, like milky yellow fireflies.

"I know just the thing," said Arkady. "I will care for the girl. I will watch over her. You'd only get in the way." There was no question which of them he meant, but for once Steve didn't snarl. "I've told you about Ashley's friends, the ones in the other guest room. They are musicians, and they will be performing tonight at a club on Rue Decatur. The club serves the strongest drinks in all the Vieux Carré, and when you come back, everything will be over. The child will be dead, and you can take your Ann home again."

Uh-uh, thought Ghost. His brain felt edged with hysteria; he smelled strawberry incense, cheap wine, clove cigarettes. He closed his eyes. Behind his lids he saw a closet door swinging slowly open, saw a silken sleeve reaching out for him, heard a voice whispering, *Easy, Ghost . . . easy . . .* He thought, *No way. I don't want to see any band that came out of that closet. We'll find a two-dollar strip show on Bourbon Street, we'll go to the Ripley's Believe It or Not Museum, we'll do anything but see poor dead Ashley Raventon's lovers playing at some club on Decatur Street.*

But when Ghost opened his eyes again, Steve was looking morbidly interested. He had perked up at the mention of the strongest drinks in all the Vieux Carré. "That sounds pretty good," he said. "I'd like to check out the club scene here. Sure sounds better than sitting around waiting." He turned to Ghost. "You want to?"

It would make Steve happy, or at least take his mind off Ann, or at least give him an excuse to get blind drunk. What could happen in a club? Ashley's lovers couldn't fly off the stage at Ghost, flapping their silks, whispering *easy. . . .* He and Steve would be safe in the crowd.

"Okay by me," he said, hoping he sounded surer than he felt.

"Fine then," said Arkady. As he turned to leave the room, he flapped his hand toward the foot of the bed. A tangle of cotton bandages trailed onto the floor. "You'll want to wrap her up," Arkady told Steve. "Tightly enough to keep some of the blood in, but loose enough to let out the . . . matter."

Steve winced. Arkady made his exit, white robes swirling behind him.

Ghost stood there for a moment, gripping Steve's shoulder. Then he followed Arkady out of the room and shut the door, and Steve was alone with Ann.

At first she only drifted.

Her lungs felt stuffed with cotton, and there was an acrid

chemical burn in the back of her throat. She was too tired to
open her eyes: her eyelids were weighted with sand. She let
herself slip back into sleep, and she drifted. The backs of her
knees and the back of her neck turned to warm water. Her
muscles melted from her bones. Soon she began to see pictures.

They were too vivid to be dreams. Her dreams had always
been in black and white, as precise and disjointed as Fellini
films. The pictures she saw now were in virulent color. For a
time she struggled against them, trying to wake up; then she
gave in, because the pictures swelled in her brain and made
her head hurt when she struggled.

She saw her father's fragile-boned face, weirdly phosphorescent in the gloom of the living room back home. Newspapers were strewn in disarray around his feet, and an empty
coffee mug sat on the arm of his chair near his outstretched
hand. She tried to call his name, but if he heard her, he made
no response.

She saw a jack-o'-lantern lit orange against a black night,
bobbing as if some shadow-wraith carried it. The glowing
grin split open, and a great frothy rose blossomed out, with-
ering and rotting in the space of a few seconds.

She saw a girl's face with dark eyes half-hidden by a curtain of hair; then the girl's eyes rolled up white and silver,
and the girl's mouth opened impossibly wide, and a gout of
blood and whiskey tumbled down her chin.

She saw a jumble of streets laid out like a glowing map.
Neon danced and rippled: purple, green, gold. In the streets,
crowds of thin children in black frolicked. They wore studded belts and wristlets, skull-and-crossbone earrings, hair
dyed every color, teased and twisted into every conceivable
style. She saw pale faces slashed across with scarlet lipstick,
with great smudges of eyeliner. Stalking among the children,
everywhere, were corny silent-film vampires. They pulled
black silk capes up over their noses, drew back in mock
horror at crucifixes dangling from multipierced earlobes. Beside the children in their gaudy mourning, the vampires
were old-fashioned and hokey—except that all of them had
green eyes that glowed and snapped like strange acid fire.

As the final image dwindled into darkness, Ann realized
that someone was touching her. Fumbling with the button of
her skirt, sliding her tights down over her hips. She would
know that touch anywhere, would know it even if she hadn't
felt it in ten years: half-rough but trying to be gentle, half-
desperate but trying to be tender.

Steve. At first she wanted to push his hands away, but she
could not muster the will to move, so she lay quietly and let
him ease her panties down. *Those panties are really skanky,*
she thought. Then she thought, *Who cares, it's only Steve,
he's smelled me before.* Then some distant part of her mind
realized what was happening and shrieked, *Steve!*

He would not let himself part her legs to look. He knew
the warm saddle between her thighs too well, knew its perfumed scent and its tangy taste, knew just how to slide into
its warmth. For some perverse reason he had a raging, aching
hard-on. *Maybe because you haven't touched a girl in over
two months,* the demon in his mind babbled, *not even an
unconscious one.*

He knew that if he looked at her too long, he would want
her, even passed out. Yes, he could slip inside her so easily, it
would be like coming home—but what if the thing in her
womb reached a tiny hand down and grabbed him? What if it
got ahold of him with its *teeth*?

His hard-on was suddenly gone.

Steve slid one hand under Ann's hips—she was thinner,
he noticed; there was only a scant handful of flesh on each
buttock that had once been so sweetly round—and started
winding the bandages around her. Between the milk-pale
thighs, snug against the treacherous cunt, up around Ann's
slender waist and back down.

Would these keep her from bleeding to death when the
poison started to work? He didn't know. But Arkady had said
to wrap her up, and Ghost trusted Arkady because there was
no one else to trust, so Steve had to trust him too. Even if he
was a rat-faced little fuckwad.

When Ann was wrapped from her waist to the middle of
her thighs in white cotton, Steve pulled the sheet up to her

chin. The coarse cloth seemed to settle flat over Ann's body; even the rise of her swaddled pubic mound was nearly imperceptible.

Steve sat on the edge of the bed for a long time, looking at her face. She didn't look any different. Tired, that was all. They might have just made love. She might be catnapping in that lovely twilight lull that happened after good sex, waiting for him to roll over and give her one more long deep kiss.

He bowed his head and rested his cheek against her breasts. Beneath their softness he felt the trembling of her heart. *Turn back,* he thought with sudden incoherence. *Something got fucked up bad. None of this was supposed to happen. Time, turn back!*

But time would not.

He kissed her through the bandages, right at the V where her thighs met. Then he stood up and walked toward the door, and only when he saw how blurred it was did he realize his eyes were overflowing.

Steve! her mind shrieked.

But he never turned around.

30

Arkady lit a candle and started down the stairs. He would get a packet of dried leaves that needed grinding; he would sift them to dust between his fingers as he sat beside Ann's bed. He would bring up an old fragile book that he had not looked at in too long, and the decanter of sherry that rested beneath the altar with Ashley.

He would keep vigil beside the girl all night, or at least until Steve and Ghost returned. He would mark her bleeding, watch her temperature, daub her forehead with ice. He would take good care of her.

And he would think about the way Ghost had slighted him, rejected him, made a fool of him. He would think about the way Steve had shown him nothing but sullenness and discourtesy. He would sit beside the beautiful unconscious girl and think about these things, pondering the power he wielded over Steve and Ghost now. He would look upon the girl's pale fevered face and contemplate the administration of another poison, one for the mother instead of the child, one that would never be detected. He knew a poison made from the spleen of a certain fish, a poison that duplicated the structure of normal stomach acids. He would contemplate unwrapping the bandages that Steve had tucked so carefully around her hips, would imagine himself straightening a wire coat hanger and sliding it up inside her, as tenderly as a lover, until the sharp end punctured her womb. . . .

But no. He wielded great power over Steve and Ghost

through this helpless girl, but he must not use it. That would
be allowing the vampires to triumph. He must save her with
his poisons; otherwise the vampires would have killed her as
surely as they had killed his brother Ashley. As surely as they
had turned that lovely aristocratic face to dust, dried that
sweet white flesh, shrivelled those eyes, those *eyes* . . .

He only hoped his concoction would work. He had told
Ghost he'd developed it after the death of Richelle, and this
was true; but he had neglected to mention that it had never
been tested on anyone.

Something wavered at the foot of the stairs. His shadow,
huge and unsteady in the flickering light of his candle.
Arkady stepped on it—a trick he had learned long ago, stepping on one's own shadow, good for nothing but show—and
ducked under the velvet curtain into the back room of the
shop. *Mullein-leaf,* he thought. *I must bring the mullein-leaf
to be crumbled, and the book and the sherry.* Drawing near
the altar, he bent to retrieve the decanter—and stopped, his
dry lips hissing air, his hands frozen in their movement
toward the dropcloth.

He always kept Ashley's skull beneath the altar, safe in the
dark. Sometimes in the night he would wander downstairs to
speak to Ashley and stroke the smooth ivory curve, but he
always put Ashley back in his resting place. Why, then, was
the skull here on top of the altar, nestled among the relics
and offerings?

Some of the other objects had been displaced as well: the
floor at the foot of the altar was littered with dead flowers,
stray coins, the powdery ash of incense sticks. One of the
plaster saints had toppled over, but the candles still burned,
two on either side of Ashley, dripping pink and black wax
onto the altar. Arkady reached out to touch what was left of
his brother, hoping the contact might give him an answer, or
at least lessen his confusion and his fear.

The skull was as cold as a November wind, as cold as
frozen earth.

"What?" he whispered. "What's wrong? What's happening?"

The eye sockets retained their velvety tragic darkness; the

teeth did not meet in reply. But as Arkady stroked the dome of the skull, all the candles—the four upon the altar, and the one he was carrying—suddenly flickered and then burned stronger than before. But now their flames were a bright, cold blue.

A sure sign of evil spirits present in the room.

"Ashley?" he whispered. "My brother? Is it you?" But that made no sense. Ashley was not evil. Ashley would never hurt him. Arkady groped under the altar for the sherry. He would need it tonight. When his fingers found the faceted glass of the decanter, he clutched it and started for the stairs.

But just before he was about to sweep the velvet curtain aside, he paused, then turned and went back to get Ashley. This meant he must abandon his candle and ascend the stairs in darkness, but Arkady would not leave his brother down here alone with whatever spirits roamed tonight.

The first stair tread creaked when he rested his weight upon it. With his bare toes he felt for the edge of the next stair, tried to ease his foot onto it without making a sound. His eyes strained against the dark. His shoulder brushed the wall—or did the wall lean in to crush him? Under his feet the boards felt unpleasantly dry, almost furry. He climbed two more stairs, three, four.

He was halfway to the top when he heard the light footsteps coming up behind him.

The stairs were dark, but the two faces seemed lit by an unhealthy glow from within. Arkady could make out their sharp features, their drawn mouths, the tired gleam of their eyes through the cheap sunglasses they wore. "It's only you two," he said. "You gave me a turn."

They started up the stairs toward him.

"Look at us, Arkady," said one of them. His voice was only a rustle, like a voice sifting through dried moth wings.

"We've waited too long," said the other, and his voice was like a wind that blew from far away over a stagnant sea. "We can't find anyone. We can't even look in the mirror. And we have a show to do. . . ."

Arkady kept backing up the stairs. He heard his own breath sobbing in and out of his throat. "What do you want?"

"It's time, Arkady," said the first one. He smiled, and
patches of ivory skin flaked away from his cheeks, powdering
the stairs, mingling with the dust.

The other one smiled too. His lips were caked with dry
rouge, once red, now faded to dusty orange. Even in this dim
light, Arkady could see the delicate tracery of lines that
webbed the twins' faces and disappeared beneath their sunglasses.

"We need you," said the first one.

"It's easy. You can join your brother."

"There's a girl upstairs," Arkady heard himself say.
"Young, pretty. You can have her—"

The first one shook his head in mock reproach. His ruby
hair whipped his face. "No, Arkady. We don't want your
pretty girl, not yet anyway. Next you'll be telling us to go find
a whore on Bourbon Street. We're hungry. We know you. We
need you."

"We love you, Arkady," said the other, smiling even more
widely. One of his upper front teeth fell out of its socket and
landed with a tiny *plink* on the stairs. He picked it up and
fitted it back into the ragged hole in his gum, still smiling.
There was no blood, not a drop. "You see? Would you have
our beauty wither and crack as your brother's did? You can
help us, Arkady. You can feed us. You know it's easy."

"Easy . . ." echoed the other.

They ascended the stairs toward him. Arkady could not
run, could not move; already his feet and his ankles felt
withered, useless. He wondered how they would feed. Did
they have a sort of proboscis that would thrust deep into his
body to search out every last drop of life? Or would they just
bury their mouths in him, rend him with their teeth and let
his life force flow into them?

Whatever it was, Ashley had felt it too; it was the last thing
Ashley had felt, apart from a rope around his neck. The
thought gave Arkady a sick sort of comfort. He would try not
to be afraid.

The twins kept climbing toward him. Now he could see
the silver sheen of their eyes behind their sunglasses. He
could see the minute cracks that glazed the surface of their

skin. He could see the thin layer of dust that coated their tongues.

When their graceful hands were almost upon him, he uttered a low desperate cry and hurled Ashley's skull at them. It struck the redhead's chest and bounced away. As the first dry hand touched his cheek, Arkady saw the skull tumbling from stair to stair, down into the darkness.

The twins fed for two hours. They pressed themselves close against Arkady's body, and every crack and pore of their skin became a tiny mouth, a minuscule suckhole, questing deep into Arkady's tissue to extract every drop of moisture, of vitality, of whatever love might still be buried in Arkady's bitter heart. They stopped occasionally to stretch toward each other and exchange long kisses oiled and flavored by the inner workings of Arkady. Sex was only a stopgap measure for them now, a means to an end. The usual sorts of lovemaking seemed pallid, tame. Feeding was ever so much more sensual.

Eventually the redhead sat up and yawned. The blond stopped sucking and regarded Arkady with mild curiosity. Arkady's fingers were little more than bone now, but they still scraped weakly against the wooden floor of the landing where the twins had dragged him. The husk of his head still creaked from side to side in blind denial; the dried leaf of his tongue still thrust from his crumbling mouth, questing for a drop of moisture. There was no drop of moisture left anywhere in Arkady's ruined body; the blond twin knew that. But they always took so long to die.

It was sort of interesting.

The redhead glanced over his shoulder, back toward the warren of rooms down the hall. "Arkady said there was a girl," he suggested.

The blond smirked at him. "Greedy, greedy."

"I don't care. . . ."

"Let's have a look, then."

They tiptoed into Steve and Ghost's room and stood on either side of the bed. There was a strong smell of blood. Arkady had left no light on, and their eyesight was not as

strong as their other senses, but they did not really need it.
They leaned over the bed and breathed in deep, going past
the girl's odor of sweat, blood, and sorrow, trying to scent out
the pulse of life still beating.

Then they looked at each other and shook their heads.

"This girl belonged to Ghost, you know," said the blond.
"Who?"

"*Ghost!* Don't you remember? The beautiful dreamer?"

"Oh! I didn't like him. Not our sort. Too . . ."

"Too asexual?"

"Too *pure*," said the redhead, and they both giggled. But
their laughter died as they stared at the indistinct curled
form on the bed. Arkady had been so *dry.*

"A shame."

"A pity. But we have a show to do."

What Arkady had said about the twins' being musicians
was not precisely true. They were dilettantes who welcomed
any chance to perform almost any act in public. Currently
they had captured the affections of a local band whose
Gothic act had failed to ignite the French Quarter club
scene. The guitarist and former singer, Pearl, was a lovely
young woman with opalescent skin, masses of dyed and
crimped blue-black hair, and no hint of a brain in her head.
"You'll inject some *life* into the act," she enthused. With a
perfectly straight face, the blond twin had replied, "And perhaps you will inject some life into us, too."

Pearl and the other members of Midnight Sun had agreed
to let the twins front their act for as long as they wished to.
Audiences were enthralled; club owners loved them. The
band particularly liked the fact that the twins never took
their cut of the door. They had no use for money.

At the foot of Ann's bed they embraced. Their brittle hair
drifted together; their eyes glittered silver behind the sunglasses they still wore.

"Let's leave after the show tonight," the redhead murmured. "Let's blow this town."

"But Pearl . . ." The blond had taken a particular liking
to the empty-headed, lush-bodied guitarist.

"We can do her later. I don't care. But let's leave after that. My darling? Please?"

"Of course, then, anything you want. But why so suddenly?"

The redhead glanced at the bloody hump on the bed. Then he tilted his head back and smiled into his brother's silver eyes. His grin was warm, lazy, insouciant. "Don't you see what happened to *her*?" he asked. "Where's the elegance in that? This is a trashy town.

"Too many damned bloodsuckers here."

Out on the landing Arkady's fingers still scraped uselessly at the floorboards. Flakes of parchment skin sifted from him with every feeble twitch. "Goodbye, Arkady dear," said the redhead unconcernedly.

The twins picked up Ashley's skull at the bottom of the stairs and took it with them as they left.

31

"I think this is the place," said Steve.

They'd been out since dusk hitting all the Bourbon Street bars they had missed before. Now it was almost midnight, and they were staggering along Decatur searching for the club Arkady had told them about.

Steve backed up, stumbled into the gutter, and stared blearily up at a big black sign above a set of ironwork doors. The sign was written in enormous Gothic letters that dripped lurid red blood, the corners decorated with a delicate spiderweb motif: *PASKO'S*. Steve narrowed his eyes, trying to make the swimming letters come together. "Is this the place?"

"I think so," said Ghost, swaying as a breeze from the river brushed his face. The breeze was warmer than the night air, and it smelled of oysters and pearls, of bones, of dark mud. It made him nervous and thirsty. "Um—maybe we ought to walk down to that big café and get some coffee first."

"Yeah, us and a million tourists. Let's go on in. We can get some more beer." Steve shoved the doors open and dragged Ghost in.

The kid working the door was dressed entirely in black. Somehow Ghost wasn't surprised. His skin was so pale that it glowed in the blue light of the club; his eyes were nearly obscured by smudges of greasy black makeup.

"Fi' dollar cover tonight," he said.

Ghost rummaged through his pockets. Things sifted out—
leaves, rose petals, everything but money. The kid's sneer
deepened. He looked like Billy Idol at the end of a long,
rough night. There was a tic in his right eye, barely noticeable but constant. "You fags gonna pay or what?" He spoke
less with malice than extreme indifference.

Steve leaned against the wall and produced a crumpled
ten-dollar bill. The kid snatched it. With courtesy exaggerated to the point of great sarcasm, he waved them in.

As soon as they entered the club, Ghost was struck by the
likeness of this place to the Sacred Yew back home in Missing Mile. It surprised him. The Yew was only a little hole-in-
the-wall, more progressive than most of its kind. But this was
a nightclub in the big city, in the heart of the French Quarter. Ghost had vaguely expected more glitter, more jazz.
Revellers in spangled cat's-eye masks, maybe, shaking con-
fetti from their hair. But here were only the same sorts of
kids that haunted the Sacred Yew. More of them, sure, but
with the same dark-rimmed eyes, the studded ears, the pale
jewelled throats. The sweet smell of clove cigarettes was familiar, and their smoke swirling through blue light.

There were differences too. Pasko's served mixed drinks;
Ghost saw mysterious crimson concoctions in fancy plastic
goblets full of skewered fruit and paper parasols. And they
had a decent PA here, one that not even Steve would be able
to bitch about. Right now it was blasting Bauhaus at shattering volume. Ghost recognized the grave, guttural voice of the
lead singer.

Ann had listened to them. Ghost couldn't remember the
singer's name or the name of the album, upon which all the
songs twined together to tell a kind of horror story. Nothing
would know. Ghost wondered whether Nothing would be
here tonight; all the children looked like him. Their long
dark raincoats or too-big leather jackets enveloped their fragile bones like shadow. Most of them looked so small, so frail,
ready to break like soap bubbles if you touched them. But in
all those black-smudged eyes lurked a certain hardness, a
wall of glass to mask their terrible vulnerability. *Show me*

what you can, those eyes said. *Hurt me if you want to. I've seen it all, or I think I have, and where's the difference?*

Steve was already at the bar ordering them a couple of Dixie beers. In the past few days he had developed a taste for the brand; sometimes he drank it as a chaser for his whiskey. Ghost would rather have gone to one of the all-night groceries on Bourbon Street and bought a flask of scuppernong wine. Wild Irish Rose or Night Train. He liked the syrupy thickness of the wine, and the way the fermented, rotten-sweet flavor of the grapes melted over his tongue. It reminded him of the elixirs his grandmother had mixed for him long ago: the spoonful at bedtime, the tiny liqueur glass that often sat by his plate at breakfast. He remembered her saying *Drink that right down, every drop. That will stop your cough. That one will put rose petals in your cheeks.* And the one he had drunk most eagerly, the one he now knew had been mostly fruit juice and sugar-syrup: *This one will keep you from growing all the way up. It will preserve the child in you forever.*

Fruit juice and sugar-syrup.

Well, mostly.

Steve was coming back toward him with a dripping bottle in each hand. Ghost reached out to grab a beer and their fingers touched briefly, and Steve was grinning his old easy drunken grin, and for a moment it was as if they were back at the Yew, taking a break between sets, catching a buzz together. For a moment everything was all right.

That was when the band began to play.

The Bauhaus singer's voice plunged from the heights of psychosexual ecstasy to the sepulchral depths of despair. Then the song cut off as abruptly as if a cancer had seized its throat. There came a ripple of wooden drums as the band took the stage, and a growling bass . . . and then the very air of the club was transfixed by an unearthly, blood-chilling, double-throated howl.

From where they stood near the back of the club, Steve and Ghost could not see the stage. They glanced at each other when they heard the howl, which vibrated through the layers of smoke, through the ivory bones of all the children, through the spray-painted walls of the club. As the first line of the opening song came whispering through the smoky air, the crowd rippled and parted. Now there was a clear path all the way to the stage, and Ghost got his first look at Ashley's lovers. Ashley's *twin* lovers.

He felt his nerves draw him rigid, taut as wire. His beer slipped from his hand and fell foaming on the sticky floor. Dimly he was aware of wetness soaking through his sneakers, of Steve staring at him, saying "What the fuck," bending to rescue the bottle of Dixie before it all foamed away. He wanted to reach out and grab Steve's wrist—for warning, for protection, for the simple feeling of warm familiar skin under his fingers.

But he could not move. He could only stare at the two figures onstage, could only watch their lips as they began to whisper into their microphones: *"Death is easy . . ."*

They hadn't changed much since the night on the hill up by Roxboro. Since the night Ghost had dreamed of them. The only difference was the dark glasses both of them wore, even here in this dim club, in this air thick with smoke like blue cream. If anything, they were more beautiful than they had been in his dream, lusher than they had been up at the hill.

No more were they dry and brittle. No more did their skin look as if it might flake away from their bones at the lightest touch. Tonight their lips shone purple with rouge, and the ripe insides of their mouths glistened pink. Their skin was the smooth white of almonds. Their colored silks writhed around them. They clutched each other with their bird-boned hands and pressed their hollow cheeks together. Their hair twined together, long strands of ruby-red and yellow-white like mingling flames. Their faces echoed each other in a perfection that was at once opulent and dissolute.

As the twins' song touched Ghost, he thought he caught their scent too, their heady bouquet of strawberry incense, clove cigarettes, wine and blood and rain and the sweat of passion. All the things they had loved when they were alive,

the things that had dragged them down and carved the rich
white flesh from their bones, the things that sustained them
now. Incense and spice, wine and blood, sex and rain . . .
and the juice of other lives, sucked away to saturate their
brittle tissues, to restore them.

They whispered their song to him.

> Death is dark, death is sweet.
> Death is eternal beauty—
> A lover with a thousand tongues—
> A thousand insect caresses—
> Death is easy.
> Death is easy . . .
> DEATH IS EASY . . . DEATH IS EASY . . .
> DEATH . . . IS . . . EASSSSSSY.

The patrons of the club must have seen these twins perform before, must have heard this susurrant song many
times. They took up the chant. "Death is easy," they wailed.

A girl near Ghost raised her arms, swaying. She wore a
little black hat with a tattered veil that hung down over her
face. A mourning hat. Beside her, a boy draped in fishnet and
leather—a boy about Nothing's age—wrapped his thin arms
around himself. Ghost saw tears glistening on the boy's fine-
boned face.

"Death is easy," the children whispered, and Ghost closed
his eyes, but he could not keep their minds from brushing
his. He knew that they believed those words. Why else did
they shroud themselves in funeral garb; why else were their
thin wrists scarred with razor-tracery delicate as spiderwebs?
Why else did they make trysts in graveyards, starve themselves and then kill their hunger with cigarettes, suck down
their drinks and swallow their exotic drugs with all the en-
thusiasm of children turned loose in a candy store?

Why else did they love the vampires?

If Arkady had spoken truly, the twins were vampires of a
different sort. They did not live on blood, like Zillah and his
pair of lollipop thugs, like Christian and Nothing. These

vampires sucked lives. They had sucked Ashley Raventon's life out, or so Arkady implied. They had left Ashley a dry husk, a skeleton bound together by withered skin, with only the strength to finish what they had begun. Ghost could see the withered body suspended in the tower, slowly turning.

The twins shared a microphone now, giving it head, taunting the crowd with their erotic narcissism. Their hands twined in each other's hair; their ripe lips nearly touched. The rest of the band was obscured, cast into shadow; all eyes were on the twins.

Suddenly, through the fog of drunkenness that clouded Ghost's brain, suspicion flared. Why were they so opulent tonight? Why did their lips shine so wetly; why did their bright hair writhe, alive with color? What had they found to sate them before the show?

Now the redheaded twin had a skull in his hands. He held it up and slowly turned it, letting the colored stagelights play over its ivory surface. The eye sockets caught two beams of golden light, and a ripple of pleasure went through the crowd. Now all the lights went off except the ones shining directly on the skull. It hung above the stage, suspended in darkness, revolving slowly.

Ghost thought he recognized it.

Had the twins been back to the shop tonight?

And if they had, who was taking care of Ann?

Steve was watching the band and the audience, transfixed if not actually enjoying himself. Ghost grabbed his elbow. Steve swayed a little as he turned; somehow his drinking had gotten ahead of Ghost's. He rolled his eyes. "We never shoulda trusted Arkady's taste in music. You heard enough of this Gothic crap? You wanna go find a bar?"

"No," said Ghost. He tightened his grip on Steve's arm. "Listen. I think we better go back to Arkady's. I think something might be wrong."

At any other time the look Steve gave him would have hurt like hell. But there was no time to worry about himself. Ghost only stared back, and at last Steve dropped his gaze and muttered, "Okay. Whatever you say, man."

* * *

"Death is easy!" a boy with red lipstick smudged around his eyes shouted into Steve's face. Steve shoved the boy out of his way and continued toward the door. The kid stumbled backward, as drunkenly limp as a rag doll, and spilled his fancy cocktail all over his friend. The friend's cigarette sputtered out.

Steve didn't give a fuck. He stared at the back of Ghost's head, at the pale hair that straggled over the collar of Ghost's army jacket. For a second—just for a second—Steve wanted to grab a handful of that dirty, tangled, silky hair and yank it as hard as he could. He stuffed his hands in the pockets of his jeans.

Not for the first time, and surely not for the last, Steve found himself wishing he could reach inside Ghost's skull and pull out the magic there. He wished he could grind it under his boot, leave it smeared across the beer-sticky floor. He'd been standing there minding his own damn business, drunk enough to groove on the stupid music, a beer in each hand. For a couple of hours Steve had managed to forget Ann and everything else. Now they were tearing off on some mission that could only mean more pain and trouble. Ghost's thoughts brushed Steve's, Ghost's fear was in him, and for a second he hated Ghost. If Ghost really did have a shining eye in his heart, as Arkady had said, Steve wished he could gouge it out.

"Have a nice night," the doorman called nastily after them as they left the club.

When the cool night air touched his face, Steve calmed down a little. Crazy shit to be thinking about. What did he love best about Ghost? What had he *always* loved about Ghost? The magic. The weird, illogical, irritating magic.

"I'm sorry," he said, bumping into Ghost, hugging him. For one more moment they were safe, they did not have to hurt. Neither wanted to move.

But finally Ghost stepped away and pulled Steve by the arm. "Come on," he said. "We got to get back."

Steve knew there was more trouble ahead. More stupid shit and agony. But he could not hate Ghost, no way, nohow. He followed his best friend—maybe his only friend—

through the maze of streets and alleys that led back to
Arkady's shop, and the wind that fingered their hair blew off
the river, smelling of oysters and pearls, of dark mud and the
bones of children.

32

"I'm dying," Molochai moaned. The floor beside him was spattered with fresh blood.

"I already died," Twig told him. "I'm a zombie, I wanna eat your BRAINS—" He lunged at Molochai, got a mouthful of hair. Molochai began to choke. After a moment he vomited a long stream of blood, some of which soaked the front of Twig's jacket. They collapsed across the floor.

"Not again—"

"I can't *help* it—"

"SHUT UP!" screeched Zillah. The room fell silent except for the sound of Molochai and Twig softly gagging. At the first onset of the sickness Zillah had collapsed in a corner, shivering madly. He would let no one near him; no one wanted to go near him.

Nothing lay on the bed bathed in icy sweat. Long streaks of crimson marked the side of the mattress where he had vomited.

Christian stood at the window. His back was rigid, his face drawn with disgust. The shade was pulled down. When he had tried to raise it, the others shrieked piteously at the faint light that filtered up from the gas lamps far below. At last, when the retching had subsided, he said, "Do none of you possess the sense of smell?"

No one replied.

"Do none of you possess the sense of *taste*?"

Still no answer.

"Because if his cancer was far enough along to make all of you this sick, Wallace Creech must have reeked like a fresh grave. Or were you so eager to make your kill—in our alley, under our *window*—that you paid no attention to the very things that give you power? ARE YOU ALL MAD?" Wild-eyed, Christian surveyed the room for a moment. Then, as if he knew the answer to his own question, he turned back to the window.

Nothing's voice wavered toward him in the darkness. "Are we gonna die?"

Christian snorted. "No. You're going to—how would you put it?—puke your guts out. For about twenty-four hours. Then you'll be weak and tired for twenty-four more. Essentially, you have food poisoning. A fine way to spend your first full night in the French Quarter, no?"

"You're so smug," hissed Zillah from the corner. "But what happens when you drink *our* poisons? Give you a double shot of Chartreuse and you'd be flat on your back just like us."

"Yes." Christian permitted himself a faint cold smile. "But I would be wise enough not to drink a double shot of Char-treuse." He remembered a time when he had not been so wise, and phantom pain shot through him. If they were hurting that badly, they deserved more sympathy. After all, he supposed they had thought they were doing him a favor.

But Zillah didn't want sympathy. He hauled himself up on his elbows and glared at Christian. His eyes snapped green fire, visible from across the room. "Yeah?" he whispered. "Yeah? You know what *I* think? I think if we have to be sick, then you should be sick too."

Christian hesitated, wary. "What do you mean?"

"I mean . . . maybe you should have a *drink*, Chrissy."

Molochai giggled. "Have a drink, Chrissy."

Twig took up the chant. "Have a drink . . . Chrissy, have a drink . . ." Their voices chased each other around the room. Only Nothing was silent. He lay absolutely still against the red-streaked sheets. Christian saw the shadow of his ribs under his white skin.

"You can't make me," said Christian, but cold fear trickled down his spine.

"Twenty-four hours puking our guts out," mused Zillah. "Then twenty-four more to recover. We could be on the road by the next night. The van's gassed up. Twig has the keys."

"There's no Chartreuse," said Christian wildly.

Zillah waved a languid hand. "In your bag. The closet, top shelf. Three bottles."

Then he leaned over, coughed, and vomited a great gob of blood. It cascaded down his chin and trailed onto the floor. When he straightened up, his face was as serene as ever. "Have a drink, Chrissy," he said. His voice was almost casual.

Could he live like this, with Zillah always threatening him, dangling the constant specter of loneliness over his head? Christian considered the alternative. If they left, he would lose not only them but Nothing too. His heart clenched at the thought of never seeing that fine fragile face again. His only moments of love would be those he spent with the children, matching their caresses with his own before he tore their pale throats out and stole their lives.

Whether he could live with Zillah's threats Christian did not know. But he knew he could not live alone again. Numbly, as if in a dream from which he hoped to wake, he moved toward the closet.

"Don't make me do this," he said when he had the bottle in his hand. He spoke calmly, but it was a plea born of desperation.

Zillah only stared at him, eyes still flaring. His breath hissed in and out through his teeth—quick, jagged, painful.

"Have a drink, Chrissy," he said.

The first shot blazed green agony as it went down.

And then Zillah made him drink another.

And then another.

33

By the time they got back to Arkady's shop, Steve was running full tilt. Ghost lost his breath trying to keep up. Cold drops of sweat flew from them, catching the light of the street-lamps. Ghost licked salt off his lips. The sweat in Steve's hair sparkled, as if his hair were full of a million tiny diamonds.

"Hurry up," Steve panted as they swung into the alley. "You've got the key."

Ghost fumbled with the key Arkady had given him, aware of Steve behind him wanting to wrest it out of his hand. At last the door swung open. The shop was very cold. There was some other smell beneath the herbs and candles and incense, something dry, ready to crumble. *The mummy smell,* Ghost thought. *That's what they smelled like.* Ghost had never seen a mummy, but his grandmother had looked at a bunch of them in a museum once. *They were all in glass boxes,* she told him. *You couldn't smell them, but I knew just how they would smell. Like spice kept in a jar too long. Like rags hung up to dry for a thousand years.*

Pink and black candle wax had melted onto the velvet dropcloth of the altar. Steve took the stairs three at a time, kicking aside a heap of rags that lay across the top tread. Ghost followed slowly. There was a bad feeling here, a feeling of stillness, of nothing left alive. He didn't want to go upstairs, but he knew he had to.

At the top of the stairs he nudged the heap of rags with the toe of his sneaker. It rolled over and gaped up at him, lips stretched tight over teeth like chips of ivory. A tiny half-dried trickle of blood seeped from the torn socket of its right eye. Arkady must have summoned the last of his strength to pull the knife out of his robe and drive it into his eye socket. Ghost had seen the knife on Arkady's nightstand, a long, lethal-looking thing with a jewelled handle and a ten-inch tapered blade. His hands were still folded around the haft. Ghost saw the gleam of precious stones between fingers like dry kindling.

Steve's boot had punched a sizable hole in Arkady's brittle rib cage. Inside the body cavity, withered organs hung like empty wineskins, grayish-brown, already coated with a fine layer of dust. *How the twins must have loved Arkady,* Ghost thought; *how many wild nights they must have spent with him, to be able to suck him so utterly dry.* How could this bundle of shrivelled tissues have lived long enough to drive a knife into its own eye?

But the knife protruded from the socket in mute testimony. Gently, Ghost pried Arkady's brittle fingers from the haft, drew the blade from Arkady's eye, and tried to tuck the white robe around the desiccated little body. He closed Arkady's withered eyelids as carefully as he could, but they still flaked away beneath his fingers.

Then he made himself go into the bedroom.

The light was as flat and dead as neon, though it was only the light of the moon shining through the window. Steve sat on the edge of the bed. Beside him was a hump swathed in bloody sheets. Steve's face had gone an absolute, eerie white. Thick blood coated his hands. He raked his fingers through his hair, matting it and streaking his forehead. "She's dead," he said.

"Are you sure?"

Steve laughed the most hopeless laugh Ghost had ever heard. "Oh yeah. I'm sure. Come here and get a good look, why don't you?" Ghost stepped closer to the bed, and Steve yanked the sheet back.

Ann lay on her side, twisted into an attitude that was painful to look at. Her neck craned stiffly back. Her face was a grimace of pain. Crusted rivulets of blood ran from the corners of her mouth. Her hands were thrust between her out-stretched legs as if she had been clawing at herself. Blood slimed her arms to the elbows like gory gloves. Most of the bandages had come unravelled, or Ann had torn them away. They lay in a sodden heap beside the bed. The sheet beneath Ann's hips was a black nightmare of blood. She had bled so much that the sheet and the mattress could not absorb it all; the overflow pooled in the wrinkles and depressions of the bedclothes, clotting as thick and dark as jelly.

Cupped in Ann's hands, half-encased in a glob of gelatinous blood, Ghost saw a pale shape no larger than a red bean: the dot of an eye, the veined bubble of a skull, tiny fingers like the petals of sea anemones. He looked away.

Four A.M. is when all my dreams die, Ann had told him. It would always be four A.M. for her now; nothing could ever get her through this last, longest night.

"You know what?" Steve laughed again and shoved his bloody hair back. "There's even blood on her eyeballs. How the fuck did it get on her *eyeballs*? What did he give her? What did *we* give her?" He stared wildly around the room, at the dusty walls, the cobwebbed ceiling. He met Ghost's eyes, but there was no sign of recognition in his empty stare. A long shudder ran through him.

Then he seemed to pull himself together. His eyes were no longer blank; they shone with the glaze of alcohol and unhealthy resolve. "I'm gonna kill them," he said. "You found Ann. You can find where they live. And you're gonna take me there and help me kill them all."

Ghost had to moisten his lips before he spoke. "I don't want to kill anybody," he said.

"Yeah?" Steve grinned his humorless grin. "Then how come you're holding *that*?"

Ghost looked down at his hand. He was holding Arkady's jewelled knife. The slender blade was dazzling in the cold neon light.

Ghost raised his eyes back to Steve's. Slowly he shook his head.

"*Fuck you, then!*" Steve jumped up and bolted onto the landing, heading for the stairs. Ghost started to follow.

But before he reached the door, he turned back and dug a handkerchief out of one of his pockets. Quickly, without thinking much about it, he took the head of the foetus between thumb and forefinger and extracted it from the lump of congealed blood. The back of his hand brushed Ann's inner thigh; it was scaly with dried gore.

The tiny skull was still warm, and for a moment the sticky skin seemed to twitch between his fingers. But that was only his hand trembling. He wrapped the foetus in his handkerchief and tucked the bundle into his pocket.

Out on the landing, Steve snatched Arkady's withered corpse up by the front of its robe and slammed it against the wall. The brittle cranium shattered. Dust sifted from the cavity, powdered Steve's hands, mingled with Ann's blood.

"What'd you do to her?" Steve yelled into the ruined face. "What was that stuff? Drāno? Why did we trust you?"

He kicked the body down the stairs. At the bottom it crumbled, the white robe settling over a pile of dust and splintered bones. Steve followed it.

Ghost ran down after him and tried to grab him, but Steve was already raging through the shop. He kicked Arkady's altar, and it crashed over, though Ashley's skull was nowhere to be seen. He tore the beaded curtain down. Bright bits of plastic skittered across the floor. He swept rows of bottles and boxes off the shelves. Strange pungent smells wafted up from the spilt substances.

"Fucker," said Steve helplessly. "Goddamn shithead fucker." He might have been speaking of God or Arkady or himself. He stood with his feet splayed and his eyes rolling wildly, looking for something else to destroy, something whose broken fragments might magically recoalesce into a whole, living Ann. He grabbed the knife from Ghost's hand and raised it high above his head.

Ghost saw plainly what Steve intended to do next: he was going to bring the heavy handle down on the glass case where Arkady's bowls and jars were laid out. Several hundred pounds of shattering glass, even in a back alley of the French Quarter late at night, might attract attention. And with Ann lying in her own blood upstairs and the proprietor smashed to powder in the back room, attention was not what they wanted. "Don't do that," Ghost said, and caught Steve's arm.

Steve whirled on him. For a moment Ghost thought Steve would bring the knife down in his face. But Steve only stood poised to attack, the muscles of his arms trembling.

"Listen," Ghost said as calmly as he could. "It wasn't your fault. It wasn't even Arkady's fault. Ann made her own choice." *Bewitched,* he thought, but that wouldn't help Steve.

Steve's lips worked soundlessly. His eyes were red and desperate. But ever so slowly he lowered the knife. In that moment, despite the dark smears of blood on his forehead and the lines of exhaustion bracketing his mouth, Steve's face looked younger and more vulnerable than ever. It was the face of the eleven-year-old kid Ghost had once known, wanting badly to believe what Ghost was telling him, wanting to trust Ghost but not quite able.

At last Steve said, "You don't think it was my fault?"

"It was never your goddamn fault."

"Or Arkady's, even? You don't think she died because of the poison we gave her?"

"She would've died no matter what, Steve. Arkady told us she couldn't have an abortion. And the baby would have killed her. It wasn't our fault. Not a damn thing could have helped her."

"The vampires did it." Soft, but simmering with rage and pain. "Yeah. Vampires. So what if they are? Does that mean they can just roll into town, fuck up my life, then go off and party some more? I was fucking up my life just fine on my own. I didn't need them. Ann didn't need them. I still loved her—I would've—I would've—"

"I know you would've."

"But now I can't." Steve spread his hands wide. "There's no choice anymore. Everything I wanted, everything *she* ever wanted—none of it can ever happen now. And how come? Because some vampire was *horny?*" He hefted the knife. "No. It's not gonna be that way. You can find them, Ghost. You can take me to their lair.

"And I'm gonna kick some vampire ass."

Christian clawed the bathroom door open and felt his way back along the landing. His good night vision could not help him now, because his eyes were squeezed shut against the pain. It washed over him again, a green nausea that felt as if it were turning his guts into bloody lace, a sickness that clutched the softest core of him and squeezed.

Twice already he had made his way to the bathroom. His fastidiousness would not allow him to vomit on the floor as the others were doing, though now he was far sicker than any of them, except possibly Nothing.

He swore at himself. *Stupid, stupid—falling for Zillah's tricks, trying to buy their love. You can never be like them. They are young and strong and wild. To them the blood is just another path to drunken gratification. You are old, and for you the blood is life itself.*

But as the Chartreuse blazed down, he had felt as if he were drinking those eyes, Zillah's eyes. Zillah had made him drink half the bottle. Molochai and Twig egged him on between bouts of retching. Nothing lay silent, slit-eyed, beaded with icy sweat.

Christian pushed the door shut, stumbled across the room, and fell on the bed beside Nothing. He heard no gagging or moaning; everyone else seemed to be asleep. The blaze of green pain lessened a little. Christian opened his eyes and studied the delicate pattern of water marks on the ceiling, following their lines, wondering if they formed maps that someone might travel. Wondering if they formed the map that had brought him and Nothing and the others here, to this city, to this room.

Soon his eyes closed, and he slept dark dreamless sleep.

His feet sore from all the night's running, his heart ready to burst with Steve's pain and his own, Ghost led Steve along Chartres Street. Steve had jammed the dagger into the waistband of his jeans. The jewelled handle protruded obscenely.

Ghost was pretty sure he knew where Nothing and the others were staying. He didn't have to be psychic to use the phone book, and Christian's bar was still listed. *But how do you know about the bar, the long-ago nights empty even at Mardi Gras? How do you know about the room upstairs where a girl gave birth to her own death?* These were questions best asked in dreams. Ghost let his feet lead him along.

He shouldn't be taking Steve on this fool mission at all, putting them both in danger. He should lead him to a dead end, an empty room somewhere. Or a bar. But Steve had been put through enough bullshit tonight. Something in Ghost rebelled at lying to him. Anyway, the vampires would surely be out drinking somewhere. Steve could go upstairs and bang on the door until he saw the room was empty. Then there would be no reason to stay.

Steve saw the boarded-up window, the shabby door with the faded sign above it that still said *CHRISTIAN'S.* Beside it, an unmarked door stood open; a long staircase ascended into darkness.

"Is this it?" Steve didn't wait for an answer; the truth was in Ghost's eyes. He put his hand on the jewelled haft and started up.

Halfway to the top, the darkness took on a velvety tangibility, as if Ghost might stroke it with his hand. Above him he heard Steve feeling his way up the stairs, banging his head against the walls, missing a step and stumbling when he finally reached the landing. Up here there was a little light, dim and watery, as if the moon shone in through an unseen hole in the roof.

"This door?" Steve asked. There were three.

"Yeah, but—" Ghost stared at the door. He had thought the room would be empty, but it didn't *feel* empty.

Steve twisted the knob and gave the door a vicious kick with the toe of his boot. It swung open, and before Ghost could react, Steve had stepped inside.

It was even darker in the apartment. Steve couldn't see the bed or its two shadowy occupants until he was upon them. His knees hit the edge of the mattress, and he nearly lost his balance. Only the thought of falling into bed with two vampires steadied him.

The room reeked of blood and vomit. Steve's stomach clenched, and all the beer he had drunk earlier threatened to make itself known to him again. But he was past being sick. There was another smell too, something herbal and alcoholic. It was coming, he realized, from one of the figures on the bed. It was on his breath.

Steve pulled the knife out. The haft felt good in his hand, heavy and sure. It would cleave straight through the mother-fucker's heart—blood for Ann's blood. And then he would keep carving. He would take out as many of them as he could.

The weight of the knife tugged at Steve's arm, as if the thin sharp blade were hungry for blood. A thread of doubt touched him. Blood for blood: that was right. But somewhere in him he knew that this was not the one who had killed Ann. This was not Zillah. Did they all have to die for Zillah's sins?

Steve wavered, nearly dropped the knife. But then the demon in his mind began to whisper. Not his old familiar demon. This was a new one, darker and more twisted, with a dark shapeless mouth and eyes that wept blood. *Ann died like a roadkill,* it told him. *And you know it was your fault. Fuck what Ghost says, you know the part you played. If you can't do this, you might as well carry her bloody corpse back to Missing Mile slung over your shoulders.*

Steve's hands tightened convulsively around the haft of the knife. The sharp facets of the jewels cut into his palms. Zillah was somewhere in this room, he knew that. And Zillah would be next.

Then the demon was pulling his arms down, and Steve screamed his exultant rage as the blade cracked the vam-pire's breastbone and sank into his soft dark heart.

Nothing struggled to wake up. Something was wrong. His body felt sheathed in dry sweat, and he could not force his eyelids open.

He had been so sick from Wallace's blood. They all had.

The smell of vomit was still strong in the room, vomit and Chartreuse and beer . . .

No one had drunk beer tonight. That much he was certain of. Nothing managed to open his eyes.

He had just enough time to see Steve standing over the bed, his face terrified but crazily exultant, his arms raised high above his head—and then Nothing saw the blade plunge down into Christian's body beside him. Christian's black blood arced up from his chest, splattering the moonlight, soaking into the carpet to mingle with the faded blood of Jessy.

The impact brought Christian up from sleep.

For a moment there was pain, deep and cold. But compared with the sickness he had felt earlier, the pain was not very bad. It was like being adrift on a river, one that smelled of mud and bones like the Mississippi, but this river was green. Its gentle luminescence bathed him and soaked through him. At last he was drunk. The river made him drunk, and his mind grew dim and began to rest.

Heartblood welled up in his mouth, and he licked it from his lips. The taste was sweet, dark, familiar, and it would stay with him forever; it was the essence of him. Through the bright film that washed over his eyes, he saw a face above him: translucent hair hanging like a waterfall, pale eyes wide and stricken.

As Christian sank beneath the green waters of his death, he thought, *Three hundred and eighty-three years. And he was as beautiful as he should have been. He was lovely.*

There were too many words in Ghost's mouth, ready to spill into the silence of the room. *Murderer,* he wanted to say, *my best friend, my only brother. I once saw you run your car off the road to keep from hitting a stray dog. How could you stab someone through the heart? How could you bear it as you looked into his eyes?*

But in the end he didn't say any of those words, because the silence erupted around them.

Ghost had come up beside the bed. He was standing a

little behind Steve, and he never saw Zillah coming. Steve must have seen him, because he stepped backward.

There was only a heart-stopping blur of motion launching itself out of the darkness. Then the razor flashed, and every speck of light in the room seemed to coalesce along its deadly edge. Wetness hit Ghost's face, hot and stinging. The taste was in his mouth, in his throat. Blood. Steve's blood, spraying.

Zillah had Steve around the chest, forcing him down. Steve bucked and clawed at him. But Zillah's free hand had the razor, and now it was swinging down, toward Steve's throat.

The knife still protruded from Christian's chest, jewels glittering dully in the faint light. Ghost reached out and pulled it free. Christian's heart made a faint sucking sound as the blade came away. Blood seeped from the wound.

Ghost felt that he moved in slow motion: the razor was still swinging down. He took two steps forward. Easily, he slid his left arm around Zillah's neck; effortlessly he pulled Zillah's chin up and back.

Then he drove the knife straight into Zillah's temple, and that was the hardest thing he had ever done.

Nothing saw it all. He was still on the bed, half-propped on his elbows, naked except for the vomit-stained sheet that covered him. He saw Steve bring the knife down into Christian's chest, and he had not even had time to react to that when Zillah flew like a demented bat out of the corner and whipped his razor across Steve's upraised forearms.

Then the most extraordinary thing of all happened: Ghost took the knife, stepped forward, and lifted Zillah straight off the floor. He only had one arm around Zillah's neck, but Nothing saw Zillah's feet dangling an inch above the floorboards. Ghost hoisted Zillah around so that he was facing the bed.

And Zillah's eyes met Nothing's as the knife went in.

There was no love in them, no sorrow. Only pain and blame and blind rage. This was not the way Zillah had planned it. Through all the stupid risks he took he had never

considered the possibility of his own death. *This is your fault,*
those eyes told Nothing. *You brought me to this, and this
should be happening to you.*

Then the green light blazed once and went out. Zillah's
eyes were as dead as a blown light bulb. But their message
had burned itself into Nothing, had hardened him faster and
better than anything else could.

Zillah's feet kicked and shuffled an inch above the floor.
Blood began to seep around the handle of the knife, then
from his nostrils and the corners of his eyes. His mouth fell
open, and a fountain of blood tumbled down his chin,
washed over Ghost's arm and hand. That seemed to wake
Ghost. The strain of Zillah's weight hit him, and he let the
body fall. He stared unbelievingly at his hands.

"Steve?" he said in a small voice. "What . . . ?"

Steve was slumped against the bed. He had taken off his
shirt and was pressing it between his arms, trying to stop the
bleeding from his slashed wrists. Tiredly, he looked up at
Ghost.

"I owe you another one," he said.

Nothing glanced around the room. Where were Molochai
and Twig? He saw them huddled against the far wall, heard
them puking more violently than ever. He didn't know if
they had seen Zillah die. Right now they sounded as if they
were beyond caring.

He looked at Ghost. Ghost stared back. His eyes were
clear and very pale.

"I could kill you, you know," Nothing heard himself say. "I
could make them get up and kill you."

Ghost didn't move. "I know you could."

"I could make them kill both of you."

"It'll be me first, then," said Ghost.

Nothing looked at Zillah's body sprawled on the floor. Rivulets of blood crawled along the cracks between the floorboards where Zillah's head had fallen. He thought of never
feeling those strong veined hands on him again, of never
kissing that lush mouth.

He thought of never again having anyone tell him what to do.

"Take that thing out of him," he said.

Ghost knelt and pulled the knife out of Zillah's skull. He had to wiggle the blade free, but Nothing didn't look away. The knife left a clean narrow wound in Zillah's temple. A pale, slightly cloudy fluid began to trickle from it.

"Now get out," said Nothing.

Steve and Ghost only stared at him.

"*Now.* If they get up, I'll let them kill you. They loved Zillah too." Nothing wasn't sure if he meant this. Could he really watch Steve and Ghost die, even now? He thought of the cold message he had seen in Zillah's eyes and wondered whether he would ever have known the truth if Zillah had lived.

Still, his father had loved him in his way. In the way of decadence and self-gratification. But even that was worth something. Nothing was amazed at how calm he felt. He never knew his face was wet with tears.

Life was his now. When he was on the road he would want to think about Steve and Ghost, to know they were alive somewhere. He hadn't wanted Ann's baby to die either, not really. It would have been his brother or his sister. He would have taken care of it. He would have held it on his knees so it could look out the windows of the van and dabbed wine and blood on its soft little gums.

He knew Ann must be dead. Why else would Steve have come on this murdering rampage? But if he never asked, he would be able to pretend the baby was alive somewhere, growing up without its family just as he had done. Maybe someday they'd be driving along some country road and suddenly there would be Zillah's child, Nothing's brother or sister, sticking out a hopeful thumb.

Maybe.

"Go on," he told Ghost more gently. "Steve's hurt. Get him to a hospital. Take him home."

Ghost pulled Steve up, and they left without a word. Nothing didn't watch them go. He had enough goodbyes to say.

Toward morning, when the sky was beginning to go from

purple to transparent violet, Molochai and Twig awakened from their nauseated daze. At first they were frightened when they saw the bodies. Then they got mad, but Nothing only clamped his arms across his chest and stared them down.

"Zillah would have killed them," said Twig sullenly.

"Zillah tried," said Nothing. He knew how cold his words sounded. But if he could make Molochai and Twig feel his power now, in these first few minutes, he did not think they would challenge him again.

"I did it the way I wanted to," he told them, and no one had anything to say to that.

All of them knew what to do for their dead. There was not much blood left in Christian's body; the tapered blade of the knife had pierced his heart and crushed it, and most of his blood had drained into the mattress. They licked what they could from his face, his hands, his chest. They sucked at the edges of the wound. With a wet snuffling sound, Molochai buried his face in the hole the knife had made. He nibbled at Christian's torn heart and pronounced it bitter.

Tenderly they laid Zillah out on the bed and used his pearl-handled razor to slit him open from sternum to pubic bone. Nothing saw strangely shaped organs glistening in the pale aperture. They lifted the organs out and arranged them carefully, lovingly, on the bed around him. Then, one by one, they thrust their heads into the long wound and licked the husk of Zillah clean.

As the sun rose, shedding its wan light upon the proud old buildings of the French Quarter and the trash in its gutters, they left Christian's room and filed down the stairs. The black van was parked two blocks away. Nothing hated to leave so soon. He had spent only two nights here, one of them puking his guts out. It wasn't fair.

He smiled, though it barely touched his lips. *Fair?* How long had it been since he expected things to be fair? If you wanted something, you didn't wait for the world to deal it out to you; you took it. If he had learned nothing else during his time with Zillah, he had learned that. And anyway, it didn't matter that he had to leave New Orleans so soon. The city was in his blood. He would be back; there was always time.

Nothing had left his long black raincoat behind, draped over the bodies like a shroud. In its place he wore Zillah's jacket with its purple silk lining. The fresh bloodstains were like badges. The smell of them twisted his heart, but he wore them with pride.

Just before they left the room, Nothing had pulled the shade up. As the first ray of light touched the bodies of Zillah and Christian, their flesh began to smolder and crumble. In less than an hour it was only ash.

34

Steve got his arms stitched and bandaged at Charity Hospital on the edge of the French Quarter. The doctors on duty in the emergency room suspected a suicide attempt, but Steve kept telling his story over and over, and Ghost kept backing him up. They'd been out drinking; a gang of kids had jumped them; one of the kids pulled a razor. Steve flung his arms up to protect his face and got slashed.

They had to talk to a policeman, and Ghost could see Steve getting ready to break down: it was in the corners of his mouth, the way his shoulders sagged. Ghost closed his eyes and tried to send Steve strength. At last they were allowed to go.

For a few minutes they stood outside the hospital in the cool dawn. Steve stared at his gauze-swathed arms. "If I wanted to kill myself," he muttered, "I wouldn't have slashed my goddamn *wrists* like some kind of half-assed moron." Ghost started walking back toward the car. After a moment Steve followed. "I'd get a shotgun. Straight through the brain." Ghost shuddered, but Steve didn't notice. "Or I'd drive up to the mountains and run my car over a guardrail. A thousand feet down and BAM! you're spread out over a mile of rocks."

They reached the car. Steve stood staring around him, seeming to search for something in the faces of the old buildings, maybe just having a final look at the place that had

claimed so much from him. Ghost wondered if they would
ever come back here.

Ghost drove all the way back to Missing Mile. The muscles of his shoulders and upper arms were sore. The palms of
his hands tingled faintly, and he kept wiping them on his
knees, on the fabric of the seat. Again and again he felt the
knife going into Zillah's skull, the terrible lack of resistance
as it slid through Zillah's brain. He had heard Zillah's final
shriek of rage and agony in his mind. He'd had to do it; Steve
would be dead now if he hadn't, his throat sliced wide open
and his life bled away. Still Ghost felt the knife going in.

Somewhere in the Louisiana swamps Steve said, "Pull
over." Ghost killed the ignition. In the dark phosphorescence
of the swamp Steve's tears shone as clear and bright as crystal. Blindly he reached for Ghost, pressed his face into
Ghost's hair, rubbed his hands over Ghost's face, gathered
the fabric of Ghost's clothes between his fingers. "You're
here," he gasped. "I know you're here—I can feel you—I
can *smell* you—you're not gonna go away—"

"Steve," said Ghost, "oh, Steve . . ." He could hardly
speak. Just to hold each other was not enough; again he
wished that their hearts could be joined. Maybe that would
clean some of the blood from their hands.

Back in Missing Mile they were a little puzzled when their
friends did not greet them with astonishment. It was hard to
realize that they had only been gone a few days. Terry told
them that Simon Bransby had been found dead in an easy
chair in his living room. The house, Terry said with mild
bemusement, was full of crazy shit—cat guts pickled in form-
aldehyde, terrariums full of toads that bounced off the glass
as if they were tripping on high-grade acid. Simon had died
of a Valium overdose, and everybody thought it was suicide,
presumably because his only daughter had finally left home
for good.

Ann was never heard from, and only a handful of people in
Missing Mile—R.J., Terry, Monica—knew anything about
what had happened to her. Not even they knew the whole
tale.

* * *

They discovered that even in the face of pain that seems unbearable, even in the face of pain that wrings the last drop of blood out of your heart and leaves its scrimshaw tracery on the inside of your skull, life goes on. And pain grows dull, and begins to fade.

Steve went back to work at the Whirling Disc, played his guitar obsessively. Kinsey Hummingbird hired him to tend bar a couple of times a week at the Sacred Yew. Sometimes Steve would start screaming in the night. He would wake sobbing, clawing at the darkness in front of his face. Ghost held him and tried to warm the chill of nightmare out of his bones.

By day, Ghost wandered around town picking up leaves and bits of colored glass, talking to the old men who had moved their checker game inside the hardware store for winter. They kidded him about the bad times he'd said were coming, but stopped when they saw the look on his face.

One day he rode his bike out to Miz Catlin's and told her everything. At the end of the hour it took him, he was sobbing. Miz Catlin patted his hand and said the things Ghost had known she would say: she believed it, every word, and his grandmother would be proud of him.

Then she told him something he hadn't known. "That Raventon fellow was a fake and a liar."

"Huh?"

"Pennyroyal, yarrow, brooklime." Miz Catlin flapped a wrinkled hand. "All those things are good to start a pessary with, but they wouldn't do a damn thing together. Not strong enough. The girl would have died anyway, Ghost."

Ghost wondered. But when he was lying awake at night, staring at the stars on his ceiling and thinking about everything, Miz Catlin's words made him feel better.

One December day Ghost found himself out on Violin Road near the trailer where Christian and the others had lived. The tangle of rosebushes still grew wild in the backyard, and though Missing Mile was deep in winter, one rose blossomed in the heart of the thicket. When Ghost reached

for it, a thorn sank like a tooth into the ball of his thumb.
Bright drops of his blood spattered the frozen ground.

"Blood for blood," he whispered. Again he remembered
how the knife had felt going into Zillah's skull.

On an evening in early spring Steve and Ghost walked out
to the old graveyard. Beside Miles Hummingbird's weathered tombstone, unmarked, was a soft spot in the ground
where Ghost had buried the foetus still wrapped in his handkerchief. He wished he could have placed Ann's body here
too, but this was part of her; this would have to do.

Ghost wondered where Ann was now. He wished he could
ask Miles, but he would not. *What goes on between the dead,*
his grandmother had told him, *is the dead's own business.*

Steve rolled a joint, lit it, passed it to Ghost, and began to
talk lovingly about what a piece of shit the T-bird was. He
was going to sell it to the junkyard, he said, and throw a party
to celebrate. Whenever Steve started talking that way, it
meant he was thinking about a road trip. That might do them
both good.

Steve was quiet for a while. When the joint had burned
down to a ragged end, he turned to Ghost. "Listen . . ."

"What?"

"Everything that happened last fall . . . I know it was
real. I mean, I was there. But it's still hard, Ghost." Steve
spread his arms wide. "What does it do to *you*? How do you
deal with it? Doesn't it fuck you up, to know that we touched
something evil, that it's still out there in the world?"

Steve was letting himself think about those days again. For
a long time he had refused to. His world was visibly torn
apart, but he would not acknowledge what had sundered it.
Ghost held him during his night terrors and never tried to
make him talk.

But a postcard had come in the mail last week, a brightly
colored postcard, its edges ragged, its message blurred with
the grime of small-town post offices. Ghost knew Steve had
seen it. *You are safe,* the card had said. *You will be safe as
long as I live: forever, or nearly so. I love you.* And the signature was scrawled large across the bottom, the *t* like a dagger

thrusting down, the *N* and the loop of the *g* swooping like bats' wings: *Nothing*.

"I don't know," Ghost said at last. "Maybe they were evil, like Miz Catlin says. My grandmother told me you shouldn't try to define evil, that the minute you think you've got it all pinned down, a kind of evil you never even thought of will sneak up behind you and jump inside your head. I don't think anyone knows what evil is. I don't think anyone has the right to say.

"So maybe they were just like us. I hate what they did, what they do. But they'd hate our lives too. Maybe they did what they had to do to live, and tried to get a little love and have a little fun before the darkness took them."

"I love you, Ghost."

Ghost felt his heart expand. "Love you too."

He accepted the last of the joint from Steve, sucked at it, closed his eyes. When the smoke was gone, he stretched out on the pine needles, his head in Steve's lap. Steve stroked his hair, and through those guitar-callused fingertips Ghost caught Steve's mood: lonely, but not alone. Bitter, but not destroyed. They had made it through the winter.

They stayed in the graveyard, talking sometimes, drifting off to sleep and waking to see their breath plume in the air, watching the sky until it grew pale with the first light of morning.

EPILOGUE

Fifty Years Later

Night.
Black night in a club, 4:00 A.M. relieved only by the watery neon pulse that filters through the holes in the ceiling. The club is in the basement of a burned-out building, so most of the light is lost in the charred and rusted skeleton of steel that towers seventeen stories into the night. But some light filters through, purplish and flat.

Night in a club. These dives have changed very little. The walls are painted black, scorched in spots, crawling with arcane graffiti: spiky insignia, dripping band emblems sprayed in gold and red. This club is located a few blocks from the edge of the French Quarter, and Mardi Gras week has just begun. Less than a mile away the endless party rages through the streets, the bright costumes swirl by, the liquor flows like milk.

They will be there soon enough.

On the tiny stage, separated from the dance floor by strands of barbed wire, two members of a snuff-rock band are packing up their equipment: the cords and effects, the violin bows and bone-saws, the ampules of blood the audience thinks is fake. They mix it with alcohol to keep it from coagulating too quickly; they have not forgotten their old customs. Their faces are smudged white, with rows of tiny, slightly raised black dots in elaborate patterns of scarification. They wear their hair twisted into hundreds of matted, filthy little braids. Their eyes are ringed in gray. They still bleed from the slashes made by the singer's chrome-tipped whip upon their hands and faces and naked pierced chests, but they are healing fast.

On a steel bench that runs along the wall, a young man is curled on his side, asleep: the band's singer. His fist is pressed against his mouth, and his lips make a slight sucking motion. He looks perhaps twenty, too thin for his height. His face has taken on a cool ivory beauty: the high sharp cheekbones, the twin black arches of his eyebrows sweeping toward his temples, the flickering dark pools of his eyes as he dreams. His hair falls across his forehead in a straight, smooth sheaf, blue-black. The air in the club is colder than the semitropical night outside, and in his sleep the young man has pulled his purple-lined coat tightly around him.

He has good reason to be tired. He runs a tight crew, and he has kept them alive, well fed, and sated for half a century.

The band have finished packing up. At the sound of their footsteps approaching the young man comes awake, blinking up at them. At first his vision makes them hazy, and he thinks there are three of them—three clumps of hair, three faces defined in blots of dark makeup—but slowly they come clear, and there are only two.

The memory of singing tonight returns to him. He gives strange performances, alternately whispering his words and shrieking them, his hands clenched at his sides, then flung out gesturing at the crowd as if he would conjure them all into hell. He swirls his whip through the smoky air and watches the audience bleed. And sometimes as he sings, he remembers another night at a different club, a night when a pale-eyed wraith clung to a microphone as if the crowd would drown him. He remembers a hoarse golden voice.

But the show is over. He smiles up at them and asks, "What did you bring me?"

Molochai pulls his hand out of his pocket and opens his fingers. Lying on his grubby palm is a hypodermic needle full of blood. Nothing opens his mouth. Molochai places the sharp tip of the needle—carefully, ever so carefully—on Nothing's tongue and pushes the plunger. The blood trickles down Nothing's throat, rich and sweet.

"We saved the last for you," Twig tells him.

"We can get more," says Nothing. The others nod in agreement.

"We can *always* get more," says Nothing.

A smile of happy anticipation spreads across Molochai's scarified face, and he jabs Twig in the ribs. Twig returns the jab with a tug on one of Molochai's tiny braids.

"Because we have time," Nothing tells them. "Forever and ever." For the first time in years he thinks of Christian, his smooth impassive face, his coldly tragic eyes. He believes Christian would be proud of him now.

"Or nearly so," he whispers a beat later. But the others have already turned away.

The stage lights have been turned off, and the neon of the buzz-vendors flickers only fitfully. Nothing leads his family out of the club in darkness. They are headed for Bourbon Street. Nothing knows how to get there, and where they can pick up a bottle of Chartreuse along the way.

Molochai is playing with a heavy silver doubloon of the same shape and size as those thrown from Mardi Gras parade floats along with all the other colored trinkets. But this coin is older than any Mardi Gras doubloon. Molochai keeps tossing it into the air and catching it.

Nothing snatches the coin in midair and looks at it. Over the years Molochai's sticky fingerprints have worn away some of the carving: the man's lips no longer appear so full, and his sharp teeth are barely visible.

"Let me see that, kiddo," says Twig, making a grab for the coin.

They bandy it about for a few moments, tossing it back and forth, trying to spin it on the ends of their fingers. As they climb the stairs to street level, the sound of their boots on the cement echoes back along the graffiti-swarming corridor, up through the spiderwebs and the maze of burned-out girders, out into the night.

Night. And they are gone.

The footsteps, still echoing.

Then silent.

Then black.

Missing Mile, North Carolina, in the summer of 1972 was
scarcely more than a wide spot in the road. The main street was
shaded by a few great spreading pecans and oaks, flanked by a
few even larger, more sprawling southern homes too far off any
beaten path to have fallen to the scourge of the Civil War. The
ravages and triumphs of the past decade seemed to have
touched the town not at all, not at first glance. You might think
that here was a place adrift in a gentler time, a place where Peace
reigned naturally, and did not have to be blazoned on banners or
worn around the neck.

You might think that, if you were just driving through. Stay
long enough, and you would begin to see signs. Literal ones like
the posters in the window of the record store that would later
become the Whirling Disc, but was now still known as the
Spin'n'Spur. Despite the name and the plywood cowboy boot

above the door, those who wanted songs about God, guns, and glory went to Ronnie's Record Barn down the highway in Corinth. The Spin'n'Spur had been taken over, and the posters in the window swarmed with psychedelic patterns and colors, shouted crazy, angry words.

And the graffiti: STOP WAR with a lurid red fist thrusting halfway up the side of a building, HE IS RISEN with a sketchy, sulkily sensual face beneath that might have been Jesus Christ or Jim Morrison. Literal signs.

Or figurative ones, like the shattered boy who now sat with the old men outside the Farmers Hardware Store on clear days. In another life his name had been Johnny Wiegers, and he had been an open-faced, sweet-natured kid; most of the old-timers remembered buying him a candy bar or a soda at some point over the years, or later cadging from him a couple of beers. Now his mother wheeled him down Firehouse Street every day and propped him up so he could hear their talk and watch the endless rounds of checkers they played with a battered board and a set of purple and orange Nehi caps. So far none of them had had the heart to ask her not to do it anymore. Johnny Wiegers sat quietly. He had to. He had stepped on a Vietcong land mine, and breathed fire, which took out his tongue and his vocal cords. His face was gone to unrecognizable meat, save for one eye glittering mindlessly in all that ruin, like the eye of a bird or a reptile. Both arms and his right leg were gone; the left leg ended just above the knee, and Miz Wiegers *would* insist on rolling his trouser cuff up over it to air out the fresh scar. The old-timers hunched over their checkers game, talking less than usual, glancing every now and then at the raw, pitiful stump or the gently heaving torso, never at the mangled face. All of them hoped Johnny Wiegers would die soon.

Literal signs of the times, and figurative ones. The decade of love was gone, its gods dead or disillusioned, its fury beginning to mutate into a kind of self-absorbed unease. The only constant was the war.

If Trevor McGee knew any of this, it was only in the fuzziest of ways, sensing it through osmosis rather than any conscious effort. He had just turned five. He had seen Vietnam broadcasts on the news, though his family did not now have a TV. He knew that his parents believed the war was wrong, but they spoke of it as something that could not be changed, like a rainy day when you wanted to play outside or an elbow already skinned.

Momma told stories of peace marches she'd gone to before the boys were born. She listened to records that reminded her of those days, made her happy. When Daddy listened to his records now, they seemed to make him sad. Trevor liked all the music, especially the jazz saxophonist Charlie Parker, who Daddy always called Bird. And the song Janis Joplin sang with his daddy's name in it. "Me and Bobby McGee."

Trev wished he could remember all the words, and sing the song himself. Then he could pretend it was just him and his daddy driving along this road, without Momma or Didi, just the two of them. Then he could ride up front with Daddy, not stuck in the back with Didi like a baby.

He made himself stop thinking that. Where would Momma and Didi be, if not here? Back in Texas, or the place they had left two days ago, New Orleans? If he wasn't careful he would make himself cry. He didn't want his mother or his little brother to be in New Orleans. That city had given him a bad feeling. The streets and the buildings were dark and old, the kind of place where ghosts could live. Daddy said there were real witches there, and maybe zombies.

And Daddy had gotten drunk. Momma had sent him out alone to do it, said it might be good for him. But Daddy had come back with blood on his T-shirt and a sick smell about him. And while Trev huddled in the hotel bed with his arms around his brother and his face buried in Didi's soft hair, Daddy had put his head in Momma's lap and cried.

Not just a few tears either, the way he'd done when their old dog Flakey died back in Austin. Big gulping, trembling sobs that turned his face bright red and made snot run out of his nose onto Momma's leg. That was the way Didi cried when he was hurt or scared really bad. But Didi was only three. Daddy was thirty-five.

No, Trev didn't want to go back to New Orleans, and he didn't want Momma or Didi to be there either. He wanted them all with him, going wherever they were going right now. When they passed the sign that said MISSING MILE TOWN LIMITS, Trevor read it out loud. He'd learned to read last year and was teaching Didi now.

"Great," said Daddy. "Fucking great. We did *better* than miss the highway by a mile—*we found the goddamn mile.*" Trevor wanted to laugh, but Daddy didn't sound as if he was joking. Momma didn't say anything at all, though Trev knew she had lived around here when she was a little girl his age. He wondered if she was glad to be back. He thought North Carolina was pretty, all the giant trees and green hills and long, curvy roads like black ribbons unwinding beneath the wheels of their Rambler.

Momma had told him about a place she remembered, though, something called the Devil's Tramping Ground. Trevor hoped they wouldn't see it. It was a round track in a field where no grass or flowers grew, where animals wouldn't go. If you put trash or sticks in the circle at night, they would be gone in the morning, as if a cloven hoof had kicked them out of its way and they had landed all the way down in Hell. Momma said it was supposed to be the place where the Devil walked round and round all night, plotting his evil for the next day.

("That's right, teach them the fucking Christian dichotomy, poison their brains," Daddy had said, and Momma had flipped him The Bird. For a long time Trevor had thought The Bird was something like the peace sign—it meant you liked Charlie Parker, maybe—and he had gone around happily flipping people off until Momma explained it to him.)

But Trevor couldn't blame even the Devil for wanting to live around here. He thought it was the prettiest place he had ever seen.

Now they were driving through the town. The buildings looked old, but not scary like the ones in New Orleans. Most of these were built of wood, which gave them a soft-edged, friendly look. He saw an old-fashioned gas pump and a fence made out of wagon wheels. On the other side of the street, Momma spied a group of teenagers in beads and ripped denim. One of them, a boy, flipped back long luxuriant hair. The kids paused on the sidewalk for a moment before entering the record store, and Momma pointed them out to Daddy. "There must be some kind of a scene here. This might be a good place to stop."

Daddy scowled. "This is Buttfuckville. I hate these little Southern towns—you move in, and three days later everybody knows where you came from and how you make a living and who you're sleeping with." He caressed the steering wheel; then his fingers tightened convulsively around it. "I think we can make it through to New York."

"Bobby, no!" Momma reached over, put a hand on his shoulder. Her silver rings caught the sunlight. "You know the car can't do it. Let's not get stranded on the highway somewhere. I don't want to hitch with the kids."

"No? You'd rather be stranded *here*?" Now Daddy looked away from the road to glare at Momma through the black sunglasses that hid his pale blue eyes, so like Trevor's eyes. Didi had eyes like Momma's, huge and nearly black. "What would we do here, Rosena? Huh? What would *I* do?"

"The same thing you do anywhere. You'd draw." Momma wasn't looking at Daddy; her hand still rested on his shoulder, but her head was turned toward the window, looking out at Missing Mile. "We'd find a place to rent and I'd get a job somewhere. And you'd stay at home with the kids, and there'd be nowhere to get drunk, and you'd start doing comics again."

At one time Trev would have chimed in his support for Momma, perhaps even tried to enlist Didi's help. He wanted to stay here. Just looking at the place made him feel relaxed inside, not cramped up and hurting the way New Orleans and sometimes Texas had made him feel. He could tell it made Momma happy too, at least as happy as she ever felt anymore.

But he knew better than to interrupt his parents while they were "discussing." Instead he stared out the window and hoped as hard as he could that they would stop. If only Momma needed cigarettes, or Didi had to go pee, or something. His brother was toying with the frayed cuff of his shorts, dreaming, not even seeing the town. Trev poked his arm. "Didi," he whispered out the corner of his mouth, "you need to pee again?"

"Uh-uh," said Didi solemnly, too loudly. "I peed last time."

Daddy slammed his hands against the wheel. "Goddammit, Trevor, don't encourage his weak bladder! You know what it means if I have to stop the car every hour? It means I have to start it again too. And you know what starting the car does? It uses extra gas. And that gas costs money. So you take your pick, Trev—do you want to stop and take a piss, or do you want to eat tonight?"

"Eat tonight," Trevor said. He felt tears trying to start in his eyes. But he knew that if he cried, Daddy would keep picking on him. He hadn't always been like that, but he was now. If Trev stood up to Daddy and answered back—even if the answer was giving in—Daddy might be ashamed and leave him alone.

"OK, then, leave Didi alone." Daddy made the car go faster. Trevor could tell Daddy hated the little town as much as he and Momma liked it. Didi, as usual, was lost in space.

Daddy wouldn't stop on purpose now, not for any reason. Trevor knew the car was going to break down soon; at least, Momma said so. If that was true, he wished it would go ahead and break down here. He thought a place like this might be good for Daddy if he would only give it a chance.

"God *DAMN*!" Daddy was wrestling with the shift stick, slamming it with the heel of his hand. Something in the guts of the car banged and shuddered horribly; then greasy black smoke came streaming around the edges of the hood. The car coasted to a stop on the grassy shoulder of the road.

Trevor felt like crying again. What if Daddy knew he had been wishing for the car to break down *right that very second*? What would Daddy do? Trevor looked down at his lap, noticed how tightly his fists were clenched against the knees of his jeans. Cautiously he opened one hand, then the other. His fingernails had made stinging red half-moons in the soft flesh of his palms.

Daddy kicked the Rambler's door open and flung himself out. They had already passed through downtown, and now the road was flanked by farmland, green and wet-smelling. Trevor saw a few patches of writhing vine dotted with tiny purple flowers that smelled like grape soda. They had been seeing this plant for miles. Momma called it kudzu, and said it only flowered once every seven years. Daddy snorted and said it was a goddamn crop-killing pest that wouldn't even die if you burned it with gasoline.

Daddy walked away from the car toward a cluster of trees not far from the road. He stopped and stood with his back to the Rambler, his hands clenched at his sides. Even from a distance Trevor could tell Daddy was shaking. Momma said Daddy was a bundle of nerves, wouldn't even fix him coffee anymore because it just made him nervous. But sometimes Daddy was worse than nervous. When he got like this, Trevor could feel a blind red rage pulsing from him, hotter than the car's engine, a rage that did not know words like *wife* and *sons*.

It was because Daddy couldn't draw anymore. But why was that? How could a thing you'd had all your life, the thing you loved to do most, suddenly just be *gone*?

Momma's door swung open. When Trevor glanced up, her long blue-jeaned legs were already out of the car, and she was looking at him over the back of the seat. "Please watch Didi for a few minutes," she said. "Do some reading with him if you're up to it." The door slammed and she was striding across the green verge toward the taut, trembling figure of Daddy.

Trevor watched them come together, watched Momma's arms go around Daddy's from behind. He knew her gentle, cool hands would be stroking Daddy's chest, she would be whispering meaningless soothing words in her soft Southern voice, the way she did for Trevor or Didi when they woke from nightmares. His mind framed a still shot of his parents standing together under the trees, a picture he would remember for a long time: his father, Robert Fredric McGee, a smallish, sharp-featured man with black wraparound sunglasses and a wispy shock of ginger hair that stood straight up on top, the lines of his body tight as a violin string; his mother, Rosena Parks McGee, a slender woman dressed as becomingly as the fashions of the day would allow in faded, embroidered jeans and a loose green Indian shirt with tiny mirrors at the collar and sleeves, her long wavy hair twisted into a braid that hung halfway down her back, a thick cable shot through with wheat and corn silk and autumn gold.

Trevor's hair was the same color as his father's. Didi's was still the palest silk-spun blond, the color of the lightest hairs on Momma's head, but Momma said Trev's hair had been that color too and Didi's would likely darken to ginger by the time he was Trevor's age.

Trevor wondered if Momma was out there soothing Daddy, convincing him that it didn't matter if the car was broken, that this would be a good place to stay. He hoped so. Then he picked up the closest reading material at hand, a Robert Crumb comic, and slid across the seat to his brother. Didi didn't understand all the things that happened in these stories—neither did Trevor, for that matter—but both boys loved the drawings and thought the girls with giant butts were funny.

Back in Texas, Daddy used to joke that Momma had a classic Crumb butt, and Momma would smack him with a sofa pillow. There had been a big, comfortable green sofa in that house. Sometimes Trevor and Didi would join in the pillow fights too. If Momma and Daddy were really stoned, they'd wind up giggling so hard that they'd lose their breath, and Trevor and Didi could win.

Daddy didn't make jokes about Momma's butt anymore. Daddy didn't even read his Robert Crumb comics anymore; he'd given them all to Trevor. And Trev couldn't remember the last time they had all had a pillow fight.

He rolled the window down to let in the green-smelling air. Though it was still faintly rank with the odor of the frying engine, it was fresher than the inside of the car, which smelled of smoke and sour milk and Didi's last accident. Then he started reading the comic aloud, pointing to each word as he spoke it, making Didi follow along after him. His brother kept trying to see what Momma and Daddy were doing. Trevor saw out of the corner of his eye that Daddy had pulled away from Momma and was taking long strides down the highway, away from the car, away from the town. Momma was hurrying after him, not quite running. Trevor pulled Didi against him and forced himself not to look, to concentrate on the words and pictures and the stories they formed.

After a few panels it was easy: the comic was all about Mr. Natural, his favorite Crumb character. The sight of the clever old hippie-sage comforted him, made him forget Daddy's anger and Momma's pain, made him forget he was reading the words for Didi. The story took him away.

Besides, he knew they would come back. They always did. Your parents couldn't just walk away and leave you in the back seat, not when it would be dark soon, not when you were in a strange place and there was nothing to eat and nowhere to sleep and you were only five years old.

Could they?

Momma and Daddy were far down the road now, small gesturing shapes in the distance. But Trevor could see that they had stopped walking, that they were just standing there. Arguing, yes. Yelling, probably. Maybe crying. But not going away.

Trevor looked down at the page and fell back into the story.

* * *

It turned out they couldn't go anywhere. Daddy called a mechanic, an immensely tall, skinny young man who was still almost a teenager, with a face as long and pale and kindly as that of the Man in the Moon. Stitched in bright orange thread on the pocket of his greasy overalls was the improbable name *Kinsey*.

Kinsey said the Rambler had thrown a rod that had probably been ready to go since New Orleans, and unless they were prepared to drop several hundred bucks into that tired old engine, they might as well push the car off the road and be glad they'd broken down close to a town. After all, Kinsey pointed out, they might be staying awhile.

Daddy helped him roll the car forward a few feet so that it was completely off the blacktop. The body sagged on its tires, two-toned paint a faded turquoise above the dusty strip of chrome that ran along the side, dirty white below. Trevor thought the Rambler already looked dead. Daddy's face was very pale, almost bluish, sheened with oily-looking sweat. When he took off his sunglasses, Trevor saw smudgy purple shadows in the hollows of his eyes.

"How much do we owe you?" Daddy said. It was obvious from his voice that he dreaded the answer.

Kinsey looked at Momma, at Trevor and Didi in the crooks of her arms, at their clothes and other belongings heaped in the back seat, the duffel bags bulging up from under the roped-down lid of the trunk, the three mattresses strapped to the roof. His quick blue eyes, as bright as Trevor's and Daddy's were pale, seemed to take in the situation at a glance. "For coming out? Nothing. My time isn't that valuable, believe me."

He lowered his head a little to peer into Daddy's face. Trevor thought suddenly of an inquisitive giraffe. "But don't I know you? You wouldn't be . . . no . . . not Robert McGee? 'The cartoonist who blew the brainpan off the American underground' in the words of Saint Crumb himself? . . . No, no, of course not. Not in Missing Mile. Silly of me, sorry."

He was already turning away, and Daddy wasn't going to say anything. Trevor couldn't stand it. He wanted to run to the tall young man, to yell up into that kind, curious face, *Yes, it is him, it is Robert McGee and he's everything you said and he's MY DADDY TOO!* In that moment Trevor felt he would burst with pride for his father.

But Momma's arm tightened around him, holding him back. One long, lacquered nail tapped a warning on his forearm. *"Shh,"* he heard her say softly.

And Daddy, Robert McGee, *Bobby* McGee, creator of the crazed, sick, beautiful comic *Birdland,* whose work had appeared beside Crumb's and Shelton's, in *Zap!* and the L.A. *Free Press* and the *East Village Other* and everywhere in between, all across the country . . . who had received and refused offers from the same Hollywood he had once drawn as a giant blood-swollen tick still clinging to the rotten corpse of a dog labeled *Art* . . . who had once had a steady hand and a pure, scathing vision . . .

Daddy only shook his head and looked away.

Just past downtown Missing Mile, a road splits off to the left from Firehouse Street and meanders away into scrubby country-side. The fields out here are nearly barren, the soil gone infertile —most believe from overfarming and lack of crop rotation. Only the oldest residents of town still say these fields are cursed and were once sowed with salt. The good land is on the other side of town, the side toward Corinth, out where the abandoned rail yard and the deep woods are. Firehouse Street runs into State Highway 42. The road that splits off to the left soon becomes gravel, then dirt. This is the poorest part of Missing Mile, the place called Violin Road.

Out here the best places to live are decrepit farmhouses, big rambling places with high ceilings and large cool rooms, most of which were abandoned or sold as the crops went bad. A step below these are the aluminum trailers and tarpaper shacks, their dirt yards choked with broken toys, rusting hulks of autos, and other trash, their peripheries negligently guarded by slat-sided, soporific hounds.

Out here only the wild things are healthy, the old trees whose roots find sustenance far below the ill-used layer of topsoil, the occasional rosebush gone to green thicket and thorns, the un-stoppable kudzu. It is as if they have decided to take back the land for their own.

Trevor loved it. It was where he discovered that *he* could draw even if Daddy couldn't.

Momma talked to a real estate agent in town and figured out that they could afford to rent one of the dilapidated farmhouses for a month. By that time, she said, she would find a job in Missing Mile and Daddy would be drawing. Sure enough, a few days after they moved their things into the house, a dress shop hired Momma as a salesgirl. The job was no fun—she couldn't wear jeans to work, which left her with a choice of one Indian-print skirt and blouse or one patchwork dress—but she ate lunch at the diner in town and sometimes stopped for coffee after her shift. Soon she met some of the kids they'd seen going into the record store, and others like them.

If she could drive to Raleigh or Chapel Hill, they told Momma, she could make good money modeling for university art classes. Momma talked to Kinsey at the garage, who let her set up a payment plan. A week later the Rambler had a brand-new engine, and Momma quit the dress shop and started driving to Raleigh several times a week.

Daddy had his things set up in a tiny fourth bedroom at the back of the house, his untidy jumble of inks and brushes and his drawing table, the one piece of furniture they had brought from Austin. He went in there and shut the door every morning after Momma left, and he stayed in there most of the day. Trevor had no idea whether he was drawing or not.

But Trevor was. He had found an old sketchbook of Daddy's when Momma unpacked the car. Most of the pages had been torn out, but there were still a few blank sheets left. Trevor usually took Didi outside to play in the daytime—Momma had assured him that the Devil's Tramping Ground was more than forty miles away, so he didn't have to worry about accidentally coming upon the pacing, muttering demon.

When Didi was napping—something he seemed to do more and more often these days—Trevor wandered through the house, looking at the bare floorboards and the water-stained walls, wondering if anyone had ever loved this house. One afternoon he found himself in the dim, shabby kitchen, perched on one of the rickety chairs that had come with the house, a felt-tip pen in his hand, the sketchbook on the table before him. He had no idea what he was going to draw. He had hardly ever thought about drawing before; that was what Daddy did. Trevor could remember scribbling with crayons on cheap newsprint when he was Didi's age, making great round heads with stick arms and legs coming straight out of them, as small children do. This circle with five dots in it is Mommy, this one is Daddy, that one's me. But he hadn't drawn for at least a year—not since Daddy stopped.

Daddy had told him once that the trick was *not* to think about it, not in your sketchbook anyway. You just had to find the path between your hand and your heart and your brain and see what came out. Trevor uncapped the pen and put its tip against the unblemished (though slightly yellowed) page of the sketchbook. The ink began to bleed into the paper, making a small spreading dot, a tiny black sun in a pale void. Then, slowly, Trevor's hand began to move.

He soon discovered he was drawing Skeletal Sammy, a character from Daddy's comic book, *Birdland*. Sammy was all straight lines and sharp points: easy to draw. The half-leering, half-desperate face, the long black coat that hung on Sammy's shoulders like a pair of broken wings, the spidery hands and the long, thin legs and the exaggerated bulge of Sammy's kneecaps beneath his black stovepipe pants—all began to take shape.

Trevor sat back and looked at the drawing. It was nowhere near as good as Daddy's Sammy, of course; the lines weren't straight, the black inking was more like scribbling. But it was no circle with five dots, either. It was immediately recognizable as Skeletal Sammy.

Daddy recognized it as soon as he walked into the kitchen.

He leaned over Trevor's shoulder for several moments looking at the drawing. One hand rested lightly on Trev's back; the other tapped the table nervously, fingers as long and thin as Sammy's, faint lavender veins visible beneath the pale skin, silver wedding ring too loose on the third finger. For a moment Trevor feared Daddy might snatch the drawing, the whole sketchbook; he felt as if he had been caught doing something wrong.

But Daddy only kissed the top of Trevor's head. "You draw a mean junkie, kiddo," he whispered into Trevor's ginger hair. And he was gone from the kitchen silently, like a ghost, without getting the beer or glass of water or whatever he had come for, leaving his elder son half elated and half dreadfully, mysteriously shamed.

The carefully drawn fingers of Sammy's left hand were blurring. A drop of moisture on the page, making the ink bleed and furl. Trevor touched the wetness, then put his finger to his lips. Salty. A tear.

Daddy's, or his own?

The worst thing happened the following week. It turned out Daddy *had* been drawing in his cramped little studio. Had finally finished a story, only a page long, and sent it off to one of his papers. Trevor couldn't remember if it was the *Barb* or the *Freep* or maybe one of the others—he got them mixed up sometimes.

The paper rejected the story. Daddy read the letter aloud in a hollow, mocking voice. It had been a difficult decision, the editor said, considering his reputation and the selling power of his name. However, he simply didn't feel the story approached the quality of Daddy's previous work, and he thought publishing it would be bad both for the paper and for Daddy's career.

It was the kindest way the editor could find to say, *This comic is a piece of shit.*

The next day, Daddy walked into town and called the publisher of *Birdland*. The stories for the fourth issue were already nearly a year overdue. Daddy told the publisher there would be no more stories, not now, not ever. Then he hung up the pay phone and walked a mile across town to the liquor store. By the time he got home, he had already cracked the seal on a gallon jug of bourbon.

Momma had begun staying later and later in the city after her modeling jobs—having drinks with some of the other models one night, going to someone's apartment to get stoned the next. Daddy didn't like that, had even refused to smoke the joint she brought him as a present from her friends. She said they wanted to meet him and the kids, but Daddy wouldn't go into Raleigh and told her not to invite them out.

Trevor had gone into Raleigh with Momma one day. He brought his sketchbook and sat in a corner of the big airy studio that smelled of paint thinner and charcoal dust. Momma stood gracefully naked on a wooden podium at the front of the room, joking with the students when she took her breaks. Some of them laughed at him, bent over his sketchbook so quiet and serious. Their laughter faltered when they saw the likenesses he had produced of them during the class period: the stringy-haired girl whose granny glasses pinched her beaky nose like some torture device made of wire; the droopy-eyed boy whose patchy beard grew straight down into the collar of his black turtleneck because he had no chin.

But on this day Trevor had stayed home. Daddy sat in the living room all evening, sprawled in a threadbare recliner that had come with the house, his feet tapping out a meaningless tattoo on the warped floorboards. He had the turntable hooked up and kept playing record after record, anything that his hand fell upon, Sarah Vaughan, Country Joe and the Fish, frenetic band music from the twenties that sounded like something skeletons might jitterbug to—it all ran together in one long musical cry of pain. Most of all Trevor remembered Daddy searching obsessively for a set of Charlie Parker records: Bird with Miles, Bird on Fifty-second Street, Bird at Birdland. He found them, slammed one onto the turntable. The saxophone spiraled through the old house, found the cracks in the walls, and spun out into the night, an exalted sound, terribly sad but somehow free. Free as a bird in Birdland.

Daddy hefted the bottle and chugged bourbon straight from it. A moment later he let out a long, wet, rippling belch. Trevor got up from the corner where he'd been sitting, keeping an eye out for Momma's headlights, and started to leave the room. He didn't want to see Daddy get sick. He'd seen it before and it had nearly made him sick too, not even so much the sight of the thin, stringy whiskey vomit as that of his father's helplessness and shame.

His foot struck a loose piece of wood and sent it skittering across the floor. Daddy had been doing repairs around the house a few days earlier, nailing down a board that had begun to curl away from the wall. Long silver nails and a hammer were still scattered around the hall doorway. Trevor began to gather up the nails, thinking Didi might step on one, then stopped. Didi was smart enough not to go around the house barefoot, with all the splinters in the floorboards. Maybe Daddy would need the nails. Maybe he would still finish the repairs.

At the sound of the nails chinking together, Daddy looked up from his bottle. His eyes focused on Trevor, pinned him to the spot where he stood. "Trev. What're you doin'?"

"Going to bed."

"Thass good. I'll fixyer juice." Momma usually gave the boys fruit juice to take to bed with them, when there was any in the house. Daddy got up and stumbled past Trevor into the kitchen, slapping one hand against the door frame to support himself. Trevor heard the refrigerator opening, bottles rattling. Daddy came back in and handed him a glass of grapefruit juice. A few drops sloshed over the side, trickled over Trevor's fingers. He put his hand to his mouth and licked them away. Grapefruit was his favorite, because of the interestingly sour, almost salty taste. But there was an extra bitterness to this juice, as if it had begun to spoil in the bottle.

He must have made a face, because Daddy kept staring at him. "Something wrong?"

Trevor shook his head.

"You gonna drink that or not?"

He raised the glass to his lips and drank half of it, took a deep breath, and finished it off. The bitter taste shivered over his tongue, lingered in the back of his throat.

"There you go." Daddy reached out, pulled Trevor into his embrace. Daddy smelled of stinging liquor and old sweat and dirty clothes. Trevor hugged back anyway. As the side of his head pressed against Daddy's, a panicky terror flooded through him, though he didn't know why. He clutched at Daddy's shoulders, tried to wrap his arms around Daddy's neck.

But after a moment, Daddy pried him off and gently pushed him away.

Trevor went down the hall, glancing into Didi's dark bedroom. Sometimes Didi got scared at night, but now he was fast asleep despite the punishing volume of the music, his face burrowed into his pillow, the faint light from the hallway casting a halo on his pale hair. Back in Austin the brothers had shared a room; this was the first time they had slept apart. Trevor missed waking up to the soft sound of Didi's breathing, to the scent of talcum powder and candy when Didi crawled in bed with him. For a moment he thought he might sleep with Didi tonight, might wrap his arms around his brother and not have to fall asleep alone.

But he didn't want to wake Didi. Daddy was being too scary. Instead Trevor walked down the hall to his own bedroom, trailing his hand along the wall. The old boards were damp, faintly sticky. He wiped his fingers on the front of his T-shirt.

His own room was nearly as bare as Didi's. They had been able to bring none of their furniture from Austin, and hardly any of their toys. Trevor's mattress lay flat on the floor, a rumpled blanket thrown over it. He had pinned up some of his drawings on the walls, though he hadn't put up Skeletal Sammy and he hadn't tried to draw any of Daddy's other characters. More drawings lay scattered on the floor, along with the comics he had scrounged from Daddy. He picked up a Fabulous Furry Freak Brothers book, thinking he might read it in bed. The antics of those friendly fools might make him forget Daddy sprawled in the chair, pouring straight whiskey on top of his pain.

But he was too tired; his eyes were already closing. Trevor turned off his bedside lamp and crawled under the blanket. The familiar contours of his mattress cradled him like a welcoming hand. From the living room he heard Charlie Parker run down a shimmering scale. *Birdland,* he thought again. That was the place where you could work magic, the place where no one else could touch you. It might be an actual spot in the world; it might be a place deep down inside you. Daddy could only reach his Birdland by drinking now. Travor had begun to believe his own Birdland might be the pen moving over the paper, the weight of the sketchbook in his hands, the creation of worlds out of ink and sweat and love.

He slept, and the music wove uneasily in and out of his dreams. He heard Janis Joplin singing "Me and Bobby McGee," and remembered suddenly that she had died last year. From drugs, Momma had told him, taking care to explain that the drugs Janis had been using were much worse than the pot she and Daddy sometimes smoked. An image came to him of Daddy walking hand in hand with a girl shorter and more rounded than Momma, a girl who wore bright feathers in her hair. She turned to Daddy, and Trevor saw that her face was a swollen purple mass of flesh, the holes of her eyes black and depthless behind the big round glasses, her ruined features split in the semblance of a smile as she leaned in to give his father a deep soul kiss.

And Daddy kissed back . . .

Sunlight woke him, streaming through the dirty panes of his window, trickling into the corners of his eyes. His head ached slightly, felt somehow too heavy on his neck. Trevor rolled over, stretched, and looked around the room, silently greeting his drawings. There was one of the house, one of Momma holding Didi, a whole series of ones that he was pretty sure were going to turn into a comic. He knew he could never draw the slick, tawdry world of *Birdland* the way Daddy had, but he could make his own world. He needed to practice writing smaller so he could do the letters.

His head slightly logy but full of ideas, Trevor rolled off the mattress, pushed open the door of his room, and walked down the hall toward the kitchen.

He saw the blood on the walls before he saw Momma.

It would come out in the autopsy report—which Trevor did not read until years later—that Daddy had attacked her near the front door, that they must have argued, that there had been a struggle and he had driven her back toward the hall before he killed her. That was where he would have picked up the hammer.

Momma was crumpled in the doorway that led from the living room into the hall. Her back rested against the frame. Her head lolled on the fragile stem of her neck. Her eyes were open, and as Trevor edged around her body, they seemed to fix on him. For a heart-stopping second he thought she was alive. Then he saw that the eyes were cloudy and filmed with blood.

Her arms were a mass of blood and bruises, silver rings sparkling amid the ruin of her hands. (Seven fingers broken, the autopsy report would say, along with most of the small bones in her palms, as she raised her hands to ward off the blows of the hammer.) There was a deep gouge in her left temple, another in the center of her forehead. Her hair was loose, fanned around her shoulders, stiff with blood. A clear fluid had seeped from her head wounds and dried on her face, making silvery tracks through the mask of red.

And on the wall above her, a confusion of bloody handprints trailing down, down . . .

Trevor spun and ran back down the hall, toward his brother's room. He did not know that his bladder had let go, did not feel the hot urine spilling down his legs. He did not hear the sound he was making, a long, high moan.

The door of Didi's room was closed. Trevor had not closed it when he looked in on Didi last night. High up on the door was a tiny smudge of blood, barely noticeable. It told Trevor everything he needed to know. He went in anyway.

The room was thick with the smell of blood and shit. The two odors together were cloying, almost sweet. Trevor went to the bed. Didi lay in the same position Trevor had left him in last night, his head burrowed into the pillow, one small hand curled into a fist near his mouth. The back of Didi's head was like a swamp, a dark mush of splintered bone and thick clotted blood. Sometime during the night—because of the heat, or in the spasms of death—Didi had kicked off his covers. Trevor saw the dark brown stain between his legs. That was where the smell came from.

Trevor lifted the blanket and pulled it over Didi, covering the stain, the ruined head, the unbearable curled hand. The blanket settled over the small still form. Where it covered the head, a blotch of red appeared.

He had to find Daddy. His mind clung to some tiny, glittering hope that maybe Daddy hadn't done this at all, that maybe some crazy person had broken into their house and killed Momma and Didi and left him alive for some reason, that Daddy might still be alive too.

He stumbled out of Didi's room, felt his way along the hall, sprawled headlong into the bathroom.

That was where Momma's friends found him hours later, when they drove out to see why Momma hadn't shown up to model that day; she was so reliable that they became worried immediately. The front door was unlocked. They saw Momma's body first, and had nearly worked themselves into hysterics when someone heard the high toneless keening.

They found Trevor squeezed into a tiny space between the toilet and the old porcelain sink, curled as compact as a fetus, his eyes fixed on the body of his father. Bobby McGee hung from the shower curtain rod. It was the old-fashioned kind bolted into the wall, and had held his weight all night and all day. He was naked. His penis hung limp and dry as a dead leaf; there had been no last orgasm in death for him. His body was thin nearly to the point of emaciation, luminously pale, his hands and feet gravid with blood, his face was so swollen as to be featureless except for the eyes bulging halfway out of their sockets. The rough strand of hemp cut a deep slash in his neck. His hands and his torso were still stained with the blood of his family.

As someone lifted him and carried him out, still curled into the smallest possible ball, Trevor had his first coherent thought in hours, and the last he would have for several days.

He needn't have worried about accidentally coming upon the Devil's Tramping Ground, he realized.

The Devil's Tramping Ground had come to him.